PEACOCK BOOKS

Editor: Kaye Webb

ANNE OF AVONLEA

This story begins five years after the lonely red-haired orphan Anne arrived at Green Gables. She is now sixteen and quite grown up (except for occasions when she starts imagining things and getting into difficulties, just like the old Anne).

Gentle, kind Uncle Matthew has died, but in every other way it is a year of beginnings and new responsibilities for Anne. She is a moving spirit in a society for improving Avonlea, and she has her first job, as the teacher in her own old school, where most of the children still remember her as a pupil. She has new friends too; the peppery old bachelor Mr Harrison, graceful Lavendar Lewis of Echo Lodge, and the six-year-old twins – wicked, loving little Davy and his model sister Dora – whom she and Marilla welcome into their home.

It will be a pleasure for any devotee of that impetuous heroine in *Anne of Green Gables* to read more of her doings, and to see how much of the old harum scarum Anne remains in this new Anne, so much wiser than she used to be, yet still leaping into more peculiar scrapes than the Avonlea average, still dreaming her impossible dreams, even though she *is* beginning to be more aware of a certain familiar pleasant young man, so unlike the dark, proud, melancholy lover she had always imagined for herself.

For readers of twelve and over.

L. M. MONTGOMERY

Anne of Avonlea

—

Flowers spring to blossom where she walks
  The careful ways of duty,
Our hard, stiff lines of life with her
  Are flowing curves of beauty.

– WHITTIER

PENGUIN BOOKS

Penguin Books Ltd, Harmondsworth, Middlesex, England

—

First published in Great Britain by Harrap 1925
Published in Peacock Books 1975

—

Made and printed in Great Britain by
Cox & Wyman Ltd,
London, Reading and Fakenham
Set in Intertype Times

To
my former teacher
Hattie Gordon Smith
in grateful remembrance of her
sympathy and encouragement

Contents

CHAPTER 1

An Irate Neighbour

A TALL, slim girl, 'half past sixteen', with serious grey eyes and hair which her friends called auburn, had sat down on the broad red sandstone doorstep of a Prince Edward Island farmhouse one ripe afternoon in August, firmly resolved to construe so many lines of Virgil.

But an August afternoon, with blue hazes scarfing the harvest slopes, little winds whispering elfishly in the poplars, and a dancing splendour of red poppies outflaming against the dark coppice of young firs in a corner of the cherry orchard was fitter for dreams than dead languages. The Virgil soon slipped unheeded to the ground, and Anne, her chin propped on her clasped hands, and her eyes on the splendid mass of fluffy clouds that were heaping up just over Mr J. A. Harrison's house like a great white mountain, was far away in a delicious world where a certain school-teacher was doing a wonderful work, shaping the destinies of future statesmen, and inspiring youthful minds and hearts with high and lofty ambitions.

To be sure, if you came down to harsh facts ... which, it must be confessed, Anne seldom did until she had to ... it did not seem likely that there was much promising material for celebrities in Avonlea school; but you could never tell what might happen if a teacher used her influence for good. Anne had certain rose-tinted ideals of what a teacher might accomplish if she only went the right way about it; and she was in the midst of a delightful scene, forty years hence, with a famous personage ... just exactly what he was to be famous for was left in convenient haziness, but Anne thought it would be rather nice to have him a college president or a Canadian premier ... bowing low over her wrinkled hand and assuring her that it was she who had first kindled his ambition, and that all his success in life was due to the lessons she had instilled so long ago in Avon-

lea school. The pleasant vision was shattered by a most unpleasant interruption.

A demure little Jersey cow came scuttling down the lane, and
five seconds later Mr Harrison arrived . . . if 'arrived' be not too
mild a term to describe the manner of his irruption into the
yard.

He bounced over the fence without waiting to open the gate,
and angrily confronted astonished Anne, who had risen to her
feet and stood looking at him in some bewilderment. Mr Harrison was their new right-hand neighbour, and she had never met
him before, although she had seen him once or twice.

In early April, before Anne had come home from Queen's,
Mr Robert Bell, whose farm adjoined the Cuthbert place on the
west, had sold out and moved to Charlottetown. His farm had
been bought by a certain Mr J. A. Harrison; whose name, and
the fact that he was a New Brunswick man, were all that was
known about him. But before he had been a month in Avonlea
he had won the reputation of being an odd person . . . a 'crank'
Mrs Rachel Lynde said. Mrs Rachel was an outspoken lady, as
those of you who may have already made her acquaintance will
remember. Mr Harrison was certainly different from other
people . . . and that is the essential characteristic of a crank, as
everybody knows.

In the first place he kept house for himself, and had publicly
stated that he wanted no fools of women around his diggings.
Feminine Avonlea took its revenge by the gruesome tales it
related about his housekeeping and cooking. He had hired little
John Henry Carter of White Sands, and John Henry started the
stories. For one thing, there was never any stated time for meals
in the Harrison establishment. Mr Harrison 'got a bite' when he
felt hungry, and if John Henry were around at the time, he
came in for a share, but if he were not, he had to wait until Mr
Harrison's next hungry spell. John Henry mournfully averred
that he would have starved to death if it wasn't that he got
home on Sundays and got a good filling up, and that his mother
always gave him a basket of 'grub' to take back with him on
Monday mornings.

As for washing dishes, Mr Harrison never made any pretence

of doing it unless a rainy Sunday came. Then he went to work and washed them all at once in the rainwater hogshead, and left them to drain dry.

Again, Mr Harrison was 'close'. When he was asked to subscribe to the Rev. Mr Allan's salary he said he'd wait and see how many dollars' worth of good he got out of his preaching first ... *he* didn't believe in buying a pig in a poke. And when Mrs Lynde went to ask for a contribution to missions ... and incidentally to see the inside of the house ... he told her there were more heathens among the old woman gossips in Avonlea than anywhere else he knew of, and he'd cheerfully contribute to a mission for Christianizing them if she'd undertake it. Mrs Rachel got herself away and said it was a mercy poor Mrs Robert Bell was safe in her grave, for it would have broken her heart to see the state of her house, in which she used to take so much pride.

'Why, she scrubbed the kitchen floor every second day,' Mrs Lynde told Marilla Cuthbert indignantly, 'and if you could see it now! I had to hold up my skirts as I walked across it.'

Finally, Mr Harrison kept a parrot called Ginger. Nobody in Avonlea had ever kept a parrot before; consequently that proceeding was considered barely respectable. And such a parrot! If you took John Henry Carter's word for it, never was such an unholy bird. It swore terribly. Mrs Carter would have taken John Henry away at once if she had been sure she could get another place for him. Besides, Ginger had bitten a piece right out of the back of John Henry's neck one day when he had stooped down too near the cage. Mrs Carter showed everybody the mark when the luckless John Henry went home on Sundays.

All these things flashed through Anne's mind as Mr Harrison stood, quite speechless with wrath apparently, before her. In his most amiable mood Mr Harrison could not have been considered a handsome man; he was short and fat and bald; and now, with his round face purple with rage and his prominent blue eyes almost sticking out of his head, Anne thought he was really the ugliest person she had ever seen.

All at once Mr Harrison found his voice.

'I'm not going to put up with this,' he spluttered, 'not a day longer, do you hear, miss. Bless my soul, this is the third time, miss . . . the third time! Patience has ceased to be a virtue, miss. I warned your aunt the last time not to let it occur again . . . and she's let it . . . she's done it . . . what does she mean by it, that is what I want to know. That is what I'm here about, miss.'

'Will you explain what the trouble is?' asked Anne, in her most dignified manner. She had been practising it considerably of late to have it in good working order when school began; but it had no apparent effect on the irate J. A. Harrison.

'Trouble, is it? Bless my soul, trouble enough, I should think. The trouble is, miss, that I found that Jersey cow of your aunt's in my oats again, not half an hour ago. The third time, mark you. I found her in last Tuesday and I found her in yesterday. I came here and told your aunt not to let it occur again. She *has* let it occur again. Where's your aunt, miss? I just want to see her for a minute and give her a piece of my mind . . . a piece of J. A. Harrison's mind, miss.'

'If you mean Miss Marilla Cuthbert, she is *not* my aunt, and she has gone down to East Grafton to see a distant relative of hers who is very ill,' said Anne, with due increase of dignity at every word. 'I am very sorry that my cow should have broken into your oats . . . she *is* my cow and not Miss Cuthbert's . . . Matthew gave her to me three years ago when she was a little calf and he bought her from Mr Bell.'

'Sorry, miss! Sorry isn't going to help matters any. You'd better go and look at the havoc that animal has made in my oats . . . trampled them from centre to circumference, miss.'

'I am very sorry,' repeated Anne firmly, 'but perhaps if you kept your fences in better repair Dolly might not have broken in. It is your part of the line fence that separates your oat-field from our pasture, and I noticed the other day that it was not in a very good condition.'

'My fence is all right,' snapped Mr Harrison, angrier than ever at this carrying of the war into the enemy's country. 'The gaol fence couldn't keep a demon of a cow like that out. And I can tell you, you red-headed snippet, that if the cow is yours, as you say, you'd be better employed in watching her out of other people's grain than in sitting round reading yellow-covered novels' ... with a scathing glance at the innocent tan-coloured Virgil by Anne's feet.

Something at that moment was red besides Anne's hair ... which had always been a tender point with her.

'I'd rather have red hair than none at all except a little fringe round my ears,' she flashed.

The shot told, for Mr Harrison was really very sensitive about his bald head. His anger choked him up again, and he could only glare speechlessly at Anne, who recovered her temper and followed up her advantage.

'I can make allowance for you, Mr Harrison, because I have an imagination. I can easily imagine how very trying it must be to find a cow in your oats, and I shall not cherish any hard feelings against you for the things you've said. I promise you that Dolly shall never break into your oats again. I give you my word of honour on *that* point.'

'Well, mind you she doesn't,' muttered Mr Harrison in a somewhat subdued tone; but he stamped off angrily enough, and Anne heard him growling to himself until he was out of earshot.

Grievously disturbed in mind, Anne marched across the yard and shut the naughty Jersey up in the milking-pen.

'She can't possibly get out of that unless she tears the fence down,' she reflected. 'She looks pretty quiet now. I dare say she has sickened herself on those oats. I wish I'd sold her to Mr Shearer when he wanted her last week, but I thought it was just as well to wait until we had the auction of the stock and let them all go together. I believe it is true about Mr Harrison being a crank. Certainly there's nothing of the kindred spirit about *him*.'

Anne had always a weather eye open for kindred spirits.

Marilla Cuthbert was driving into the yard as Anne returned to the house, and the latter flew to get tea ready. They discussed the matter at the tea-table.

'I'll be glad when the auction is over,' said Marilla. 'It is too much responsibility having so much stock about the place and nobody but that unreliable Martin to look after them. He has never come back yet, and he promised that he would certainly be back last night if I'd give him the day off to go to his aunt's funeral. I don't know how many aunts he has got, I am sure. That's the fourth that's died since he hired here a year ago. I'll be more than thankful when the crop is in and Mr Barry takes over the farm. We'll have to keep Dolly shut up in the pen till Martin comes, for she must be put in the back pasture, and the fences there have to be fixed. I declare it is a world of trouble, as Rachel says. Here's poor Mary Keith dying, and what is to become of those two children of hers is more than I know. She has a brother in British Columbia and she has written to him about them, but she hasn't heard from him yet.'

'What are the children like? How old are they?'

'Six past ... they're twins.'

'Oh, I've always been especially interested in twins ever since Mrs Hammond had so many,' said Anne eagerly. 'Are they pretty?'

'Goodness, you couldn't tell ... they were too dirty. Davy had been out making mud pies and Dora went out to call him in. Davy pushed her head first into the biggest pie and then, because she cried, he got into it himself and wallowed in it to show her it was nothing to cry about. Mary said Dora was really a very good child, but that Davy was full of mischief. He has never had any bringing up, you might say. His father died when he was a baby and Mary has been sick almost ever since.'

'I'm always sorry for children that have had no bringing up,' said Anne soberly. 'You know *I* hadn't any till you took me in hand. I hope their uncle will look after them. Just what relation is Mrs Keith to you?'

'Mary? None in the world. It was her husband ... he was our third cousin. There's Mrs Lynde coming through the yard. I thought she'd be up to hear about Mary.'

'Don't tell her about Mr Harrison and the cow,' implored Anne.

Marilla promised; but the promise was quite unnecessary, for Mrs Lynde was no sooner fairly seated than she said:

'I saw Mr Harrison chasing your Jersey out of his oats today

when I was coming home from Carmody. I thought he looked
pretty mad. Did he make much of a rumpus?'

Anne and Marilla furtively exchanged amused smiles. Few
things in Avonlea ever escaped Mrs Lynde. It was only that
morning Anne had said: 'If you went to your own room at
midnight, locked the door, pulled down the blind, and *sneezed*,
Mrs Lynde would ask you the next day how your cold was!'

'I believe he did,' admitted Marilla. 'I was away. He gave
Anne a piece of his mind.'

'I think he is a very disagreeable man,' said Anne, with a
resentful toss of her ruddy head.

'You never said a truer word,' said Mrs Rachel solemnly. 'I
knew there'd be trouble when Robert Bell sold his place to a
New Brunswick man, that's what. I don't know what Avonlea is
coming to, with so many strange people rushing into it. It'll
soon not be safe to go to sleep in our beds.'

'Why, what other strangers are coming in?' asked Marilla.

'Haven't you heard? Well, there's a family of Donnells, for
one thing. They've rented Peter Sloane's old house. Peter has
hired the man to run his mill. They belong down east and
nobody knows anything about them. Then that shiftless Timothy Cotton family are going to move up from White Sands,
and they'll simply be a burden on the public. He is in consumption ... when he isn't stealing ... and his wife is a slack-
twisted creature that can't turn her hand to a thing. She washes
her dishes *sitting down*. Mrs George Pye has taken her husband's orphan nephew, Anthony Pye. He'll be going to school
to you, Anne, so you may expect trouble, that's what. And
you'll have another strange pupil too. Paul Irving is coming
from the States to live with his grandmother. You remember his
father, Marilla ... Stephen Irving, him that jilted Lavendar
Lewis over at Grafton?'

'I don't think he jilted her. There was a quarrel ... I suppose
there was blame on both sides.'

'Well, anyway, he didn't marry her, and she's been as queer
as possible ever since, they say ... living all by herself in that
little stone house she calls Echo Lodge. Stephen went off to the
States and went into business with his uncle and married a

Yankee. He's never been home since, though his mother has been up to see him once or twice. His wife died two years ago and he's sending the boy home to his mother for a spell. He's ten years old, and I don't know if he'll be a very desirable pupil. You can never tell about those Yankees.'

Mrs Lynde looked upon all people who had the misfortune to be born or brought up elsewhere than in Prince Edward Island with a decided can-any-good-thing-come-out-of-Nazareth air. They *might* be good people, of course; but you were on the safe side in doubting it. She had a special prejudice against 'Yankees'. Her husband had been cheated out of ten dollars by an employer for whom he had once worked in Boston, and neither angels nor principalities nor powers could have convinced Mrs Rachel that the whole United States was not responsible for it.

'Avonlea school won't be the worse for a little new blood,' said Marilla dryly, 'and if this boy is anything like his father he'll be all right. Steve Irving was the nicest boy that was ever raised in these parts, though some people did call him proud. I should think Mrs Irving would be very glad to have the child. She has been very lonesome since her husband died.'

'Oh, the boy may be well enough, but he'll be different from Avonlea children,' said Mrs Rachel, as if that clinched the matter. Mrs Rachel's opinions concerning any person, place, or thing were always warranted to wear. 'What's this I hear about your going to start up a Village Improvement Society, Anne?'

'I was just talking it over with some of the girls and boys at the last Debating Club,' said Anne, flushing. 'They thought it would be rather nice ... and so do Mr and Mrs Allan. Lots of villages have them now.'

'Well, you'll get into no end of hot water if you do. Better leave it alone, Anne, that's what. People don't like being improved.'

'Oh, we are not going to try to improve the *people*. It is Avonlea itself. There are lots of things which might be done to make it prettier. For instance, if we could coax Mr Levi Boulter to pull down that dreadful old house on his upper farm, wouldn't that be an improvement?'

'It certainly would,' admitted Mrs Rachel. 'That old ruin has been an eyesore to the settlement for years. But if you Improvers can coax Levi Boulter to do anything for the public that he isn't to be paid for doing, may I be there to see and hear the process, that's what. I don't want to discourage you, Anne, for there may be something in your idea, though I suppose you did get it out of some rubbishy Yankee magazine; but you'll have your hands full with your school, and I advise you as a friend not to bother with your improvements, that's what. But there, I know you'll go ahead with it if you've set your mind on it. You were always one to carry a thing through somehow.'

Something about the firm outlines of Anne's lips told that Mrs Rachel was not far astray in this estimate. Anne's heart was bent on forming the Improvement Society. Gilbert Blythe, who was to teach in White Sands, but would always be home from Friday night to Monday morning, was enthusiastic about it; and most of the other young folks were willing to go in for anything that meant occasional meetings, and consequently some 'fun'. As for what the 'improvements' were to be, nobody had any very clear idea except Anne and Gilbert. They had talked them over and planned them out until an ideal Avonlea existed in their minds, if nowhere else.

Mrs Rachel had still another item of news.

'They've given the Carmody school to a Priscilla Grant. Didn't you go to Queen's with a girl of that name, Anne?'

'Yes, indeed. Priscilla to teach at Carmody! How perfectly lovely!' exclaimed Anne, her grey eyes lighting up until they looked like evening stars, causing Mrs Lynde to wonder anew if she would ever get it settled to her satisfaction whether Anne Shirley were really a pretty girl or not.

CHAPTER 2

Selling in Haste and Repenting at Leisure

ANNE drove over to Carmody on a shopping expedition the next afternoon and took Diana Barry with her. Diana was, of course, a pledged member of the Improvement Society, and the two girls talked about little else all the way to Carmody and back.

'The very first thing we ought to do when we get started is to have that hall painted,' said Diana, as they drove past the Avonlea hall, a rather shabby building set down in a wooded hollow, with spruce-trees hooding it about on all sides. 'It's a disgraceful-looking place and we must attend to it even before we try to get Mr Levi Boulter to pull his house down. Father says we'll never succeed in doing *that* ... Levi Boulter is too mean to spend the time it would take.'

'Perhaps he'll let the boys take it down if they promise to haul the boards and split them up for him for kindling wood,' said Anne hopefully. 'We must do our best and be content to go slowly at first. We can't expect to improve everything all at once. We'll have to educate public sentiment first, of course.'

Diana wasn't exactly sure what educating public sentiment meant; but it sounded fine, and she felt rather proud that she was going to belong to a society with such an aim in view.

'I thought of something last night that we could do, Anne. You know that three-cornered piece of ground where the roads from Carmody and Newbridge and White Sands meet? It's all grown over with young spruce; but wouldn't it be nice to have them all cleared out, and just leave the two or three birch-trees that are on it?'

'Splendid,' agreed Anne gaily. 'And have a rustic seat put under the birches. And when spring comes we'll have a flower-bed made in the middle of it and plant geraniums.'

'Yes; only we'll have to devise some way of getting old Mrs Hiram Sloane to keep her cow off the road, or she'll eat our geraniums up,' laughed Diana. 'I begin to see what you mean by educating public sentiment, Anne. There's the old Boulter house now. Did you ever see such a rookery? And perched right close to the road too. An old house with its windows gone always makes me think of something dead with its eyes picked out.'

'I think an old, deserted house is such a sad sight,' said Anne dreamily. 'It always seems to me to be thinking about its past and mourning for its old-time joys. Marilla says that a large family was raised in that old house long ago, and that it was a really pretty place, with a lovely garden and roses climbing all over it. It was full of little children and laughter and songs; and now it is empty, and nothing ever wanders through it but the wind. How lonely and sorrowful it must feel! Perhaps they all come back on moonlit nights ... the ghosts of the little children of long ago and the roses and the songs ... and for a little while the old house can dream it is young and joyous again.'

Diana shook her head.

'I never imagine things like that about places now, Anne. Don't you remember how cross Mother and Marilla were when we imagined ghosts into the Haunted Wood? To this day I can't go through that bush comfortably after dark; and if I began imagining such things about the old Boulter house I'd be frightened to pass it too. Besides, those children aren't dead. They're all grown up and doing well ... and one of them is a butcher. And flowers and songs couldn't have ghosts anyhow.'

Anne smothered a little sigh. She loved Diana dearly and they had always been good comrades. But she had long ago learned that when she wandered into the realm of fancy she must go alone. The way to it was by an enchanted path where not even her dearest might follow her.

A thunder-shower came up while the girls were at Carmody; it did not last long, however, and the drive home, through the lanes where the raindrops sparkled on the boughs and little leafy valleys where the drenched ferns gave out spicy odours, was delightful. But just as they turned into the Cuthbert lane Anne saw something that spoiled the beauty of the landscape for her.

Before them on the right extended Mr Harrison's broad, grey-green field of late oats, wet and luxuriant; and there, standing squarely in the middle of it, up to her sleek sides in the lush growth and blinking at them calmly over the intervening tassels, was a Jersey cow!

Anne dropped the reins and stood up with a tightening of the lips that boded no good to the predatory quadruped. Not a word said she, but she climbed nimbly down over the wheels, and whisked across the fence before Diana understood what had happened.

'Anne, come back,' shrieked the latter, as soon as she found her voice. 'You'll ruin your dress in that wet grain ... ruin it. She doesn't hear me! Well, she'll never get that cow out by herself. I must go and help her, of course.'

Anne was charging through the grain like a mad thing. Diana hopped briskly down, tied the horse securely to a post, turned the skirt of her pretty gingham dress over her shoulders, mounted the fence, and started in pursuit of her frantic friend. She could run faster than Anne, who was hampered by her clinging and drenched skirt, and soon overtook her. Behind them they left a trail that would break Mr Harrison's heart when he should see it.

'Anne, for mercy's sake, stop,' panted poor Diana. 'I'm right out of breath, and you are wet to the skin.'

'I must ... get ... that cow ... out ... before ... Mr Harrison ... sees her,' gasped Anne. 'I don't ... care ... if I'm ... drowned ... if we ... can ... only ... do that.'

But the Jersey cow appeared to see no good reason for being hustled out of her luscious browsing-ground. No sooner had the two breathless girls got near her than she turned and bolted squarely for the opposite corner of the field.

'Head her off' screamed Anne. 'Run, Diana, run.'

Diana did run. Anne tried to, and the wicked Jersey went round the field as if she were possessed. Privately, Diana thought she was. It was fully ten minutes before they headed her off and drove her through the corner gap into the Cuthbert lane.

There is no denying that Anne was in anything but an angelic temper at that precise moment. Nor did it soothe her in the least to behold a buggy halted just outside the lane, wherein sat Mr Shearer of Carmody and his son, both of whom wore a broad smile.

'I guess you'd better have sold me that cow when I wanted to buy her last week, Anne,' chuckled Mr Shearer.

'I'll sell her to you now, if you want her,' said her flushed and dishevelled owner. 'You may have her this very minute.'

'Done. I'll give you twenty for her as I offered before, and Jim here can drive her right over to Carmody. She'll go to town with the rest of the shipment this evening. Mr Read of Brighton wants a Jersey cow.'

Five minutes later Jim Shearer and the Jersey cow were marching up the road, and impulsive Anne was driving along the Green Gables lane with her twenty dollars.

'What will Marilla say?' asked Diana.

'Oh, she won't care. Dolly was my own cow and it isn't likely she'd bring more than twenty dollars at the auction. But oh, dear, if Mr Harrison sees that grain he will know she has been in again, and after my giving him my word of honour that I'd never let it happen! Well, it has taught me a lesson not to give my word of honour about cows. A cow that could jump over or break through our milk-pen fence couldn't be trusted anywhere.'

Marilla had gone down to Mrs Lynde's, and when she returned knew all about Dolly's sale and transfer, for Mrs Lynde had seen most of the transaction from her window and guessed the rest.

'I suppose it's just as well she's gone, though you *do* do things in a dreadful headlong fashion, Anne. I don't see how she got out of the pen, though. She must have broken some of the boards off.'

'I didn't think of looking,' said Anne, 'but I'll go and see now. Martin has never come back yet. Perhaps some more of his aunts have died. I think it's something like Mr Peter Sloane and the octogenarians. The other evening Mrs Sloane was reading the newspaper and she said to Mr Sloane, "I see here that another octogenarian has just died. What *is* an octogenarian, Peter?" And Mr Sloane said he didn't know, but they must be very sickly creatures, for you never heard tell of them but they were dying. That's the way with Martin's aunts.'

'Martin's just like all the rest of those French,' said Marilla in disgust. 'You can't depend on them for a day.'

Marilla was looking over Anne's Carmody purchases when she heard a shrill shriek in the barnyard. A minute later Anne dashed into the kitchen, wringing her hands.

'Anne Shirley, what's the matter now?'

'Oh, Marilla, whatever shall I do? This is terrible. And it's all my fault. Oh, will I *ever* learn to stop and reflect a little before doing reckless things? Mrs Lynde always told me I would do something dreadful some day, and now I've done it!'

'Anne, you are the most exasperating girl! *What* is it you've done?'

'Sold Mr Harrison's Jersey cow ... the one he bought from Mr Bell ... to Mr Shearer! Dolly is out in the milking-pen this very minute.'

'Anne Shirley, are you dreaming?'

'I only wish I were. There's no dream about it, though it's very like a nightmare. And Mr Harrison's cow is in Charlottetown by this time. Oh, Marilla, I thought I'd finished getting into scrapes, and here I am in the very worst one I ever was in my life. What can I do?'

'Do? There's nothing to do, child, except go and see Mr Harrison about it. We can offer him our Jersey in exchange if he doesn't want to take the money. She is just as good as his.'

'I'm sure he'll be awfully cross and disagreeable about it, though,' moaned Anne.

'I dare say he will. He seems to be an irritable sort of a man. I'll go and explain to him if you like.'

'No, indeed, I'm not as mean as that,' exclaimed Anne. 'This is all my fault and I'm certainly not going to let you take my punishment. I'll go myself and I'll go at once. The sooner it's over the better, for it will be terribly humiliating.'

Poor Anne got her hat and her twenty dollars and was passing out when she happened to glance through the open pantry door. On the table reposed a nut cake which she had baked that morning ... a particularly toothsome concoction iced with pink icing and adorned with walnuts. Anne had intended it for Friday evening, when the youth of Avonlea were to meet at Green Gables to organize the Improvement Society. But what were they compared to the justly offended Mr Harrison? Anne thought that cake ought to soften the heart of any man, especially one who had to do his own cooking, and she promptly popped it into a box. She would take it to Mr Harrison as a peace-offering.

'That is, if he gives me a chance to say anything at all,' she thought ruefully, as she climbed the lane fence and started on a short cut across the fields, golden in the light of the dreamy August evening. 'I know now just how people feel who are being led to execution.'

CHAPTER 3

Mr Harrison at Home

MR HARRISON'S house was an old-fashioned, low-eaved, whitewashed structure, set against a thick spruce grove.

Mr Harrison himself was sitting on his vine-shaded veranda, in his shirt-sleeves, enjoying his evening pipe. When he realized who was coming up the path he sprang suddenly to his feet, bolted into the house, and shut the door. This was merely the uncomfortable result of his surprise, mingled with a good deal of shame over his outburst of temper the day before. But nearly swept the remnant of her courage from Anne's heart.

'If he's so cross now what will he be when he hears what I've done,' she reflected miserably, as she rapped at the door.

But Mr Harrison opened it, smiling sheepishly, and invited her to enter in a tone quite mild and friendly, if somewhat nervous. He had laid aside his pipe and donned his coat; he offered Anne a very dusty chair very politely, and her reception would have passed off pleasantly enough if it had not been for that tell-tale of a parrot who was peering through the bars of his cage with wicked golden eyes. No sooner had Anne seated herself than Ginger exclaimed:

'Bless my soul, what's that red-headed snippet coming here for?'

It would be hard to say whose face was the redder, Mr Harrison's or Anne's.

'Don't you mind that parrot,' said Mr Harrison, casting a furious glance at Ginger. 'He's . . . he's always talking nonsense. I got him from my brother who was a sailor. Sailors don't always use the choicest language, and parrots are very imitative birds.'

'So I should think,' said poor Anne, the remembrance of her errand quelling her resentment. She couldn't afford to snub Mr Harrison under the circumstances, that was certain. When you had just sold a man's Jersey cow offhand, without his knowledge or consent, you must not mind if his parrot repeated uncomplimentary things. Nevertheless, the 'red-headed snippet' was not quite so meek as she might otherwise have been.

'I've come to confess something to you, Mr Harrison,' she said resolutely. 'It's . . . it's about . . . that Jersey cow.'

'Bless my soul,' exclaimed Mr Harrison nervously, 'has she gone and broken into my oats again? Well, never mind . . . never mind if she has. It's no difference . . . none at all. I . . . I was too hasty yesterday, that's a fact. Never mind if she has.'

'Oh, if it were only that,' sighed Anne. 'But it's ten times worse. I don't . . .'

'Bless my soul, do you mean to say she's got into my wheat?'

'No . . . no. . . . not the wheat. But . . .'

'Then it's the cabbages? She's broken into my cabbages that I was raising for exhibition, hey?'

'It's *not* the cabbages, Mr Harrison. I'll tell you everything . . . that is what I came for – but please don't interrupt me. It makes me so nervous. Just let me tell my story and don't say anything till I get through – and then no doubt you'll say plenty,' Anne concluded, but in thought only.

'I won't say another word,' said Mr Harrison, and he didn't. But Ginger was not bound by any contract of silence and kept ejaculating, 'Red-headed snippet' at intervals until Anne felt quite wild.

'I shut my Jersey cow up in our pen yesterday. This morning I went to Carmody and when I came back I saw a Jersey cow in your oats. Diana and I chased her out and you can't imagine what a hard time we had. I was so dreadfully wet and tired and vexed – and Mr Shearer came by that very minute and offered to buy the cow. I sold her to him on the spot for twenty dollars. It was wrong of me. I should have waited and consulted Marilla, of course. But I'm dreadfully given to doing things without thinking – everybody who knows me will tell you that. Mr

Shearer took the cow right away to ship her on the afternoon train.'

'Red-headed snippet,' quoth Ginger in a tone of profound contempt.

At this point Mr Harrison arose and, with an expression that would have struck terror into any bird but a parrot, carried Ginger's cage into an adjoining room and shut the door. Ginger shrieked, swore, and otherwise conducted himself in keeping with his reputation, but, finding himself left alone, relapsed into sulky silence.

'Excuse me and go on,' said Mr Harrison, sitting down again. 'My brother the sailor never taught that bird any manners.'

'I went home and after tea I went out to the milking-pen. Mr Harrison' . . . Anne leaned forward, clasping her hands with her old childish gesture, while her big grey eyes gazed imploringly into Mr Harrison's embarrassed face . . . 'I found my cow still shut up in the pen. It was *your* cow I had sold to Mr Shearer.'

'Bless my soul,' exclaimed Mr Harrison, in blank amazement at this unlooked-for-conclusion. 'What a *very* extraordinary thing!'

'Oh, it isn't in the least extraordinary that I should be getting myself and other people into scrapes,' said Anne mournfully. 'I'm noted for that. You might suppose I'd have grown out of it by this time . . . I'll be seventeen next March . . . but it seems that I haven't. Mr Harrison, is it too much to hope that you'll forgive me? I'm afraid it's too late to get your cow back, but here is the money for her . . . or you can have mine in exchange if you'd rather. She's a very good cow. And I can't express how sorry I am for it all.'

'Tut, tut,' said Mr Harrison briskly, 'don't say another word about it, miss. It's of no consequence . . . no consequence whatever. Accidents will happen. I'm too hasty myself sometimes, miss . . . far too hasty. But I can't help speaking out just what I think, and folks must take me as they find me. If that cow had been in my cabbages now . . . but never mind, she wasn't, so it's all right. I think I'd rather have your cow in exchange, since you want to be rid of her.'

Oh, thank you, Mr Harrison. I'm so glad you are not vexed. I was afraid you would be.'

'And I suppose you were scared to death to come here and tell me, after the fuss I made yesterday, hey? But you mustn't mind me. I'm a terrible outspoken old fellow, that's all ... awful apt to tell the truth, no matter if it is a bit plain.'

'So is Mrs Lynde,' said Anne, before she could prevent herself.

'Who? Mrs Lynde? Don't you tell me I'm like that old gossip,' said Mr Harrison irritably. 'I'm not ... not a bit. What have you got in that box?'

'A cake,' said Anne archly. In her relief at Mr Harrison's unexpected amiability her spirits soared upward feather-light. 'I brought it over for you ... I thought perhaps you didn't have cake very often.'

'I don't, that's a fact, and I'm mighty fond of it, too. I'm much obliged to you. It looks good on top. I hope it's good all the way through.'

'It is,' said Anne, gaily confident. 'I have made cakes in my time that were *not*, as Mrs Allan could tell you, but this one is all right. I made it for the Improvement Society, but I can make another for them.'

'Well, I'll tell you what, miss, you must help me eat it. I'll put the kettle on and we'll have a cup of tea. How will that do?'

'Will you let me make the tea?' said Anne dubiously.

Mr Harrison chuckled.

'I see you haven't much confidence in my ability to make tea. You're wrong ... I can brew up as good a jorum of tea as you ever drank. But go ahead yourself. Fortunately it rained last Sunday, so there's plenty clean dishes.'

Anne hopped briskly up and went to work. She washed the teapot in several waters before she put the tea to steep. Then she swept the stove and set the table, bringing the dishes out of the pantry. The state of that pantry horrified Anne, but she wisely said nothing. Mr Harrison told her where to find the bread and butter and a can of peaches. Anne adorned the table with a bouquet from the garden and shut her eyes to the stains on the tablecloth. Soon the tea was ready and Anne found herself sitting opposite Mr Harrison at his own table, pouring his tea for him, and chatting freely to him about her school and friends and plans. She could hardly believe the evidence of her senses.

Mr Harrison had brought Ginger back, averring that the poor bird would be lonesome; and Anne, feeling that she could forgive everybody and everything, offered him a walnut. But Ginger's feelings had been grievously hurt and he rejected all overtures of friendliness. He sat moodily on his perch and ruffled his feathers up until he looked like a mere ball of green and gold.

'Why do you call him Ginger?' asked Anne, who liked appropriate names and thought Ginger accorded not at all with such gorgeous plumage.

'My brother the sailor named him. Maybe it had some reference to his temper. I think a lot of that bird though . . . you'd be surprised if you knew how much. He has his faults of course. That bird has cost me a good deal one way and another. Some people object to his swearing habits, but he can't be broken of them. I've tried . . . other people have tried. Some folks have prejudices against parrots. Silly, ain't it? I like them myself. Ginger's a lot of company to me. Nothing would induce me to give that bird up . . . nothing in the world, miss.'

Mr Harrison flung the last sentence at Anne as explosively as if he suspected her of some latent design of persuading him to give Ginger up. Anne, however, was beginning to like the queer, fussy, fidgety little man, and before the meal was over they were quite good friends. Mr Harrison found out about the Improvement Society and was disposed to approve of it.

'That's right. Go ahead. There's lots of room for improvement in this settlement . . . and in the people too.'

'Oh, I don't know,' flashed Anne. To herself, or to her particular cronies, she might admit that there were some small imperfections, easily removable, in Avonlea and its inhabitants. But to hear a practical outsider like Mr Harrison saying it was an entirely different thing. 'I think Avonlea is a lovely place; and the people in it are very nice, too.'

'I guess you've got a spice of temper,' commented Mr Harrison, surveying the flushed cheeks and indignant eyes opposite him. 'It goes with hair like yours, I reckon. Avonlea is a pretty decent place or I wouldn't have located here; but I suppose even you will admit that it has *some* faults?'

'I like it all the better for them,' said loyal Anne. 'I don't like places or people either that haven't any faults. I think a truly perfect person would be very uninteresting. Mrs Milton White says she never met a perfect person, but she'd heard enough about one . . . her husband's first wife. Don't you think it must be very uncomfortable to be married to a man whose first wife was perfect?'

'It would be more uncomfortable to be married to the perfect wife,' declared Mr Harrison, with a sudden and inexplicable warmth.

When tea was over Anne insisted on washing the dishes, although Mr Harrison assured her that there were enough in the house to do for weeks yet. She would dearly have loved to sweep the floor also, but no broom was visible and she did not like to ask where it was for fear there wasn't one at all.

'You might run across and talk to me once in a while,' suggested Mr Harrison when she was leaving. ' 'Tisn't far and folks ought to be neighbourly. I'm kind of interested in that society of yours. Seems to me there'll be some fun in it. Who are you going to tackle first?'

'We are not going to meddle with *people* . . . it is only *places* we mean to improve,' said Anne, in a dignified tone. She rather suspected that Mr Harrison was making fun of the project.

When she had gone Mr Harrison watched her from the window . . . a lithe, girlish shape, tripping light-heartedly across the fields in the sunset afterglow.

'I'm a crusty, lonesome, crabbed old chap,' he said aloud, 'but there's something about that little girl makes me feel young again . . . and it's such a pleasant sensation I'd like to have it repeated once in a while.'

'Red-headed snippet,' croaked Ginger mockingly.

Mr Harrison shook his fist at the parrot.

'You ornery bird,' he muttered. 'I almost wish I'd wrung your neck when my brother the sailor brought you home. Will you never be done getting me into trouble?'

Anne ran home blithely and recounted her adventures to Marilla, who had been not a little alarmed by her long absence and was on the point of starting out to look for her.

'It's a pretty good world, after all, isn't it, Marilla?' concluded Anne happily. 'Mrs Lynde was complaining the other day that it wasn't much of a world. She said whenever you looked forward to anything pleasant you were sure to be more or less disappointed ... that nothing ever came up to your expectations. Well, perhaps that is true. But there is a good side to it too. The bad things don't always come up to your expectations either ... they nearly always turn out ever so much better than you think. I looked forward to a dreadfully unpleasant experience when I went over to Mr Harrison's tonight; and instead he was quite kind and I had almost a nice time. I think we're going to be real good friends if we make plenty of allowances for each other, and everything has turned out for the best. But all the same, Marilla, I shall certainly never again sell a cow before making sure to whom she belongs. And I do not like parrots!'

CHAPTER 4

Different Opinions

ONE evening at sunset, Jane Andrews, Gilbert Blythe, and Anne Shirley were lingering by a fence in the shadow of gently swaying spruce-boughs, where a wood cut known as the Birch Path joined the main road. Jane had been up to spend the afternoon with Anne, who walked part of the way home with her; at the fence they met Gilbert, and all three were now talking about the fateful morrow; for that morrow was the first of September and the schools would open. Jane would go to Newbridge and Gilbert to White Sands.

'You both have the advantage of me,' sighed Anne. 'You're going to teach children who don't know you, but I have to teach my own old schoolmates, and Mrs Lynde says she's afraid they won't respect me as they would a stranger unless I'm very cross from the first. But I don't believe a teacher should be cross. Oh, it seems to me such a responsibility!'

'I guess we'll get on all right,' said Jane, comfortably. Jane was not troubled by any aspirations to be an influence for good. She meant to earn her salary fairly, please the trustees, and get her name on the School Inspector's roll of honour. Further ambitions Jane had none. 'The main thing will be to keep order and a teacher has to be a little cross to do that. If my pupils won't do as I tell them I shall punish them.'

'How?'

'Give them a good whipping, of course.'

'Oh, Jane, you wouldn't,' cried Anne, shocked. 'Jane, you *couldn't*!'

'Indeed I could and would, if they deserved it,' said Jane decidedly.

'I could *never* whip a child,' said Anne with equal decision. 'I don't believe in it *at all*. Miss Stacy never whipped any of us and she had perfect order; and Mr Phillips was always whipping and he had no order at all. No, if I can't get along without whipping I shall not try to teach school. There are better ways of managing. I shall try to win my pupils' affections and then they will *want* to do what I tell them.'

'But suppose they don't?' said practical Jane.

'I wouldn't whip them, anyhow. I'm sure it wouldn't do any good. Oh, don't whip your pupils, Jane, dear, no matter what they do.'

'What do you think about it, Gilbert?' demanded Jane. 'Don't you think there are some children who really need a whipping now and then?'

'Don't you think it's a cruel, barbarous thing to whip a child ... *any* child?' exclaimed Anne, her face flushing with earnestness.

'Well,' said Gilbert slowly, torn between his real convictions and his wish to measure up to Anne's ideal, 'there's something to be said on both sides. I don't believe in whipping children *much*. I think, as you say, Anne, that there are better ways of managing as a rule, and that corporal punishment should be a last resort. But on the other hand, as Jane says, I believe there is an occasional child who can't be influenced in any other way and who, in short, needs a whipping and would be improved by it. Corporal punishment as a last resort is to be my rule.'

Gilbert, having tried to please both sides, succeeded, as is usual and eminently right, in pleasing neither. Jane tossed her head.

'I'll whip my pupils when they're naughty. It's the shortest and easiest way of convincing them.'

Anne gave Gilbert a disappointed glance.

'I shall never whip a child,' she repeated firmly. 'I feel sure it isn't either right or necessary.'

'Suppose a boy sauced you back when you told him to do something?' said Jane.

'I'd keep him in after school and talk kindly and firmly to him,' said Anne. 'There is some good in every person if you can find it. It is a teacher's duty to find and develop it. That is what our School Management professor at Queen's told us, you know. Do you suppose you could find any good in a child by whipping him? It's far more important to influence the children aright than it is even to teach them the three R's, Professor Rennie says.'

'But the Inspector examines them in the three R's, mind you, and he won't give you a good report if they don't come up to his standard,' protested Jane.

'I'd rather have my pupils love me and look back to me in after years as a real helper than be on the roll of honour,' asserted Anne decidedly.

'Wouldn't you punish children at all, when they misbehaved?' asked Gilbert.

'Oh, yes, I suppose I shall have to, although I know I'll hate to do it. But you can keep them in at recess or stand them on the floor or give them lines to write.'

'I suppose you won't punish the girls by making them sit with the boys?' said Jane slyly.

Gilbert and Anne looked at each other and smiled rather foolishly. Once upon a time, Anne had been made to sit with Gilbert for punishment, and sad and bitter had been the consequences thereof.

'Well, time will tell which is the best way,' said Jane philosophically as they parted.

Anne went back to Green Gables by way of the Birch Path,

shadowy, rustling, fern-scented, through Violet Vale and past Willowmere, where dark and light kissed each other under the firs, and down through Lovers' Lane ... spots she and Diana had so named long ago. She walked slowly, enjoying the sweetness of wood and field and the starry summer twilight, and thinking soberly about the new duties she was to take up on the morrow. When she reached the yard at Green Gables Mrs Lynde's loud, decided tones floated out through the open kitchen window.

'Mrs Lynde has come up to give me good advice about tomorrow,' thought Anne with a grimace, 'but I don't believe I'll go in. Her advice is much like pepper, I think ... excellent in small quantities but rather scorching in her doses. I'll run over and have a chat with Mr Harrison instead.'

This was not the first time Anne had run over and chatted with Mr Harrison since the notable affair of the Jersey cow. She had been there several evenings and Mr Harrison and she were very good friends, although there were times and seasons when Anne found the outspokenness on which he prided himself rather trying. Ginger still continued to regard her with suspicion, and never failed to greet her sarcastically as 'red-headed snippet'. Mr Harrison had tried vainly to break him of the habit by jumping excitedly up whenever he saw Anne coming and exclaiming,

'Bless my soul, here's that pretty little girl again,' or something equally flattering. But Ginger saw through the scheme and scorned it. Anne was never to know how many compliments Mr Harrison paid her behind her back. He certainly never paid her any to her face.

'Well, I suppose you've been back in the woods laying in a supply of switches for tomorrow?' was his greeting as Anne came up the veranda steps.

'No, indeed,' said Anne indignantly. She was an excellent target for teasing because she always took things so seriously. 'I shall never have a switch in my school, Mr Harrison. Of course, I shall have to have a pointer, but I shall use it for pointing *only*.'

So you mean to strap them instead? Well, I don't know but

you're right. A switch stings more at the time but the strap smarts longer, that's a fact.'

'I shall not use anything of the sort. I'm not going to whip my pupils.'

'Bless my soul,' exclaimed Mr Harrison in genuine astonishment, 'how do you lay out to keep order then?'

'I shall govern by affection, Mr Harrison.'

'It won't do,' said Mr Harrison, 'won't do at all, Anne. "Spare the rod and spoil the child." When I went to school the master whipped me regular every day because he said if I wasn't in mischief just then I was plotting it.'

'Methods have changed since your schooldays, Mr Harrison.'

'But human nature hasn't. Mark my words, you'll never manage the young fry unless you keep a rod in pickle for them. The thing is impossible.'

'Well, I'm going to try my way first,' said Anne, who had a fairly strong will of her own and was apt to cling very tenaciously to her theories.

'You're pretty stubborn, I reckon,' was Mr Harrison's way of putting it. 'Well, well, we'll see. Some day when you get riled up ... and people with hair like yours are desperate apt to get riled ... you'll forget all your pretty little notions and give some of them a whaling. You're too young to be teaching anyhow ... far too young and childish.'

Altogether, Anne went to bed that night in a rather pessimistic mood. She slept poorly and was so pale and tragic at breakfast next morning that Marilla was alarmed and insisted on making her take a cup of scorching ginger tea. Anne sipped it patiently, although she could not imagine what good ginger tea would do. Had it been some magic brew, potent to confer age and experience, Anne would have swallowed a quart of it without flinching.

'Marilla, what if I fail!'

'You'll hardly fail completely in one day and there's plenty more days coming,' said Marilla. 'The trouble with you, Anne, is that you'll expect to teach those children everything and reform all their faults right off, and if you can't you'll think you've failed.'

CHAPTER 5

A Full-fledged Schoolma'am

WHEN Anne reached the school that morning . . . for the first time in her life she had traversed the Birch Path deaf and blind to its beauties . . . all was quiet and still. The preceding teacher had trained the children to be in their places at her arrival, and when Anne entered the schoolroom she was confronted by prim rows of 'shining morning faces' and bright, inquisitive eyes. She hung up her hat and faced her pupils, hoping that she did not look as frightened and foolish as she felt and that they would not perceive how she was trembling.

She had sat up until nearly twelve the preceding night composing a speech she meant to make to her pupils upon opening the school. She had revised and improved it painstakingly, and then she had learned it off by heart. It was a very good speech and had some very fine ideas in it, especially about mutual help and earnest striving after knowledge. The only trouble was that she could not now remember a word of it.

After what seemed to her a year . . . about ten seconds in reality . . . she said faintly, 'Take your Testaments, please,' and sank breathlessly into her chair under cover of the rustle and clatter of desk lids that followed. While the children read their verses Anne marshalled her shaky wits into order and looked over the array of little pilgrims to the Grown-up Land.

Most of them were, of course, quite well known to her. Her own classmates had passed out in the preceding year but the rest had all gone to school with her, excepting the primer class and ten newcomers to Avonlea. Anne secretly felt more interest in these ten than in those whose possibilities were already fairly well mapped out to her. To be sure, they might be just as commonplace as the rest; but on the other hand there *might* be a genius among them. It was a thrilling idea.

Sitting by himself at a corner desk was Anthony Pye. He had a dark, sullen little face, and was staring at Anne with a hostile expression in his black eyes. Anne instantly made up her mind that she would win that boy's affection and discomfit the Pyes utterly.

In the other corner another strange boy was sitting with Arty Sloane . . . a jolly-looking little chap, with a snub nose, freckled face, and big, light blue eyes, fringed with whitish lashes . . . probably the Donnell boy; and if resemblance went for anything, his sister was sitting across the aisle with Mary Bell. Anne wondered what sort of a mother the child had, to send her to school dressed as she was. She wore a faded pink silk dress, trimmed with a great deal of cotton lace, soiled white kid slippers, and silk stockings. Her sandy hair was tortured into innumerable kinky and unnatural curls, surmounted by a flamboyant bow of pink ribbon bigger than her head. Judging from her expression she was very well satisfied with herself.

A pale little thing, with smooth ripples of fine, silky, fawn-coloured hair flowing over her shoulders, must, Anne thought, be Annetta Bell, whose parents had formerly lived in the New-bridge school district, but, by reason of hauling their house fifty yards north of its old site, were now in Avonlea. Three pallid little girls crowded into one seat were certainly Cottons; and there was no doubt that the small beauty with the long brown curls and hazel eyes, who was casting coquettish looks at Jack Gillis over the edge of her Testament, was Prillie Rogerson, whose father had recently married a second wife and brought Prillie home from her grandmother's in Grafton. A tall, awkward girl in a back seat, who seemed to have too many feet and hands, Anne could not place at all, but later on discovered that her name was Barbara Shaw, and that she had come to live with an Avonlea aunt. She was also to find that if Barbara ever managed to walk down the aisle without falling over her own or somebody else's feet the Avonlea scholars wrote the unusual fact up on the porch wall to commemorate it.

But when Anne's eyes met those of the boy at the front desk facing her own, a queer little thrill went over her, as if she had found her genius. She knew this must be Paul Irving and that Mrs Rachel Lynde had been right for once when she prophesied that he would be unlike the Avonlea children. More than that, Anne realized that he was unlike other children anywhere, and

35

that there was a soul subtly akin to her own gazing at her out of the very dark blue eyes that were watching her so intently.

She knew Paul was ten but he looked no more than eight. He had the most beautiful little face she had ever seen in a child ... features of exquisite delicacy and refinement, framed in a halo of chestnut curls. His mouth was delicious, being full without pouting, the crimson lips just softly touching and curving into finely finished little corners that narrowly escaped being dimpled. He had a sober, grave, meditative expression, as if his spirit was much older than his body; but when Anne smiled softly at him it vanished in a sudden answering smile, which seemed an illumination of his whole being, as if some lamp had suddenly kindled into flame inside him, irradiating him from top to toe. Best of all, it was involuntary, born of no external effort or motive, but simply the outflashing of a hidden personality, rare and fine and sweet. With that quick interchange of smiles Anne and Paul were fast friends for ever before a word had passed between them.

The day went by like a dream. Anne could never clearly recall it afterwards. It almost seemed as if it were not she who was teaching but somebody else. She heard classes and worked sums and set copies mechanically. The children behaved quite well; only two cases of discipline occurred. Morley Andrews was caught driving a pair of trained crickets in the aisle. Anne stood Morley on the platform for an hour and ... which Morley felt much more keenly ... confiscated his crickets. She put them in a box and on the way from school set them free in Violet Vale; but Morley believed, then and ever afterwards, that she took them home and kept them for her own private amusement.

The other culprit was Anthony Pye, who poured the last drops of water from his slate-bottle down the back of Aurelia Clay's neck. Anne kept Anthony in at recess and talked to him about what was expected of gentlemen, admonishing him that they never poured water down ladies' necks. She wanted all her boys to be gentlemen, she said. Her little lecture was quite kind and touching; but unfortunately Anthony remained absolutely untouched. He listened to her in silence, with the same sullen expression, and whistled scornfully as he went out. Anne sighed; and then cheered herself up by remembering that winning a Pye's affections, like the building of Rome, wasn't the work of a day. In fact, it was doubtful whether some of the Pyes had any affections to win; but Anne hoped better things of Anthony, who looked as if he might be a rather nice boy if one ever got behind his sullenness.

When school was dismissed and the children had gone Anne dropped wearily into her chair. Her head ached and she felt woefully discouraged. There was no real reason for discouragement, since nothing very dreadful had occurred; but Anne was very tired and inclined to believe that she would never learn to like teaching. And how terrible it would be to be doing something you didn't like every day for . . . well, say forty years. Anne was of two minds whether to have her cry out then and there, or wait till she was safely in her own white room at home. Before she could decide there was a click of heels and a silken swish on the porch floor, and Anne found herself confronted by a lady whose appearance made her recall a recent criticism of Mr Harrison's on an over-dressed female he had seen in a Charlottetown store. 'She looked like a head-on collision between a fashion plate and a nightmare.'

The newcomer was gorgeously arrayed in a pale blue summer silk, puffed, frilled, and shirred wherever puff, frill, or shirring could possibly be placed. Her head was surmounted by a huge white chiffon hat, bedecked with three long but rather stringy ostrich feathers. A veil of pink chiffon, lavishly sprinkled with huge black dots, hung like a flounce from the hat brim to her shoulders and floated off in two airy streamers behind her. She wore all the jewellery that could be crowded on one small woman, and a very strong odour of perfume attended her.

'I am Mrs Don*nell* . . . Mrs H. B. Don*nell*,' announced this vision, 'and I have come in to see you about something Clarice Almira told me when she came home to dinner today. It annoyed me *excessively*.'

'I'm sorry,' faltered Anne, vainly trying to recollect any incident of the morning connected with the Donnell children.

'Clarice Almira told me that you pronounced our name

*Don*nell. Now, Miss Shirley, the correct pronunciation of our name is Don*nell* ... accent on the last syllable. I *hope* you'll remember this in future.'

'I'll try to,' gasped Anne, choking back a wild desire to laugh. 'I know by experience that it's very unpleasant to have one's name *spelled* wrong and I suppose it must be even worse to have it pronounced wrong.'

'Certainly it is. And Clarice Almira also informed me that you call my son Jacob.'

'He told me his name was Jacob,' protested Anne.

'I might have expected that,' said Mrs H. B. Don*nell*, in a tone which implied that gratitude in children was not to be looked for in this degenerate age. 'That boy has such plebeian tastes, Miss Shirley. When he was born I wanted to call him St Clair ... it sounds *so* aristocratic, doesn't it? But his father insisted he should be called Jacob after his uncle. I yielded, because Uncle Jacob was a rich old bachelor. And what do you think, Miss Shirley? When our innocent boy was five years old Uncle Jacob actually went and got married and now he has three boys of his own. Did you ever hear of such ingratitude? The moment the invitation to the wedding ... for he had the impertinence to send us an invitation, Miss Shirley ... came to the house I said, "No more Jacobs for me, thank you." From that day I called my son St Clair, and St Clair I am determined he shall be called. His father obstinately continues to call him Jacob, and the boy himself has a perfectly unaccountable preference for the vulgar name. But St Clair he is and St Clair he shall remain. You will kindly remember this, Miss Shirley, will you not? *Thank* you. I told Clarice Almira that I was sure it was only a misunderstanding and that a word would set it right. Don*nell* ... accent on last syllable ... and St Clair ... on *no* account Jacob. You'll remember? *Thank* you.'

When Mrs H. B. Don*nell* had skimmed away Anne locked the school door and went home. At the foot of the hill she found Paul Irving by the Birch Path. He held out to her a cluster of the dainty little wild orchids which Avonlea children called 'rice lilies'.

'Please, teacher, I found these in Mr Wright's field,' he said shyly, 'and I came back to give them to you because I thought you were the kind of lady that would like them, and because' . . . he lifted his big, beautiful eyes . . . 'I like you, teacher.'

'You darling,' said Anne, taking the fragrant spikes. As if Paul's words had been a spell of magic, discouragement and weariness passed from her spirit, and hope upwelled in her heart like a dancing fountain. She went through the Birch Path light-footedly, attended by the sweetness of her orchids as by a benediction.

'Well, how did you get along?' Marilla wanted to know.

'Ask me that a month later and I may be able to tell you. I can't now . . . I don't know myself . . . I'm too near it. My thoughts feel as if they had been all stirred up until they were thick and muddy. The only thing I feel really sure of having accomplished today is that I taught Cliffie Wright that A is A. He never knew it before. Isn't it something to have started a soul along a path that may end in Shakespeare and *Paradise Lost*?'

Mrs Lynde came up later on with more encouragement. That good lady had waylaid the schoolchildren at her gate and demanded of them how they liked their new teacher.

'And every one of them said they liked you splendid, Anne, except Anthony Pye. I must admit he didn't. He said you "weren't any good, just like all girl teachers." There's the Pye leaven for you. But never mind.'

'I'm not going to mind,' said Anne quietly, 'and I'm going to make Anthony Pye like me yet. Patience and kindness will surely win him.'

'Well, you can never tell about a Pye,' said Mrs Rachel cautiously. 'They go by contraries, like dreams, often as not. As for that *Don*nell woman, she'll get no Don*nell*ing from me, I can assure you. The name is *Don*nell and always has been. The woman is crazy, that's what. She has a pug dog she calls Queenie and it has its meals at the table along with the family, eating off a china plate. I'd be afraid of a judgement if I was her. Thomas says Donnell himself is a sensible, hard-working man, but he hadn't much gumption when he picked out a wife, that's what.'

CHAPTER 6

All Sorts and Conditions of Men . . . and Women

A SEPTEMBER day on Prince Edward Island Hills; a crisp wind blowing up over the sand dunes from the sea; a long red road, winding through fields and woods, now looping itself about a corner of thick-set spruces, now threading a plantation of young maples with great feathery sheets of ferns beneath them, now dipping down into a hollow where a brook flashed out of the woods and into them again, now basking in open sunshine between ribbons of goldenrod and smoke-blue asters; athrill with the pipings of myriads of crickets, those glad little pensioners of the summer hills; a plump brown pony ambling along the road; two girls behind him, full to the lips with the simple, priceless joy of youth and life.

'Oh, this is a day left over from Eden, isn't it, Diana?' . . . and Anne sighed for sheer happiness. 'The air has magic in it. Look at the purple in the cup of that harvest valley, Diana. And oh, do smell the dying fir! It's coming up from that little sunny hollow where Mr Eben Wright has been cutting fence poles. Bliss is it on such a day to be alive; but to smell dying fir is very heaven. That's two thirds Wordsworth and one third Anne Shirley. It doesn't seem possible that there should be dying fir in heaven, does it? And yet it doesn't seem to me that heaven would be quite perfect if you couldn't get a whiff of dead fir as you went through its woods. Perhaps we'll have the odour there without the death. Yes, I think that will be the way. That delicious aroma must be the souls of the firs . . . and of course it will be just souls in heaven.'

'Trees haven't souls,' said practical Diana, 'but the smell of dead fir is certainly lovely. I'm going to make a cushion and fill it with fir needles. You'd better make one too, Anne.'

'I think I shall . . . and use it for my naps. I'd be certain to dream I was a dryad or a wood-nymph then. But just this minute I'm well content to be Anne Shirley, Avonlea schoolma'am, driving over a road like this on such a sweet, friendly day.'

'It's a lovely day but we have anything but a lovely task before us,' sighed Diana. 'Why on earth did you offer to canvass this road, Anne? Almost all the cranks in Avonlea live along it, and we'll probably be treated as if we were begging for ourselves. It's the very worst road of all.'

'That is why I chose it. Of course Gilbert and Fred would have taken this road if we had asked them. But you see, Diana, I feel myself responsible for the A.V.I.S., since I was the first to suggest it, and it seems to me that I ought to do the most disagreeable things. I'm sorry on your account; but you needn't say a word at the cranky places. I'll do all the talking ... Mrs Lynde would say I was well able to. Mrs Lynde doesn't know whether to approve of our enterprise or not. She inclines to, when she remembers that Mr and Mrs Allan are in favour of it, but the fact that village improvement societies first originated in the States is a count against it. So she is halting between two opinions and only success will justify us in Mrs Lynde's eyes. Priscilla is going to write a paper for our next Improvement meeting, and I expect it will be good, for her aunt is such a clever writer and no doubt it runs in the family. I shall never forget the thrill it gave me when I found out that Mrs Charlotte E. Morgan was Priscilla's aunt. It seemed so wonderful that I was a friend of the girl whose aunt wrote *Edgewood Days* and *The Rosebud Garden*.'

'Where does Mrs Morgan live?'

'In Toronto. And Priscilla says she is coming to the Island for a visit next summer, and if it is possible Priscilla is going to arrange to have us meet her. That seems almost too good to be true – but it's something pleasant to imagine after you go to bed.'

The Avonlea Village Improvement Society was an organized fact. Gilbert Blythe was president, Fred Wright vice-president, Anne Shirley secretary, and Diana Barry treasurer. The 'Improvers', as they were promptly christened, were to meet once a fortnight at the homes of the members. It was admitted that they could not expect to effect many improvements so late in the season; but they meant to plan the next summer's campaign, collect and discuss ideas, write and read papers, and, as Anne said, educate public sentiment generally.

There was some disapproval, of course, and ... which the Improvers felt much more keenly ... a good deal of ridicule. Mr Elisha Wright was reported to have said that a more appropriate name for the organization would be Courting Club. Mrs Mirian Sloane declared she had heard the Improvers meant to plough up all the roadsides and set them out with geraniums. Mr Levi Boulter warned his neighbours that the Improvers would insist that everybody pull down his house and rebuild it after plans approved by the society. Mr James Spencer sent them word that he wished they would kindly shovel down the church hill. Eben Wright told Anne that he wished the Improvers could induce old Josiah Sloane to keep his whiskers trimmed. Mr Lawrence Bell said he would whitewash his barns if nothing else would please them but he would *not* hang lace curtains in his cow-stable windows. Mr Major Spencer asked Clifton Sloane, an Improver who drove the milk to the Carmody cheese factory, if it was true that everybody would have to have his milk-stand hand-painted next summer and keep an embroidered centre-piece on it.

In spite of ... or perhaps, human nature being what it is, because of ... this, the Society went gamely to work at the only improvement they could hope to bring about that fall. At the second meeting, in the Barry parlour, Oliver Sloane moved that they start a subscription to re-shingle and paint the hall; Julia Bell seconded it, with an uneasy feeling that she was doing something not exactly lady-like. Gilbert put the motion, it was carried unanimously, and Anne gravely recorded it in her minutes. The next thing was to appoint a committee, and Gertie Pye, determined not to let Julia Bell carry off all the laurels, boldly moved that Miss Jane Andrews be chairman of said committee. This motion being also duly seconded and carried, Jane returned the compliment by appointing Gertie on the committee, along with Gilbert, Anne, Diana, and Fred Wright. The committee chose their routes in private conclave. Anne and Diana were told off for the Newbridge road, Gilbert and Fred for the White Sands road, and Jane and Gertie for the Carmody road.

'Because,' explained Gilbert to Anne, as they walked home

together through the Haunted Wood, 'the Pyes all live along that road and they won't give a cent unless one of themselves canvasses them.'

The next Saturday Anne and Diana started out. They drove to the end of the road and canvassed homeward, calling first on the 'Andrews girls'.

'If Catherine is alone we may get something,' said Diana, 'but if Eliza is there we won't.'

Eliza was there . . . very much so . . . and looked even grimmer than usual. Miss Eliza was one of those people who give you the impression that life is indeed a vale of tears, and that a smile, never to speak of a laugh, is a waste of nervous energy truly reprehensible. The Andrews girls had been 'girls' for fifty odd years and seemed likely to remain girls to the end of their earthly pilgrimage. Catherine, it was said, had not entirely given up hope, but Eliza, who was born a pessimist, had never had any. They lived in a little brown house built in a sunny corner scooped out of Mark Andrews' beech woods. Eliza complained that it was terrible hot in summer, but Catherine was wont to say it was lovely and warm in winter.

Eliza was sewing patchwork, not because it was needed but simply as a protest against the frivolous lace Catherine was crocheting. Eliza listened with a frown and Catherine with a smile, as the girls explained their errand. To be sure, whenever Catherine caught Eliza's eye she discarded the smile in guilty confusion; but it crept back the next moment.

'If I had money to waste,' said Eliza grimly, 'I'd burn it up and have the fun of seeing a blaze maybe; but I wouldn't give it to that hall, not a cent. It's no benefit to the settlement . . . just a place for young folks to meet and carry on when they'd better be home in their beds.'

'Oh, Eliza, young folks must have some amusement,' protested Catherine.

'I don't see the necessity. *We* didn't gad about to halls and places when we were young, Catherine Andrews. This world is getting worse every day.'

'I think it's getting better,' said Catherine firmly.

'*You* think!' Miss Eliza's voice expressed the utmost contempt. 'It doesn't signify what you *think*, Catherine Andrews. Facts is facts.'

'Well, I always like to look on the bright side, Eliza.'

'There isn't any bright side.'

'Oh, indeed there is,' cried Anne, who couldn't endure such heresy in silence. 'Why, there are ever so many bright sides, Miss Andrews. It's really a beautiful world.'

'You won't have such a high opinion of it when you've lived as long in it as I have,' retorted Miss Eliza sourly, 'and you won't be so enthusiastic about improving it either. How is your mother, Diana? Dear me, but she has failed of late. She looks terrible run down. And how long is it before Marilla expects to be stone blind, Anne?'

'The doctor thinks her eyes will not get any worse if she is very careful,' faltered Anne.

Eliza shook her head.

'Doctors always talk like that just to keep people cheered up. I wouldn't have much hope if I was her. It's best to be prepared for the worst.'

'But oughtn't we to be prepared for the best too?' pleaded Anne. 'It's just as likely to happen as the worst.'

'Not in my experience, and I've fifty-seven years to set against your sixteen,' retorted Eliza. 'Going, are you? Well, I hope this new society of yours will be able to keep Avonlea from running any further downhill but I haven't much hope of it.'

Anne and Diana got themselves thankfully out, and drove away as fast as the fat pony could go. As they rounded the curve below the beech wood a plump figure came speeding over Mr Andrews' pasture, waving to them excitedly. It was Catherine Andrews, and she was so out of breath that she could hardly speak, but she thrust a couple of quarters into Anne's hand.

'That's my contribution to painting the hall,' she gasped. 'I'd like to give you a dollar but I don't dare take more from my egg money, for Eliza would find it out if I did. I'm real interested in your society and I believe you're going to do a lot of good. I'm an optimist. I *have* to be, living with Eliza. I must hurry back before she misses me . . . she thinks I'm feeding the hens. I hope you'll have good luck canvassing, and don't be cast down over what Eliza said. The world *is* getting better . . . it certainly is.'

The next house was Daniel Blair's.

'Now, it all depends on whether his wife is home or not,' said Diana, as they jolted along a deep-rutted lane. 'If she is we won't get a cent. Everybody says Dan Blair doesn't dare have his hair cut without asking her permission; and it's certain she's very close, to state it moderately. She says she has to be just before she's generous. But Mrs Lynde says she's so much "before" that generosity never catches up with her at all.'

Anne related their experience at the Blair place to Marilla that evening.

'We tied the horse and then rapped at the kitchen door. Nobody came, but the door was open and we could hear somebody in the pantry, going on dreadfully. We couldn't make out the words but Diana says she knows they were swearing by the sound of them. I can't believe that of Mr Blair, for he is always so quiet and meek; but at least he had great provocation, for, Marilla, when that poor man came to the door, red as a beet, with perspiration streaming down his face, he had on one of his wife's big gingham aprons. "I can't get this durned thing off," he said, "for the strings are tied in a hard knot, and I can't bust 'em, so you'll have to excuse me, ladies." We begged him not to mention it and went in and sat down. Mr Blair sat down too; he twisted the apron around to his back and rolled it up, but he did look so ashamed and worried that I felt sorry for him, and Diana said she feared we had called at an inconvenient time. "Oh, not at all," said Mr Blair, trying to smile . . . you know he is always very polite . . . "I'm a little busy . . . getting ready to bake a cake as it were. My wife got a telegram today that her sister from Montreal is coming tonight and she's gone to the train to meet her and left orders for me to make a cake for tea. She writ out the recipe and told me what to do, but I've clean forgot half the directions already. And it says, 'flavour according to taste.' What does that mean? How can you tell? And what if my taste doesn't happen to be other people's taste? Would a tablespoon of vanilla be enough for a small layer cake?"

'I felt sorrier than ever for the poor man. He didn't seem to be in his proper sphere at all. I had heard of henpecked husbands and now I felt that I saw one. It was on my lips to say, "Mr Blair, if you'll give us a subscription for the hall I'll mix up your cake for you." But I suddenly thought it wouldn't be neighbourly to drive too sharp a bargain with a fellow creature in distress. So I offered to mix the cake for him without any conditions at all. He just jumped at my offer. He said he'd been used to making his own bread before he was married but he feared cake was beyond him, and yet he hated to disappoint his wife. He got me another apron, and Diana beat the eggs and I mixed the cake. Mr Blair ran about and got us the materials. He had forgotten all about his apron and when he ran it streamed out behind him and Diana said she thought she would die to see it. He said he could bake the cake all right . . . he was used to that . . . and then he asked for our list and he put down four dollars. So you see we were rewarded. But even if he hadn't given a cent I'd always feel that we had done a truly Christian act in helping him.'

Theodore White's was the next stopping-place. Neither Anne nor Diana had ever been there before, and they had only a very slight acquaintance with Mrs Theodore, who was not given to hospitality. Should they go to the back or front door? While they held a whispered consultation Mrs Theodore appeared at the front door with an armful of newspapers. Deliberately she laid them down one by one on the porch floor and the porch steps, and then down the path to the very feet of her mystified callers.

'Will you please wipe your feet carefully on the grass and then walk on these papers?' she said anxiously. 'I've just swept the house all over and I can't have any more dust tracked in. The path's been real muddy since the rain yesterday.'

'Don't you dare laugh,' warned Anne in a whisper, as they marched along the newspapers. 'And I implore you, Diana, not to look at me, no matter what she says, or I shall not be able to keep a sober face.'

The papers extended across the hall and into a prim, fleckless parlour. Anne and Diana sat down gingerly on the nearest chairs and explained their errand. Mrs White heard them politely, interrupting only twice, once to chase out an adventurous fly, and once to pick up a tiny wisp of grass that had fallen on the carpet from Anne's dress. Anne felt wretchedly guilty; but Mrs White subscribed two dollars and paid the money down . . . 'to prevent us from having to go back for it,' Diana said when they got away. Mrs White had the newspapers gathered up before they had their horses untied, and as they drove out of the yard they saw her busily wielding a broom in the hall.

'I've always heard that Mrs Theodore White was the neatest woman alive and I'll believe it after this,' said Diana, giving way to her suppressed laughter as soon as it was safe.

'I am glad she has no children,' said Anne solemnly. 'It would be dreadful beyond words for them if she had.'

At the Spencers' Mrs Isabella Spencer made them miserable by saying something ill-natured about every one in Avonlea. Mr Thomas Boulter refused to give anything because the hall, when it had been built, twenty years before, hadn't been built on the site he recommended. Mrs Esther Bell, who was the picture of health, took half an hour to detail all her aches and pains, and sadly put down fifty cents because she wouldn't be there that time next year to do it . . . no, she would be in her grave.

Their worst reception, however, was at Simon Fletcher's. When they drove into the yard they saw two faces peering at them through the porch window. But although they rapped and waited patiently and persistently nobody came to the door. Two decidedly ruffled and indignant girls drove away from Simon Fletcher's. Even Anne admitted that she was beginning to feel discouraged. But the tide turned after that. Several Sloane homesteads came next, where they got liberal subscriptions, and from that to the end they fared well, with only an occasional snub. Their last place of call was at Robert Dickson's by the pond bridge. They stayed to tea here, although they were nearly home, rather than risk offending Mrs Dickson, who had the reputation of being a very 'touchy' woman.

While they were there old Mrs James White called in.

'I've just been down to Lorenzo's,' she announced. 'He's the proudest man in Avonlea this minute. What do you think? There's a brand new boy there ... and after seven girls that's quite an event, I can tell you.'

Anne pricked up her ears, and when they drove away she said,

'I'm going straight to Lorenzo White's.'

'But he lives on the White Sands road and it's quite a distance out of our way,' protested Diana. 'Gilbert and Fred will canvass him.'

'They are not going around until next Saturday and it will be too late by then,' said Anne firmly. 'The novelty will be worn off. Lorenzo White is dreadfully mean but he will subscribe to *anything* just now. We mustn't let such a golden opportunity slip, Diana.'

The result justified Anne's foresight. Mr White met them in the yard, beaming like the sun upon an Easter day. When Anne asked for a subscription he agreed enthusiastically.

'Certain, certain. Just put me down for a dollar more than the highest subscription you've got.'

'That will be five dollars ... Mr Daniel Blair put down four,' said Anne, half afraid. But Lorenzo did not flinch.

'Five it is ... and here's the money on the spot. Now, I want you to come into the house. There's something in there worth seeing ... something very few people have seen as yet. Just come in and pass *your* opinion.'

'What will we say if the baby isn't pretty?' whispered Diana in trepidation as they followed the excited Lorenzo into the house.

'Oh, there will certainly be something else nice to say about it,' said Anne easily. 'There always is about a baby.'

The baby *was* pretty, however, and Mr White felt that he got his five dollars' worth out of the girls' honest delight over the plump little newcomer. But that was the first, last, and only time that Lorenzo White ever subscribed to anything.

Anne, tired as she was, made one more effort for the public weal that night, slipping over the fields to interview Mr Harrison, who was as usual smoking his pipe on the veranda with Ginger beside him. Strictly speaking he was on the Carmody road; but Jane and Gertie, who were not acquainted with him save by doubtful report, had nervously begged Anne to canvass him.

Mr Harrison, however, flatly refused to subscribe a cent, and all Anne's wiles were in vain.

'But I thought you approved of our society, Mr Harrison,' she mourned.

'So I do ... so I do ... but my approval doesn't go as deep as my pocket, Anne.'

'A few more experiences such as I have had today would make me as much of a pessimist as Miss Eliza Andrews,' Anne told her reflection in the east gable mirror at bedtime.

CHAPTER 7

The Pointing of Duty

ANNE leaned back in her chair one mild October evening and sighed. She was sitting at a table covered with textbooks and exercises, but the closely written sheets of paper before her had no apparent connection with studies or school work.

'What is the matter?' asked Gilbert, who had arrived at the open kitchen door just in time to hear the sigh.

Anne coloured, and thrust her writing out of sight under some school compositions.

'Nothing very dreadful. I was just trying to write out some of my thoughts, as Professor Hamilton advised me, but I couldn't get them to please me. They seem so stiff and foolish directly they're written down on white paper with black ink. Fancies are like shadows ... you can't cage them, they're such wayward dancing things. But perhaps I'll learn the secret some day if I keep on trying. I haven't a great many spare moments, you know. By the time I finish correcting school exercises and compositions, I don't always feel like writing any of my own.'

'You are getting on splendidly in school, Anne. All the children like you,' said Gilbert, sitting down on the stone step.

'No, not all. Anthony Pye doesn't and *won't* like me. What is worse, he doesn't respect me . . . no, he doesn't. He simply holds me in contempt, and I don't mind confessing to you that it worries me miserably. It isn't that he is so very bad . . . he is only rather mischievous, but no worse than some of the others. He seldom disobeys me; but he obeys with a scornful air of toleration as if it wasn't worth while disputing the point or he would . . . and it has a bad effect on the others. I've tried every way to win him but I'm beginning to fear I never shall. I want to, for he's rather a cute little lad, if he *is* a Pye, and I could like him if he'd let me.'

'Probably it's merely the effect of what he hears at home.'

'Not altogether. Anthony is an independent little chap and makes up his own mind about things. He has always gone to men before and he says girl teachers are no good. Well, we'll see what patience and kindness will do. I like overcoming difficulties and teaching is really very interesting work. Paul Irving makes up for all that is lacking in the others. That child is a perfect darling, Gilbert, and a genius into the bargain. I'm persuaded the world will hear of him some day,' concluded Anne in a tone of conviction.

'I like teaching, too,' said Gilbert. 'It's good training, for one thing. Why, Anne, I've learned more in the weeks I've been teaching the young ideas of White Sands than I learned in all the years I went to school myself. We all seem to be getting on pretty well. The Newbridge people like Jane, I hear; and I think White Sands is tolerably satisfied with your humble servant . . . all except Mr Andrew Spencer. I met Mrs Peter Blewett on my way home last night and she told me she thought it her duty to inform me that Mr Spencer didn't approve of my methods.'

'Have you ever noticed,' asked Anne reflectively, 'that when people say it is their duty to tell you a certain thing you may prepare for something disagreeable? Why is it that they never seem to think it a duty to tell you the pleasant things they hear about you? Mrs H. B. Don*nell* called at the school again yesterday and told me she thought it *her* duty to inform me that Mrs Harmon Andrews didn't approve of my reading fairy tales to the children, and that Mr Rogerson thought Prillie wasn't coming on fast enough in arithmetic. If Prillie would spend less time making eyes at the boys over her slate she might do better. I feel quite sure that Jack Gillis works her class sums for her, though I've never been able to catch him red-handed.'

'Have you succeeded in reconciling Mrs Donnell's hopeful son to his saintly name?'

'Yes,' laughed Anne, 'but it was really a difficult task. At first, when I called him "St Clair" he would not take the least notice until I'd spoken two or three times; and then, when the other boys nudged him, he would look up with such an aggrieved air, as if I'd called him John or Charlie and he couldn't be expected to know I meant him. So I kept him in after school one night and talked kindly to him. I told him his mother wished me to call him St Clair and I couldn't go against her wishes. He saw it when it was all explained out ... he's really a very reasonable little fellow ... and he said *I* could call him St Clair but that he'd "lick the stuffing" out of any of the boys that tried it. Of course, I had to rebuke him again for using such shocking language. Since then *I* call him St Clair and the boys call him Jake and all goes smoothly. He informs me that he means to be a carpenter, but Mrs Donnell says I am to make a college professor out of him.'

The mention of college gave a new direction to Gilbert's thoughts, and they talked for a time of their plans and wishes ... gravely, earnestly, hopefully, as youth loves to talk, while the future is yet an untrodden path full of wonderful possibilities.

Gilbert had finally made up his mind that he was going to be a doctor.

'It's a splendid profession,' he said enthusiastically. 'A fellow has to fight something all through life ... didn't somebody once define man as a fighting animal? ... and I want to fight disease and pain and ignorance ... which are all members one of another. I want to do my share of honest, real work in the world, Anne ... add a little to the sum of human knowledge that all the good men have been accumulating since it began. The folks who lived before me have done so much for me that I want to show my gratitude by doing something for the folks who will live after me. It seems to me that is the only way a fellow can get square with his obligations to the race.'

'I'd like to add some beauty to life,' said Anne dreamily. 'I don't exactly want to make people *know* more ... though I know that *is* the noblest ambition ... but I'd love to make them have a pleasanter time because of me ... to have some little joy or happy thought that would never have existed if I hadn't been born.'

'I think you're fulfilling that ambition every day,' said Gilbert admiringly.

And he was right. Anne was one of the children of light by birthright. After she had passed through a life with a smile or a word thrown across it like a gleam of sunshine the owner of that life saw it, for the time being at least, as hopeful and lovely and of good report.

Finally Gilbert rose regretfully.

'Well, I must run up to MacPhersons'. Moody Spurgeon came home from Queen's today for Sunday and he was to bring me out a book Professor Boyd is lending me.'

'And I must get Marilla's tea. She went to see Mrs Keith this evening and she will soon be back.'

Anne had tea ready when Marilla came home; the fire was crackling cheerily, a vase of frost-bleached ferns and ruby-red maple leaves adorned the table, and delectable odours of ham and toast pervaded the air. But Marilla sank into her chair with a deep sigh.

'Are your eyes troubling you? Does your head ache?' queried Anne anxiously.

'No. I'm only tired ... and worried. It's about Mary and those children. Mary is worse ... she can't last much longer. And as for the twins, *I* don't know what is to become of them.'

'Hasn't their uncle been heard from?'

'Yes, Mary had a letter from him. He's working in a lumber camp and "shacking it", whatever that means. Anyway, he says he can't possibly take the children till the spring. He expects to be married then and will have a home to take them to; but he says she must get some of the neighbours to keep them for the winter. She says she can't bear to ask any of them. Mary never got on any too well with the East Grafton people and that's a fact. And the long and short of it is, Anne, that I'm sure Mary wants me to take those children ... she didn't say so but she *looked* it.'

'Oh!' Anne clasped her hands, all athrill with excitement. 'And of course you will, Marilla, won't you?'

'I haven't made up my mind,' said Marilla rather tartly. 'I don't rush into things in your headlong way, Anne. Third cousinship is a pretty slim claim. And it will be a fearful responsibility to have two children of six years to look after ... twins, at that.'

Marilla had an idea that twins were just twice as bad as single children.

'Twins are very interesting ... at least one pair of them,' said Anne. 'It's only when there are two or three pairs that it gets monotonous. And I think it would be real nice for you to have something to amuse you when I'm away in school.'

'I don't reckon there'd be much amusement in it ... more worry and bother than anything else, I should say. It wouldn't be so risky if they were even as old as you were when I took you. I wouldn't mind Dora so much ... she seems good and quiet. But that Davy is a limb.'

Anne was fond of children and her heart yearned over the Keith twins. The remembrance of her own neglected childhood was very vivid with her still. She knew that Marilla's only vulnerable point was her stern devotion to what she believed to be her duty, and Anne skilfully marshalled her arguments along this line.

'If Davy is naughty it's all the more reason why he should have good training, isn't it, Marilla? If we don't take them we don't know who will, nor what kind of influences may surround them. Suppose Mrs Keith's next-door neighbours, the Sprotts, were to take them. Mrs Lynde says Henry Sprott is the most profane man that ever lived and you can't believe a word his children say. Wouldn't it be dreadful to have the twins learn anything like that? Or suppose they went to the Wiggins'. Mrs Lynde says that Mr Wiggins sells everything off the place that can be sold and brings his family up on skim milk. You wouldn't like your relations to be starved, even if they were only third cousins, would you? It seems to me, Marilla, that it is our duty to take them.'

'I suppose it is,' assented Marilla gloomily. 'I daresay I'll tell Mary I'll take them. You needn't look so delighted, Anne. It will mean a good deal of extra work for you. I can't sew a stitch on account of my eyes, so you'll have to see to the making and mending of their clothes. And you don't like sewing.'

'I hate it,' said Anne calmly, 'but if you are willing to take those children from a sense of duty surely I can do their sewing from a sense of duty. It does people good to have to do things they don't like . . . in moderation.'

CHAPTER 8

Marilla Adopts Twins

MRS RACHEL LYNDE was sitting at her kitchen window, knitting a quilt, just as she had been sitting one evening several years previously when Matthew Cuthbert had driven down over the hill with what Mrs Rachel called 'his imported orphan'. But that had been in springtime; and this was late autumn, and all the woods were leafless and the fields sere and brown. The sun was just setting with a great deal of purple and golden pomp behind the dark woods west of Avonlea when a buggy drawn by a comfortable brown nag came down the hill. Mrs Rachel peered at it eagerly.

'There's Marilla getting home from the funeral,' she said to her husband, who was lying on the kitchen lounge. Thomas Lynde lay more on the lounge nowadays than he had been used to do, but Mrs Rachel, who was so sharp at noticing anything beyond her own household, had not as yet noticed this. 'And she's got the twins with her, . . . yes, there's Davy leaning over the dashboard grabbing at the pony's tail and Marilla jerking him back. Dora's sitting up on the seat as prim as you please. She always looks as if she'd just been starched and ironed. Well, poor Marilla is going to have her hands full this winter and no mistake. Still, I don't see that she could do anything less than take them, under the circumstances, and she'll have Anne to help her. Anne's tickled to death over the whole business, and she has a real knacky way with children, I must say. Dear me, it doesn't seem a day since poor Matthew brought Anne herself home and everybody laughed at the idea of Marilla bringing up a child. And now she has adopted twins. You're never safe from being surprised till you're dead.'

The fat pony jogged over the bridge in Lynde's Hollow and along the Green Gables lane. Marilla's face was rather grim. It was ten miles from East Grafton and Davy Keith seemed to be possessed with a passion for perpetual motion. It was beyond Marilla's power to make him sit still and she had been in an agony the whole way lest he fall over the back of the wagon and break his neck, or tumble over the dashboard under the pony's heels. In despair she finally threatened to whip him soundly when she got him home. Whereupon Davy climbed into her lap, regardless of the reins, flung his chubby arms about her neck and gave her a bear-like hug.

'I don't believe you mean it,' he said, smacking her wrinkled cheek affectionately. 'You don't *look* like a lady who'd whip a little boy just 'cause he couldn't keep still. Didn't you find it awful hard to keep still when you was only 's old as me?'

'No, I always kept still when I was told,' said Marilla, trying to speak sternly, albeit she felt her heart waxing soft within her under Davy's impulsive caresses.

'Well, I s'pose that was 'cause you was 'a girl,' said Davy, squirming back to his place after another hug. 'You *was* a girl once, I s'pose, though it's awful funny to think of it. Dora can sit still . . . but there ain't much fun in it *I* don't think. Seems to me it must be slow to be a girl. Here, Dora, let me liven you up a bit.'

Davy's method of 'livening up' was to grasp Dora's curls in his fingers and give them a tug. Dora shrieked and then cried.

'How can you be such a naughty boy and your poor mother just laid in her grave this very day?' demanded Marilla despairingly.

'But she was glad to die,' said Davy confidentially. 'I know, 'cause she told me so. She was awful tired of being sick. We'd a long talk the night before she died. She told me you was going to take me and Dora for the winter and I was to be a good boy. I'm going to be good, but can't you be good running round just as well as sitting still? And she said I was always to be kind to Dora and stand up for her, and I'm going to.'

'Do you call pulling her hair being kind to her?'

'Well, I ain't going to let anybody else pull it,' said Davy, doubling up his fists and frowning. 'They'd just better try it. I didn't hurt her much ... she just cried 'cause she's a girl. I'm glad I'm a boy but I'm sorry I'm a twin. When Jimmy Sprott's sister conterdicks him he just says, "I'm oldern you, so of course I know better," and that settles *her*. But I can't tell Dora that, and she just goes on thinking diffrunt from me. You might let me drive the gee-gee for a spell, since I'm a man.'

Altogether, Marilla was a thankful woman when she drove into her own yard, where the wind of the autumn night was dancing with the brown leaves. Anne was at the gate to meet them and lift the twins out. Dora submitted calmly to be kissed, but Davy responded to Anne's welcome with one of his hearty hugs and the cheerful announcement, 'I'm Mr Davy Keith.'

At the supper table Dora behaved like a little lady, but Davy's manners left much to be desired.

'I'm so hungry I ain't got time to eat p'litely,' he said when Marilla reproved him. 'Dora ain't half as hungry as I am. Look at all the ex'cise I took on the road here. That cake's awful nice and plummy. We haven't had any cake at home for ever'n ever so long, 'cause Mother was too sick to make it and Mrs Sprott said it was as much as she could do to bake our bread for us. And Mrs Wiggins never puts any plums in *her* cakes. Catch her! Can I have another piece?'

Marilla would have refused but Anne cut a generous second slice. However, she reminded Davy that he ought to say 'Thank you' for it. Davy merely grinned at her and took a huge bite. When he had finished the slice he said,

'If you'll give me *another* piece I'll say "Thank you" for *it*.'

'No, you have had plenty of cake,' said Marilla in a tone which Anne knew and Davy was to learn to be final.

Davy winked at Anne, and then, leaning over the table,

snatched Dora's first piece of cake, from which she had just taken one dainty little bite, out of her very fingers and, opening his mouth to the fullest extent, crammed the whole slice in. Dora's lip trembled and Marilla was speechless with horror. Anne promptly exclaimed, with her best 'schoolma'am' air, 'Oh, Davy, gentlemen don't do things like that.'

'I know they don't,' said Davy, as soon as he could speak, 'but I ain't a gemplum.'

'But don't you want to be?' said shocked Anne.

'Course I do. But you can't be a gemplum till you grow up.'

'Oh, indeed you can,' Anne hastened to say, thinking she saw a chance to sow good seed betimes. 'You can begin to be a gentleman when you are a little boy. And gentlemen *never* snatch things from ladies . . . or forget to say thank you . . . or pull anybody's hair.'

'They don't have much fun, that's a fact,' said Davy frankly. 'I guess I'll wait till I'm grown up to be one.'

Marilla, with a resigned air, had cut another piece of cake for Dora. She did not feel able to cope with Davy just then. It had been a hard day for her, what with the funeral and the long drive. At that moment she looked forward to the future with a pessimism that would have done credit to Eliza Andrews herself.

The twins were not noticeably alike, although both were fair. Dora had long sleek curls that never got out of order. Davy had a crop of fuzzy little yellow ringlets all over his round head. Dora's hazel eyes were gentle and mild; Davy's were as roguish and dancing as an elf's. Dora's nose was straight, Davy's was a positive snub; Dora had a 'prunes and prisms' mouth, Davy's was all smiles; and besides, he had a dimple in one cheek and none in the other, which gave him a dear, comical, lop-sided look when he laughed. Mirth and mischief lurked in every corner of his little face.

'They'd better go to bed,' said Marilla, who thought it was the easiest way to dispose of them. 'Dora will sleep with me and you can put Davy in the west gable. You're not afraid to sleep alone, are you, Davy?'

'No; but I ain't going to bed for ever so long yet,' said Davy comfortably.

'Oh, yes, you are.' That was all the much-tried Marilla said, but something in her tone squelched even Davy. He trotted obediently upstairs with Anne.

'When I'm grown up the very first thing I'm going to do is stay up *all* night just to see what it would be like,' he told her confidentially.

In after-years Marilla never thought of that first week of the twins, sojourn at Green Gables without a shiver. Not that it really was so much worse than the weeks that followed it; but it seemed so by reason of its novelty. There was seldom a waking minute of any day when Davy was not in mischief or devising it; but his first notable exploit occurred two days after his arrival, on Sunday morning . . . a fine, warm day, as hazy and mild as September. Anne dressed him for church while Marilla attended to Dora. Davy at first objected strongly to having his face washed.

'Marilla washed it yesterday . . . and Mrs Wiggins scoured me with hard soap the day of the funeral. That's enough for one week. I don't see the good of being so awful clean. It's lots more comfable being dirty.'

'Paul Irving washes his face every day of his own accord,' said Anne astutely.

Davy had been an inmate of Green Gables for little over forty-eight hours; but he already worshipped Anne and hated Paul Irving, whom he had heard Anne praising enthusiastically the day after his arrival. If Paul Irving washed his face every day, that settled it. He, Davy Keith, would do it too, if it killed him. The same consideration induced him to submit meekly to the other details of his toilet, and he was really a handsome little lad when all was done. Anne felt an almost maternal pride in him as she led him into the old Cuthbert pew.

Davy behaved quite well at first, being occupied in casting covert glances at all the small boys within view and wondering which was Paul Irving. The first two hymns and the Scripture reading passed off uneventfully. Mr Allan was praying when the sensation came.

Lauretta White was sitting in front of Davy, her head slightly bent and her fair hair hanging in two long braids, between which a tempting expanse of white neck showed, encased in a loose lace frill. Lauretta was a fat, placid-looking child of eight, who had conducted herself irreproachably in church from the very first day her mother carried her there, an infant of six months.

Davy thrust his hand into his pocket and produced ... a caterpillar, a furry, squirming caterpillar. Marilla saw and clutched at him but she was too late. Davy dropped the caterpillar down Lauretta's neck.

Right into the middle of Mr Allan's prayer burst a series of piercing shrieks. The minister stopped appalled and opened his eyes. Every head in the congregation flew up. Lauretta White was dancing up and down in her pew, clutching frantically at the back of her dress.

'Ow ... mommer ... mommer ... ow ... take it off ... ow ... get it out ... ow ... that bad boy put it down my neck ... ow ... mommer ... it's going further down ... ow ... ow ... ow ...'

Mrs White rose and with a set face carried the hysterical, writhing Lauretta out of church. Her shrieks died away in the distance and Mr Allan proceeded with the service. But everybody felt that it was a failure that day. For the first time in her life Marilla took no notice of the text and Anne sat with scarlet cheeks of mortification.

When they got home Marilla put Davy to bed and made him stay there for the rest of the day. She would not give him any dinner but allowed him a plain tea of bread and milk. Anne carried it to him and sat sorrowfully by him while he ate it with an unrepentant relish. But Anne's mournful eyes troubled him.

'I s'pose,' he said reflectively, 'that Paul Irving wouldn't have dropped a caterpillar down a girl's neck in church, would he?'

'Indeed he wouldn't,' said Anne sadly.

'Well, I'm kind of sorry I did it, then,' conceded Davy. 'But it was such a jolly big caterpillar ... I picked him up on the church steps just as we went in. It seemed a pity to waste him. And say, wasn't it fun to hear that girl yell?'

Tuesday afternoon the Aid Society met at Green Gables. Anne hurried home from school, for she knew that Marilla would need all the assistance she could give. Dora, neat and proper, in her nicely starched white dress and black sash, was sitting with the members of the Aid in the parlour, speaking demurely when spoken to, keeping silence when not, and in every way comporting herself as a model child. Davy, blissfully dirty, was making mud-pies in the barnyard.

'I told him he might,' said Marilla wearily. 'I thought it would keep him out of worse mischief. He can only get dirty at that. We'll have our teas over before we call him to his. Dora can have hers with us, but I would never dare to let Davy sit down at the table with all the Aids here.'

When Anne went to call the Aids to tea she found that Dora was not in the parlour. Mrs Jasper Bell said Davy had come to the front door and called her out. A hasty consultation with Marilla in the pantry resulted in a decision to let both children have their teas together later on.

Tea was half over when the dining-room was invaded by a forlorn figure. Marilla and Anne stared in dismay, the Aids in amazement. Could that be Dora ... that sobbing nondescript in a drenched, dripping dress and hair from which the water was streaming on Marilla's new coin-spot rug?

'Dora, what has happened to you?' cried Anne, with a guilty glance at Mrs Jasper Bell, whose family was said to be the only one in the world in which accidents never occurred.

'Davy made me walk the pig-pen fence,' wailed Dora. 'I didn't want to but he called me a fraid-cat. And I fell off into the pig-pen and my dress got all dirty and the pig runned right over me. My dress was just awful but Davy said if I'd stand under the pump he'd wash it clean, and I did and he pumped water all over me but my dress ain't a bit cleaner and my pretty sash and shoes is all spoiled.'

Anne did the honours of the table alone for the rest of the meal while Marilla went upstairs and redressed Dora in her old clothes. Davy was caught and sent to bed without any supper. Anne went to his room at twilight and talked to him seriously ... a method in which she had great faith, not altogether unjustified by results. She told him she felt very badly over his conduct.

'I feel sorry now myself,' admitted Davy, 'but the trouble is I never feel sorry for doing things till after I've did them. Dora wouldn't help me make pies 'cause she was afraid of messing her clo'es, and that made me hopping mad. I s'pose Paul Irving wouldn't have made *his* sister walk a pig-pen fence if he knew she'd fall in?'

'No, he would never dream of such a thing. Paul is a perfect little gentleman.'

Davy screwed his eyes tight shut and seemed to meditate on this for a time. Then he crawled up and put his arms about Anne's neck, snuggling his flushed little face down on her shoulder.

'Anne, don't you like me a little bit, even if I ain't a good boy like Paul?'

'Indeed I do,' said Anne sincerely. Somehow, it was impossible to help liking Davy. 'But I'd like you better still if you weren't so naughty.'

'I . . . did something else today,' went on Davy in a muffled voice. 'I'm sorry now but I'm awful scared to tell you. You won't be very cross, will you? And you won't tell Marilla, will you?'

'I don't know, Davy. Perhaps I ought to tell her. But I think I can promise you I won't if you promise me that you will never do it again, whatever it is.'

'No, I never will. Anyhow, it's not likely I'd find any more of them this year. I found this one on the cellar steps.'

'Davy, what is it you've done?'

'I put a toad in Marilla's bed. You can go and take it out if you like. But say, Anne, wouldn't it be fun to leave it there?'

'Davy Keith!' Anne sprang from Davy's clinging arms and flew across the hall to Marilla's room. The bed was slightly rumpled. She threw back the blankets in nervous haste and there in very truth was the toad, blinking at her from under a pillow.

'How can I carry that awful thing out?' moaned Anne with a shudder. The fire shovel suggested itself to her as she crept down to get it while Marilla was busy in the pantry. Anne had her own troubles carrying that toad downstairs, for it hopped off the shovel three times and once she thought she had lost it in the hall. When she finally deposited it in the cherry orchard she drew a long breath of relief.

'If Marilla knew she'd never feel safe getting into bed again in her life. I'm so glad that little sinner repented in time. There's Diana signalling to me from her window. I'm glad ... I really feel the need of some diversion, for what with Anthony Pye in school and Davy Keith at home my nerves have had about all they can endure for one day.'

CHAPTER 9

A Question of Colour

'THAT old nuisance of a Rachel Lynde was here again today, pestering me for a subscription towards buying a carpet for the vestry room,' said Mr Harrison wrathfully. 'I detest that woman more than anybody I know. She can put a whole sermon, text, comment, and application into six words, and throw it at you like a brick.'

Anne, who was perched on the edge of the veranda, enjoying the charm of a mild west wind blowing across a newly ploughed field on a grey November twilight and piping a quaint little melody among the twisted firs below the garden, turned her dreamy face over her shoulder.

'The trouble is, you and Mrs Lynde don't understand one another,' she explained. 'That is always what is wrong when people don't like each other. I didn't like Mrs Lynde at first either; but as soon as I came to understand her I learned to.'

'Mrs Lynde may be an acquired taste with some folks; but I didn't keep on eating bananas because I was told I'd learn to like them if I did,' growled Mr Harrison. 'And as for understanding her, I understand that she is a confirmed busybody and I told her so.'

'Oh, that must have hurt her feelings very much,' said Anne

reproachfully. 'How could you say such a thing? *I* said some dreadful things to Mrs Lynde long ago but it was when I had lost my temper. I couldn't say them *deliberately*.'

'It was the truth and I believe in telling the truth to everybody.'

'But you don't tell the whole truth,' objected Anne. 'You only tell the disagreeable part of the truth. Now, you've told me a dozen times that my hair was red, but you've never once told me that I had a nice nose.'

'I daresay you know it without any telling,' chuckled Mr Harrison.

'I know I have red hair too ... although it's *much* darker than it used to be ... so there's no need of telling me that either.'

'Well, well, I'll try and not mention it again since you're so sensitive. You must excuse me, Anne. I've got a habit of being outspoken and folks mustn't mind it.'

'But they can't help minding it. And I don't think it's any help that it's your habit. What would you think of a person who went about sticking pins and needles into people and saying, "Excuse me, you mustn't mind it ... it's just a habit I've got." You'd think he was crazy, wouldn't you? And as for Mrs Lynde being a busybody, perhaps she is. But did you tell her she had a very kind heart and always helped the poor, and never said a word when Timothy Cotton stole a crock of butter out of her dairy and told his wife he'd bought it from her? Mrs Cotton cast it up to her the next time they met that it tasted of turnips and Mrs Lynde just said she was sorry it had turned out so poorly.'

'I suppose she has some good qualities,' conceded Mr Harrison grudgingly. 'Most folks have. I have some myself, though you might never suspect it. But anyhow I ain't going to give anything to that carpet. Folks are everlasting begging for money here, it seems to me. How's your project of painting the hall coming on?'

'Splendidly. We had a meeting of the A.V.I.S. last Friday night and found that we had plenty of money subscribed to paint the hall and shingle the roof too. *Most* people gave very liberally, Mr Harrison.'

Anne was a sweet-souled lass, but she could instil some venom into innocent italics when occasion required.

'What colour are you going to have it?'

'We have decided on a very pretty green. The roof will be dark red, of course. Mr Roger Pye is going to get the paint in town today.'

'Who's got the job?'

'Mr Joshua Pye of Carmody. He has nearly finished the shingling. We had to give him the contract, for every one of the Pyes ... and there are four families, you know ... said they wouldn't give a cent unless Joshua got it. They had subscribed twelve dollars between them and we thought that was too much to lose, although some people think we shouldn't have given it to the Pyes. Mrs Lynde says they try to run everything.'

'The main question is will this Joshua do his work well. If he does I don't see that it matters whether his name is Pye or Pudding.'

'He has the reputation of being a good workman, though they say he's a very peculiar man. He hardly ever talks.'

'He's peculiar enough all right then,' said Mr Harrison dryly. 'Or at least, folks here will call him so. I never was much of a talker till I came to Avonlea and then I had to begin in self-defence or Mrs Lynde would have said I was dumb and started a subscription to have me taught sign-language. You're not going yet, Anne?'

'I must. I have some sewing to do for Dora this evening. Besides, Davy is probably breaking Marilla's heart with some new mischief by this time. This morning the first thing he said was, "Where does the dark go, Anne? I want to know." I told him it went around to the other side of the world but after breakfast he declared it didn't ... that it went down the well. Marilla says she caught him hanging over the well-box four times today, trying to reach down to the dark.'

'He's a limb,' declared Mr Harrison. 'He came over here yesterday and pulled six feathers out of Ginger's tail before I could get in from the barn. The poor bird has been moping ever since. Those children must be a sight of trouble to you folks.'

'Everything that's worth having is some trouble,' said Anne, secretly resolving to forgive Davy's next offence, whatever it might be, since he had avenged her on Ginger.

Mr Roger Pye brought the hall paint home that night and Mr Joshua Pye, a surly, taciturn man, began painting the next day. He was not disturbed in his task. The hall was situated on what was called 'the lower road'. In late autumn this road was always muddy and wet, and people going to Carmody travelled by the longer 'upper' road. The hall was so closely surrounded by fir woods that it was invisible unless you were near it. Mr Joshua Pye painted away in the solitude and independence that was so dear to his unsociable heart.

On Friday afternoon he finished his job and went home to Carmody. Soon after his departure Mrs Rachel Lynde drove by, having braved the mud of the lower road out of curiosity to see what the hall looked like in its new coat of paint. When she rounded the spruce curve she saw.

The sight affected Mrs Lynde oddly. She dropped the reins, held up her hands, and said 'Gracious Providence!' She stared as if she could not believe her eyes. Then she laughed almost hysterically.

'There must be some mistake ... there *must*. I knew those Pyes would make a mess of things.'

Mrs Lynde drove home, meeting several people on the road and stopping to tell them about the hall. The news flew like wildfire. Gilbert Blythe, poring over a textbook at home, heard it from his father's hired boy at sunset, and rushed breathlessly to Green Gables, joined on the way by Fred Wright. They found Diana Barry, Jane Andrews, and Anne Shirley, despair personified, at the yard gate of Green Gables, under the big leafless willows.

'It isn't true surely, Anne?' exclaimed Gilbert.

'It *is* true,' answered Anne, looking like the muse of tragedy. 'Mrs Lynde called on her way from Carmody to tell me. Oh, it is simply dreadful! *What* is the use of trying to improve anything?'

'What is dreadful?' asked Oliver Sloane, arriving at this moment with a bandbox he had brought from town for Marilla.

'Haven't you heard?' said Jane wrathfully. 'Well, it's simply this ... Joshua Pye *has gone and painted the hall blue instead of green* ... a deep, brilliant blue, the shade they use for painting carts and wheelbarrows. And Mrs Lynde says it is the most hideous colour for a building, especially when combined with a red roof, that she ever saw or imagined. You could simply have knocked me down with a feather when I heard it. It's heart-breaking, after all the trouble we've had.'

'How on earth could such a mistake have happened?' wailed Diana.

The blame of this unmerciful disaster was eventually narrowed down to the Pyes. The Improvers had decided to use Morton-Harris paints and the Morton-Harris paint cans were numbered according to a colour card. A purchaser chose his shade on the card and ordered by the accompanying number. Number 147 was the shade of green desired and when Mr Roger Pye sent word to the Improvers by his son, John Andrew, that he was going to town and would get their paint for them, the Improvers told John Andrew to tell his father to get 147. John Andrew always averred that he did so, but Mr Roger Pye as staunchly declared that John Andrew told him 157; and there the matter stands to this day.

That night there was blank dismay in every Avonlea house where an Improver lived. The gloom at Green Gables was so intense that it quenched even Davy. Anne wept and would not be comforted.

'I *must* cry, even if I am almost seventeen, Marilla,' she sobbed. 'It's so mortifying. And it sounds the death knell of our society. We'll simply be laughed out of existence.'

In life, as in dreams, however, things often go by contraries. The Avonlea people did not laugh; they were too angry. *Their* money had gone to paint the hall and consequently *they* felt themselves bitterly aggrieved by the mistake. Public indignation centred on the Pyes. Roger Pye and John Andrew had bungled the matter between them; and as for Joshua Pye, he must be a born fool not to suspect there was something wrong when he opened the cans and saw the colour of the paint. Joshua Pye, when thus animadverted upon, retorted that the

Avonlea taste in colours was no business of his, whatever his private opinion of it might be; he had been hired to paint the hall, not to talk about it; and he meant to have his money for it.

The Improvers paid him his money in bitterness of spirit, after consulting Mr Peter Sloane, who was a magistrate.

'You'll have to pay it,' Peter told them. 'You can't hold him responsible for the mistake, since he claims he was never told what the colour was supposed to be but just given the cans and told to go ahead. But it's a burning shame and that hall certainly does look awful.'

The luckless Improvers expected that Avonlea would be more prejudiced than ever against them; but instead, public sympathy veered around in their favour. People thought the eager, enthusiastic little band who had worked so hard for their object had been badly used. Mrs Lynde told them to keep on and show the Pyes that there really were people in the world who could do things without making a muddle of them. Mr Major Spencer sent them word that he would clean out all the stumps along the road front of his farm and seed it down with grass at his own expense; and Mrs Hiram Sloane called at the school one day and beckoned Anne mysteriously out into the porch to tell her that if the 'Sassiety' wanted to make a geranium bed at the cross roads in the spring they needn't be afraid of her cow, for she would see that the marauding animal was kept within safe bounds. Even Mr Harrison chuckled, if he chuckled at all, in private, and was all sympathy outwardly.

'Never mind, Anne. Most paints fade uglier every year but that blue is as ugly as it can be to begin with, so it's bound to fade prettier. And the roof is shingled and painted all right. Folks will be able to sit in the hall after this without being leaked on. You've accomplished so much anyhow.'

'But Avonlea's blue hall will be a byword in all the neighbouring settlements from this time out,' said Anne bitterly.

And it must be confessed that it was.

CHAPTER 10

Davy in Search of a Sensation

ANNE, walking home from school through the Birch Path one
November afternoon, felt convinced afresh that life was a very
wonderful thing. The day had been a good day; all had gone
well in her little kingdom. St Clair Donnell had *not* fought any
of the other boys over the question of his name; Prillie Rogerson's face had been so puffed up from the effects of toothache
that she did not once try to coquette with the boys in her vicin-
ity. Barbara Shaw had met with only *one* accident . . . spilling a
dipper of water over the floor . . . and Anthony Pye had not
been in school at all.

'What a nice month this November has been!' said Anne,
who had never quite got over her childish habit of talking to
herself. 'November is usually such a disagreeable month . . . as
if the year had suddenly found out that she was growing old and
could do nothing but weep and fret over it. This year is growing
old gracefully . . . just like a stately old lady who knows she can
be charming even with grey hair and wrinkles. We've had lovely
days and delicious twilights. This last fortnight has been so
peaceful, and even Davy has been almost well-behaved. I really
think he is improving a great deal. How quiet the woods are
today . . . not a murmur except that soft wind purring in the
tree-tops! It sounds like surf on a far-away shore. How dear
the woods are! You beautiful trees! I love every one of you as a
friend.'

Anne paused to throw her arm about a slim young birch and
kiss its cream-white trunk. Diana, rounding a curve in the path,
saw her and laughed.

'Anne Shirley, you're only pretending to be grown up. I believe when you're alone you're as much a little girl as you ever
were.'

'Well, one can't get over the habit of being a little girl all at
once,' said Anne gaily. 'You see, I was little for fourteen years
and I've only been grown-uppish for scarcely three. I'm sure I

shall always feel like a child in the woods. These walks home
from school are almost the only time I have for dreaming ...
except the half hour or so before I go to sleep. I'm so busy with
teaching and studying and helping Marilla with the twins that I
haven't another moment for imagining things. You don't
know what splendid adventures I have for a little while after I
go to bed in the east gable every night. I always imagine I'm
something very brilliant and triumphant and splendid ... a
great prima donna or a Red Cross nurse or a queen. Last night I
was a queen. It's really splendid to imagine you are a queen.
You have all the fun of it without any of the inconveniences
and you can stop being a queen whenever you want to, which
you couldn't in real life. But here in the woods I like best to
imagine quite different things ... I'm a dryad living in an old
pine, or a little brown wood-elf hiding under a crinkled leaf.
The white birch you caught me kissing is a sister of mine. The
only difference is, she's a tree and I'm a girl, but that's no real
difference. Where are you going, Diana?'

'Down to the Dicksons. I promised to help Alberta cut out
her new dress. Can't you walk down in the evening, Anne, and
come home with me?'

'I might ... since Fred Wright is away in town,' said Anne
with a rather too innocent face.

Diana blushed, tossed her head, and walked on. She did not
look offended, however.

Anne fully intended to go down to the Dicksons' that evening, but she did not. When she arrived at Green Gables she
found a state of affairs which banished every other thought
from her mind. Marilla met her in the yard ... a wild-eyed
Marilla.

'Anne, Dora is lost!'

'Dora! Lost!' Anne looked at Davy, who was swinging on the
yard gate, and detected merriment in his eyes. 'Davy, do you
know where she is?'

'No, I don't,' said Davy stoutly. 'I haven't seen her since
dinner-time, cross my heart.'

'I've been away ever since one o'clock,' said Marilla.
'Thomas Lynde took sick all of a sudden and Rachel sent up for

me to go at once. When I left here Dora was playing with her doll in the kitchen and Davy was making mud-pies behind the barn. I only got home half an hour ago ... and no Dora to be seen. Davy declares he never saw her since I left.'

'Neither I did,' avowed Davy solemnly.

'She must be somewhere around,' said Anne. 'She would never wander far away alone ... you know how timid she is. Perhaps she has fallen asleep in one of the rooms.'

Marilla shook her head.

'I've hunted the whole house through. But she may be in some of the buildings.'

A thorough search followed. Every corner of house, yard, and outbuildings was ransacked by those two distracted people. Anne roved the orchards and the Haunted Wood, calling Dora's name. Marilla took a candle and explored the cellar. Davy accompanied each of them in turn, and was fertile in thinking of places where Dora could possibly be. Finally they met again in the yard.

'It's a most mysterious thing,' groaned Marilla.

'Where can she be?' said Anne miserably.

'Maybe she's tumbled into the well,' suggested Davy cheerfully.

Anne and Marilla looked fearfully into each other's eyes. The thought had been with them both through their entire search but neither had dared to put it into words.

'She ... she might have,' whispered Marilla.

Anne, feeling faint and sick, went to the well-box and peered over. The bucket sat on the shelf inside. Far down below was a tiny glimmer of still water. The Cuthbert well was the deepest in Avonlea. If Dora ... but Anne could not face the idea. She shuddered and turned away.

'Run across for Mr Harrison,' said Marilla, wringing her hands.

'Mr Harrison and John Henry are both away ... they went to town today. I'll go for Mr Barry.'

Mr Barry came back with Anne, carrying a coil of rope to which was attached a claw-like instrument that had been the business end of a grubbing-fork. Marilla and Anne stood by, cold and shaken with horror and dread, while Mr Barry dragged the well, and Davy, astride the gate, watched the group with a face indicative of huge enjoyment.

Finally Mr Barry shook his head, with a relieved air.

'She can't be down there. It's a mighty curious thing where she could have got to, though. Look here, young man, are you sure you've no idea where your sister is?'

'I've told you a dozen times that I haven't,' said Davy, with an injured air. 'Maybe a tramp come and stole her.'

'Nonsense,' said Marilla sharply, relieved from her horrible fear of the well. 'Anne, do you suppose she could have strayed over to Mr Harrison's? She has always been talking about his parrot ever since that time you took her over.'

'I can't believe Dora would venture so far alone, but I'll go over and see,' said Anne.

Nobody was looking at Davy just then or it would have been seen that a very decided change came over his face. He quietly slipped off the gate and ran, as fast as his fat legs could carry him, to the barn.

Anne hastened across the fields to the Harrison establishment in no very hopeful frame of mind. The house was locked, the window shades were down, and there was no sign of anything living about the place. She stood on the veranda and called Dora loudly.

Ginger, in the kitchen behind her, shrieked and swore with sudden fierceness; but between his outbursts Anne heard a plaintive cry from the little building in the yard which served Mr Harrison as a toolhouse. Anne flew to the door, unhasped it, and caught up a small mortal with a tear-stained face who was sitting forlornly on an upturned nail-keg.

'Oh, Dora, Dora, what a fright you have given us! How came you to be here?'

'Davy and I come over to see Ginger,' sobbed Dora, 'but we couldn't see him after all, only Davy made him swear by kicking the door. And then Davy brought me here and run out and shut the door; and I couldn't get out. I cried and cried, I was so frightened, and oh, I'm so hungry and cold; and I thought you'd never come, Anne.'

'Davy?' But Anne could say no more. She carried Dora home with a heavy heart. Her joy at finding the child safe and sound was drowned out in the pain caused by Davy's behaviour. The freak of shutting Dora up might easily have been pardoned. But Davy had told falsehoods ... downright cold-blooded false-hoods about it. That was the ugly fact and Anne could not shut her eyes to it. She could have sat down and cried with sheer disappointment. She had grown to love Davy dearly ... how dearly she had not known until this minute ... and it hurt her unbearably to discover that he was guilty of deliberate false-hood.

Marilla listened to Anne's tale in a silence that boded no good Davy-ward; Mr Barry laughed and advised that Davy be sum-marily dealt with. When he had gone home Anne soothed and warmed the sobbing, shivering Dora, got her her supper, and put her to bed. Then she returned to the kitchen, just as Marilla came grimly in, leading, or rather pulling, the reluctant, cob-webby Davy, whom she had just found hidden away in the darkest corner of the stable.

She jerked him to the mat on the middle of the floor and then went and sat down by the east window. Anne was sitting limply by the west window. Between them stood the culprit. His back was towards Marilla and it was a meek, subdued, frightened back; but his face was towards Anne and although it was a little shamefaced there was a gleam of comradeship in Davy's eyes, as if he knew he had done wrong and was going to be punished for it, but could count on a laugh over it all with Anne later on.

But no half-hidden smile answered him in Anne's grey eyes, as there might have done had it been only a question of mis-chief. There was something else ... something ugly and repul-sive.

'How could you behave so, Davy?' she asked sorrowfully.

Davy squirmed uncomfortably.

'I just did it for fun. Things have been so awful quiet here for so long that I thought it would be fun to give you folks a big scare. It was, too.'

In spite of fear and a little remorse Davy grinned over the recollection.

'But you told a falsehood about it, Davy,' said Anne, more sorrowfully than ever.

Davy looked puzzled.

'What's a falsehood? Do you mean a whopper?'

'I mean a story that was not true.'

'Course I did,' said Davy frankly. 'If I hadn't you wouldn't have been scared. I *had* to tell it.'

Anne was feeling the reaction from her fright and exertions. Davy's impenitent attitude gave the finishing touch. Two big tears brimmed up in her eyes.

'Oh, Davy, how could you?' she said, with a quiver in her voice. 'Don't you know how wrong it was?'

Davy was aghast. Anne crying ... he had made Anne cry! A flood of real remorse rolled like a wave over his warm little heart and engulfed it. He rushed to Anne, hurled himself into her lap, flung his arms around her neck, and burst into tears.

'I didn't know it was wrong to tell whoppers,' he sobbed. 'How did you expect me to know it was wrong? All Mr Sprott's children told them *regular* every day, and cross their hearts too. I s'pose Paul Irving never tells whoppers and here I've been trying awful hard to be as good as him, but now I s'pose you'll never love me again. I'm awfully sorry I've made you cry, Anne, and I'll never tell a whopper again.'

Davy buried his face in Anne's shoulder and cried stormily. Anne, in a sudden glad flash of understanding, held him tight and looked over his curly thatch at Marilla.

'He didn't know it was wrong to tell falsehoods, Marilla. I think we must forgive him for that part of it this time if he will promise never to say what isn't true again.'

'I never will, now that I know it's bad,' asseverated Davy between sobs. 'If you ever catch me telling a whopper again you can ...' Davy groped mentally for a suitable penance ... 'you can skin me alive, Anne.'

'Don't say "whopper", Davy ... say "falsehood",' said the schoolma'am.

'Why?' queried Davy, settling comfortably down and looking up with a tear-stained, investigating face. 'Why ain't whopper as good as falsehood? I want to know. It's just as big a word.'

'It's slang; and it's wrong for little boys to use slang.'

'There's an awful lot of things it's wrong to do,' said Davy with a sigh. 'I never s'posed there was so many. I'm sorry it's wrong to tell whop . . . falsehoods, 'cause it's awful handy, but since it is I'm never going to tell any more. What are you going to do to me for telling them this time? I want to know.' Anne looked beseechingly at Marilla.

'I don't want to be too hard on the child,' said Marilla. 'I dare say nobody ever did tell him it was wrong to tell lies, and those Sprott children were no fit companions for him. Poor Mary was too sick to train him properly and I presume you couldn't expect a six-year-old child to know things like that by instinct. I suppose we'll just have to assume he doesn't know *anything* right and begin at the beginning. But he'll have to be punished for shutting Dora up, and I can't think of any way except to send him to bed without his supper and we've done that so often. Can't you suggest something else, Anne? I should think you ought to be able to, with that imagination you're always talking of.'

'But punishments are so horrid and I like to imagine only pleasant things,' said Anne, cuddling Davy. 'There are so many unpleasant things in the world already that there is no use of imagining any more.'

In the end Davy was sent to bed, as usual, there to remain until noon next day. He evidently did some thinking, for when Anne went up to her room a little later she heard him calling her name softly. Going in, she found him sitting up in bed, with his elbows on his knees and his chin propped on his hands.

'Anne,' he said solemnly, 'is it wrong for everybody to tell whop . . . falsehoods? I want to know.'

'Yes, indeed.'

'Is it wrong for a grown-up person?'

'Yes.'

'Then,' said Davy decidedly, 'Marilla is bad, for *she* tells them. And she's worse'n me, for I didn't know it was wrong but she does.'

'Davy Keith, Marilla never told a story in her life,' said Anne indignantly.

'She did so. She told me last Tuesday that something dreadful would happen to me if I didn't say my prayers every night. And I haven't said them for over a week, just to see what *would* happen ... and nothing has,' concluded Davy in an aggrieved tone.

Anne choked back a mad desire to laugh with the conviction that it would be fatal, and then earnestly set about saving Marilla's reputation.

'Why, Davy Keith,' she said solemnly, 'something dreadful *has* happened to you this very day.'

Davy looked sceptical.

'I s'pose you mean being sent to bed without any supper,' he said scornfully, 'but *that* isn't dreadful. Course, I don't like it, but I've been sent to bed so much since I come here that I'm getting used to it. And you don't save anything by making me go without supper either, for I always eat twice as much for breakfast.'

'I don't mean your being sent to bed. I mean the fact that you told a falsehood today. And, Davy,' ... Anne leaned over the footboard of the bed and shook her finger impressively at the culprit ... 'for a boy to tell what isn't true is almost the worst thing that *could* happen to him ... almost the very worst. So you see Marilla told you the truth.'

'But I thought the something bad would be exciting,' protested Davy in an injured tone.

'Marilla isn't to blame for what you thought. Bad things aren't always exciting. They've very often just nasty and stupid.'

'It was awful funny to see Marilla and you looking down the well, though,' said Davy, hugging his knees.

Anne kept a sober face until she got downstairs, and then she collapsed on the sitting-room lounge and laughed until her sides ached.

'I wish you'd tell me the joke,' said Marilla, a little grimly. 'I haven't seen much to laugh at today.'

'You'll laugh when you hear this,' assured Anne. And Marilla did laugh, which showed how much her education had advanced since the adoption of Anne. But she sighed immediately afterwards.

'I suppose I shouldn't have told him that, although I heard a minister say it to a child once. But he did aggravate me so. It was that night you were at the Carmody concert and I was putting him to bed. He said he didn't see the good of praying until he got big enough to be of some importance to God. Anne, I do not know what we are going to do with that child. I never saw his beat. I'm feeling clean discouraged.'

'Oh, don't say that, Marilla. Remember how bad I was when I came here.'

'Anne, you never were bad ... *never*. I see that now, when I've learned what real badness is. You were always getting into terrible scrapes, I'll admit, but your motive was always good. Davy is just bad from sheer love of it.'

'Oh, no, I don't think it is real badness with him either,' pleaded Anne. 'It's just mischief. And it is rather quiet for him here, you know. He has no other boys to play with and his mind has to have something to occupy it. Dora is so prim and proper she is no good for a boy's playmate. I really think it would be better to let them go to school, Marilla.'

'No,' said Marilla resolutely, 'my father always said that no child should be cooped up in the four walls of a school until it was seven years old, and Mr Allan says the same thing. The twins can have a few lessons at home but go to school they shan't till they're seven.'

'Well, we must try to reform Davy at home then,' said Anne cheerfully. 'With all his faults he's really a dear little chap. I can't help loving him. Marilla, it may be a dreadful thing to say, but honestly, I like Davy better than Dora, for all she's so good.'

'I don't know but that I do myself,' confessed Marilla, 'and it isn't fair, for Dora isn't a bit of trouble. There couldn't be a better child and you'd hardly know she was in the house.'

'Dora is too good,' said Anne. 'She'd behave just as well if there wasn't a soul to tell her what to do. She was born already brought up, so she doesn't need us; and I think,' concluded Anne, hitting on a very vital truth, 'that we always love best the people who need us. Davy needs us badly.'

'He certainly needs something,' agreed Marilla. 'Rachel Lynde would say it was a good spanking.'

CHAPTER 11

Facts and Fancies

'TEACHING is really very interesting work,' wrote Anne to a Queen's Academy chum. 'Jane says she thinks it is monotonous but I don't find it so. Something funny is almost sure to happen every day, and the children say such amusing things. Jane says she punishes her pupils when they make funny speeches, which is probably why she finds teaching monotonous. This afternoon little Jimmy Andrews was trying to spell "speckled" and couldn't manage it. "Well," he said finally, "I can't spell it but I know what it means."

' "What?" I asked.

' "St Clair Donnell's face, miss."

'St Clair is certainly very much freckled, although I try to prevent the others from commenting on it . . . for *I* was freckled once and well do I remember it. But I don't think St Clair minds. It was because Jimmy called him "St Clair" that St Clair pounded him on the way home from school. I heard of the pounding, but not officially, so I don't think I'll take any notice of it.

'Yesterday I was trying to teach Lottie Wright to do addition. I said, "If you had three candies in one hand and two in the other, how many would you have altogether?" "A mouthful," said Lottie. And in the nature study class, when I asked them to give me a good reason why toads shouldn't be killed, Benjie Sloane gravely answered, "Because it would rain the next day."

'It's so hard not to laugh, Stella. I have to save up all my amusement until I get home, and Marilla says it makes her nervous to hear wild shrieks of mirth proceeding from the east gable without any apparent cause. She says a man in Grafton went insane once, and that was how it began.

'Did you know that Thomas à Becket was canonized as a *snake*? Rose Bell says he was . . . also that William Tyndale *wrote* the New Testament. Claude White says a "glacier" is a man who puts in window frames!

77

'I think the most difficult thing in teaching, as well as the most interesting, is to get the children to tell you their real thoughts about things. One stormy day last week I gathered them around me at dinner hour and tried to get them to talk to me just as if I were one of themselves. I asked them to tell me the things they most wanted. Some of the answers were commonplace enough ... dolls, ponies, and skates. Others were decidedly original. Hester Boulter wanted "to wear her Sunday dress every day and eat in the sitting-room". Hannah Bell wanted "to be good without having to take any trouble about it". Marjory White, aged ten, wanted to be a *widow*. Questioned why, she gravely said that if you weren't married people called you an old maid, and if you were your husband bossed you; but if you were a widow there'd be no danger of either. The most remarkable wish was Sally Bell's. She wanted a "honeymoon". I asked her if she knew what it was, and she said she thought it was an extra nice kind of bicycle because her cousin in Montreal went on a honeymoon when he was married and he had always had the very latest in bicycles.

'Another day I asked them all to tell me the naughtiest thing they had ever done. I couldn't get the older ones to do so, but the third class answered quite freely. Eliza Bell had "set fire to her aunt's carded rolls". Asked if she meant to do it she said, "not altogether". She just tried a little end to see how it would burn and the whole bundle blazed up in a jiffy. Emerson Gillis had spent ten cents for candy when he should have put it in his missionary box. Annetta Bell's worst crime was "eating some blueberries that grew in the graveyard". Willie White had "slid down the sheephouse roof a lot of times with his Sunday trousers on". "But I was punished for it 'cause I had to wear patched pants to Sunday School all summer, and when you're punished for a thing you don't have to repent of it," declared Willie.

'I wish you could see some of their compositions ... so much do I wish it that I'll send you copies of some written recently. Last week I told the fourth class I wanted them to write me letters about anything they pleased, adding by way of suggestion that they might tell me of some place they had visited or some interesting thing or person they had seen. They were to write the letters on real note-paper, seal them in an envelope, and address them to me, all without any assistance from other people. Last Friday morning I found a pile of letters on my desk and that evening I realized afresh that teaching has its pleasures as well as its pains. Those compositions would atone for much. Here is Ned Clay's, address, spelling, and grammar as originally penned.

> Miss teacher ShiRley
> > Green gabels.
> > > p. e. Island can
> > > > birds

Dear teacher I think I will write you a composition about birds. birds is very useful animals. my cat catches birds. His name is William but pa calls him tom. He is oll striped and he got one of his ears froz of last winter. only for that he would be a good-looking cat. My unkle has adopted a cat. it come to his house one day and woudent go away and unkle says it has forgot more than most people ever knowed. he lets it sleep on his rocking chare and my aunt says he thinks more of it than he does of his children. that is not right. we ought to be kind to cats and give them new milk but we ought not to be better to them than to our children. this is oll I can think of so no more at present from

> > > > edward blake ClaY.

'St Clair Donnell's is, as usual, short and to the point. St Clair never wastes words. I do not think he chose his subject or added the postscript out of malice aforethought. It is just that he has not a great deal of tact or imagination.

Dear Miss Shirley,

You told us to describe something strange we have seen. I will describe the Avonlea Hall. It has two doors, an inside one and an outside one. It has six windows and a chimney. It has two ends and two sides. It is painted blue. That is what makes it strange. It is built on the lower Carmody road. It is the third most important building in Avonlea. The others are the church and the blacksmith shop. They hold debating clubs and lectures in it and concerts.

> > > Yours truly.
> > > > Jacob Donnell.

P.S. The hall is a very bright blue.

'Annetta Bell's letter was quite long, which surprised me, for writing essays is not Annetta's *forte*, and hers are generally as brief as St Clair's. Annetta is a quiet little puss and a model of good behaviour, but there isn't a shadow of originality in her. Here is her letter:

Dearest teacher,

I think I will write you a letter to tell you how much I love you. I love you with my whole heart and soul and mind ... with all there is of me to love ... and I want to serve you for ever. It would be my highest privilege. That is why I try so hard to be good in school and learn my lessuns.

You are so beautiful, my teacher. Your voice is like music and your eyes are like pansies when the dew is on them. You are like a tall stately queen. Your hair is like rippling gold. Anthony Pye says it is red, but you needn't pay any attention to Anthony.

I have only known you for a few months but I cannot realize that there was ever a time when I did not know you ... when you had not come into my life to bless and hallow it. I will always look back to this year as the most wonderful in my life because it brought you to me. Besides, it's the year we moved to Avonlea from newbridge. My love for you has made my life very rich and it has kept me from much of harm and evil. I owe this all to you, my sweetest teacher.

I shall never forget how sweet you looked the last time I saw you in that black dress with flowers in your hair. I shall see you like that for ever, even when we are both old and gray. You will always be young and fair to me, dearest teacher. I am thinking of you all the time ... in the morning and at the noontide and at the twilight. I love you when you laugh and when you sigh ... even when you look disdainful. I never saw you look cross though Anthony Pye says you always look so but I don't wonder you look cross at him for he deserves it. I love you in every dress ... you seem more adorable in each new dress than the last.

Dearest teacher, good night. The sun has set and the stars are shining ... stars that are as bright and beautiful as your eyes. I kiss your hands and face, my sweet. May God watch over you and protect you from all harm.

Your afecksionate pupil
Annetta Bell.

'This extraordinary letter puzzled me not a little. I knew Annetta couldn't have composed it any more than she could fly.

When I went to school the next day I took her for a walk down to the brook at recess and asked her to tell me the truth about the letter. Annetta cried and 'fessed up freely. She said she had never written a letter and she didn't know how to, or what to say, but there was a bundle of love letters in her mother's top bureau drawer which had been written to her by an old beau.

' "It wasn't Father," sobbed Annetta, "it was some one who was studying for a minister, and so he could write lovely letters, but Ma didn't marry him after all. She said she couldn't make out what he was driving at half the time. But I thought the letters were sweet and that I'd just copy things out of them here and there to write you. I put 'teacher' where he put 'lady' and I put in something of my own when I could think of it and changed some words. I put 'dress' in place of 'mood'. I didn't know just what a 'mood' was, but I s'posed it was something to wear. I didn't s'pose you'd know the difference. I don't see how you found out it wasn't all mine. You must be awful clever, teacher."

'I told Annetta it was very wrong to copy another person's letter and pass it off as her own. But I'm afraid that all Annetta repented of was being found out.

' "And I *do* love you, teacher," she sobbed. "It was all true, even if the minister wrote it first. I do love you with all my heart."

'It's very difficult to scold anybody properly under such circumstances.

'Here is Barbara Shaw's letter. I can't reproduce the blots of the original.

Dear teacher,
    You said we might write about a visit. I never visited but once. It was at my Aunt Mary's last winter. My Aunt Mary is a very particular woman and a great housekeeper. The first night I was there we were at tea. I knocked over a jug and broke it. Aunt Mary said she had had that jug ever since she was married and nobody had ever broken it before. When we got up I stepped on her dress and all the gathers tore out of the skirt. The next morning when I got up I hit the pitcher against the basin and cracked them both and I upset a cup of tea on the tablecloth at breakfast. When I was helping

81

Aunt Mary with the dinner dishes I dropped a china plate and it smashed. That evening I fell downstairs and sprained my ankle and had to stay in bed for a week. I heard Aunt Mary tell Uncle Joseph it was a mercy or I'd have broken everything in the house. When I got better it was time to go home. I don't like visiting very much. I like going to school better, especially since I came to Avonlea.

Yours respectfully,
Barbara Shaw.

'Willie White's began:

Respected Miss,

I want to tell you about my Very Brave Aunt. She lives in Ontario and one day she went out to the barn and saw a dog in the yard. The dog had no business there so she got a stick and whacked him hard and drove him into the barn and shut him up. Pretty soon a man came looking for an imaginary lion [query – did Willie mean a menagerie lion?] that had run away from a circus. And it turned out that the dog was a lion and my Very Brave Aunt had druv him into the barn with a stick. It is a wonder she was not et up but she was very brave. Emerson Gillis says if she thought it was a dog she wasn't any braver than if it really was a dog. But Emerson is jealous because he hasn't got a Brave Aunt himself, nothing but uncles.

'I have kept the best for the last. You laugh at me because I think Paul is a genius, but I am sure his letter will convince you that he is a very uncommon child. Paul lives away down near the shore with his grandmother and he has no playmates . . . no *real* playmates. You remember our School Management professor told us that we must not have "favourites" among our pupils, but I can't help loving Paul Irving the best of all mine. I don't think it does any harm, though, for everybody loves Paul, even Mrs Lynde, who says she could never have believed she'd get so fond of a Yankee. The other boys in school like him too. There is nothing weak or girlish about him in spite of his dreams and fancies. He is very manly and can hold his own in all games. He fought St Clair Donnell recently because St Clair said the Union Jack was away ahead of the Stars and Stripes as a flag. The result was a drawn battle and a mutual agreement to respect each other's patriotism henceforth. St Clair says he can hit the hardest but Paul can hit the *oftenest*.

'Paul's letter:

My dear teacher,

You told us we might write you about some interesting people we knew. I think the most interesting people I know are my rock-people and I mean to tell you about them. I have never told anybody about them except grandma and father but I would like to have you know about them because you understand things. There are a great many people who do *not* understand things so there is no use in telling them.

My rock-people live at the shore. I used to visit them almost every evening before the winter came. Now I can't go till spring, but they will be there, for people like that never change . . . that is the splendid thing about them. Nora was the first one of them I got acquainted with and so I think I love her the best. She lives in Andrews' Cove and she has black hair and black eyes, and she knows all about the mermaids and the water kelpies. You ought to hear the stories she can tell. Then there are the Twin Sailors. They don't live anywhere, they sail all the time, but they often come ashore to talk to me. They are a pair of jolly tars and they have seen everything in the world . . . and more than what is in the world. Do you know what happened to the youngest Twin Sailor once? He was sailing and he sailed right into a moonglade. A moonglade is the track the full moon makes on the water when it is rising from the sea, you know, teacher. Well, the youngest Twin Sailor sailed along the moonglade till he came right up to the moon, and there was a little golden door in the moon and he opened it and sailed right through. He had some wonderful adventures in the moon, but it would make this letter too long to tell them.

Then there is the Golden Lady of the cave. One day I found a big cave down on the shore and I went away in and after a while I found the Golden Lady. She has golden hair right down to her feet and her dress is all glittering and glistening like gold that is alive. And she has a golden harp and plays on it all day long . . . you can hear the music any time along shore if you listen carefully but most people would think it was only the wind among the rocks. I've never told Nora about the Golden Lady. I was afraid it might hurt her feelings. It even hurt her feelings if I talked too long with the Twin Sailors.

I always met the Twin Sailors at the Striped Rocks. The youngest Twin Sailor is very good-tempered but the oldest Twin Sailor can look dreadfully fierce at times. I have my suspicions about that oldest Twin. I believe he'd be a pirate if he dared. There's really something very mysterious about him. He swore once and I told him if he ever did it again he needn't come ashore to talk to me because I'd promised grandmother I'd never associate with anybody who swore. He was pretty well scared, I can tell you, and he said if I would forgive him he would take me to the sunset. So the next evening when I was sitting on the Striped Rocks the oldest Twin came sailing over the sea in an enchanted boat and I got in her. The boat was all pearly and rainbowy, like the inside of the mussel shells, and her sail was like moonshine. Well, we sailed right across to the sunset. Think of that, teacher, I've been in the sunset. And what do you suppose it is? The sunset is a land all flowers, like a great garden, and the clouds are beds of flowers. We sailed into a great harbour, all the colour of gold, and I stepped right out of the boat on a big meadow all covered with buttercups as big as roses. I stayed there for ever so long. It seemed nearly a year but the Oldest Twin says it was only a few minutes. You see, in the sunset land the time is ever so much longer than it is here.

> Your loving pupil,
>
> Paul Irving.

P.S. Of course, this letter isn't really true, teacher.

> P. I.

CHAPTER 12

A Jonah Day

IT really began the night before with a restless, wakeful vigil of grumbling toothache. When Anne arose in the dull, bitter winter morning she felt that life was flat, stale, and unprofitable.

She went to school in no angelic mood. Her cheek was swollen and her face ached. The schoolroom was cold and smoky, for the fire refused to burn and the children were huddled about it in shivering groups. Anne sent them to their seats with a sharper tone than she had ever used before. Anthony Pye strutted to his with his usual impertinent swagger and she saw him whisper something to his seat-mate and then glance at her with a grin.

Never, so it seemed to Anne, had there been so many squeaky pencils as there were that morning; and when Barbara Shaw came up to the desk with a sum she tripped over the coal scuttle with disastrous results. The coal rolled to every part of the room, her slate was broken into fragments, and when she picked herself up, her face, stained with coal dust, sent the boys into roars of laughter.

Anne turned from the second reader class which she was hearing.

'Really, Barbara,' she said icily, 'if you cannot move without falling over something you'd better remain in your seat. It is positively disgraceful for a girl of your age to be so awkward.'

Poor Barbara stumbled back to her desk, her tears combining with the coal dust to produce an effect truly grotesque. Never before had her beloved, sympathetic teacher spoken to her in such a tone or fashion, and Barbara was heart-broken. Anne herself felt a prick of conscience, but it only served to increase her mental irritation, and the second reader class remember that lesson yet, as well as the unmerciful infliction of arithmetic that followed. Just as Anne was snapping the sums out St Clair Donnell arrived breathlessly.

'You are half an hour late, St Clair,' Anne reminded him frigidly. 'Why is this?'

'Please, miss, I had to help Ma make a pudding for dinner 'cause we're expecting company and Clarice Almira's sick,' was St Clair's answer, given in a perfectly respectful voice but nevertheless provocative of great mirth among his mates.

'Take your seat and work out the six problems on page eighty-four of your arithmetic for punishment,' said Anne. St Clair looked rather amazed at her tone, but he went meekly to his desk and took out his slate. Then he stealthily passed a small parcel to Joe Sloane across the aisle. Anne caught him in the act and jumped to a fatal conclusion about that parcel.

Old Mrs Hiram Sloane had lately taken to making and selling 'nut cakes' by way of adding to her scanty income. The cakes were specially tempting to small boys and for several weeks Anne had had not a little trouble in regard to them. On their way to school the boys would invest their spare cash at Mrs Hiram's, bring the cakes along with them to school, and, if possible, eat them and treat their mates during school hours. Anne had warned them that if they brought any more cakes to school they would be confiscated; and yet here was St Clair Donnell coolly passing a parcel of them, wrapped up in the blue and white striped paper Mrs Hiram used, under her very eyes.

'Joseph,' said Anne quietly, 'bring that parcel here.'

Joe, startled and abashed, obeyed. He was a fat urchin who always blushed and stuttered when he was frightened. Never did anybody look more guilty than poor Joe at that moment.

'Throw it into the fire,' said Anne.

Joe looked very blank.

'P . . . p . . . p . . . lease, m . . . m . . . miss,' he began.

'Do as I tell you, Joseph, without any words about it.'

'B . . . b . . . but m . . . m . . . miss . . . th . . . th . . . they're . . .' gasped Joe in desperation.

'Joseph, are you going to obey me or are you *not*?' said Anne.

A bolder and more self-possessed lad than Joe Sloane would have been overawed by her tone and the dangerous flash of her eyes. This was a new Anne whom none of her pupils had ever seen before. Joe, with an agonized glance at St Clair, went to the stove, opened the big, square front door, and threw the blue and white parcel in, before St Clair, who had sprung to his feet, could utter a word. Then he dodged back just in time.

For a few moments the terrified occupants of Avonlea school did not know whether it was an earthquake or a volcanic explosion that had occurred. The innocent-looking parcel which Anne had rashly supposed to contain Mrs Hiram's nut cakes really held an assortment of firecrackers and pin-wheels for which Warren Sloane had sent to town by St Clair Donnell's father the day before, intending to have a birthday celebration that evening. The crackers went off in a thunderclap of noise and the pin-wheels bursting out of the door spun madly around the room, hissing and spluttering. Anne dropped into her chair white with dismay and all the girls climbed shrieking upon their desks. Joe Sloane stood as one transfixed in the midst of the commotion and St Clair, helpless with laughter, rocked to and fro in the aisle. Prillie Rogerson fainted and Annetta Bell went into hysterics.

It seemed a long time, although it was really only a few minutes, before the last pin-wheel subsided. Anne, recovering herself sprang to open doors and windows and let out the gas and smoke which filled the room. Then she helped the girls carry the unconscious Prillie into the porch, where Barbara Shaw, in an agony of desire to be useful, poured a pailful of half-frozen water over Prillie's face and shoulders before anyone could stop her.

It was a full hour before quiet was restored ... but it was a quiet that might be felt. Everybody realized that even the explosion had not cleared the teacher's mental atmosphere. Nobody, except Anthony Pye dared whisper a word. Ned Clay accidentally squeaked his pencil while working a sum, caught Anne's eye and wished the floor would open and swallow him up. The geography class were whisked through a continent with a speed that made them dizzy. The grammar class were parsed and analysed within an inch of their lives. Chester Sloane, spelling 'odoriferous' with two F's, was made to feel that he could never live down the disgrace of it, either in this world or in that which is to come.

Anne knew that she had made herself ridiculous and that the incident would be laughed over that night at a score of tea-tables, but the knowledge only angered her further. In a calmer mood she could have carried off the situation with a laugh, but now that was impossible; so she ignored it in icy disdain.

When Anne returned to the school after dinner all the children were as usual in their seats and every face was bent studiously over a desk except Anthony Pye's. He peered across his book at Anne, his black eyes sparkling with curiosity and mockery. Anne twitched open the drawer of her desk in search of chalk and under her very hand a lively mouse sprang out of the drawer, scampered over the desk, and leaped to the floor.

Anne screamed and sprang back, as if it had been a snake, and Anthony Pye laughed aloud.

Then a silence fell ... a very creepy, uncomfortable silence. Annetta Bell was of two minds whether to go into hysterics again or not, especially as she didn't know just where the mouse had gone. But she decided not to. Who could take any comfort out of hysterics with a teacher so white-faced and so blazing-eyed standing before one?

'Who put that mouse in my desk?' said Anne. Her voice was quite low but it made a shiver go up and down Paul Irving's spine. Joe Sloane caught her eye, felt responsible from the crown of his head to the soles of his feet, stuttered out wildly,

'N ... n ... not m ... m ... me t ... t ... teacher, n ... n ... not m ... m ... me.'

Anne paid no attention to the wretched Joseph. She looked at Anthony Pye, and Anthony Pye looked back, unabashed and unashamed.

'Anthony, was it you?'

'Yes, it was,' said Anthony insolently.

Anne took her pointer from her desk. It was a long heavy hardwood pointer.

'Come here, Anthony.'

It was far from being the most severe punishment Anthony Pye had ever undergone. Anne, even the stormy-souled Anne she was at that moment, could not have punished any child cruelly. But the pointer nipped keenly and finally Anthony's bravado failed him; he winced and the tears came to his eyes.

Anne, conscience-stricken, dropped the pointer and told Anthony to go to his seat. She sat down at her desk feeling ashamed, repentant, and bitterly mortified. Her quick anger was gone and she would have given much to have been able to seek relief in tears. So all her boasts had come to this ... she had actually whipped one of her pupils. How Jane would triumph! And how Mr Harrison would chuckle! But worse than this, bitterest thought of all, she had lost her last chance of winning Anthony Pye. Never would he like her now.

Anne, by what somebody has called 'a Herculaneum effort', kept back her tears until she got home that night. Then she shut herself in the east gable room and wept all her shame and re-

morse and disappointment into her pillows . . . wept so long that
Marilla grew alarmed, invaded the room, and insisted on knowing what the trouble was.

'The trouble is, I've got things the matter with my conscience,' sobbed Anne. 'Oh, this has been such a Jonah day,
Marilla. I'm so ashamed of myself. I lost my temper and
whipped Anthony Pye.'

'I'm glad to hear it,' said Marilla with decision. 'It's what you
should have done long ago.'

'Oh, no, no, Marilla. And I don't see how I can ever look
those children in the face again. I feel that I have humiliated
myself to the very dust. You don't know how cross and hateful
and horrid I was. I can't forget the expression in Paul Irving's
eyes . . . he looked so surprised and disappointed. Oh, Marilla, I
have tried so hard to be patient and to win Anthony's liking . . .
and now it has all gone for nothing.'

Marilla passed her hard work-worn hand over the girl's
glossy, tumbled hair with a wonderful tenderness. When Anne's
sobs grew quieter she said, very gently for her:

'You take things too much to heart, Anne. We all make mistakes . . . but people forget them. And Jonah days come to
everybody. As for Anthony Pye, why need you care if he does
dislike you? He is the only one.'

'I can't help it. I want everybody to love me and it hurts me
so when anybody doesn't. And Anthony never will now. Oh, I
just made an idiot of myself today, Marilla. I'll tell you the
whole story.'

Marilla listened to the whole story, and if she smiled at certain parts of it Anne never knew. When the tale ended, she said
briskly:

'Well, never mind. This day's done and there's a new one
coming tomorrow, with no mistakes in it yet, as you used to say
yourself. Just come downstairs and have your supper. You'll
see if a good cup of tea and those plum puffs I made today
won't hearten you up.'

'Plum puffs won't minister to a mind diseased,' said Anne
disconsolately; but Marilla thought it a good sign that she had
recovered sufficiently to adapt a quotation.

The cheerful supper table, with the twins' bright faces, and Marilla's matchless plum puffs ... of which Davy ate four ... did 'hearten her up' considerably after all. She had a good sleep that night and awakened in the morning to find herself and the world transformed. It had snowed softly and thickly all through the hours of darkness and the beautiful whiteness, glittering in the frosty sunshine, looked like a mantle of charity cast over all the mistakes and humiliations of the past.

> 'Every morn is a fresh beginning,
>   Every morn is the world made new,'

sang Anne, as she dressed.

Owing to the snow she had to go round by the road to school and she thought it was certainly an impish coincidence that Anthony Pye should come ploughing along just as she left the Green Gables lane. She felt as guilty as if their positions were reversed; but to her unspeakable astonishment Anthony not only lifted his cap ... which he had never done before ... but said easily:

'Kind of bad walking, ain't it? Can I take those books for you, teacher?'

Anne surrendered her books and wondered if she could possibly be awake. Anthony walked on in silence to the school, but when Anne took her books she smiled down at him ... not the stereotyped 'kind' smile she had so persistently assumed for his benefit but a sudden outflashing of good comradeship. Anthony smiled ... no, if the truth must be told, Anthony *grinned* back. A grin is not generally supposed to be a respectful thing; yet Anne suddenly felt that if she had not yet won Anthony's liking she had, somehow or other, won his respect.

Mrs Rachel Lynde came up the next Saturday and confirmed this.

'Well, Anne, I guess you've won over Anthony Pye, that's what. He says he believes you are some good after all, even if you are a girl. Says that whipping you gave him was "just as good as a man's".'

'I never expected to win him by whipping him, though,' said Anne, a little mournfully, feeling that her ideals had played her false somewhere. 'It doesn't seem right. I'm *sure* my theory of kindness can't be wrong.'

'No, but the Pyes are an exception to every known rule, that's what,' declared Mrs Rachel with conviction.

Mr Harrison said, 'Thought you'd come to it,' when he heard it, and Jane rubbed it in rather unmercifully.

CHAPTER 13

A Golden Picnic

ANNE, on her way to Orchard Slope, met Diana, bound for Green Gables, just where the mossy old log bridge spanned the brook below the Haunted Wood, and they sat down by the margin of the Dryad's Bubble, where tiny ferns were unrolling like curly-headed green pixy-folk wakening up from a nap.

'I was just on my way over to invite you to help me celebrate my birthday on Saturday,' said Anne.

'Your birthday? But your birthday was in March!'

'That wasn't my fault,' laughed Anne. 'If my parents had consulted me it would never have happened then. I should have chosen to be born in spring, of course. It must be delightful to come into the world with the mayflowers and violets. You would always feel that you were their foster sister. But since I didn't, the next best thing is to celebrate my birthday in the spring. Priscilla is coming over Saturday and Jane will be home. We'll all four start off to the woods and spend a golden day making the acquaintance of the spring. We none of us really know her yet, but we'll meet her back there as we never can anywhere else. I want to explore all those fields and lonely places anyhow. I have a conviction that there are scores of beautiful nooks there that have never really been *seen* although they may have been *looked* at. We'll make friends with wind and sky and sun, and bring home the spring in our hearts.'

'It *sounds* awfully nice,' said Diana, with some inward distrust of Anne's magic of words. 'But won't it be very damp in some places yet?'

'Oh, we'll wear rubbers,' was Anne's concession to practicalities. 'And I want you to come over early Saturday morning and help me prepare lunch. I'm going to have the daintiest things possible ... things that will match the spring, you understand ... little jelly tarts and lady fingers, and drop cookies frosted with pink and yellow icing, and buttercup cake. And we must have sandwiches too, though they're *not* very poetical.'

Saturday proved an ideal day for a picnic ... a day of breeze and blue, warm, sunny, with a little rollicking wind blowing across meadow and orchard. Over every sunlit upland and field was a delicate, flower-starred green.

Mr Harrison, harrowing at the back of his farm and feeling some of the spring witch-work even in his sober, middle-aged blood, saw four girls, basket-laden, tripping across the end of his field where it joined a fringing woodland of birch and fir. Their blithe voices and laughter echoed down to him.

'It's so easy to be happy on a day like this, isn't it?' Anne was saying, with true Anneish philosophy. 'Let's try to make this a really golden day, girls, a day to which we can always look back with delight. We're to seek for beauty and refuse to see anything else. 'Begone, dull care!" Jane, you are thinking of something that went wrong in school yesterday.'

'How do you know?' gasped Jane, amazed.

'Oh, I know the expression ... I've felt it often enough on my own face. But put it out of your mind, there's a dear. It will keep till Monday ... or if it doesn't so much the better. Oh, girls, girls, see that patch of violets! There's something for memory's picture gallery. When I'm eighty years old ... if I ever am ... I shall shut my eyes and see those violets just as I see them now. That's the first good gift our day has given us.'

'If a kiss could be seen I think it would look like a violet,' said Priscilla.

Anne glowed.

'I'm so glad you *spoke* that thought, Priscilla, instead of just thinking it and keeping it to yourself. This world would be a much more interesting place ... although it *is* very interesting anyhow ... if people spoke out their real thoughts.'

'It would be too hot to hold some folks,' quoth Jane sagely.

'I suppose it might be, but that would be their own faults for thinking nasty things. Anyhow, we can tell all our thoughts today because we are going to have nothing but beautiful thoughts. Everybody can say just what comes into her head. *That* is conversation. Here's a little path I never saw before. Let's explore it.'

The path was a winding one, so narrow that the girls walked in single file and even then the fir boughs brushed their faces. Under the firs were velvety cushions of moss, and further on, where the trees were smaller and fewer, the ground was rich in a variety of green growing things.

'What a lot of elephant's ears,' exclaimed Diana. 'I'm going to pick a big bunch, they're so pretty.'

'How did such graceful feathery things ever come to have such a dreadful name?' asked Priscilla.

'Because the person who first named them either had no imagination at all or else far too much,' said Anne. 'Oh, girls, look at that!'

'That' was a shallow woodland pool in the centre of a little open glade where the path ended. Later on in the season it would be dried up and its place filled with a rank growth of ferns; but now it was a glimmering placid sheet, round as a saucer and clear as crystal. A ring of slender young birches encircled it and little ferns fringed its margin.

'How sweet!' said Jane.

'Let us dance around it like wood-nymphs,' cried Anne, dropping her basket and extending her hands.

But the dance was not a success, for the ground was boggy and Jane's rubbers came off.

'You can't be a wood-nymph if you have to wear rubbers,' was her decision.

'Well, we must name this place before we leave it,' said Anne, yielding to the indisputable logic of facts. 'Everybody suggest a name and we'll draw lots. Diana?'

'Birch Pool,' suggested Diana promptly.

'Crystal Lake,' said Jane.

Anne, standing behind them, implored Priscilla with her eyes not to perpetrate another such name and Priscilla rose to the occasion with 'Glimmer-glass'. Anne's selection was 'The Fairies' Mirror'.

The names were written on strips of birch bark with a pencil Schoolma'am Jane produced from her pocket, and placed in Anne's hat. Then Priscilla shut her eyes and drew one. 'Crystal Lake,' read Jane triumphantly. Crystal Lake it was, and if Anne thought that chance had played the pool a shabby trick she did not say so.

Pushing through the undergrowth beyond, the girls came out of the young green seclusion of Mr Silas Sloane's back pasture. Across it they found the entrance to a lane striking up through the woods and voted to explore it also. It rewarded their quest with a succession of pretty surprises. First, skirting Mr Sloane's pasture, came an archway of wild cherry-trees all in bloom. The girls swung their hats on their arms and wreathed their hair with the creamy, fluffy blossoms. Then the lane turned at right angles and plunged into a spruce wood so thick and dark that they walked in a gloom as of twilight, with not a glimpse of sky or sunlight to be seen.

'This is where the bad wood-elves dwell,' whispered Anne. 'They are impish and malicious but they can't harm us, because they are not allowed to do evil in the spring. There was one peeping at us around that old twisted fir; and didn't you see a group of them on that big freckly toadstool we just passed? The good fairies always dwell in the sunshiny places.'

'I wish there really were fairies,' said Jane. 'Wouldn't it be nice to have three wishes granted you ... or even only one? What would you wish for, girls, if you could have a wish granted? I'd wish to be rich and beautiful and clever.'

'I'd wish to be tall and slender,' said Diana.

'I would wish to be famous,' said Priscilla.

Anne thought of her hair and then dismissed the thought as unworthy.

'I'd wish it might be spring all the time and in everybody's heart and all our lives,' she said.

'But that,' said Priscilla, 'would be just wishing this world were like heaven.'

'Only like a part of heaven. In the other parts there would be summer and autumn ... yes, and a bit of winter, too. I think I want glittering snowy fields, and white frosts in heaven sometimes. Don't you, Jane?'

'I ... I don't know,' said Jane uncomfortably. Jane was a good girl, a member of the church, who tried conscientiously to live up to her profession and believed everything she had been taught. But she never thought about heaven any more than she could help, for all that.

'Minnie May asked me the other day if we would wear our best dresses every day in heaven,' laughed Diana.

'And didn't you tell her we would?' asked Anne.

'Mercy, no! I told her we wouldn't be thinking of dresses at all there.'

'Oh, I think we will ... a *little*,' said Anne earnestly. 'There'll be plenty of time in all eternity for it without neglecting more important things. I believe we'll all wear beautiful dresses ... or I suppose *raiment* would be a more suitable way of speaking. I shall want to wear pink for a few centuries at first ... it would take me that long to get tired of it, I feel sure. I do love pink so and I can never wear it in *this* world.'

Past the spruces the lane dipped down into a sunny little open where a log bridge spanned a brook; and then came the glory of a sunlit beech wood where the air was like transparent golden wine, and the leaves fresh and green, and the wood floor a mosaic of tremulous sunshine. Then more wild cherries, and a little valley of lissome firs, and then a hill so steep that the girls lost their breath climbing it; but when they reached the top and came out into the open the prettiest surprise of all awaited them.

Beyond were the 'back fields' of the farms that ran out to the upper Carmody road. Just before them, hemmed in by beeches and firs but open to the south, was a little corner and in it a garden ... or what had once been a garden. A tumbledown stone dyke, overgrown with mosses and grass, surrounded it. Along the eastern side ran a row of garden cherry-trees, white as a snowdrift. There were traces of old paths still and a double line of rose-bushes through the middle; but all the rest of the space was a sheet of yellow and white narcissi, in their airiest, most lavish, wind-swayed bloom above the lush green grasses.

'Oh, how perfectly lovely!' three of the girls cried. Anne only gazed in eloquent silence.

'How in the world does it happen that there ever was a garden back here?' said Priscilla in amazement.

'It must be Hester Gray's garden,' said Diana. 'I've heard Mother speak of it but I never saw it before, and I wouldn't have supposed that it could be in existence still. You've heard the story, Anne?'

'No, but the name seems familiar to me.'

'Oh, you've seen it in the graveyard. She is buried down there in the poplar corner. You know the little brown stone with the opening gates carved on it and "Sacred to the memory of Hester Gray, aged twenty-two." Jordan Gray is buried right beside her, but there's no stone to him. It's a wonder Marilla never told you about it, Anne. To be sure, it happened thirty years ago and everybody has forgotten.'

'Well, if there's a story we must have it,' said Anne. 'Let's sit right down here among the narcissi and Diana will tell it. Why, girls, there are hundreds of them ... they've spread over everything. It looks as if the garden were carpeted with moonshine and sunshine combined. This is a discovery worth making. To think that I've lived within a mile of this place for six years and have never seen it before! Now, Diana.'

'Long ago,' began Diana, 'this farm belonged to old Mr David Gray. He didn't live on it ... he lived where Silas Sloane lives now. He had one son, Jordan, and he went up to Boston one winter to work and while he was there he fell in love with a girl named Hester Murray. She was working in a store and she hated it. She'd been brought up in the country and she always wanted to get back. When Jordan asked her to marry him she said she would if he'd take her away to some quiet spot where she'd see nothing but fields and trees. So he brought her to Avonlea. Mrs Lynde said he was taking a fearful risk in marrying a Yankee, and it's certain that Hester was very delicate and a very poor housekeeper; but Mother says she was very pretty and sweet, and Jordan just worshipped the ground she walked on. Well, Mr Gray gave Jordan this farm and he built a little house back here and Jordan and Hester lived in it for four years. She never went out much and hardly anybody went to see her except Mother and Mrs Lynde. Jordan made her this garden and she was crazy about it and spent most of her time in it. She wasn't much of a housekeeper but she had a knack with flowers. And then she got sick. Mother says she thinks she was in consumption before she ever came here. She never really laid up, but just grew weaker and weaker all the time. Jordan wouldn't have anybody to wait on her. He did it all himself and Mother says he was as tender and gentle as a woman. Every day he'd wrap her in a shawl and carry her out to the garden and she'd lie there on a bench quite happy. They say she used to make Jordan kneel down by her every night and morning and pray with her that she might die out in the garden when the time came. And her prayer was answered. One day Jordan carried her out to the bench and then he picked all the roses that were out and heaped them over her; and she just smiled up at him ... and closed her eyes ... and that,' concluded Diana softly, 'was the end.'

'Oh, what a dear story,' sighed Anne, wiping away her tears.

'What became of Jordan?' asked Priscilla.

'He sold the farm after Hester died and went back to Boston. Mr Jabez Sloane bought the farm and hauled the little house out to the road. Jordan died about ten years after and he was brought home and buried beside Hester.'

'I can't understand how she could have wanted to live back here away from everything,' said Jane.

'Oh, I can easily understand *that*,' said Anne thoughtfully. 'I wouldn't want it myself for a steady thing, because, although I love the fields and woods, I love people too. But I can understand it in Hester. She was tired to death of the noise of the big city and the crowds of people always coming and going and caring nothing for her. She just wanted to escape from it all to some still, green, friendly place where she could rest. And she got just what she wanted, which is something very few people do, I believe. She had four beautiful years before she died ... four years of perfect happiness, so I think she was to be envied more than pitied. And then to shut your eyes and fall asleep among roses, with the one you loved best on earth smiling down at you . . . oh, I think it was beautiful!'

'She set out those cherry-trees over there,' said Diana. 'She told Mother she'd never live to eat their fruit, but she wanted to think that something she had planted would go on living and helping to make the world beautiful after she was dead.'

'I'm so glad we came this way,' said Anne, the shining-eyed. 'This is my adopted birthday, you know, and this garden and its story is the birthday gift it has given me. Did your mother ever tell you what Hester Gray looked like, Diana?'

'No . . . only just that she was pretty.'

'I'm rather glad of that, because I can imagine what she looked like, without being hampered by facts. I think she was very slight and small, with softly curling dark hair and big, sweet, timid brown eyes, and a little wistful, pale face.'

The girls left their baskets in Hester's garden and spent the rest of the afternoon rambling in the woods and fields surrounding it, discovering many pretty nooks and lanes. When they got hungry they had lunch in the prettiest spot of all . . . on the steep bank of a gurgling brook where white birches shot up out of long feathery grasses. The girls sat down by the roots and did full justice to Anne's dainties, even the unpoetical sandwiches being greatly appreciated by hearty, unspoiled appetites sharpened by all the fresh air and exercise they had enjoyed. Anne had brought glasses and lemonade for her guests, but for her own part drank cold brook water from a cup fashioned out of birch bark. The cup leaked, and the water tasted of earth, as brook water is apt to do in spring; but Anne thought it more appropriate to the occasion than lemonade.

'Look, do you see that poem?' she said suddenly, pointing.

'Where?' Jane and Diana stared, as if expecting to see Runic rhymes on the birch-trees.

'There . . . down in the brook . . . that old green, mossy log with the water flowing over it in those smooth ripples that look as if they'd been combed, and that single shaft of sunshine falling right athwart it, far down into the pool. Oh, it's the most beautiful poem I ever saw.'

'I should rather call it a picture,' said Jane. 'A poem is lines and verses.'

'Oh dear me, no.' Anne shook her head with its fluffy wild-cherry coronal positively. 'The lines and verses are only the outward garments of the poem and are no more really it than your ruffles and flounces are *you*, Jane. The real poem is the soul within them ... and that beautiful bit is the soul of an unwritten poem. It is not every day one sees a soul ... even of a poem.'

'I wonder what a soul ... a person's soul ... would look like,' said Priscilla dreamily.

'Like that, I should think,' answered Anne, pointing to a radiance of sifted sunlight streaming through a birch-tree. 'Only with shape and features of course. I like to fancy souls as being made of light. And some are all shot through with rosy stains and quivers ... and some have a soft glitter like moonlight on the sea ... and some are pale and transparent like mist at dawn.'

'I read somewhere once that souls were like flowers,' said Priscilla.

'Then your soul is a golden narcissus,' said Anne, 'and Diana's is like a red, red rose. Jane's is an apple-blossom, pink and wholesome and sweet.'

'And your own is a white violet, with purple streaks in its heart,' finished Priscilla.

Jane whispered to Diana that she really could not understand what they were talking about. Could she?

The girls went home by the light of a calm golden sunset, their baskets filled with narcissus blossoms from Hester's garden, some of which Anne carried to the cemetery next day and laid upon Hester's grave. Minstrel robins were whistling in the firs and the frogs were singing in the marshes. All the basins among the hills were brimmed with topaz and emerald light.

'Well, we have had a lovely time after all,' said Diana, as if she had hardly expected to have it when she set out.

'It has been a truly golden day,' said Priscilla.

'I'm really awfully fond of the woods myself,' said Jane.

Anne said nothing. She was looking afar into the western sky and thinking of little Hester Gray.

CHAPTER 14

A Danger Averted

ANNE, walking home from the post office one Friday evening, was joined by Mrs Lynde, who was as usual cumbered with all the cares of church and state.

'I've just been down to Timothy Cotton's to see if I could get Alice Louise to help me for a few days,' she said. 'I had her last week, for, though she's too slow to stop quick, she's better than nobody. But she's sick and can't come. Timothy's sitting there, too, coughing and complaining. He's been dying for ten years and he'll go on dying for ten years more. That kind can't even die and have done with it ... they can't stick to anything, even to being sick, long enough to finish it. They're a terrible shiftless family and what is to become of them I don't know, but perhaps Providence does.'

Mrs Lynde sighed as if she rather doubted the extent of Providential knowledge on the subject.

'Marilla was in about her eyes again Tuesday, wasn't she? What did the specialist think of them?' she continued.

'He was much pleased,' said Anne brightly. 'He says there is a great improvement in them and he thinks the danger of her losing her sight completely is past. But he says she'll never be able to read much or do any fine hand-work again. How are your preparations for your bazaar coming on?'

The Ladies' Aid Society was preparing for a fair and supper, and Mrs Lynde was the head and front of the enterprise.

'Pretty well ... and that reminds me. Mrs Allan thinks it would be nice to fix up a booth like an old-time kitchen and serve a supper of baked beans, doughnuts, pie, and so on. We're collecting old-fashioned fixings everywhere. Mrs Simon Fletcher is going to lend us her mother's braided rugs and Mrs Levi Boulter some old chairs and Aunt Mary Shaw will lend us her cupboard with the glass doors. I suppose Marilla will let us have her brass candlesticks? And we want all the old dishes we can get. Mrs Allan is specially set on having a real blue willow

ware platter if we can find one. But nobody seems to have one.
Do you know where we could get one?'

'Miss Josephine Barry has one. I'll write and ask her if she'll
lend it for the occasion,' said Anne.

'Well, I wish you would. I guess we'll have supper in about
a fortnight's time. Uncle Abe Andrews is prophesying rain
and storms for about that time; and that's a pretty sure sign
we'll have fine weather.'

The said 'Uncle Abe', it may be mentioned, was at least like
other prophets in that he had small honour in his own country.
He was, in fact, considered in the light of a standing joke, for
few of his weather predictions were ever fulfilled. Mr Elisha
Wright, who laboured under the impression that he was a local
wit, used to say that nobody in Avonlea ever thought of looking
in the Charlottetown dailies for weather probabilities. No; they
just asked Uncle Abe what it was going to be tomorrow and
expected the opposite. Nothing daunted, Uncle Abe kept on
prophesying.

'We want to have the fair over before the election comes off,'
continued Mrs Lynde, 'for the candidates will be sure to come
and spend lots of money. The Tories are bribing right and left,
so they might as well be given a chance to spend their money
honestly for once.'

Anne was a red-hot Conservative, out of loyalty to Matthew's memory, but she said nothing. She knew better than to
get Mrs Lynde started on politics.

She had a letter for Marilla, postmarked from a town in
British Columbia.

'It's probably from the children's uncle,' she said excitedly,
when she got home. 'Oh, Marilla, I wonder what he says about
them.'

'The best plan might be to open it and see,' said Marilla
curtly. A close observer might have thought that she was excited also, but she would rather have died than show it.

Anne tore open the letter and glanced over the somewhat
untidy and poorly written contents.

'He says he can't take the children this spring ... he's been
sick most of the winter and his wedding is put off. He wants to

know if we can keep them till the fall and he'll try and take them then. We will, of course, won't we, Marilla?'

'I don't see that there is anything else for us to do,' said Marilla rather grimly, although she felt a secret relief. 'Anyhow they're not so much trouble as they were ... or else we've got used to them. Davy has improved a great deal.'

'His *manners* are certainly much better,' said Anne cautiously, as if she were not prepared to say as much for his morals.

Anne had come home from school the previous evening, to find Marilla away at an Aid meeting, Dora asleep on the kitchen sofa, and Davy in the sitting-room closet, blissfully absorbing the contents of a jar of Marilla's famous yellow plum preserves ... 'company jam', Davy called it ... which he had been forbidden to touch. He looked very guilty when Anne pounced on him and whisked him out of the closet.

'Davy Keith, don't you know that it is very wrong of you to be eating that jam, when you were told never to meddle with anything in that closet?'

'Yes, I knew it was wrong,' admitted Davy uncomfortably, 'but plum jam is awful nice, Anne. I just peeped in and it looked so good I thought I'd take just a weeny taste. I stuck my finger in ...' Anne groaned ... 'and licked it clean. And it was so much gooder than I'd ever thought that I got a spoon and just *sailed in.*'

Anne gave him such a serious lecture on the sin of stealing plum jam that Davy became conscience-stricken and promised with repentant kisses never to do it again.

'Anyhow, there'll be plenty of jam in heaven, that's one comfort,' he said complacently.

Anne nipped a smile in the bud.

'Perhaps there will ... if we want it,' she said, 'but what makes you think so?'

'Why, it's in the catechism,' said Davy.

'Oh, no, there is nothing like *that* in the catechism, Davy.'

'But I tell you there is,' persisted Davy. 'It was in that question Marilla taught me last Sunday. "Why should we love God?" It says, "Because He makes preserves, and redeems us." Preserves is just a holy way of saying jam.'

'I must get a drink of water,' said Anne hastily. When she came back it cost her some time and trouble to explain to Davy that a certain comma in the said catechism question made a great deal of difference in the meaning.

'Well, I thought it was too good to be true,' he said at last, with a sigh of disappointed conviction. 'And besides, I didn't see when He'd find time to make jam if it's one endless Sabbath day, as the hymn says. I don't believe I want to go to heaven. Won't there ever be any Saturdays in heaven, Anne?'

'Yes, Saturdays, and every other kind of beautiful days. And every day in heaven will be more beautiful than the one before it, Davy,' assured Anne, who was rather glad that Marilla was not by to be shocked. Marilla, it is needless to say, was bringing the twins up in the good old ways of theology, and discouraged all fanciful speculations thereupon. Davy and Dora were taught a hymn, a catechism question, and two Bible verses every Sunday. Dora learned meekly and recited like a little machine, with perhaps as much understanding or interest as if she were one. Davy, on the contrary, had a lively curiosity, and frequently asked questions which made Marilla tremble for his fate.

'Chester Sloane says we'll do nothing all the time in heaven but walk around in white dresses and play on harps; and he says he hopes he won't have to go till he's an old man, 'cause maybe he'll like it better then. And he thinks it will be horrid to wear dresses and I think so too. Why can't men angels wear trousers, Anne? Chester Sloane is interested in those things, 'cause they're going to make a minister of him. He's *got* to be a minister 'cause his grandmother left the money to send him to college and he can't have it unless he is a minister. She thought a minister was such a 'spectable thing to have in a family. Chester says he doesn't mind much ... though he'd rather be a black-smith ... but he's bound to have all the fun he can before he begins to be a minister, 'cause he doesn't expect to have much afterwards. *I* ain't going to be a minister. I'm going to be a storekeeper, like Mr Blair, and keep heaps of candy and bananas. But I'd rather like going to your kind of a heaven if they'd let me play a mouth organ instead of a harp. Do you s'pose they would?'

'Yes, I think they would if you wanted it,' was all Anne could trust herself to say.

The A.V.I.S. met at Mr Harmon Andrews' that evening and a full attendance had been requested, since important business was to be discussed. The A.V.I.S. was in a flourishing condition, and had already accomplished wonders. Early in the spring Mr Major Spencer had redeemed his promise and had stumped, graded, and seeded down all the road-front of his farm. A dozen other men, some prompted by a determination not to let a Spencer get ahead of them, others goaded into action by Improvers in their own households, had followed his example. The result was that there were long strips of smooth velvet turf where once had been unsightly undergrowth or brush. The farm fronts that had not been done looked so badly by contrast that their owners were secretly shamed into resolving to see what they could do another spring. The triangle of ground at the cross roads had also been cleared and seeded down, and Anne's bed of geraniums, unharmed by any marauding cow, was already set out in the centre.

Altogether, the Improvers thought that they were getting on beautifully, even if Mr Levi Boulter, tactfully approached by a carefully selected committee in regard to the old house on his upper farm, did bluntly tell them that he wasn't going to have it meddled with.

At this especial meeting they intended to draw up a petition to the school trustees, humbly praying that a fence be put around the school grounds; and a plan was also to be discussed for planting a few ornamental trees by the church, if the funds of the society would permit of it ... for, as Anne said, there was no use in starting another subscription as long as the hall remained blue. The members were assembled in the Andrews' parlour and Jane was already on her feet to move the appointment of a committee which should find out and report on the price of said trees, when Gertie Pye swept in, pompadoured and frilled within an inch of her life. Gertie had a habit of being late ... 'to make her entrance more effective', spiteful people said. Gertie's entrance in this instance was certainly effective, for she paused dramatically on the middle of the floor, threw up her hands, rolled her eyes, and exclaimed,

'I've just heard something perfectly awful. What *do* you think? Mr Judson Parker *is going to rent all the road fence of his farm to a patent medicine company to paint advertisements on.*'

For once in her life Gertie Pye made all the sensation she desired. If she had thrown a bomb among the complacent Improvers she could hardly have made more.

'It *can't* be true,' said Anne bluntly.

'That's just what *I* said when I heard it first, don't you know,' said Gertie, who was enjoying herself hugely. '*I* said it couldn't be true ... that Judson Parker wouldn't have the *heart* to do it, don't you know. But Father met him this afternoon and asked him about it and he said it *was* true. Just fancy! His farm is side-on to the Newbridge road and how perfectly awful it will look to see advertisements of pills and plasters all along it, don't you know?'

The Improvers *did* know, all too well. Even the least imaginative among them could picture the grotesque effect of half a mile of board fence adorned with such advertisements. All thought of church and school grounds vanished before this new danger. Parliamentary rules and regulations were forgotten, and Anne, in despair, gave up trying to keep minutes at all. Everybody talked at once and fearful was the hubbub.

'Oh, let us keep calm,' implored Anne, who was the most excited of them all, 'and try to think of some way of preventing him.'

'I don't know how you're going to prevent him,' exclaimed Jane bitterly. 'Everybody knows what Judson Parker is. He'd do *anything* for money. He hasn't a *spark* of public spirit or *any* sense of the beautiful.'

The prospect looked rather unpromising. Judson Parker and his sister were the only Parkers in Avonlea, so that no leverage could be exerted by family connections. Martha Parker was a lady of all too certain age who disapproved of young people in general and the Improvers in particular. Judson was a jovial smooth-spoken man, so uniformly good-natured and bland that it was surprising how few friends he had. Perhaps he had got the better in too many business transactions ... which seldom makes for popularity. He was reputed to be very 'sharp' and it was the general opinion that he 'hadn't much principle'.

'If Judson Parker has a chance to "turn an honest penny", as he says himself, he'll never lose it,' declared Fred Wright.

'Is there *nobody* who has any influence over him?' asked Anne despairingly.

'He goes to see Louisa Spencer at White Sands,' suggested Carrie Sloane. 'Perhaps she could coax him not to rent his fences.'

'Not she,' said Gilbert emphatically. 'I know Louisa Spencer well. She doesn't "believe" in Village Improvement Societies, but she *does* believe in dollars and cents. She'd be more likely to urge Judson on than to dissuade him.'

'The only thing to do is to appoint a committee to wait on him and protest,' said Julia Bell, 'and you must send girls, for he'd hardly be civil to boys ... but *I* won't go, so nobody need nominate me.'

'Better send Anne alone,' said Oliver Sloane. 'She can talk Judson over if anybody can.'

Anne protested. She was willing to go and do the talking; but she must have others with her 'for moral support'. Diana and Jane were therefore appointed to support her morally and the Improvers broke up, buzzing like angry bees with indignation. Anne was so worried that she didn't sleep until nearly morning, and then she dreamed that the trustees had put a fence around the school and painted 'Try Purple Pills' all over it.

The committee waited on Judson Parker the next afternoon. Anne pleaded eloquently against his nefarious design and Jane and Diana supported her morally and valiantly. Judson was sleek, suave, flattering; paid them several compliments of the delicacy of sunflowers; felt real bad to refuse such charming young ladies ... but business was business; couldn't afford to let sentiment stand in the way these hard times.

'But I'll tell what I *will* do,' he said, with a twinkle in his light, full eyes. 'I'll tell the agent he must use only handsome, tasty colours . . . red and yellow and so on. I'll tell him he mustn't paint the ads *blue* on any account.'

The vanquished committee retired, thinking things not lawfully to be uttered.

'We have done all we can do and must simply trust the rest to Providence,' said Jane, with an unconscious imitation of Mrs Lynde's tone and manner.

'I wonder if Mr Allan could do anything,' reflected Diana.

Anne shook her head.

'No, it's no use to worry Mr Allan, especially now when the baby's so sick. Judson would slip away from him as smoothly as from us, although he *has* taken to going to church quite regularly just now. That is simply because Louisa Spencer's father is an elder and very particular about such things.'

'Judson Parker is the only man in Avonlea who would dream of renting his fences,' said Jane indignantly. 'Even Levi Boulter or Lorenzo White would never stoop to that, tight-fisted as they are. They would have too much respect for public opinion.'

Public opinion was certainly down on Judson Parker when the facts became known, but that did not help matters much. Judson chuckled to himself and defied it, and the Improvers were trying to reconcile themselves to the prospect of seeing the prettiest part of the Newbridge road defaced by advertisements, when Anne rose quietly at the president's call for reports of committees on the occasion of the next meeting of the Society, and announced that Mr Judson Parker had instructed her to inform the Society that he was *not* going to rent his fences to the Patent Medicine Company.

Jane and Diana stared as if they found it hard to believe their ears. Parliamentary etiquette, which was generally very strictly enforced in the A.V.I.S., forbade them giving instant vent to their curiosity, but after the Society adjourned Anne was besieged for explanations. Anne had no explanation to give. Judson Parker had overtaken her on the road the preceding evening and told her that he had decided to humour the A.V.I.S. in its peculiar prejudice against patent medicine advertisements. That was all Anne would say, then or ever afterwards, and it was the simple truth; but when Jane Andrews, on her way home, confided to Oliver Sloane her firm belief that there was more behind Judson Parker's mysterious change of heart than Anne Shirley had revealed, she spoke the truth also.

Anne had been down to old Mrs Irving's on the shore road the preceding evening and had come home by a short cut which led her first over the low-lying shore fields, and then through the beech wood below Robert Dickson's, by a little footpath that ran out to the main road just above the Lake of Shining Waters . . . known to unimaginative people as Barry's pond.

Two men were sitting in their buggies, reined off to the side of the road, just at the entrance of the path. One was Judson Parker; the other was Jerry Corcoran, a Newbridge man against whom, as Mrs Lynde would have told you in eloquent italics, nothing shady had ever been *proved*. He was an agent for agricultural implements and a prominent personage in matters political. He had a finger . . . some people said *all* his fingers . . . in every political pie that was cooked; and as Canada was on the eve of a general election Jerry Corcoran had been a busy man for many weeks, canvassing the county in the interests of his party's candidate. Just as Anne emerged from under the overhanging beech boughs she heard Corcoran say:

'If you'll vote for Amesbury, Parker . . . well, I've a note for that pair of harrows you got in the spring. I suppose you wouldn't object to having it back, eh?'

'We . . . ll, since you put it in that way,' drawled Judson with a grin, 'I reckon I might as well do it. A man must look out for his own interests in these hard times.'

Both saw Anne at this moment and conversation abruptly ceased. Anne bowed frostily and walked on, with her chin slightly more tilted than usual. Soon Judson Parker overtook her.

'Have a lift, Anne?' he inquired genially.

'Thank you, no,' said Anne politely, but with a fine, needle-like disdain in her voice that pierced even Judson Parker's none too sensitive consciousness. His face reddened and he twitched his reins angrily; but the next second prudential considerations checked him. He looked uneasily at Anne, as she walked steadily on, glancing neither to the right nor to the left. Had she heard Corcoran's unmistakable offer and his own too plain acceptance of it? Confound Corcoran! If he couldn't put his meaning into less dangerous phrases he'd get into trouble some of these long-come-shorts. And confound red-headed schoolma'ams with a habit of popping out of beech woods where they had no business to be. If Anne had heard, Judson Parker, 'measuring her corn in his own half bushel', as the country saying went, and cheating himself thereby, as such people generally do, believed that she would tell it far and wide. Now, Judson Parker, as has been seen, was not over-regardful of public opinion; but to be known as having accepted a bribe would be a nasty thing; and if it ever reached Isaac Spencer's ears, farewell for ever to all hope of winning Louisa Jane with her comfortable prospects as the heiress of a well-to-do farmer. Judson Parker knew that Mr Spencer looked somewhat askance at him as it was; he could not afford to take any risks.

'Ahem ... Anne, I've been wanting to see you about that little matter we were discussing the other day. I've decided not to let my fences to that company after all. A society with an aim like yours ought to be encouraged.'

Anne thawed out the merest trifle.

'Thank you,' she said.

'And ... and ... you needn't mention that little conversation of mine with Jerry.'

'I have no intention of mentioning it in any case,' said Anne icily, for she would have seen every fence in Avonlea painted with advertisements before she would have stooped to bargain with a man who would sell his vote.

'Just so ... just so,' agreed Judson, imagining that they understood each other beautifully. 'I didn't suppose you would. Of course, I was only stringing Jerry ... he thinks he's so all-fired cute and smart. I've no intention of voting for Amesbury. I'm going to vote for Grant as I've always done ... you'll see that when the election comes off. I just led Jerry on to see if he would commit himself. And it's all right about the fence ... you can tell the Improvers that.'

'It takes all sorts of people to make a world, as I've often heard, but I think there are some who could be spared,' Anne told her reflection in the east gable mirror that night. 'I wouldn't have mentioned the disgraceful thing to a soul anyhow, so my conscience is clear on *that* score. I really don't know who or what is to be thanked for this. *I* did nothing to bring it about, and it's hard to believe that Providence ever works by means of the kind of politics men like Judson Parker and Jerry Corcoran have.'

CHAPTER 15

The Beginning of Vacation

ANNE locked the schoolhouse door on a still, yellow evening, when the winds were purring in the spruces around the playground, and the shadows were long and lazy by the edge of the woods. She dropped the key into her pocket with a sigh of satisfaction. The school year was ended, she had been re-engaged for the next, with many expressions of satisfaction . . . only Mr Harmon Andrews told her she ought to use the strap oftener . . . and two delightful months of a well-earned vacation beckoned her invitingly. Anne felt at peace with the world and herself as she walked down the hill with her basket of flowers in her hand. Since the earliest may-flowers Anne had never missed her weekly pilgrimage to Matthew's grave. Everybody else in Avonlea, except Marilla, had already forgotten quiet, shy, unimportant Matthew Cuthbert; but his memory was still green in Anne's heart and always would be. She could never forget the kind old man who had been the first to give her the love and sympathy her starved childhood had craved.

At the foot of the hill a boy was sitting on the fence in the shadow of the spruces . . . a boy with big, dreamy eyes and a beautiful, sensitive face. He swung down and joined Anne, smiling; but there were traces of tears on his cheeks.

'I thought I'd wait for you, teacher, because I knew you were going to the graveyard,' he said, slipping his hand into hers. 'I'm going there, too . . . I'm taking this bouquet of geraniums to put on Grandpa Irving's grave for Grandma. And look, teacher, I'm going to put this bunch of white roses beside Grandpa's grave in memory of my little mother . . . because I can't go to her grave to put it there. But don't you think she'll know all about it, just the same?'

'Yes, I am sure she will, Paul.'

'You see, teacher, it's just three years today since my little mother died. It's such a long, long time but it hurts just as much as ever . . . and I miss her just as much as ever. Sometimes it seems to me that I just can't bear it, it hurts so.'

Paul's voice quivered and his lip trembled. He looked down at his roses, hoping that his teacher would not notice the tears in his eyes.

'And yet,' said Anne, very softly, 'you wouldn't want it to stop hurting . . . you wouldn't want to forget your little mother even if you could.'

'No, indeed I wouldn't . . . that's just the way I feel. You're so good at understanding, teacher. Nobody else understands so well . . . not even Grandma, although she's so good to me. Father understood pretty well, but still I couldn't talk much to him about Mother, because it made him feel so bad. When he put his hand over his face I always knew it was time to stop. Poor Father, he must be dreadfully lonesome without me; but you see he has nobody but a housekeeper now and he thinks housekeepers are no good to bring up little boys, especially when he has to be away from home so much on business. Grandmothers are better, next to mothers. Some day, when I'm brought up, I'll go back to Father and we're never going to be parted again.'

Paul had talked so much to Anne about his mother and father that she felt as if she had known them. She thought his mother must have been very like what he was himself, in temperament and disposition; and she had an idea that Stephen Irving was a rather reserved man with a deep and tender nature which he kept hidden scrupulously from the world.

'Father's not very easy to get acquainted with,' Paul had said once. 'I never got really acquainted with him until after my little mother died. But he's splendid when you do get to know him. I love him the best in all the world, and Grandma Irving next, and then you, teacher. I'd love you next to Father, if it wasn't my *duty* to love Grandma Irving best, because she's doing so much for me. *You* know, teacher. I wish she would leave the lamp in my room till I go to sleep, though. She takes it right out as soon as she tucks me up because she says I mustn't be a coward. I'm *not* scared, but I'd *rather* have the light. My little mother used always to sit beside me and hold my hand till I went to sleep. I expect she spoiled me. Mothers do sometimes, you know.'

No, Anne did not know this, although she might imagine it. She thought sadly of *her* 'little mother', the mother who had thought her so 'perfectly beautiful' and who had died so long ago and was buried beside her boyish husband in that unvisited grave far away. Anne could not remember her mother and for this reason she almost envied Paul.

'My birthday is next week,' said Paul, as they walked up the long red hill, basking in the June sunshine, 'and Father wrote me that he is sending something that he thinks I'll like better than anything else he could send. I believe it has come already, for Grandma is keeping the bookcase drawer locked and that is something new. And when I asked her why, she just looked mysterious and said little boys mustn't be too curious. It's very exciting to have a birthday, isn't it? I'll be eleven. You'd never think it to look at me, would you? Grandma says I'm very small for my age and that it's all because I don't eat enough porridge. I do my best, but Grandma gives such *generous* platefuls ... there's nothing mean about Grandma, I can tell you. Ever since you and I had that talk about praying going home from Sunday School that day, teacher ... when you said we ought to pray about all our difficulties ... I've prayed every night that God would give me enough grace to enable me to eat every bit of my porridge in the mornings. But I've never been able to do it yet, and whether it's because I have too little grace or too much porridge I really can't decide. Grandma says Father was brought up on porridge, and it certainly did work well in his case, for you ought to see the shoulders he has. But sometimes,' concluded Paul with a sigh and a meditative air, 'I really think porridge will be the death of me.'

Anne permitted herself a smile, since Paul was not looking at her. All Avonlea knew that old Mrs Irving was bringing her grandson up in accordance with the good, old-fashioned methods of diet and morals.

'Let us hope not, dear,' she said cheerfully. 'How are your rock-people coming on? Does the oldest Twin still continue to behave himself?'

'He *has* to,' said Paul emphatically. 'He knows I won't associate with him if he doesn't. He is really full of wickedness, *I* think.'

'And has Nora found out about the Golden Lady yet?'

'No; but I think she suspects. I'm almost sure she watched me the last time I went to the cave. *I* don't mind if she finds out ... it is only for *her* sake I don't want her to ... so that her feelings won't be hurt. But if she is *determined* to have her feelings hurt it can't be helped.'

'If I were to go to the shore some night with you do you think I could see your rock-people too?'

Paul shook his head gravely.

'No, I don't think you could see *my* rock-people. I'm the only person who can see them. But you could see rock-people of your own. You're one of the kind that can. We're both that kind. *You* know, teacher,' he added, squeezing her hand chummily. 'Isn't it splendid to be that kind, teacher?'

'Splendid,' Anne agreed, grey shining eyes looking down into blue shining ones. Anne and Paul both knew

> How fair the realm
> Imagination opens to the view,

and both knew the way to that happy land. There the rose of joy bloomed immortal by dale and stream; clouds never darkened the sunny sky; sweet bells never jangled out of tune; and kindred spirits abounded. The knowledge of that land's geography ... 'east o' the sun, west o' the moon' ... is priceless lore, not to be bought in any market place. It must be the gift of the good fairies at birth and the years can never deface it or take it away.

It is better to possess it, living in a garret, than to be the inhabitant of palaces without it.

The Avonlea graveyard was as yet the grass-grown solitude it had always been. To be sure, the Improvers had an eye on it, and Priscilla Grant had read a paper on cemeteries before the last meeting of the Society. At some future time the Improvers meant to have the lichened, wayward old board fence replaced by a neat wire railing, the grass mown and the leaning monuments straightened up.

Anne put on Matthew's grave the flowers she had brought for it, and then went over to the little poplar-shaded corner where Hester Gray slept. Ever since the day of the spring picnic Anne had put flowers on Hester's grave when she visited Matthew's. The evening before she had made a pilgrimage back to the little deserted garden in the woods and brought therefrom some of Hester's own white roses.

'I thought you would like them better than any others, dear,' she said softly.

Anne was still sitting there when a shadow fell over the grass and she looked up to see Mrs Allan. They walked home together.

Mrs Allan's face was not the face of the girl-bride whom the minister had brought to Avonlea five years before. It had lost some of its bloom and youthful curves, and there were fine, patient lines about eyes and mouth. A tiny grave in that very cemetery accounted for some of them; and some new ones had come during the recent illness, now happily over, of her little son. But Mrs Allan's dimples were as sweet and sudden as ever, her eyes as clear and bright and true; and what her face lacked of girlish beauty was now more than atoned for in added tenderness and strength.

'I suppose you are looking forward to your vacation, Anne?' she said, as they left the graveyard.

Anne nodded.

'Yes, ... I could roll the word as a sweet morsel under my tongue. I think the summer is going to be lovely. For one thing, Mrs Morgan is coming to the Island in July and Priscilla is going to bring her up. I feel one of my old "thrills" at the mere thought.'

'I hope you'll have a good time, Anne. You've worked very hard this past year and you have succeeded.'

'Oh, I don't know. I've come so far short in so many things. I haven't done what I meant to do when I began to teach last fall . . . I haven't lived up to my ideals.'

'None of us ever do,' said Mrs Allan with a sigh. 'But then, Anne, you know what Lowell says, "Not failure but low aim is crime." We must have ideals and try to live up to them, even if we never quite succeed. Life would be a sorry business without them. With them it's grand and great. Hold fast to your ideals, Anne.'

'I shall try. But I have let go most of my theories,' said Anne, laughing a little. 'I had the most beautiful set of theories you ever knew when I started out as a schoolma'am, but every one of them has failed me at some pinch or another.'

'Even the theory on corporal punishment,' teased Mrs Allan. But Anne flushed.

'I shall never forgive myself for whipping Anthony.'

'Nonsense, dear, he deserved it. And it agreed with him. You have had no trouble with him since and he has come to think there's nobody like you. Your kindness won his love after the idea that a "girl was no good" was rooted out of his stubborn mind.'

'He may have deserved it, but that is not the point. If I had calmly and deliberately decided to whip him because I thought it a just punishment for him I would not feel over it as I do. But the truth is, Mrs Allan, that I just flew into a temper and whipped him because of that. I wasn't thinking whether it was just or unjust . . . even if he hadn't deserved it I'd have done it just the same. That is what humiliates me.'

'Well, we all make mistakes, dear, so just put it behind you. We should regret our mistakes and learn from them, but never carry them forward into the future with us. There goes Gilbert Blythe on his wheel . . . home from his vacation too, I suppose. How are you and he getting on with your studies?'

'Pretty well. We plan to finish the Virgil tonight . . . there are only twenty lines to do. Then we are not going to study any more until September.'

'Do you think you will ever get to college?'

'Oh, I don't know.' Anne looked dreamily afar to the opal-tinted horizon. 'Marilla's eyes will never be much better than they are now, although we are so thankful to think that they will not get worse. And then there are the twins . . . somehow I don't believe their uncle will ever really send for them. Perhaps college may be around the bend in the road, but I haven't got to the bend yet and I don't think much about it lest I might grow discontented.'

'Well, I should like to see you go to college, Anne; but if you never do, don't be discontented about it. We make our own lives wherever we are, after all . . . college can only help us to do it more easily. They are broad or narrow according to what we put into them, not what we get out. Life is rich and full here . . . everywhere . . . if we can only learn how to open our whole hearts to its richness and fullness.'

'I think I understand what you mean,' said Anne thoughtfully, 'and I know I have so much to feel thankful for . . . oh, so much . . . my work, and Paul Irving, and the dear twins, and all my friends. Do you know, Mrs Allan, I'm so thankful for friendship. It beautifies life so much.'

'True friendship is a very helpful thing indeed,' said Mrs Allan, 'and we should have a very high ideal of it, and never sully it by any failure in truth and sincerity. I fear the name of friendship is often degraded to a kind of intimacy that has nothing of real friendship in it.'

'Yes . . . like Gertie Pye's and Julia Bell's. They are very intimate and go everywhere together; but Gertie is always saying nasty things of Julia behind her back and everybody thinks she is jealous of her because she is always so pleased when anybody criticizes Julia. I think it is desecration to call *that* friendship. If we have friends we should look only for the best in them and give them the best that is in us, don't you think? Then friendship would be the most beautiful thing in the world.'

'Friendship *is* very beautiful,' smiled Mrs Allan, 'but some day . . .'

Then she paused abruptly. In the delicate, white-browned

face beside her, with its candid eyes and mobile features, there was still far more of the child than of the woman. Anne's heart so far harboured only dreams of friendship and ambition, and Mrs Allan did not wish to brush the bloom from her sweet unconsciousness. So she left her sentence for the future years to finish.

CHAPTER 16

The Substance of Things Hoped For

'ANNE,' said Davy appealingly, scrambling up on the shiny, leather-covered sofa in the Green Gables kitchen, where Anne sat, reading a letter, 'Anne, I'm *awful* hungry. You've no idea.'

'I'll get you a piece of bread and butter in a minute,' said Anne absently. Her letter evidently contained some exciting news, for her cheeks were as pink as the roses on the big bush outside, and her eyes were as starry as only Anne's eyes could be.

'But I ain't bread-and-butter hungry,' said Davy in a disgusted tone. 'I'm plum-cake hungry.'

'Oh,' laughed Anne, laying down her letter and putting her arm about Davy to give him a squeeze, 'that's a kind of hunger that can be endured very comfortably, Davy-boy. You know it's one of Marilla's rules that you can't have anything but bread and butter between meals.'

'Well, gimme a piece then . . . please.'

Davy had been at last taught to say 'please', but he generally tacked it on as an afterthought. He looked with approval at the generous slice Anne presently brought to him. 'You always put such a nice lot of butter on it, Anne. Marilla spreads it pretty thin. It slips down a lot easier when there's plenty of butter.'

The slice 'slipped down' with tolerable ease, judging from its rapid disappearance. Davy slid head first off the sofa, turned a double somersault on the rug, and then sat up and announced decidedly,

'Anne, I've made up my mind about heaven. I don't want to go there.'

'Why not?' asked Anne gravely.

' 'Cause heaven is in Simon Fletcher's garret, and I don't like Simon Fletcher.'

'Heaven in ... Simon Fletcher's garret!' gasped Anne, too amazed even to laugh. 'Davy Keith, whatever put such an extraordinary idea into your head?'

'Milty Boulter says that's where it is. It was last Sunday in Sunday School. The lesson was about Elijah and Elisha, and I up and asked Miss Rogerson where heaven was. Miss Rogerson looked awful offended. She was cross anyhow, because when she'd asked us what Elijah left Elisha when he went to heaven Milty Boulter said, "His old clo'es," and us fellows all laughed before we thought. I wish you could think first and do things afterwards, 'cause then you wouldn't do them. But Milty didn't mean to be disrespeckful. He just couldn't think of the name of the thing. Miss Rogerson said heaven was where God was and I wasn't to ask questions like that. Milty nudged me and said in a whisper, "Heaven's in Uncle Simon's garret and I'll esplain about it on the road home." So when we was coming home he esplained. Milty's a great hand at esplaining things. Even if he don't know anything about a thing he'll make up a lot of stuff and so you get it esplained all the same. His mother is Mrs Simon's sister and he went with her to the funeral when his cousin, Jane Ellen, died. The minister said she'd gone to heaven, though Milty says she was lying right before them in the coffin. But he s'posed they carried the coffin up to the garret afterwards. Well, when Milty and his mother went upstairs after it was all over to get her bonnet he asked her where heaven was that Jane Ellen had gone to, and she pointed right to the ceiling and said, "Up there." Milty knew there wasn't anything but the garret over the ceiling, so that's how *he* found out. And he's been awful scared to go to his Uncle Simon's ever since.'

Anne took Davy on her knees and did her best to straighten out this theological tangle also. She was much better fitted for the task than Marilla, for she remembered her own childhood and had an instinctive understanding of the curious ideas that seven-year-olds sometimes get about matters that are, of course, very plain and simple to grown-up people. She had just succeeded in convincing Davy that heaven was *not* in Simon Fletcher's garret when Marilla came in from the garden, where she and Dora had been picking peas. Dora was an industrious little soul and never happier than when 'helping' in various small tasks suited to her chubby fingers. She fed chickens, picked up chips, wiped dishes, and ran errands, galore. She was neat, faithful and observant; she never had to be told how to do a thing twice and never forgot any of her little duties. Davy, on the other hand, was rather heedless and forgetful; but he had the born knack of winning love, and even yet Anne and Marilla liked him the better.

While Dora proudly shelled the peas and Davy made boats of the pods, with masts of matches and sails of paper, Anne told Marilla about the wonderful contents of her letter.

'Oh, Marilla, what do you think? I've had a letter from Priscilla and she says that Mrs Morgan is on the island, and that if it is fine Thursday they are going to drive up to Avonlea and will reach here about twelve. They will spend the afternoon with us and go to the hotel at White Sands in the evening, because some of Mrs Morgan's American friends are staying there. Oh, Marilla, isn't it wonderful? I can hardly believe I'm not dreaming.'

'I daresay Mrs Morgan is a lot like other people,' said Marilla dryly, although she did feel a trifle excited herself. Mrs Morgan was a famous woman and a visit from her was no commonplace occurrence. 'They'll be here to dinner, then?'

'Yes; and oh, Marilla, may I cook every bit of the dinner myself? I want to feel that I can do something for the author of *The Rosebud Garden*, if it is only to cook a dinner for her. You won't mind, will you?'

'Goodness, I'm not so fond of stewing over a hot fire in July that it would vex me very much to have someone else do it. You're quite welcome to the job.'

'Oh, thank you,' said Anne, as if Marilla had just conferred a tremendous favour. 'I'll make out the menu this very night.'

'You'd better not try to put on too much style,' warned

Marilla, a little alarmed by the high-flown sound of 'menu'. 'You'll likely come to grief if you do.'

'Oh, I'm not going to put on any "style", if you mean trying to do or have things we don't usually have on festal occasions,' assured Anne. 'That would be affectation, and, although I know I haven't as much sense and steadiness as a girl of seventeen and a school teacher ought to have, I'm not so silly as *that*. But I want to have everything as nice and dainty as possible. Davy-boy, don't leave those peapods on the back stairs ... someone might slip on them. I'll have a light soup to begin with ... you know I can make lovely cream-of-onion soup ... and then a couple of roast fowls. I'll have the two white roosters. I have a real affection for those roosters and they've been pets ever since the grey hen hatched out just the two of them ... little balls of yellow down. But I know they would have to be sacrificed sometime, and surely there couldn't be a worthier occasion than this. But oh, Marilla, *I* cannot kill them ... not even for Mrs Morgan's sake. I'll have to ask John Henry Carter to come over and do it for me.'

'I'll do it,' volunteered Davy, 'if Marilla'll hold them by the legs, 'cause I guess it'd take both my hands to manage the axe. It's awful jolly fun to see them hopping about after their heads are cut off.'

'Then I'll have peas and beans and creamed potatoes and a lettuce salad, for vegetables,' resumed Anne, 'and for dessert, lemon pie with whipped cream, and coffee and cheese and lady fingers. I'll make the pies and lady fingers tomorrow and do up my white muslin dress. And I must tell Diana tonight, for she'll want to do up hers. Mrs Morgan's heroines are nearly always dressed in white muslin, and Diana and I have always resolved that that was what we would wear if we ever met her. It will be such a delicate compliment, don't you think? Davy, dear, you mustn't poke peapods into the cracks of the floor. I must ask Mr and Mrs Allan and Miss Stacy to dinner, too, for they're all very anxious to meet Mrs Morgan. It's so fortunate she's coming while Miss Stacy is here. Davy dear, don't sail the peapods in the water-bucket ... go out to the trough. Oh, I do hope it will be fine Thursday, and I think it will, for Uncle Abe said last night when he called at Mr Harrison's that it was going to rain most of this week.'

'That's a good sign,' agreed Marilla.

Anne ran across to Orchard Slope that evening to tell the news to Diana, who was also very much excited over it, and they discussed the matter in the hammock swung under the big willow in the Barry garden.

'Oh, Anne, mayn't I help you cook the dinner?' implored Diana. 'You know I can make splendid lettuce salad.'

'Indeed you may,' said Anne unselfishly. 'And I shall want you to help me decorate too. I mean to have the parlour simply a *bower* of blossoms ... and the dining-table is to be adorned with wild roses. Oh, I do hope everything will go smoothly. Mrs Morgan's heroines *never* get into scrapes or are taken at a disadvantage, and they are always so self-possessed and such good housekeepers. They seem to be *born* good housekeepers. You remember that Gertrude in *Edgewood Days* kept house for her father when she was only eight years old. When I was eight years old I hardly knew how to do a thing except bring up children. Mrs Morgan must be an authority on girls when she has written so much about them, and I do want her to have a good opinion of us. I've imagined it all out a dozen different ways ... what she'll look like, and what she'll say, and what I'll say. And I'm so anxious about my nose. There are seven freckles on it, as you can see. They came at the A.V.I.S. picnic, when I went around in the sun without my hat. I suppose it's ungrateful of me to worry over them, when I should be thankful they're not spread all over my face as they once were; but I do wish they hadn't come ... all Mrs Morgan's heroines have such perfect complexions. I can't recall a freckled one among them.'

'Yours are not very noticeable,' comforted Diana. 'Try a little lemon juice on them tonight.'

The next day Anne made her pies and lady fingers, did up her muslin dress, and swept and dusted every room in the house ... a quite unnecessary proceeding, for Green Gables was, as usual, in the apple-pie order dear to Marilla's heart. But Anne felt that a fleck of dust would be a desecration in a house that was to be honoured by a visit from Charlotte E. Morgan. She even cleaned out the 'catch-all' closet under the stairs, although there was not the remotest possibility of Mrs Morgan's seeing its interior.

'But I want to *feel* that it is in perfect order, even if she isn't to see it,' Anne told Marilla. 'You know, in her book, *Golden Keys*, she makes her two heroines Alice and Louisa take for their motto that verse of Longfellow's,

> "In the elder days of Art,
>   Builders wrought with greatest care
> Each minute and unseen part;
>   For the Gods see everywhere."

and so they always kept their cellar stairs scrubbed and never forgot to sweep under the beds. I should have a guilty conscience if I thought this closet was in disorder when Mrs Morgan was in the house. Ever since we read *Golden Keys*, last April, Diana and I have taken that verse for our motto too.'

That night John Henry Carter and Davy between them contrived to execute the two white roosters, and Anne dressed them, the usually distasteful task quite glorified in her eyes by the destination of the plump birds.

'I don't like picking fowls,' she told Marilla, 'but isn't it fortunate we don't have to put our souls into what our hands may be doing? I've been picking chickens with my hands but in imagination I've been roaming the Milky Way.'

'I thought you'd scattered more feathers over the floor than usual,' remarked Marilla.

Then Anne put Davy to bed and made him promise that he would behave perfectly the next day.

'If I'm as good as good can be all day tomorrow will you let me be just as bad as I like all the next day?' asked Davy.

'I couldn't do that,' said Anne discreetly, 'but I'll take you and Dora for a row in the flat right to the bottom of the pond, and we'll go ashore on the sandhills and have a picnic.'

'It's a bargain,' said Davy. 'I'll be good, you bet. I meant to go over to Mr Harrison's and fire peas from my new pop-gun at

Ginger but another day'll do as well. I espect it will be just like
Sunday, but a picnic at the shore'll make up for *that*.'

CHAPTER 17

A Chapter of Accidents

ANNE woke three times in the night and made pilgrimages to
her window to make sure that Uncle Abe's prediction was not
coming true. Finally the morning dawned pearly and lustrous in
a sky full of silver sheen and radiance, and the wonderful day
had arrived.

Diana appeared soon after breakfast, with a basket of flowers
over one arm and *her* muslin dress over the other ... for it
would not do to don it until all the dinner preparations were
completed. Meanwhile she wore her afternoon pink print and a
lawn apron fearfully and wonderfully ruffled and frilled; and
very neat and pretty and rosy she was.

'You look simply sweet,' said Anne admiringly.

Diana sighed.

'But I've had to let out every one of my dresses *again*. I weigh
four pounds more than I did in July. Anne, *where* will this end?
Mrs Morgan's heroines are all tall and slender.'

'Well, let's forget our troubles and think of our mercies,' said
Anne gaily. 'Mrs Allan says that whenever we think of anything that is a trial to us we should also think of something nice
that we can set over against it. If you are slightly too plump
you've got the dearest dimples; and if I have a freckled nose the
shape of it is all right. Do you think the lemon juice did any
good?'

'Yes, I really think it did,' said Diana critically; and, much
elated, Anne led the way to the garden, which was full of airy
shadows and wavering golden lights.

'We'll decorate the parlour first. We have plenty of time, for
Priscilla said they'd be here about twelve or half past at the
latest, so we'll have dinner at one.'

There may have been two happier and more excited girls somewhere in Canada or the United States at that moment, but I doubt it. Every snip of the scissors, as rose and peony and bluebell fell, seemed to chirp, 'Mrs Morgan is coming today.' Anne wondered how Mr Harrison *could* go on placidly mowing hay in the field across the lane, just as if nothing were going to happen.

The parlour at Green Gables was a rather severe and gloomy apartment, with rigid horsehair furniture, stiff lace curtains, and white antimacassars that were always laid at a perfectly correct angle, except at such times as they clung to unfortunate people's buttons. Even Anne had never been able to infuse much grace into it, for Marilla would not permit any alterations. But it is wonderful what flowers can accomplish if you give them a fair chance; when Anne and Diana finished with the room you would not have recognized it.

A great blue bowlful of snowballs overflowed on the polished table. The shining black mantelpiece was heaped with roses and ferns. Every shelf of the whatnot held a sheaf of bluebells; the dark corners on either side of the grate were lighted up with jars full of glowing crimson peonies, and the grate itself was aflame with yellow poppies. All this splendour and colour, mingled with the sunshine falling through the honeysuckle vines at the windows in a leafy riot of dancing shadows over walls and floor, made of the usually dismal little room the veritable 'bower' of Anne's imagination, and even extorted a tribute of admiration from Marilla, who came in to criticize and remained to praise.

'Now, we must set the table,' said Anne, in the tone of a priestess about to perform some sacred rite in honour of a divinity. 'We'll have a big vaseful of wild roses in the centre and one single rose in front of everybody's plate – and a special bouquet of rosebuds only by Mrs Morgan's – an allusion to *The Rosebud Garden*, you know.'

The table was set in the sitting-room with Marilla's finest linen and the best china, glass, and silver. You may be perfectly certain that every article placed on it was polished or scoured to the highest possible perfection of gloss and glitter.

Then the girls tripped out to the kitchen, which was filled with appetizing odours emanating from the oven, where the chickens were already sizzling splendidly. Anne prepared the potatoes and Diana got the peas and beans ready. Then, while Diana shut herself into the pantry to compound the lettuce salad, Anne, whose cheeks were already beginning to glow crimson, as much with excitement as from the heat of the fire, prepared the bread sauce for the chickens, minced her onions for the soup, and finally whipped the cream for her lemon pies.

And what about Davy all this time? Was he redeeming his promise to be good? He was, indeed. To be sure, he insisted on remaining in the kitchen, for his curiosity wanted to see all that went on. But as he sat quietly in a corner, busily engaged in untying the knots in a piece of herring net he had brought home from his last trip to the shore, nobody objected to this.

At half past eleven the lettuce salad was made, the golden circles of the pies were heaped with whipped cream, and everything was sizzling and bubbling that ought to sizzle and bubble.

'We'd better go and dress now,' said Anne, 'for they may be here by twelve. We must have dinner at sharp one, for the soup must be served as soon as it's done.'

Serious indeed were the toilet rites presently performed in the east gable. Anne peered anxiously at her nose and rejoiced to see that its freckles were not at all prominent, thanks either to the lemon juice or to the unusual flush on her cheeks. When they were ready they looked quite as sweet and trim and girlish as ever did any of 'Mrs Morgan's heroines'.

'I do hope I'll be able to say something once in a while, and not sit like a mute,' said Diana anxiously. 'All Mrs Morgan's heroines converse so beautifully. But I'm afraid I'll be tongue-tied and stupid. And I'll be sure to say "I seen". I haven't often said it since Miss Stacy taught here; but in moments of excitement it's sure to pop out. Anne, if I were to say "I seen" before Mrs Morgan I'd die of mortification. And it would be almost as bad to have nothing to say.'

'I'm nervous about a good many things,' said Anne, 'but I don't think there is much fear that I won't be able to *talk*.'

And, to do her justice, there wasn't.

Anne shrouded her muslin glories in a big apron and went down to concoct her soup. Marilla had dressed herself and the twins, and looked more excited than she had ever been known to look before. At half past twelve the Allans and Miss Stacy came. Everything was going well but Anne was beginning to feel nervous. It was surely time for Priscilla and Mrs Morgan to arrive. She made frequent trips to the gate and looked as anxiously down the lane as ever her namesake in the Bluebeard story peered from the tower casement.

'Suppose they don't come at all?' she said piteously.

'Don't suppose it. It would be too mean,' said Diana, who, however, was beginning to have uncomfortable misgivings on the subject.

'Anne,' said Marilla, coming out from the parlour, 'Miss Stacy wants to see Miss Barry's willow-ware platter.'

Anne hastened to the sitting-room closet to get the platter. She had, in accordance with her promise to Mrs Lynde, written to Miss Barry of Charlottetown, asking for the loan of it. Miss Barry was an old friend of Anne's, and she promptly sent the platter out, with a letter exhorting Anne to be very careful of it, for she had paid twenty dollars for it. The platter had served its purpose at the Aid bazaar and had then been returned to the Green Gables closet, for Anne would not trust anybody but herself to take it back to town.

She carried the platter carefully to the front door where her guests were enjoying the cool breeze that blew up from the brook. It was examined and admired; then, just as Anne had taken it back into her own hands, a terrific crash and clatter sounded from the kitchen pantry. Marilla, Diana, and Anne fled out, the latter pausing only long enough to set the precious platter hastily down on the second step of the stairs.

When they reached the pantry a truly harrowing spectacle met their eyes ... a guilty-looking small boy scrambling down from the table, with his clean print blouse liberally plastered with yellow filling, and on the table the shattered remnants of what had been two brave, becreamed lemon pies.

Davy had finished ravelling out his herring net and had

wound the twine into a ball. Then he had gone into the pantry to put it on the shelf above the table, where he already kept a score or so of similar balls, which, so far as could be discovered, served no useful purpose save to yield the joy of possession. Davy had to climb on the table and reach over to the shelf at a dangerous angle ... something he had been forbidden by Marilla to do, as he had come to grief once before in the experiment. The result in this instance was disastrous. Davy slipped and came sprawling squarely down on the lemon pies. His clean blouse was ruined for that time and the pies for all time. It is, however, an ill wind that blows nobody good, and the pig was eventually the gainer by Davy's mischance.

'Davy Keith,' said Marilla, shaking him by the shoulder, 'didn't I forbid you to climb up on that table again? Didn't I?'

'I forgot,' whimpered Davy. 'You've told me not to do such an awful lot of things that I can't remember them all.'

'Well, you march upstairs and stay there till after dinner. Perhaps you'll get them sorted out in your memory by that time. No, Anne, never you mind interceding for him. I'm not punishing him because he spoiled your pies ... that was an accident. I'm punishing him for his disobedience. Go, Davy, I say.'

'Ain't I to have any dinner?' wailed Davy.

'You can come down after dinner is over and have yours in the kitchen.'

'Oh, all right,' said Davy, somewhat comforted. 'I know Anne'll save some nice bones for me, won't you, Anne? 'Cause you know I didn't mean to fall on the pies. Say, Anne, since they *are* spoiled can't I take some of the pieces upstairs with me?'

'No, no lemon pie for you, Master Davy,' said Marilla, pushing him towards the hall.

'What shall we do for dessert?' asked Anne, looking regretfully at the wrack and ruin.

'Get out a crock of strawberry preserves,' said Marilla consolingly. 'There's plenty of whipped cream left in the bowl for it.'

One o'clock came ... but no Priscilla or Mrs Morgan. Anne

was in an agony. Everything was done to a turn and the soup was just what soup should be, but couldn't be depended on to remain so for any length of time.

'I don't believe they're coming after all,' said Marilla crossly.

Anne and Diana sought comfort in each other's eyes.

At half past one Marilla again emerged from the parlour.

'Girls, we *must* have dinner. Everybody is hungry and it's no use waiting any longer. Priscilla and Mrs Morgan are not coming, that's plain, and nothing is being improved by waiting.'

Anne and Diana set about lifting the dinner, with all the zest gone out of the performance.

'I don't believe I'll be able to eat a mouthful,' said Diana dolefully.

'Nor I. But I hope everything will be nice for Miss Stacy's and Mr and Mrs Allan's sakes,' said Anne listlessly.

When Diana dished the peas she tasted them and a very peculiar expression crossed her face.

'Anne, did *you* put sugar in these peas?'

'Yes,' said Anne, mashing the potatoes with the air of one expected to do her duty. 'I put a spoonful of sugar in. We always do. Don't you like it?'

'But *I* put a spoonful in too, when I set them on the stove,' said Diana.

Anne dropped her masher and tasted the peas also. Then she made a grimace.

'How awful! I never dreamed you had put sugar in, because I knew your mother never does. I happened to think of it, for a wonder ... I'm always forgetting it ... so I popped a spoonful in.'

'It's a case of too many cooks, I guess,' said Marilla, who had listened to this dialogue with a rather guilty expression. 'I didn't think you'd remember about the sugar, Anne, for I'm perfectly certain you never did before ... so *I* put in a spoonful.'

The guests in the parlour heard peal after peal of laughter from the kitchen, but they never knew what the fun was about. There were no green peas on the dinner table that day, however.

'Well,' said Anne, sobering down again with a sigh of recollection, 'we have the salad anyhow and I don't think anything has happened to the beans. Let's carry the things in and get it over.'

It cannot be said that the dinner was a notable success socially. The Allans and Miss Stacy exerted themselves to save the situation and Marilla's customary placidity was not noticeably ruffled. But Anne and Diana, between their disappointment and the reaction from their excitement of the forenoon, could neither talk nor eat. Anne tried heroically to bear her part in the conversation for the sake of her guests; but all the sparkle had been quenched in her for the time being, and, in spite of her love for the Allans and Miss Stacy, she couldn't help thinking how nice it would be when everybody had gone home and she could bury her weariness and disappointment in the pillows in the east gable.

There is an old proverb that really seems at times to be inspired . . . 'it never rains but it pours'. The measure of that day's tribulations was not yet full. Just as Mr Allan had finished returning thanks there arose a strange, ominous sound on the stairs, as of some hard, heavy object bounding from step to step, finishing up with a grand smash at the bottom. Everybody ran out into the hall. Anne gave a shriek of dismay.

At the bottom of the stairs lay a big pink conch shell amid the fragments of what had been Miss Barry's platter; and at the top of the stairs knelt a terrified Davy, gazing down with wide-open eyes at the havoc.

'Davy,' said Marilla ominously, 'did you throw that conch down *on purpose*?'

'No, I never did,' whimpered Davy. 'I was just kneeling here, quiet as quiet, to watch you folks through the banisters, and my foot struck that old thing and pushed it off . . . and I'm awful hungry . . . and I do wish you'd lick a fellow and have done with it, instead of always sending him upstairs to miss all the fun.'

'Don't blame Davy,' said Anne, gathering up the fragments with trembling fingers. 'It was my fault. I set that platter there and forgot all about it. I am properly punished for my carelessness; but oh, what will Miss Barry say?'

'Well, you know she only bought it, so it isn't the same as if it was an heirloom,' said Diana, trying to console.

The guests went away soon after, feeling that it was the most tactful thing to do, and Anne and Diana washed the dishes, talking less than they had ever been known to do before. Then Diana went home with a headache and Anne went with another to the east gable, where she stayed until Marilla came home from the post office at sunset, with a letter from Priscilla, written the day before. Mrs Morgan had sprained her ankle so severely that she could not leave her room.

'And oh, Anne dear,' wrote Priscilla, 'I'm so sorry, but I'm afraid we won't get up to Green Gables at all now, for by the time Aunty's ankle is well she will have to go back to Toronto. She has to be there by a certain date.'

'Well,' sighed Anne, laying the letter down on the red sandstone step of the back porch, where she was sitting, while the twilight rained down out of a dappled sky, 'I always thought it was too good to be true that Mrs Morgan should really come. But there ... that speech sounds as pessimistic as Miss Eliza Andrews and I'm ashamed of making it. After all, it was *not* too good to be true ... things just as good and far better are coming true for me all the time. And I suppose the events of today have a funny side too. Perhaps when Diana and I are old and grey we shall be able to laugh over them. But I feel that I can't expect to do it before then, for it has truly been a bitter disappointment.'

'You'll probably have a good many more and worse disappointments than that before you get through life,' said Marilla, who honestly thought she was making a comforting speech. 'It seems to me, Anne, that you are never going to outgrow your fashion of setting your heart so on things and then crashing down into despair because you don't get them.'

'I know I'm too much inclined that way,' agreed Anne ruefully. 'When I think something nice is going to happen I seem to fly right up on the wings of anticipation; and then the first thing I realize, I drop down to earth with a thud. But really, Marilla, the flying part *is* glorious as long as it lasts ... it's like soaring through a sunset. I think it almost pays for the thud.'

'Well, maybe it does,' admitted Marilla. 'I'd rather walk

calmly along and do without both flying and thud. But every-body has her own way of living. I used to think there was only one right way ... but since I've had you and the twins to bring up I don't feel so sure of it. What are you going to do about Miss Barry's platter?'

'Pay her back the twenty dollars she paid for it, I suppose. I'm so thankful it wasn't a cherished heirloom because then no money could replace it.'

'Maybe you could find one like it somewhere and buy it for her.'

'I'm afraid not. Platters as old as that are very scarce. Mrs Lynde couldn't find one anywhere for the supper. I only wish I could, for of course Miss Barry would just as soon have one platter as another, if both were equally old and genuine. Marilla, look at that big star over Mr Harrison's maple grove, with all that holy hush of silvery sky about it. It gives me a feel-ing that is like a prayer. After all, when one can see stars and skies like that, little disappointments and accidents can't matter so much, can they?'

'Where's Davy?' said Marilla, with an indifferent glance at the star.

'In bed. I've promised to take him and Dora to the shore for a picnic tomorrow. Of course, the original agreement was that he must be good. But he *tried* to be good ... and I hadn't the heart to disappoint him.'

'You'll drown yourself or the twins, rowing about the pond in that flat,' grumbled Marilla. 'I've lived here for sixty years and I've never been on the pond yet.'

'Well, it's never too late to mend,' said Anne roguishly. 'Sup-pose you come with us tomorrow. We'll shut Green Gables up and spend the whole day at the shore, daffing the world aside.'

'No, thank you,' said Marilla, with indignant emphasis. 'I'd be a nice sight, wouldn't I, rowing down the pond in a flat? I think I hear Rachel pronouncing on it. There's Mr Harrison driving away somewhere. Do you suppose there is any truth in the gossip that Mr Harrison is going to see Isabella Andrews?'

'No, I'm sure there isn't. He just called there one evening on business with Mr Harmon Andrews, and Mrs Lynde saw him and said she knew he was courting because he had a white collar on. I don't believe Mr Harrison will ever marry. He seems to have a prejudice against marriage.'

'Well, you can never tell about those old bachelors. And if he had a white collar on I'd agree with Rachel that it looks suspicious, for I'm sure he never was seen with one before.'

'I think he only put it on because he wanted to conclude a business deal with Harmon Andrews,' said Anne. 'I've heard him say that's the only time a man needs to be particular about his appearance, because if he looks prosperous the party of the second part won't be so likely to try to cheat him. I really feel sorry for Mr Harrison; I don't believe he feels satisfied with his life. It must be very lonely to have no one to care about except a parrot, don't you think? But I notice Mr Harrison doesn't like to be pitied. Nobody does, I imagine.'

'There's Gilbert coming up the lane,' said Marilla. 'If he wants you to go for a row on the pond mind you put on your coat and rubbers. There's a heavy dew tonight.'

CHAPTER 18

An Adventure on the Tory Road

'ANNE,' said Davy, sitting up in bed and propping his chin on his hands, 'Anne, where is sleep? People go to sleep every night, and of course I know it's the place where I do the things I dream, but I want to know *where* it is and how I get there and back without knowing anything about it ... and in my nightie too. Where is it?'

Anne was kneeling at the west gable window watching the sunset sky that was like a great flower with petals of crocus and a heart of fiery yellow. She turned her head at Davy's question and answered dreamily:

> 'Over the mountains of the moon,
> Down the valley of the shadow.'

Paul Irving would have known the meaning of this, or made

132

a meaning out of it for himself, if he didn't; but practical Davy, who, as Anne often despairingly remarked, hadn't a particle of imagination, was only puzzled and disgusted.

'Anne, I believe you're just talking nonsense.'

'Of course I was, dear boy. Don't you know that it is only very foolish folk who talk sense all the time?'

'Well, I think you might give a sensible answer when I ask a sensible question,' said Davy in an injured tone.

'Oh, you are too little to understand,' said Anne. But she felt rather ashamed of saying it; for had she not, in keen remembrance of many similar snubs administered in her own early years, solemnly vowed that she would never tell any child it was too little to understand? Yet here she was doing it ... so wide sometimes is the gulf between theory and practice.

'Well, I'm doing my best to grow,' said Davy, 'but it's a thing you can't hurry much. If Marilla wasn't so stingy with her jam I believe I'd grow a lot faster.'

'Marilla is not stingy, Davy,' said Anne severely. 'It is very ungrateful of you to say such a thing.'

'There's another word that means the same thing and sounds a lot better, but I don't just remember it,' said Davy, frowning intently. 'I heard Marilla say she was it, herself, the other day.'

'If you mean *economical*, it's a *very* different thing from being stingy. It is an excellent trait in a person if she is economical. If Marilla had been stingy she wouldn't have taken you and Dora when your mother died. Would you have liked to live with Mrs Wiggins?'

'You just bet I wouldn't!' Davy was emphatic on that point. 'Nor I don't want to go out to Uncle Richard neither. I'd far rather live here, even if Marilla is that long-tailed word when it comes to jam, 'cause *you're* here, Anne. Say, Anne, won't you tell me a story 'fore I go to sleep? I don't want a fairy story. They're all right for girls, I s'pose, but I want something exciting ... lots of killing and shooting in it, and a house on fire, and in'trusting things like that.'

Fortunately for Anne, Marilla called out at this moment from her room,

'Anne, Diana's signalling at a great rate. You'd better see what she wants.'

Anne ran to the east gable and saw flashes of light coming through the twilight from Diana's window in groups of five, which meant, according to their old childish code, 'Come over at once, for I have something important to reveal.' Anne threw her white shawl over her head and hastened through the Haunted Wood and across Mr Bell's pasture corner to Orchard Slope.

'I've good news for you, Anne,' said Diana. 'Mother and I have just got home from Carmody, and I saw Mary Sentner from Spencervale in Mr Blair's store. She says the old Copp girls on the Tory Road have a willow-ware platter and she thinks it's exactly like the one we had at the supper. She says they'll likely to sell it, for Martha Copp has never been known to keep anything she *could* sell; but if they won't there's a platter at Wesley Keyson's at Spencervale and she knows they'd sell it, but she isn't sure it's just the same kind as Aunt Josephine's.'

'I'll go right over to Spencervale after it tomorrow,' said Anne resolutely, 'and you must come with me. It will be such a weight off my mind, for I have to go to town the day after tomorrow and how can I face your Aunt Josephine without a willow-ware platter? It would be even worse than the time I had to confess about jumping on the spare room bed.'

Both girls laughed over the old memory ... concerning which, if any of my readers are ignorant and curious, I must refer them to Anne's earlier history.

The next afternoon the girls fared forth on their platter-hunting expedition. It was ten miles to Spencervale and the day was not especially pleasant for travelling. It was very warm and windless, and the dust on the road was such as might have been expected after six weeks of dry weather.

'Oh, I do wish it would rain soon,' sighed Anne. 'Everything is so parched up. The poor fields just seem pitiful to me and the trees seem to be stretching out their hands pleading for rain. As for my garden, it hurts me every time I go into it. I suppose I shouldn't complain about a garden when the farmers' crops are suffering so. Mr Harrison says his pastures are so scorched up that his poor cows can hardly get a bite to eat and he feels guilty of cruelty to animals every time he meets their eyes.'

After a wearisome drive the girls reached Spencervale and turned down the 'Tory' Road ... a green, solitary highway where the strips of grass between the wheel tracks bore evidence to lack of travel. Along most of its extent it was lined with thick-set young spruces crowding down to the roadway, with here and there a break where the back field of a Spencervale farm came out to the fence or an expanse of stumps was aflame with fireweed and goldenrod.

'Why is it called the Tory Road?' asked Anne.

'Mr Allan says it is on the principle of calling a place a grove because there are no trees in it,' said Diana, 'for nobody lives along the road except the Copp girls and old Martin Bovyet at the further end, who is a Liberal. The Tory government ran the road through when they were in power just to show they were doing something.'

Diana's father was a Liberal, for which reason she and Anne never discussed politics. Green Gables folk had always been Conservatives.

Finally the girls came to the old Copp homestead . . . a place of such exceeding external neatness that even Green Gables would have suffered by contrast. The house was a very old-fashioned one, situated on a slope, which fact had necessitated the building of a stone basement under one end. The house and outbuildings were all whitewashed to a condition of blinding perfection and not a weed was visible in the prim kitchen garden surrounded by its white paling.

'The shades are all down,' said Diana ruefully. 'I believe that nobody is home.'

This proved to be the case. The girls looked at each other in perplexity.

'I don't know what to do,' said Anne. 'If I were sure the platter was the right kind I would not mind waiting until they came home. But if it isn't it may be too late to go to Wesley Keyson's afterwards.'

Diana looked at a certain little square window over the basement.

'That is the pantry window, I feel sure,' she said, 'because this house is just like Uncle Charles' at Newbridge, and that is their pantry window. The shade isn't down, so if we climbed up on the roof of that little house we could look into the pantry and might be able to see the platter. Do you think it would be any harm?'

'No, I don't think so,' decided Anne, after due reflection, 'since our motive is not idle curiosity.'

This important point of ethics being settled, Anne prepared to mount the aforesaid 'little house', a construction of lathes, with a peaked roof, which had in times past served as a habitation for ducks. The Copp girls had given up keeping ducks . . . 'because they were such untidy birds' . . . and the house had not been in use for some years, save as an abode of correction for setting hens. Although scrupulously whitewashed it had become somewhat shaky, and Anne felt rather dubious as she scrambled up from the vantage point of a keg placed on a box.

'I'm afraid it won't bear my weight,' she said as she gingerly stepped on the roof.

'Lean on the window sill,' advised Diana, and Anne accordingly leaned. Much to her delight, she saw, as she peered through the pane, a willow-ware platter, exactly such as she was in quest of, on the shelf in front of the window. So much she saw before the catastrophe came. In her joy Anne forgot the precarious nature of her footing, incautiously ceased to lean on the window sill, gave an impulsive little hop of pleasure . . . and the next moment she had crashed through the roof up to her arm-pits, and there she hung, quite unable to extricate herself. Diana dashed into the duck-house and, seizing her unfortunate friend by the waist, tried to draw her down.

'Ow . . . don't,' shrieked poor Anne. 'There are some long splinters sticking into me. See if you can put something under my feet . . . then perhaps I can draw myself up.'

Diana hastily dragged in the previously mentioned keg and Anne found that it was just sufficiently high to furnish a secure resting place for her feet. But she could not release herself.

'Could I pull you out if I crawled up?' suggested Diana.

Anne shook her head hopelessly.

'No ... the splinters hurt too badly. If you can find an axe you might chop me out, though. Oh dear, I do really begin to believe that I was born under an ill-omened star.'

Diana searched faithfully but no axe was to be found.

'I'll have to go for help,' she said, returning to the prisoner.

'No, indeed, you won't,' said Anne vehemently. 'If you do the story of this will get out everywhere and I shall be ashamed to show my face. No, we must just wait until the Copp girls come home and bind them to secrecy. They'll know where the axe is and get me out. I'm not uncomfortable as long as I keep perfectly still ... not uncomfortable in *body* I mean. I wonder what the Copp girls value this house at. I shall have to pay for the damage I've done, but I wouldn't mind that if I were only sure they would understand my motive in peeping in at their pantry window. My sole comfort is that the platter is just the kind I want and if Miss Copp will only sell it to me I shall be resigned to what has happened.'

'What if the Copp girls don't come home until after night ... or till tomorrow?' suggested Diana.

'If they're not back by sunset you'll have to go for other assistance, I suppose,' said Anne reluctantly, 'but you mustn't go until you really have to. Oh dear, this is a dreadful predicament. I wouldn't mind my misfortunes so much if they were romantic, as Mrs Morgan's heroines' always are, but they are always just simply ridiculous. Fancy what the Copp girls will think when they drive into their yard and see a girl's head and shoulders sticking out of the roof of one of their outhouses. Listen ... is that a wagon? No, Diana, I believe it is thunder.'

Thunder it was undoubtedly, and Diana, having made a hasty pilgrimage around the house, returned to announce that a very black cloud was rising rapidly in the north-west.

'I believe we're going to have a heavy thunder-shower,' she exclaimed in dismay. 'Oh, Anne, what will we do?'

'We must prepare for it,' said Anne tranquilly. A thunderstorm seemed a trifle in comparison with what had already happened. 'You'd better drive the horse and buggy into that open shed. Fortunately my parasol is in the buggy. Here ... take my hat with you. Marilla told me I was a goose to put on my best hat to come to the Tory Road and she was right, as she always is.

Diana untied the pony and drove into the shed, just as the first heavy drops of rain fell. There she sat and watched the resulting downpour, which was so thick and heavy that she could hardly see Anne through it, holding the parasol bravely over her bare head. There was not a great deal of thunder, but for the best part of an hour the rain came merrily down. Occasionally Anne slanted back her parasol and waved an encouraging hand to her friend; but conversation at that distance and under the circumstances was quite out of the question. Finally the rain ceased, the sun came out, and Diana ventured across the puddles of the yard.

'Did you get very wet?' she asked anxiously.

'Oh, no,' returned Anne cheerfully. 'My head and shoulders are quite dry and my skirt is only a little damp where the rain beat through the lathes. Don't pity me, Diana, for I haven't minded it at all. I kept thinking how much good the rain will do and how glad my garden must be for it, and imagining what the flowers and buds would think when the drops began to fall. I imagined out a most interesting dialogue between the asters and the sweet-peas and the wild canaries in the lilac-bush and the guardian spirit of the garden. When I go home I mean to write it down. I wish I had a pencil and paper to do it now, because I daresay I'll forget the best parts before I reach home.'

Diana the faithful had a pencil and discovered a sheet of wrapping paper in the box of the buggy. Anne folded up her dripping parasol, put on her hat, spread the wrapping paper on a shingle Diana handed up, and wrote out her garden idyll under conditions that could hardly be considered as favourable to literature. Nevertheless, the result was quite pretty, and Diana was 'enraptured' when Anne read it to her.

'Oh, Anne, it's sweet ... just sweet. *Do* send it to the *Canadian Woman*.'

Anne shook her head.

'Oh, no, it wouldn't be suitable at all. There is no *plot* in it, you see. It's just a string of fancies. I like writing such things, but of course nothing of the sort would ever do for publication, for editors insist on plots, so Priscilla says. Oh, there's Miss Sarah Copp now. Please, Diana, go and explain.'

Miss Sarah Copp was a small person, garbed in shabby black, with a hat chosen less for vain adornment than for qualities that would wear well. She looked as amazed as might be expected on seeing the curious tableau in her yard, but when she heard Diana's explanation she was all sympathy. She hurriedly unlocked the back door, produced the axe, and with a few skilful blows set Anne free. The latter, somewhat tired and stiff, ducked down into the interior of her prison and thankfully emerged into liberty once more.

'Miss Copp,' she said earnestly, 'I assure you I looked into your pantry window *only* to discover if you had a willow-ware platter. I didn't see anything else – I didn't *look* for anything else.'

'Bless you, that's all right,' said Miss Sarah amiably. 'You needn't worry – there's no harm done. Thank goodness, we Copps keep our pantries presentable at all times and don't care who sees into them. As for that old duck-house, I'm glad it's smashed, for maybe now Martha will agree to having it taken down. She never would before for fear it might come in handy some time and I've had to whitewash it every spring. But you might as well argue with a post as with Martha. She went to town today . . . I drove her to the station. And you want to buy my platter. Well, what will you give for it?'

'Twenty dollars,' said Anne, who was never meant to match business wits with a Copp, or she would not have offered her price at the start.

'Well, I'll see,' said Miss Sarah cautiously. 'That platter is mine fortunately, or I'd never dare to sell it when Martha wasn't here. As it is, I daresay she'll raise a fuss. Martha's the boss of this establishment, I can tell you. I'm getting awful tired of living under another woman's thumb. But come in, come in. You must be real tired and hungry. I'll do the best I can for you in the way of tea but I warn you not to expect anything but bread and butter and some cowcumbers. Martha locked up all the cake and cheese and preserves afore she went. She always does, because she says I'm too extravagant with them if company comes.'

The girls were hungry enough to do justice to any fare, and they enjoyed Miss Sarah's excellent bread and butter and 'cowcumbers' thoroughly. When the meal was over Miss Sarah said,

'I don't know as I mind selling the platter. But it's worth twenty-five dollars. It's a very old platter.'

Diana gave Anne's foot a gentle kick under the table, meaning, 'Don't agree ... she'll let it go for twenty if you hold out.' But Anne was not minded to take any chances in regard to that precious platter. She promptly agreed to give twenty-five and Miss Sarah looked as if she felt sorry she hadn't asked for thirty.

'Well, I guess you may have it. I want all the money I can scare up just now. The fact is ...' Miss Sarah threw up her head importantly, with a proud flush on her thin cheeks ... 'I'm going to be married ... to Luther Wallace. He wanted me twenty years ago. I liked him real well but he was poor then and Father packed him off. I s'pose I shouldn't have let him go so meek but I was timid and frightened of Father. Besides, I didn't know men were so skurse.'

When the girls were safely away, Diana driving and Anne holding the coveted platter carefully on her lap, the green, rain-freshened solitudes of the Tory Road were enlivened by ripples of girlish laughter.

'I'll amuse your Aunt Josephine with the "strange eventful history" of this afternoon when I go to town tomorrow. We've had a rather trying time, but it's over now. I've got the platter, and that rain has laid the dust beautifully. So "all's well that ends well".'

'We're not home yet,' said Diana rather pessimistically, 'and there's no telling what may happen before we are. You're such a girl to have adventures, Anne.'

'Having adventures comes natural to some people,' said Anne serenely. 'You just have a gift for them or you haven't.'

CHAPTER 19

Just a Happy Day

'AFTER all,' Anne had said to Marilla once, 'I believe the nicest and sweetest days are not those on which anything very splendid or wonderful or exciting happens, but just those that bring simple little pleasures, following one another softly, like pearls slipping off a string.'

Life at Green Gables was full of just such days, for Anne's adventures and misadventures, like those of other people, did not all happen at once, but were sprinkled over the year, with long stretches of harmless, happy days between, filled with work and dreams and laughter and lessons. Such a day came late in August. In the forenoon Anne and Diana rowed the delighted twins down the pond to the sandshore to pick 'sweet grass' and paddle in the surf, over which the wind was harping an old lyric learned when the world was young.

In the afternoon Anne walked down to the old Irving place to see Paul. She found him stretched out on the grassy bank beside the thick fir grove that sheltered the house on the north, absorbed in a book of fairy tales. He sprang up radiantly at the sight of her.

'Oh, I'm so glad you've come, teacher,' he said eagerly, 'because Grandma's away. You'll stay and have tea with me, won't you? It's so lonesome to have tea all by oneself. *You* know, teacher. I've had serious thoughts of asking Young Mary Joe to sit down and eat her tea with me, but I expect Grandma wouldn't approve. She says the French have to be kept in their place. And, anyhow, it's difficult to talk with Young Mary Joe. She just laughs and says, "Well, yous do beat all de kids I ever knowed." That isn't my idea of conversation.'

'Of course I'll stay to tea,' said Anne gaily. 'I was dying to be asked. My mouth has been watering for some more of your Grandma's delicious shortbread ever since I had tea here before.'

Paul looked very sober.

'If it depended on me, teacher,' he said, standing before Anne with his hands in his pockets and his beautiful little face shadowed with sudden care, 'you should have shortbread with a right good will. But it depends on Mary Joe. I heard Grandma tell her before she left that she wasn't to give me any shortcake because it was too rich for little boys' stomachs. But maybe Mary Joe will cut some for you if I promise I won't eat any. Let us hope for the best.'

'Yes, let us,' agreed Anne, whom this cheerful philosophy suited exactly, 'and if Mary Joe proves hard-hearted and won't give me any shortbread it doesn't matter in the least, so you are not to worry over that.'

'You're sure you won't mind if she doesn't?' said Paul anxiously.

'Perfectly sure, dear heart.'

'Then I won't worry,' said Paul with a long breath of relief, 'especially as I really think Mary Joe will listen to reason. She's not a naturally unreasonable person, but she has learned by experience that it doesn't do to disobey Grandma's orders. Grandma is an excellent woman but people must do as she tells them. She was very much pleased with me this morning because I managed at last to eat all my plateful of porridge. It was a great effort but I succeeded. Grandma says she thinks she'll make a man of me yet. But, teacher, I want to ask you a very important question. You will answer it truthfully, won't you?'

'I'll try,' promised Anne.

'Do you think I'm wrong in my upper storey?' asked Paul, as if his very existence depended on her reply.

'Goodness, no, Paul,' exclaimed Anne in amazement. 'Certainly you're not. What put such an idea into your head?'

'Mary Joe ... but she didn't know I heard her. Mrs Peter Sloane's hired girl, Veronica, came to see Mary Joe last evening and I heard them talking in the kitchen as I was going through the hall. I heard Mary Joe say, "Dat Paul, he is de queeres' leetle boy. He talks dat queer. I tink dere's someting wrong in his upper storey." I couldn't sleep last night for ever so long, thinking of it, and wondering if Mary Joe was right. I couldn't bear to ask Grandma about it somehow, but I made up my mind I'd ask you. I'm so glad you think I'm all right in my upper storey.'

'Of course you are. Mary Joe is a silly, ignorant girl, and you are never to worry about anything she says,' said Anne indignantly, secretly resolving to give Mrs Irving a discreet hint as to the advisability of restraining Mary Joe's tongue.

'Well, that's a weight off my mind,' said Paul. 'I'm perfectly happy now, teacher, thanks to you. It wouldn't be nice to have something wrong in your upper storey, would it, teacher? I suppose the reason Mary Joe imagines I have is because I tell her what I think about things sometimes.'

'It *is* a rather dangerous practice,' admitted Anne, out of the depths of her own experience.

'Well, by and by I'll tell you the thoughts I told Mary Joe and you can see for yourself if there's anything queer in them,' said Paul, 'but I'll wait till it begins to get dark. That is the time I ache to tell people things, and when nobody else is handy I just *have* to tell Mary Joe. But after this I won't, if it makes her imagine I'm wrong in my upper storey. I'll just ache and bear it.'

'And if the ache gets too bad you can come up to Green Gables and tell me your thoughts,' suggested Anne, with all the gravity that endeared her to children, who so dearly love to be taken seriously.

'Yes, I will. But I hope Davy won't be there when I go because he makes faces at me. I don't mind *very* much because he is such a little boy and I am quite a big one, but still it is not pleasant to have faces made at you. And Davy makes such terrible ones. Sometimes I am frightened he will never get his face straightened out again. He makes them at me in church when I ought to be thinking of sacred things. Dora likes me though, and I like her, but not so well as I did before she told Minnie May Barry that she meant to marry me when I grew up. I may marry somebody when I grow up but I'm far too young to be thinking of it yet, don't you think, teacher?'

'Rather young,' agreed teacher.

'Speaking of marrying, reminds me of another thing that has

been troubling me of late,' continued Paul. 'Mrs Lynde was down here one day last week having tea with Grandma, and Grandma made me show her my little mother's picture ... the one Father sent me for my birthday present. I didn't exactly want to show it to Mrs Lynde. Mrs Lynde is a good kind woman, but she isn't the sort of person you want to show your mother's picture to. *You* know, teacher. But of course I obeyed Grandma. Mrs Lynde said she was very pretty but kind of actressy looking, and must have been an awful lot younger than Father. Then she said, "Some of these days your pa will be marrying again likely. How will you like to have a new ma, Master Paul?" Well, the idea almost took my breath away, teacher, but I wasn't going to let Mrs Lynde see *that*. I just looked her straight in the face ... like this ... and I said, "Mrs Lynde, Father made a pretty good job of picking out my first mother and I could trust him to pick out just as good a one the second time." And I *can* trust him, teacher. But still, I hope, if he ever does give me a new mother, he'll ask my opinion about her before it's too late. There's Mary Joe coming to call us to tea. I'll go and consult with her about the shortbread.'

As a result of the 'consultation', Mary Joe cut the shortbread and added a dish of preserves to the bill of fare. Anne poured the tea and she and Paul had a very merry meal in the dim old sitting-room whose windows were open to the gulf breezes, and they talked so much 'nonsense' that Mary Joe was quite scandalized and told Veronica the next evening that 'de school mees' was as queer as Paul. After tea Paul took Anne up to his room to show her his mother's picture, which had been the mysterious birthday present kept by Mrs Irving in the bookcase. Paul's little low-ceilinged room was a soft whirl of ruddy light from the sun that was setting over the sea and swinging shadows from the fir-trees that grew close to the square, deep-set window. From out this soft glow and glamour shone a sweet, girlish face, with tender mother eyes, that was hanging on the wall at the foot of the bed.

'That's my little mother,' said Paul with loving pride. 'I got Grandma to hang it there where I'd see it as soon as I opened my eyes in the morning. I never mind not having the light when

I go to bed now, because it just seems as if my little mother was right here with me. Father knew just what I would like for a birthday present, although he never asked me. Isn't it wonderful how much fathers do know?'

'Your mother was very lovely, Paul, and you look a little like her. But her eyes and hair are darker than yours.'

'My eyes are the same colour as Father's,' said Paul, flying about the room to heap all available cushions on the window seat, 'but Father's hair is grey. He has lots of it, but it is grey. You see, Father is nearly fifty. That's ripe old age, isn't it? But it's only *outside* he's old. *Inside* he's just as young as anybody. Now, teacher, please sit here; and I'll sit at your feet. May I lay my head against your knee? That's the way my little mother and I used to sit. Oh, this is real splendid, I think.'

'Now, I want to hear those thoughts which Mary Joe pronounces so queer,' said Anne, patting the mop of curls at her side. Paul never needed any coaxing to tell his thoughts ... at least, to congenial souls.

'I thought them out in the fir grove one night,' he said dreamily. 'Of course I didn't *believe* them but I *thought* them. *You* know, teacher. And then I wanted to tell them to somebody and there was nobody but Mary Joe. Mary Joe was in the pantry setting bread and I sat down on the bench beside her and I said, "Mary Joe, do you know what I think? I think the evening star is a lighthouse on the land where the fairies dwell." And Mary Joe said, "Well, yous are de queer one. Dare ain't no such ting as fairies." I was very much provoked. Of course, I knew there are no fairies; but that needn't prevent my thinking there is. *You* know, teacher. But I tried again quite patiently. I said, "Well then, Mary Joe, do you know what I think? I think an angel walks over the world after the sun sets ... a great, tall, white angel, with silvery folded wings ... and sings the flowers and birds to sleep. Children can hear him if they know how to listen." Then Mary Joe held up her hands all over flour and said, "Well, yous are de queer leetle boy. Yous makes me feel scare." And she really did look scared. I went out then and whispered the rest of my thoughts to the garden. There was a little birch-tree in the garden and it died. Grandma says the salt spray killed it; but I think the dryad belonging to it was a foolish dryad who wandered away to see the world and got lost. And the little tree was so lonely it died of a broken heart.'

'And when the poor, foolish little dryad gets tired of the world and comes back to her tree *her* heart will break,' said Anne.

'Yes, but if dryads are foolish they must take the consequences, just as if they were real people,' said Paul gravely. 'Do you know what I think about the new moon, teacher? I think it is a little golden boat full of dreams.'

'And when it tips on a cloud some of them spill out and fall into your sleep.'

'Exactly, teacher. Oh, you *do* know. And I think the violets are little snips of the sky that fell down when the angels cut out holes for the stars to shine through. And the buttercups are made out of old sunshine; and I think the sweet peas will be butterflies when they go to heaven. Now, teacher, do you see anything so very queer about those thoughts?'

'No, laddie dear, they are not queer at all; they are strange and beautiful thoughts for a little boy to think, and so people who couldn't think anything of the sort themselves, if they tried for a hundred years, think them queer. But keep on thinking them, Paul ... some day you are going to be a poet, I believe.'

When Anne reached home she found a very different type of boyhood waiting to be put to bed. Davy was sulky; and when Anne had undressed him he bounced into bed and buried his face in the pillow.

'Davy, you have forgotten to say your prayers,' said Anne rebukingly.

'No, I didn't forget,' said Davy defiantly, 'but I ain't going to say my prayers any more. I'm going to give up trying to be good, 'cause no matter how good I am you'd like Paul Irving better. So I might as well be bad and have the fun of it.'

'I don't like Paul Irving *better*,' said Anne seriously. 'I like you just as well, only in a different way.'

'But I want you to like me the same way,' pouted Davy.

'You can't like different people the same way. You don't like Dora and me the same way, do you?'

Davy sat up and reflected.

'No . . . o . . . o,' he admitted at last, 'I like Dora because she's my sister, but I like you because you're *you*.'

'And I like Paul because he is Paul and Davy because he is Davy,' said Anne gaily.

'Well, I kind of wish I'd said my prayers then,' said Davy, convinced by this logic. 'But it's too much bother getting out now to say them. I'll say them twice in the morning, Anne. Won't that do as well?'

No, Anne was positive it would not do as well. So Davy scrambled out and knelt down at her knee. When he had finished his devotions he leaned back on his little, bare, brown heels and looked up at her.

'Anne, I'm gooder than I used to be.'

'Yes, indeed you are, Davy,' said Anne, who never hesitated to give credit where credit was due.

'I *know* I'm gooder,' said Davy confidently, 'and I'll tell you how I know it. Today Marilla give me two pieces of bread and jam, one for me and one for Dora. One was a good deal bigger than the other and Marilla didn't say which was mine. But I give the biggest piece to Dora. That was good of me, wasn't it?'

'Very good, and very manly, Davy.'

'Of course,' admitted Davy, 'Dora wasn't very hungry and she only et half her slice and then she give the rest to me. But I didn't know she was going to do that when I give it to her, so I was good, Anne.'

In the twilight Anne sauntered down to the Dryad's Bubble and saw Gilbert Blythe coming down through the dusky Haunted Wood. She had a sudden realization that Gilbert was a schoolboy no longer. And how manly he looked – the tall, frank-faced fellow, with the clear, straightforward eyes and the broad shoulders. Anne thought Gilbert was a very handsome lad, even though he didn't look at all like her ideal man. She and Diana had long ago decided what kind of a man they admired and their tastes seemed exactly similar. He must be very tall and distinguished-looking, with melancholy, inscrutable eyes, and a melting, sympathetic voice. There was nothing either melancholy or inscrutable in Gilbert's physiognomy, but of course that didn't matter in friendship!

Gilbert stretched himself out on the ferns beside the Bubble and looked approvingly at Anne. If Gilbert had been asked to describe his ideal woman the description would have answered point for point to Anne, even to those seven tiny freckles whose obnoxious presence still continued to vex her soul. Gilbert was as yet little more than a boy; but a boy has his dreams as have others, and in Gilbert's future there was always a girl with big, limpid grey eyes, and a face as fine and delicate as a flower. He had made up his mind, also, that his future must be worthy of its goddess. Even in quiet Avonlea there were temptations to be met and faced. White Sands youth were a rather 'fast' set, and Gilbert was popular wherever he went. But he meant to keep himself worthy of Anne's friendship and perhaps some distant day her love; and he watched over word and thought and deed as jealously as if her clear eyes were to pass judgement on it. She held over him the unconscious influence that every girl, whose ideals are high and pure, wields over her friends; an influence which would endure as long as she was faithful to those ideals and which she would as certainly lose if she were ever false to them. In Gilbert's eyes Anne's greatest charm was the fact that she never stooped to the petty practices of so many of the Avonlea girls – the small jealousies, the little deceits and rivalries, the palpable bids for favour. Anne held herself apart from all this, not consciously or of design, but simply because anything of the sort was utterly foreign to her transparent, impulsive nature, crystal clear in its motives and aspirations.

But Gilbert did not attempt to put his thoughts into words, for he had already too good reason to know that Anne would mercilessly and frostily nip all attempts at sentiment in the bud – or laugh at him, which was ten times worse.

'You look like a real dryad under that birch-tree,' he said teasingly.

'I love birch-trees,' said Anne, laying her cheek against the creamy satin of the slim bole, with one of the pretty caressing gestures that came so natural to her.

'Then you'll be glad to hear that Mr Major Spencer has decided to set out a row of white birches all along the road-front of his farm, by way of encouraging the A.V.I.S.,' said Gilbert. 'He was talking to me about it today. Major Spencer is the most progressive and public-spirited man in Avonlea. And Mr William Bell is going to set out a spruce hedge along his road-front and up his lane. Our Society is getting on splendidly, Anne. It is past the experimental stage and is an accepted fact. The older folks are beginning to take an interest in it and the White Sands people are talking of starting one too. Even Elisha Wright has come around since that day the Americans from the hotel had the picnic at the shore. They praised our roadsides so highly and said they were so much prettier than in any other part of the Island. And when, in due time, the other farmers follow Mr Spencer's good example and plant ornamental trees and hedges along their road-fronts Avonlea will be the prettiest settlement in the province.'

'The Aids are talking of taking up the graveyard,' said Anne, 'and I hope they will, because there will have to be a subscription for that, and it would be no use for the Society to try it after the hall affair. But the Aids would never have stirred in the matter if the Society hadn't put it into their thoughts unofficially. Those trees we planted on the church grounds are flourishing, and the trustees have promised me that they will fence in the school grounds next year. If they do I'll have an arbour day and every scholar shall plant a tree; and we'll have a garden in the corner by the road.'

'We've succeeded in almost all our plans so far, except in getting the old Boulter house removed,' said Gilbert, 'and I've given *that* up in despair. Levi won't have it taken down just to vex us. There's a contrary streak in all the Boulters and it's strongly developed in him.'

'Julia Bell wants to send another committee to him, but I think the better way will just be to leave him severely alone,' said Anne sagely.

'And trust to Providence, as Mrs Lynde says,' smiled Gilbert. 'Certainly, no more committees. They only aggravate him. Julia Bell thinks you can do anything, if you only have a committee to attempt it. Next spring, Anne, we must start an agitation for nice lawns and grounds. We'll sow good seed betimes this winter. I've a treatise here on lawns and lawn-making and I'm going to prepare a paper on the subject soon. Well, I suppose our vacation is almost over. School opens Monday. Has Ruby Gillis got the Carmody school?'

'Yes; Priscilla wrote that she had taken her own home school, so the Carmody trustees gave it to Ruby. I'm sorry Priscilla is not coming back, but since she can't I'm glad Ruby has got the school. She will be home for Saturdays and it will seem like old times, to have her and Jane and Diana and myself all together again.'

Marilla, just home from Mrs Lynde's, was sitting on the back porch step when Anne returned to the house.

'Rachel and I have decided to have our cruise to town tomorrow,' she said. 'Mr Lynde is feeling better this week and Rachel wants to go before he has another sick spell.'

'I intend to get up extra early tomorrow morning, for I've ever so much to do,' said Anne virtuously. 'For one thing, I'm going to shift the feathers from my old bed-tick to the new one. I ought to have done it long ago but I've just kept putting it off ... it's such a detestable task. It's a very bad habit to put off disagreeable things, and I never mean to again, or else I can't comfortably tell my pupils not to do it. That would be inconsistent. Then I want to make a cake for Mrs Harrison and finish my paper on gardens for the A.V.I.S., and write Stella, and wash and starch my muslin dress, and make Dora's new apron.'

'You won't get half done,' said Marilla, pessimistically. 'I never yet planned to do a lot of things but something happened to prevent me.'

CHAPTER 20

The Way it Often Happens

ANNE rose betimes the next morning and blithely greeted the fresh day, when the banners of the sunrise were shaken triumphantly across the pearly skies. Green Gables lay in a pool of sunshine, flecked with the dancing shadows of poplar and willow. Beyond the lane was Mr Harrison's wheat-field, a great, wind-rippled expanse of pale gold. The world was so beautiful that Anne spent ten blissful minutes hanging idly over the garden gate drinking the loveliness in.

After breakfast Marilla made ready for her journey. Dora was to go with her, having been long promised this treat.

'Now, Davy, you try to be a good boy and don't bother Anne,' she straitly charged him. 'If you are good I'll bring you a striped candy cane from town.'

For alas, Marilla had stooped to the evil habit of bribing people to be good!

'I won't be bad on purpose, but s'posen I'm bad zacksident-ally?' Davy wanted to know.

'You'll have to guard against accidents,' admonished Marilla. 'Anne, if Mr Shearer comes today get a nice roast and some steak. If he doesn't you'll have to kill a fowl for dinner tomorrow.'

Anne nodded.

'I'm not going to bother cooking any dinner for just Davy and myself today,' she said. 'That cold ham bone will do for noon lunch and I'll have some steak fried for you when you come home at night.'

'I'm going to help Mr Harrison haul dulse this morning,' announced Davy. 'He asked me to, and I guess he'll ask me to dinner too. Mr Harrison is an awful kind man. He's a real sociable man. I hope I'll be like him when I grow up. I mean *behave* like him ... I don't want to *look* like him. But I guess there's no danger, for Mrs Lynde says I'm a very handsome child. Do you s'pose it'll last, Anne? I want to know.'

'I dare say it will,' said Anne gravely. 'You *are* a handsome boy, Davy' ... Marilla looked volumes of disapproval ... 'but you must live up to it and be just as nice and gentlemanly as you look to be.'

'And you told Minnie May Barry the other day, when you found her crying 'cause someone said she was ugly, that if she was nice and kind and loving people wouldn't mind her looks,' said Davy discontentedly. 'Seems to me you can't get out of being good in this world for some reason or 'nother. You just have to behave.'

'Don't you want to be good?' asked Marilla, who had learned a great deal but had not yet learned the futility of asking such questions.

'Yes, I want to be good but not *too* good,' said Davy cautiously. 'You don't have to be very good to be a Sunday School superintendent. Mr Bell's that, and he's a real bad man.'

'Indeed he's not,' said Marilla indignantly.

'He is . . . he says he is himself,' asseverated Davy. 'He said it when he prayed in Sunday School last Sunday. He said he was a vile worm and a miserable sinner and guilty of the blackest 'niquity. What did he do that was so bad, Marilla? Did he kill anybody? Or steal the collection cents? I want to know.'

Fortunately Mrs Lynde came driving up the lane at this moment and Marilla made off, feeling that she had escaped from the snare of the fowler, and wishing devoutly that Mr Bell were not quite so highly figurative in his public petitions, especially in the hearing of small boys who were always 'wanting to know'.

Anne, left alone in her glory, worked with a will. The floor was swept, the beds made, the hens fed, the muslin dress washed and hung out on the line. Then Anne prepared for the transfer of feathers. She mounted to the garret and donned the first old dress that came to hand . . . a navy blue cashmere she had worn at fourteen. It was decidedly on the short side and as 'skimpy' as the notable wincey Anne had worn upon the occasion of her debut at Green Gables; but at least it would not be materially injured by down and feathers. Anne completed her toilet by tying a big red and white spotted handkerchief that had belonged to Matthew over her head, and thus accoutred, betook herself to the kitchen chamber, whither Marilla, before her departure, had helped her carry the feather bed.

A cracked mirror hung by the chamber window and in an unlucky moment Anne looked into it. There were those seven freckles on her nose, more rampant than ever, or so it seemed in the glare of light from the unshaded window.

'Oh, I forgot to rub that lotion on last night,' she thought. 'I'd better run down to the pantry and do it now.'

Anne had already suffered many things trying to remove those freckles. On one occasion the entire skin had peeled off her nose but the freckles remained. A few days previously she had found a recipe for a freckle lotion in a magazine and, as the ingredients were within her reach, she straightway compounded it, much to the disgust of Marilla, who thought that if Providence had placed freckles on your nose it was your bounden duty to leave them there.

Anne scurried down to the pantry, which, always dim from the big willow growing close to the window, was now almost dark by reason of the shade drawn to exclude the flies. Anne caught the bottle containing the lotion from the shelf and copiously anointed her nose therewith by means of a little sponge sacred to the purpose. This important duty done, she returned to her work. Anyone who has ever shifted feathers from one tick to another will not need to be told that when Anne finished she was a sight to behold. Her dress was white with down and fluff, and her front hair, escaping from under the handkerchief, was adorned with a veritable halo of feathers. At this auspicious moment a knock sounded at the kitchen door.

'That must be Mr Shearer,' thought Anne. 'I'm in a dreadful mess, but I'll have to run down as I am, for he's always in a hurry.'

Down flew Anne to the kitchen door. If ever a charitable floor did open to swallow up a miserable, befeathered damsel the Green Gables porch floor should promptly have engulfed Anne at that moment. On the doorstep were standing Priscilla Grant, golden and fair in silk attire, a short, stout, grey-haired lady in a tweed suit, and another lady, tall, stately, wonderfully gowned, with a beautiful, high-bred face and large, black-lashed violet eyes, who Anne 'instinctively felt', as she would have said in her earlier days, to be Mrs Charlotte E. Morgan.

In the dismay of the moment one thought stood out from the confusion of Anne's mind and she grasped at it as at the proverbial straw. All Mrs Morgan's heroines were noted for 'rising to the occasion'. No matter what their troubles were, they invariably rose to the occasion and showed their superiority over all ills of time, space, and quantity. Anne therefore felt it was *her* duty to rise to the occasion and she did it, so perfectly that Priscilla afterwards declared she never admired Anne Shirley more than at that moment. No matter what her outraged feelings were she did not show them. She greeted Priscilla and was introduced to her companions as calmly and composedly as if she had been arrayed in purple and fine linen. To be sure, it was somewhat of a shock to find that the lady she had instinctively felt to be Mrs Morgan was not Mrs Morgan at all, but an unknown Mrs Pendexter, while the stout, little, grey-haired woman was Mrs Morgan; but in the greater shock the lesser lost its power. Anne ushered her guests to the spare room and thence into the parlour, where she left them while she hastened out to help Priscilla unharness her horse.

'It's dreadful to come upon you so unexpectedly as this,' apologized Priscilla, 'but I did not know till last night that we were coming. Aunt Charlotte is going away Monday and she had promised to spend today with a friend in town. But last night her friend telephoned to her not to come because they were quarantined for scarlet fever. So I suggested we came here instead, for I knew you were longing to see her. We called at the White Sands Hotel and brought Mrs Pendexter with us. She is a friend of Aunt's and lives in New York, and her husband is a millionaire. We can't stay very long, for Mrs Pendexter has to be back at the hotel by five o'clock.'

Several times while they were putting away the horse Anne caught Priscilla looking at her in a furtive, puzzled way.

'She needn't stare at me so,' Anne thought a little resentfully. 'If she doesn't *know* what it is to change a feather bed she might imagine it.'

When Priscilla had gone to the parlour, and before Anne could escape upstairs, Diana walked into the kitchen. Anne caught her astonished friend by the arm.

'Diana Barry, who do you suppose is in that parlour at this very moment? Mrs Charlotte E. Morgan ... and a New York millionaire's wife ... and here I am like *this* ... and *not a thing in the house for dinner but a cold ham bone*, Diana!'

By this time Anne had become aware that Diana was staring

at her in precisely the same bewildered fashion as Priscilla had done. It was really too much.

'Oh, Diana, don't look at me so,' she implored. '*You*, at least, must know that the neatest person in the world couldn't empty feathers from one tick into another and remain neat in the process.'

'It ... it ... isn't the feathers,' hesitated Diana, 'it's ... it's ... your nose, Anne.'

'My nose? Oh, Diana, surely nothing has gone wrong with it?'

Anne rushed to the little looking-glass over the sink. One glance revealed the fatal truth. Her nose was a brilliant scarlet!

Anne sat down on the sofa, her dauntless spirit subdued at last.

'What is the matter with it?' asked Diana, curiosity overcoming delicacy.

'I thought I was rubbing my freckle lotion on it, but I must have used that red dye Marilla has for marking the pattern on her rugs,' was the despairing response. 'What shall I do?'

'Wash it off,' said Diana practically.

'Perhaps it won't wash off. First I dye my hair; then I dye my nose. Marilla cut my hair off when I dyed it, but that remedy would hardly be practicable in this case. Well, this is another punishment for vanity, and I suppose I deserve it ... though there's not much comfort in *that*. It is really almost enough to make one believe in ill-luck, though Mrs Lynde says there is no such thing, because everything is foreordained.'

Fortunately the dye washed off easily and Anne, somewhat consoled, betook herself to the east gable while Diana ran home. Presently Anne came down again, clothed and in her right mind. The muslin dress she had fondly hoped to wear was bobbing merrily about on the line outside, so she was forced to content herself with her black lawn. She had the fire on and tea steeping when Diana returned; the latter wore *her* muslin, at least, and carried a covered platter in her hand.

'Mother sent you this,' she said, lifting the cover and displaying a nicely carved and jointed chicken to Anne's grateful eyes.

The chicken was supplemented by light new bread, excellent butter and cheese, Marilla's fruit cake and a dish of preserved plums, floating in their golden syrup as in congealed summer sunshine. There was a big bowlful of pink-and-white asters also, by way of decoration; yet the spread seemed very meagre beside the elaborate one formerly prepared for Mrs Morgan.

Anne's hungry guests, however, did not seem to think anything was lacking and they ate the simple viands with apparent enjoyment. But after the first few moments Anne thought no more of what was or was not on her bill of fare. Mrs Morgan's appearance might be somewhat disappointing, as even her loyal worshippers had been forced to admit to each other; but she proved to be a delightful conversationalist. She had travelled extensively and was an excellent story-teller. She had seen much of men and women, and crystallized her experiences into witty little sentences and epigrams which made her hearers feel as if they were listening to one of the people in clever books. But under all her sparkle there was a strongly felt undercurrent of true, womanly sympathy and kind-heartedness which won affection as easily as her brilliancy won admiration. Nor did she monopolize the conversation. She could draw others out as skilfully and fully as she could talk herself, and Anne and Diana found themselves chattering freely to her. Mrs Pendexter said little; she merely smiled with her lovely eyes and lips, and ate chicken and fruit cake and preserves with such exquisite grace that she conveyed the impression of dining on ambrosia and honeydew. But then, as Anne said to Diana later on, anybody so divinely beautiful as Mrs Pendexter didn't need to talk; it was enough for her just to *look*.

After dinner they all had a walk through Lovers' Lane and Violet Vale and the Birch Path, then back through the Haunted Wood to the Dryad's Bubble, where they sat down and talked for a delightful last half hour. Mrs Morgan wanted to know how the Haunted Wood came by its name, and laughed until she cried when she heard the story and Anne's dramatic account of a certain memorable walk through it at the witching hour of twilight.

'It has indeed been a feast of reason and flow of soul, hasn't it?' said Anne, when her guests had gone and she and Diana were alone again. 'I don't know which I enjoyed more ... listening to Mrs Morgan or gazing at Mrs Pendexter. I believe we had a nicer time than if we'd known they were coming and been cumbered with much serving. You must stay to tea with me, Diana, and we'll talk it all over.'

'Priscilla says Mrs Pendexter's husband's sister is married to an English earl; and yet she took a second helping of the plum preserves,' said Diana, as if the two facts were somehow incompatible.

'I dare say even the English earl himself wouldn't have turned up his aristocratic nose at Marilla's plum preserves,' said Anne proudly.

Anne did not mention the misfortune which had befallen *her* nose when she related the day's history to Marilla that evening. But she took the bottle of freckle lotion and emptied it out of the window.

'I shall never try any beautifying messes again,' she said, darkly resolute. 'They may do for careful, deliberate people; but for anyone so hopelessly given over to making mistakes as I seem to be, it's tempting fate to meddle with them.'

CHAPTER 21

Sweet Miss Lavendar

SCHOOL opened and Anne returned to her work, with fewer theories but considerably more experience. She had several new pupils, six- and seven-year-olds just venturing, round-eyed, into a world of wonder. Among them were Davy and Dora. Davy sat with Milty Boulter, who had been going to school for a year and was therefore quite a man of the world. Dora had made a compact at Sunday School the previous Sunday to sit with Lily Sloane; but Lily Sloane not coming the first day, she was temporarily assigned to Mirabel Cotton, who was ten years old and therefore, in Dora's eyes, one of the 'big girls'.

'I think school is great fun,' Davy told Marilla when he got home that night. 'You said I'd find it hard to sit still and I did . . . you mostly do tell the truth, I notice . . . but you can wriggle your legs about under the desk and that helps a lot. It's splendid to have so many boys to play with. I sit with Milty Boulter and he's fine. He's longer than me, but I'm wider. It's nicer to sit in the back seats but you can't sit there till your legs grow long enough to touch the floor. Milty drawed a picture of Anne on his slate and it was awful ugly and I told him if he made pictures of Anne like that I'd lick him at recess. I thought at first I'd draw one of him and put horns and a tail on it, but I was afraid it would hurt his feelings, and Anne says you should never hurt anyone's feelings. It seems it's dreadful to have your feelings hurt. It's better to knock a boy down than hurt his feelings if you *must* do something. Milty said he wasn't scared of me but he'd just as soon call it somebody else to 'blige me, so he rubbed out Anne's name and printed Barbara Shaw's under it. Milty doesn't like Barbara 'cause she calls him a sweet little boy and once she patted him on his head.'

Dora said primly that she liked school; but she was very quiet, even for her; and when at twilight Marilla bade her go upstairs to bed she hesitated and began to cry.

'I'm . . . I'm frightened,' she sobbed. 'I . . . I don't want to go upstairs alone in the dark.'

'What notion have you got into your head now?' demanded Marilla. 'I'm sure you've gone to bed alone all summer and never been frightened before.'

Dora still continued to cry, so Anne picked her up, cuddled her sympathetically, and whispered:

'Tell Anne all about it, sweetheart. What are you frightened of?'

'Of . . . of Mirabel Cotton's uncle,' sobbed Dora. 'Mirabel Cotton told me all about her family today in school. Nearly everybody in her family has died . . . all her grandfathers and grandmothers and ever so many uncles and aunts. They have a habit of dying, Mirabel says. Mirabel's awful proud of having so many dead relations, and she told me what they all died of, and what they said, and how they looked in their coffins. And

Mirabel says one of her uncles was seen walking around the house after he was buried. Her mother saw him. I don't mind the rest so much, but I can't help thinking about that uncle.'

Anne went upstairs with Dora and sat by her until she fell asleep. The next day Mirabel Cotton was kept in at recess and 'gently but firmly' given to understand that when you were so unfortunate as to possess an uncle who persisted in walking about houses after he had been decently interred it was not in good taste to talk about the eccentric gentleman to your deskmate of tender years. Mirabel thought this very harsh. The Cottons had not much to boast of. How was she to keep up her prestige among her schoolmates if she were forbidden to make capital out of the family ghost?

September slipped by into a gold and crimson graciousness of October. One Friday evening Diana came over.

'I'd a letter from Ella Kimball today, Anne, and she wants us to go over to tea tomorrow afternoon to meet her cousin, Irene Trent, from town. But we can't get one of our horses to go, for they'll all be in use tomorrow, and your pony is lame ... so I suppose we can't go.'

'Why can't we walk?' suggested Anne. 'If we go straight back through the woods we'll strike the West Grafton road not far from the Kimball place. I was through that way last winter and I know the road. It's no more than four miles and we won't have to walk home, for Oliver Kimball will be sure to drive us. He'll be only too glad of the excuse, for he goes to see Carrie Sloane and they say his father will hardly ever let him have a horse.'

It was accordingly arranged that they should walk, and the following afternoon they set out, going by way of Lovers' Lane to the back of the Cuthbert farm, where they found a road leading into the heart of acres of glimmering beech and maple woods, which were all in a wondrous glow of flame and gold, lying in a great purple stillness and peace.

'It's as if the year were kneeling to pray in a vast cathedral full of mellow stained light, isn't it?' said Anne dreamily. 'It doesn't seem right to hurry through it, does it? It seems irreverent, like running in a church.'

'We *must* hurry, though,' said Diana, glancing at her watch. 'We've left ourselves little enough time as it is.'

'Well, I'll walk fast, but don't ask me to talk,' said Anne, quickening her pace. 'I just want to drink the day's loveliness in ... I feel as if she were holding it out to my lips like a cup of airy wine and I'll take a sip at every step.'

Perhaps it was because she was so absorbed in 'drinking it in' that Anne took the left turning when they came to a fork in the road. She should have taken the right, but ever afterwards she counted it the most fortunate mistake of her life. They came out finally to a lonely, grassy road, with nothing in sight along it but ranks of spruce saplings.

'Why, where are we?' exclaimed Diana in bewilderment. 'This isn't the West Grafton road.'

'No, it's the base-line road in Middle Grafton,' said Anne, rather shamefacedly. 'I must have taken the wrong turning at the fork. I don't know where we are exactly, but we must be all of three miles from Kimballs' still.'

'Then we can't get there by five, for it's half-past four now,' said Diana, with a despairing look at her watch. 'We'll arrive after they have had their tea, and they'll have all the bother of getting ours over again.'

'We'd better turn back and go home,' suggested Anne humbly. But Diana, after consideration, vetoed this.

'No, we may as well go on and spend the evening, since we have come this far.'

A few yards farther on the girls came to a place where the road forked again.

'Which of these do we take?' asked Diana dubiously.

Anne shook her head.

'I don't know and we can't afford to make any more mistakes. Here is a gate and a lane leading right into the wood. There must be a house at the other side. Let us go down and inquire.'

'What a romantic old lane this is,' said Diana, as they walked along its twists and turns. It ran under patriarchal old firs whose branches met above, creating a perpetual gloom in which nothing except moss could grow. On either hand were brown wood floors, crossed here and there by fallen lances of sunlight. All was very still and remote, as if the world and the cares of the world were far away.

'I feel as if we were walking through an enchanted forest,' said Anne in a hushed tone. 'Do you suppose we'll ever find our way back to the real world again, Diana? We shall presently come to a palace with a spellbound princess in it, I think.'

Around the next turn they came in sight, not indeed of a palace, but of a little house almost as surprising as a palace would have been in this province of conventional wooden farm-houses, all as much alike in general characteristics as if they had grown from the same seed. Anne stopped short in rapture and Diana exclaimed:

'Oh, I know where we are now. That is the little stone house where Miss Lavendar Lewis lives . . . Echo Lodge, she calls it, I think. I've often heard of it, but I've never seen it before. Isn't it a romantic spot?'

'It's the sweetest, prettiest place I ever saw or imagined,' said Anne delightedly. 'It looks like a bit out of a story-book or a dream.'

The house was a low-eaved structure built of undressed blocks of red Island sandstone, with a little peaked roof out of which peered two dormer windows, with quaint wooden hoods over them, and two great chimneys. The whole house was covered with a luxuriant growth of ivy, finding easy foothold on the rough stonework and turned by autumn frosts to most beautiful bronze and wine-red tints.

Before the house was an oblong garden into which the lane gate where the girls were standing opened. The house bounded it on one side; on the three others it was enclosed by an old stone dyke, so overgrown with moss and grass and ferns that it looked like a high, green bank. On the right and left the tall, dark spruces spread their palm-like branches over it; but below it was a little meadow, green with clover aftermath, sloping down to the blue loop of the Grafton River. No other house or clearing was in sight . . . nothing but hills and valleys covered with feathery young firs.

'I wonder what sort of a person Miss Lewis is,' speculated

Diana as they opened the gate into the garden. 'They say she is very peculiar.'

'She'll be interesting then,' said Anne decidedly. 'Peculiar people are always that at least, whatever else they are or are not. Didn't I tell you we would come to an enchanted palace? I knew the elves hadn't woven magic over that lane for nothing.'

'But Miss Lavendar Lewis is hardly a spellbound princess,' laughed Diana. 'She's an old maid ... she's forty-five and quite grey, I've heard.'

'Oh, that's only part of the spell,' asserted Anne confidently. 'At heart she's young and beautiful still ... and if we only knew how to unloose the spell she would step forth radiant and fair again. But we don't know how ... it's always and only the prince who knows that ... and Miss Lavendar's prince hasn't come yet. Perhaps some fatal mischance has befallen him ... though that's against the law of all fairy tales.'

'I'm afraid he came long ago and went away again,' said Diana. 'They say she used to be engaged to Stephen Irving ... Paul's father ... when they were young. But they quarrelled and parted.'

'Hush,' warned Anne. 'The door is open.'

The girls paused in the porch under the tendrils of ivy and knocked at the open door. There was a patter of steps inside and a rather odd little personage presented herself ... a girl of about fourteen, with a freckled face, a snub nose, a mouth so wide that it did really seem as if it stretched 'from ear to ear', and two long braids of fair hair tied with two enormous bows of blue ribbon.

'Is Miss Lewis at home?' asked Diana.

'Yes, ma'am. Come in, ma'am ... this way, ma'am ... and sit down, ma'am. I'll tell Miss Lavendar you're here, ma'am. She's upstairs, ma'am.'

With this the small handmaiden whisked out of sight and the girls, left alone, looked about them with delighted eyes. The interior of this wonderful little house was quite as interesting as its exterior.

The room had a low ceiling and two square, small-paned

windows, curtained with muslin frills. All the furnishings were old-fashioned, but so well and daintily kept that the effect was delicious. But it must be candidly admitted that the most attractive feature, to two healthy girls who had just tramped four miles through autumn air, was a table, set out with pale blue china and laden with delicacies, while little golden-hued ferns scattered over the cloth gave it what Anne would have termed 'a festal air'.

'Miss Lavendar must be expecting company to tea,' she whispered. 'There are six places set. But what a funny little girl she has. She looked like a messenger from pixy-land. I suppose she could have told us the road, but I was curious to see Miss Lavendar. S . . . s . . . sh, she's coming.'

And with that Miss Lavendar Lewis was standing in the doorway. The girls were so surprised that they forgot good manners and simply stared. They had unconsciously been expecting to see the usual type of elderly spinster as known to their experience . . . a rather angular personage, with prim grey hair and spectacles. Nothing more unlike Miss Lavendar could possibly be imagined.

She was a little lady with snow-white hair beautifully wavy and thick, and carefully arranged in becoming puffs and coils. Beneath it was an almost girlish face, pink-cheeked and sweet-lipped, with big soft brown eyes and dimples . . . actually dimples. She wore a very dainty gown of cream muslin with pale-hued roses, on it . . . a gown which would have seemed ridiculously juvenile on most women of her age, but which suited Miss Lavendar so perfectly that you never thought about it all.

'Charlotta the Fourth says that you wished to see me,' she said, in a voice that matched her appearance.

'We wanted to ask the right road to West Grafton,' said Diana. 'We are invited to tea at Mr Kimball's, but we took the wrong path coming through the woods and came out to the base-line instead of the West Grafton road. Do we take the right or left turning at your gate?'

'The left,' said Miss Lavendar, with a hesitating glance at her tea-table. Then she exclaimed, as if in a sudden little burst of resolution:

'But oh, won't you stay and have tea with me? Please do. Mr Kimball's will have tea over before you get there. And Charlotta the Fourth and I will be so glad to have you.'

Diana looked mute inquiry at Anne.

'We'd like to stay,' said Anne promptly, for she had made up her mind that she wanted to know more of this surprising Miss Lavendar, 'if it won't inconvenience you. But you are expecting other guests, aren't you?'

Miss Lavendar looked at her tea-table again, and blushed.

'I know you'll think me dreadfully foolish,' she said. 'I *am* foolish . . . and I'm ashamed of it when I'm found out, but never unless I *am* found out. I'm not expecting anybody . . . I was just pretending I was. You see, I was so lonely. I love company . . . that is, the right kind of company . . . but so few people ever come here because it is so far out of the way. Charlotta the Fourth was lonely too. So I just pretended I was going to have a tea-party. I cooked for it . . . and decorated the table for it . . . and set it with my mother's wedding china . . . and I dressed up for it.'

Diana secretly thought Miss Lavendar quite as peculiar as report had pictured her. The idea of a woman of forty-five playing at having a tea-party, just as if she were a little girl! But Anne of the shining eyes exclaimed joyfully:

'Oh, do you imagine things too?'

That 'too' revealed a kindred spirit to Miss Lavendar.

'Yes, I do,' she confessed, boldly. 'Of course it's silly in anybody as old as I am. But what is the use of being an independent old maid if you can't be silly when you want to, and when it doesn't hurt anybody? A person must have some compensations. I don't believe I could live at times if I didn't pretend things. I'm not often caught at it though, and Charlotta the Fourth never tells. But I'm glad to be caught today, for you have really come and I have tea all ready for you. Will you go up to the spare room and take off your hats? It's the white door at the head of the stairs. I must run out to the kitchen and see that Charlotta the Fourth isn't letting the tea boil. Charlotta the Fourth is a very good girl but she *will* let the tea boil.'

Miss Lavendar tripped off to the kitchen on hospitable

thoughts intent and the girls found their way up to the spare room, an apartment as white as its door, lighted by the ivy-hung dormer window and looking, as Anne said, like the place where happy dreams grew.

'This is quite an adventure, isn't it?' said Diana. 'And isn't Miss Lavendar sweet, if she *is* a little odd? She doesn't look a bit like an old maid.'

'She looks just as music sounds, I think,' answered Anne.

When they went down Miss Lavendar was carrying in the teapot, and behind her, looking vastly pleased, was Charlotta the Fourth, with a plate of hot biscuits.

'Now, you must tell me your names,' said Miss Lavendar. 'I'm so glad you are young girls. I love young girls. It's so easy to pretend I'm a girl myself when I'm with them. I do hate' ... with a little grimace ... 'to believe I'm old. Now, who are you ... just for convenience' sake? Diana Barry? And Anne Shirley? May I pretend that I've known you for a hundred years and call you Anne and Diana right away?'

'You may,' the girls said both together.

'Then just let's sit comfily down and eat everything,' said Miss Lavendar happily. 'Charlotta, you sit at the foot and help the chicken. It is so fortunate that I made the sponge cake and doughnuts. Of course, it was foolish to do it for imaginary guests ... I know Charlotta the Fourth thought so, didn't you, Charlotta? But you see how well it has turned out. Of course they wouldn't have been wasted, for Charlotta the Fourth and I could have eaten them through time. But sponge cake is not a thing that improves with time.'

That was a merry and memorable meal; and when it was over they all went out to the garden, lying in the glamour of sunset.

'I do think you have the loveliest place here,' said Diana, looking round her admiringly.

'Why do you call it Echo Lodge?' asked Anne.

'Charlotta,' said Miss Lavendar, 'go into the house and bring out the little tin horn that is hanging over the clock shelf.'

Charlotta the Fourth skipped off and returned with the horn.

'Blow it, Charlotta,' commanded Miss Lavendar.

Charlotta accordingly blew, a rather raucous strident blast. There was a moment's stillness ... and then from the woods over the river came a multitude of fairy echoes, sweet, elusive, silvery, as if all the 'horns of elfland' were blowing against the sunset. Anne and Diana exclaimed in delight.

'Now laugh, Charlotta ... laugh loudly.'

Charlotta, who would probably have obeyed if Miss Lavendar had told her to stand on her head, climbed upon the stone bench and laughed loud and heartily. Back came the echoes, as if a host of pixy people were mimicking her laughter in the purple woodlands and along the fir-fringed points.

'People always admire my echoes very much,' said Miss Lavendar, as if the echoes were her personal property. 'I love them myself. They are very good company ... with a little pretending. On calm evenings Charlotta the Fourth and I often sit out here and amuse ourselves with them. Charlotta, take back the horn and hang it carefully in its place.'

'Why do you call her Charlotta the Fourth?' asked Diana, who was bursting with curiosity on this point.

'Just to keep her from getting mixed up with the other Charlottas in my thoughts,' said Miss Lavendar seriously. 'They all look so much alike there's no telling them apart. Her name isn't really Charlotta at all. It is ... let me see ... what is it? I *think* it's Leonora ... yes, it *is* Leonora. You see, it is this way. When Mother died ten years ago I couldn't stay here alone ... and I couldn't afford to pay the wages of a grown-up girl. So I got little Charlotta Bowman to come and stay with me for board and clothes. Her name really was Charlotta ... she was Charlotta the First. She was just thirteen. She stayed with me till she was sixteen and then she went away to Boston, because she could do better there. Her sister came to stay with me then. Her name was Julietta ... Mrs Bowman had a weakness for fancy names, I think ... but she looked so like Charlotta that I kept calling her that all the time ... and she didn't mind. So I just gave up trying to remember her right name. She was Charlotta the Second, and when she went away Evelina came and she was Charlotta the Third. Now I have Charlotta the Fourth; but when she is sixteen ... she's fourteen now ... she will want to go to Boston too, and what I shall do then I really do not know. Charlotta the Fourth is the last of the Bowman girls, and the best. The other Charlottas always let me see that they thought it silly of me to pretend things, but Charlotta the Fourth never does, no matter what she may really think. I don't care what people think about me if they don't let me see it.'

'Well,' said Diana looking regretfully at the setting sun, 'I suppose we must go if we want to get to Mr Kimball's before dark. We've had a lovely time, Miss Lewis.'

'Won't you come again to see me?' pleaded Miss Lavendar.

Tall Anne put her arm about the little lady.

'Indeed we shall,' she promised. 'Now that we have discovered you we'll wear out our welcome coming to see you. Yes, we must go ... "we must tear ourselves away", as Paul Irving says every time he comes to Green Gables.'

'Paul Irving?' There was a subtle change in Miss Lavendar's voice. 'Who is he? I didn't think there was anybody of that name in Avonlea.'

Anne felt vexed at her own heedlessness. She had forgotten about Miss Lavendar's old romance when Paul's name slipped out.

'He is a little pupil of mine,' she explained slowly. 'He came from Boston last year to live with his grandmother, Mrs Irving of the shore road.'

'Is he Stephen Irving's son?' Miss Lavendar asked, bending over her namesake border so that her face was hidden.

'Yes.'

'I'm going to give you girls a bunch of lavender apiece,' said Miss Lavendar brightly, as if she had not heard the answer to her question. 'It's very sweet, don't you think? Mother always loved it. She planted these borders long ago. Father named me Lavendar because he was so fond of it. The very first time he saw Mother was when he visited her home in East Grafton with her brother. He fell in love with her at first sight; and they put him in the spare room bed to sleep and the sheets were scented with lavender and he lay awake all night and thought of her. He always loved the scent of lavender after that ... and that was why he gave me the name. Don't forget to come back soon, girls, dear. We'll be looking for you, Charlotta the Fourth and I.'

She opened the gate under the firs for them to pass through. She looked suddenly old and tired; the glow and radiance had faded from her face; her parting smile was as sweet with ineradicable youth as ever, but when the girls looked back from the first curve in the lane they saw her sitting on the old stone bench under the silver poplar in the middle of the garden with her head leaning wearily on her hand.

'She does look lonely,' said Diana softly. 'We must come often to see her.'

'I think her parents gave her the only right and fitting name that could possibly be given her,' said Anne. 'If they had been so blind as to name her Elizabeth or Nellie or Muriel she must have been called Lavendar just the same, I think. It's so suggestive of sweetness and old-fashioned graces and "silk attire". Now, my name just smacks of bread and butter, patchwork and chores.'

'Oh, I don't think so,' said Diana. 'Anne seems to me real stately and like a queen. But I'd like Kerrenhappuch if it happened to be your name. I think people make their names nice or ugly just by what they are themselves. I can't bear Josie or Gertie for names now, but before I knew the Pye girls I thought them real pretty.'

'That's a lovely idea, Diana,' said Anne enthusiastically. 'Living so that you beautify your name, even if it wasn't beautiful to begin with ... making it stand in people's thoughts for something so lovely and pleasant that they never think of it by itself. Thank you, Diana.'

CHAPTER 22

Odds and Ends

'So you had tea at the Stone House with Lavendar Lewis?' said Marilla at the breakfast table next morning. 'What is she like now? It's over fifteen years since I saw her last ... it was one

Sunday in Grafton Church. I suppose she has changed a great deal. Davy Keith, when you want something you can't reach, ask to have it passed and don't spread yourself over the table in that fashion. Did you ever see Paul Irving doing that when he was here to meals?'

'But Paul's arms are longer'n mine,' grumbled Davy. 'They've had eleven years to grow and mine've only had seven. 'Sides, I *did* ask, but you and Anne was so busy talking you didn't pay any 'tention. 'Sides, Paul's never been here to any meal escept tea, and it's easier to be p'lite at tea than at breakfast. You ain't half as hungry. It's an awful long while between supper and breakfast. Now, Anne, that spoonful ain't any bigger than it was last year and *I*'m ever so much bigger.'

'Of course, I don't know what Miss Lavendar used to look like, but I don't fancy somehow that she has changed a great deal,' said Anne, after she had helped Davy to maple syrup, giving him two spoonfuls to pacify him. 'Her hair is snow-white, but her face is fresh and almost girlish, and she has the sweetest brown eyes ... such a pretty shade of wood-brown with little golden glints in them ... and her voice makes you think of white satin and tinkling water and fairy bells all mixed up together.'

'She was reckoned a great beauty when she was a girl,' said Marilla. 'I never knew her very well but I liked her as far as I did know her. Some folks thought her peculiar even then. *Davy*, if ever I catch you at such a trick again you'll be made to wait for your meals till everyone else is done, like the French.'

Most conversations between Anne and Marilla in the presence of the twins were punctuated by these rebukes Davy-ward. In this instance, Davy, sad to relate, not being able to scoop up the last drops of his syrup with his spoon, had solved the difficulty by lifting his plate in both hands and applying his small pink tongue to it. Anne looked at him with such horrified eyes that the little sinner turned red and said, half shame-facedly, half defiantly:

'There ain't any wasted that way.'

'People who are different from other people are always called peculiar,' said Anne. 'And Miss Lavendar is certainly different, though it's hard to say just where the difference comes in. Perhaps it is because she is one of those people who never grow old.'

'One might as well grow old when all your generation do,' said Marilla, rather reckless of her pronouns. 'If you don't, you don't fit in anywhere. Far as I can learn, Lavendar Lewis has just dropped out of everything. She's lived in that out-of-the-way place until everybody has forgotten her. That stone house is one of the oldest on the Island. Old Mr Lewis built it eighty years ago when he came out from England. Davy, stop joggling Dora's elbow. Oh, I saw you! You needn't try to look innocent. What does make you behave so this morning?'

'Maybe I got out of the wrong side of the bed,' suggested Davy. 'Milty Boulter says if you do that things are bound to go wrong with you all day. His grandmother told him. But which *is* the right side? And what are you to do when your bed's against the wall? I want to know.'

'I've always wondered what went wrong between Stephen Irving and Lavendar Lewis,' continued Marilla, ignoring Davy. 'They were certainly engaged twenty-five years ago and then all at once it was broken off. I don't know what the trouble was, but it must have been something terrible, for he went away to the States and never come home since.'

'Perhaps it was nothing very dreadful after all. I think the little things in life often make more trouble than the big things,' said Anne, with one of those flashes of insight which experience could not have bettered. 'Marilla, please don't say anything about my being at Miss Lavendar's to Mrs Lynde. She'd be sure to ask a hundred questions and somehow I wouldn't like it . . . nor Miss Lavendar either if she knew, I feel sure.'

'I dare say Rachel would be curious,' admitted Marilla, 'though she hasn't as much time as she used to have for looking after other people's affairs. She's tied home now on account of Thomas; and she's feeling pretty downhearted, for I think she's beginning to lose hope of his ever getting better. Rachel will be left pretty lonely if anything happens to him, with all her children settled out west, except Eliza in town; she doesn't like her husband.'

Marilla's pronouns slandered Eliza, who was very fond of her husband.

'Rachel says if he'd only brace up and exert his will-power he'd get better. But what is the use of asking a jellyfish to sit up straight?' continued Marilla. 'Thomas Lynde never had any will-power to exert. His mother ruled him till he married and then Rachel carried it on. It's a wonder he dared to get sick without asking her permission. But there, I shouldn't talk so. Rachel has been a good wife to him. He'd never have amounted to anything without her, that's certain. He was born to be ruled; and it's well he fell into the hands of a clever, capable manager like Rachel. He didn't mind her way. It saved him the bother of ever making up his own mind about anything. Davy, do stop squirming like an eel.'

'I've nothing else to do,' protested Davy. 'I can't eat any more, and it's no fun watching you and Anne eat.'

'Well, you and Dora go out and give the hens their wheat,' said Marilla. 'And don't you try to pull any more feathers out of the white rooster's tail either.'

'I wanted some feathers for an Injun headdress,' said Davy sulkily. 'Milty Boulter has a dandy one, made out of the feathers his mother give him when she killed their old white gobbler. You might let me have some. That rooster's got ever so many more'n he wants.'

'You may have the old feather duster in the garret,' said Anne, 'and I'll dye them green and red and yellow for you.'

'You do spoil that boy dreadfully,' said Marilla, when Davy, with a radiant face, had followed prim Dora out. Marilla's education had made great strides in the past six years; but she had not yet been able to rid herself of the idea that it was very bad for a child to have too many of its wishes indulged.

'All the boys of his class have Indian headdresses, and Davy wants one too,' said Anne. '*I* know how it feels ... I'll never forget how I used to long for puffed sleeves when all the other girls had them. And Davy isn't being spoiled. He is improving every day. Think what a difference there is in him since he came here a year ago.'

'He certainly doesn't get into as much mischief since he began to go to school,' acknowledged Marilla. 'I suppose he works off the tendency with the other boys. But it's a wonder to me we haven't heard from Richard Keith before this. Never a word since last May.'

'I'll be afraid to hear from him,' sighed Anne, beginning to clear away the dishes. 'If a letter should come I'd dread opening it, for fear it would tell us to send the twins to him.'

A month later a letter did come. But it was not from Richard Keith. A friend of his wrote to say that Richard Keith had died of consumption a fortnight previously. The writer of the letter was the executor of his will and by that will the sum of two thousand dollars was left to Miss Marilla Cuthbert in trust for David and Dora Keith until they came of age or married. In the meantime the interest was to be used for their maintenance.

'It seems dreadful to be glad of anything in connection with a death,' said Anne soberly. 'I'm sorry for poor Mr Keith; but I *am* glad that we can keep the twins.'

'It's a very good thing about the money,' said Marilla practically. 'I wanted to keep them, but I really didn't see how I could afford to do it, especially when they grew older. The rent of the farm doesn't do any more than keep the house and I was bound that not a cent of your money should be spent on them. You do far too much for them as it is. Dora didn't need that new hat you bought her any more than a cat needs two tails. But now the way is made clear and they are provided for.'

Davy and Dora were delighted when they heard that they were to live at Green Gables 'for good'. The death of an uncle whom they had never seen could not weigh a moment in the balance against that. But Dora had one misgiving.

'Was Uncle Richard buried?' she whispered to Anne.

'Yes, dear, of course.'

'He ... he ... isn't like Mirabel Cotton's uncle, is he?' in a still more agitated whisper. 'He won't walk about houses after being buried, will he, Anne?'

CHAPTER 23

Miss Lavendar's Romance

'I THINK I'll take a walk through to Echo Lodge this evening,' said Anne, one Friday afternoon in December.

'It looks like snow,' said Marilla dubiously.

'I'll be there before the snow comes and I mean to stay all night. Diana can't go because she has company, and I'm sure Miss Lavendar will be looking for me tonight. It's a whole fortnight since I was there.'

Anne had paid many a visit to Echo Lodge since that October day. Sometimes she and Diana drove round by the road; sometimes they walked through the woods. When Diana could not go Anne went alone. Between her and Miss Lavendar had sprung up one of those fervent, helpful friendships possible only between a woman who has kept the freshness of youth in her heart and soul, and a girl whose imagination and intuition supplied the place of experience. Anne had at last discovered a real 'kindred spirit', while into the little lady's lonely, sequestered life of dreams Anne and Diana came with the wholesome joy and exhilaration of the outer existence, which Miss Lavendar, 'the world forgetting, by the world forgot', had long ceased to share; they brought an atmosphere of youth and reality to the little stone house. Charlotta the Fourth always greeted them with her very widest smile ... and Charlotta's smiles *were* fearfully wide ... loving them for the sake of her adored mistress as well as for their own. Never had there been such 'high jinks' held in the little stone house as were held there that beautiful, late-lingering autumn, when November seemed October over again, and even December aped the sunshine and hazes of summer.

But on this particular day it seemed as if December had remembered that it was time for winter and had turned suddenly dull and brooding, with a windless hush predictive of coming snow. Nevertheless, Anne keenly enjoyed her walk through the great grey maze of the beech-lands; though alone she never

173

found it lonely; her imagination peopled her path with merry companions, and with these she carried on a gay, pretended conversation that was wittier and more fascinating than conversations are apt to be in real life, where people sometimes fail most lamentably to talk up to the requirements. In a 'make-believe' assembly of choice spirits everybody says just the thing you want her to say and so gives you the chance to say just what *you* want to say. Attended by this invisible company, Anne traversed the woods and arrived at the fir lane just as broad, feathery flakes began to flutter down softly.

At the first bend she came upon Miss Lavendar, standing under a big, broad-branching fir. She wore a gown of warm, rich red, and her head and shoulders were wrapped in a silvery grey silk shawl.

'You look like the Queen of the fir-wood fairies,' called Anne merrily.

'I thought you would come tonight, Anne,' said Miss Lavendar, running forward. 'And I'm doubly glad, for Charlotta the Fourth is away. Her mother is sick and she had to go home for the night. I should have been very lonely if you hadn't come ... even the dreams and the echoes wouldn't have been enough company. Oh, Anne, how pretty you are,' she added suddenly, looking up at the tall, slim girl with the soft rose-flush of walking on her face. 'How pretty and how young! It's so delightful to be seventeen, isn't it? I do envy you,' concluded Miss Lavendar candidly.

'But you are only seventeen at heart,' smiled Anne.

'No, I'm old ... or rather middle-aged, which is far worse,' sighed Miss Lavendar. 'Sometimes I can pretend I'm not, but at other times I realize it. And I can't reconcile myself to it as most women seem to. I'm just as rebellious as I was when I discovered my first grey hair. Now, Anne, don't look as if you were trying to understand. Seventeen *can't* understand. I'm going to pretend right away that I am seventeen too, and I can do it, now that you're here. You always bring youth in your hand like a gift. We're going to have a jolly evening. Tea first ... what do you want for tea? We'll have whatever you like. Do think of something nice and indigestible.'

There were sounds of riot and mirth in the little stone house that night. What with cooking and feasting and making candy and laughing and 'pretending', it is quite true that Miss Lavendar and Anne comported themselves in a fashion entirely unsuited to the dignity of a spinster of forty-five and a sedate schoolma'am. Then, when they were tired, they sat down on the rug before the grate in the parlour, lighted only by the soft fireshine and perfumed deliciously by Miss Lavendar's open rose-jar on the mantel. The wind had risen and was sighing and wailing around the eaves and the snow was thudding softly against the windows, as if a hundred storm sprites were tapping for entrance.

'I'm so glad you're here, Anne,' said Miss Lavendar, nibbling at her candy. 'If you weren't I should be blue ... very blue ... almost navy blue. Dreams and make-believes are all very well in the daytime and the sunshine, but when dark and storm come they fail to satisfy. One wants real things then. But you don't know this ... seventeen never knows it. At seventeen dreams *do* satisfy because you think the realities are waiting for you further on. When I was seventeen, Anne, I didn't think forty-five would find me a white-haired little old maid with nothing but dreams to fill my life.'

'But you aren't an old maid,' said Anne, smiling into Miss Lavendar's wistful wood-brown eyes. 'Old maids are *born* ... they don't become.'

'Some are born old maids, some achieve old maidenhood, and some have old maidenhood thrust upon them,' parodied Miss Lavendar whimsically.

'You are one of those who have achieved it, then,' laughed Anne, 'and you've done it so beautifully that if every old maid were like you they would come into fashion, I think.'

'I always like to do things as well as possible,' said Miss Lavendar meditatively, 'and since an old maid I had to be I was determined to be a very nice one. People say I'm odd; but it's just because I follow my own way of being an old maid and refuse to copy the traditional pattern. Anne, did anyone ever tell you anything about Stephen Irving and me?'

'Yes,' said Anne candidly, 'I've heard that you and he were engaged once.'

'So we were . . . twenty-five years ago . . . a lifetime ago. And we were to have been married the next spring. I had my wedding dress made, although nobody but Mother and Stephen ever knew *that*. We'd been engaged in a way almost all our lives, you might say. When Stephen was a little boy his mother would bring him here when she came to see my mother; and the second time he ever came . . . he was nine and I was six . . . he told me out in the garden that he had pretty well made up his mind to marry me when he grew up. I remember that I said "Thank you"; and when he was gone I told Mother very gravely that there was a great weight off my mind, because I wasn't frightened any more about having to be an old maid. How poor Mother laughed!'

'And what went wrong?' asked Anne breathlessly.

'We had just a stupid, silly, commonplace quarrel. So commonplace that, if you'll believe me, I don't even remember just how it began. I hardly know who was the more to blame for it. Stephen did really begin it, but I suppose I provoked him by some foolishness of mine. He had a rival or two, you see. I was vain and coquettish and liked to tease him a little. He was a very high-strung, sensitive fellow. Well, we parted in a temper on both sides. But I thought it would all come right; and it would have if Stephen hadn't come back too soon. Anne, my dear, I'm sorry to say' . . . Miss Lavendar dropped her voice as if she were about to confess a predilection for murdering people . . . 'that I am a dreadfully sulky person. Oh, you needn't smile . . . it's only too true. I *do* sulk; and Stephen came back before I had finished sulking. I wouldn't listen to him and I wouldn't forgive him; and so he went away for good. He was too proud to come again. And then I sulked because he didn't come. I might have sent for him perhaps, but I couldn't humble myself to do that. I was just as proud as he was . . . pride and sulkiness make a very bad combination, Anne. But I could never care for anybody else and I didn't want to. I knew I would rather be an old maid for a thousand years than marry anybody who wasn't Stephen Irving. Well, it all seems like a dream now, of course. How sympathetic you look, Anne ... as sympathetic as only seventeen can look. But don't overdo it. I'm really a very happy, contented little person in spite of my broken heart. My heart did break, if ever a heart did, when I realized that Stephen Irving was not coming back. But, Anne, a broken heart in real life isn't half as dreadful as it is in books. It's a good deal like a bad tooth ... though you won't think *that* a very romantic simile. It takes spells of aching and gives you a sleepless night now and then, but between times it lets you enjoy life and dreams and echoes and peanut candy as if there were nothing the matter with it. And now you're looking disappointed. You don't think I'm half as interesting a person as you did five minutes ago when you believed I was always the prey of a tragic memory bravely hidden beneath external smiles. That's the worst ... or the best ... of real life, Anne. It *won't* let you be miserable. It keeps on trying to make you comfortable ... and succeeding ... even when you're determined to be unhappy and romantic. Isn't this candy scrumptious? I've eaten far more than is good for me already, but I'm going to keep recklessly on.'

After a little silence Miss Lavendar said abruptly:

'It gave me a shock to hear about Stephen's son that first day you were here, Anne. I've never been able to mention him to you since, but I've wanted to know all about him. What sort of a boy is he?'

'He is the dearest, sweetest child I ever knew, Miss Lavendar ... and he pretends things too, just as you and I do.'

'I'd like to see him,' said Miss Lavendar softly, as if talking to herself. 'I wonder if he looks anything like the little dream-boy who lives here with me ... *my* little dream-boy.'

'If you would like to see Paul I'll bring him through with me some time,' said Anne.

'I *would* like it ... but not too soon. I want to get used to the thought. There might be more pain than pleasure in it ... if he looked too much like Stephen ... or if he didn't look enough like him. In a month's time you may bring him.'

Accordingly, a month later Anne and Paul walked through the woods to the stone house, and met Miss Lavendar in the lane. She had not been expecting them just then and she turned very pale.

'So this is Stephen's boy,' she said in a low tone, taking Paul's hand and looking at him as he stood, beautiful and boyish, in his smart little fur coat and cap. 'He ... he is very like his father.'

'Everybody says I'm a chip of the old block,' remarked Paul, quite at his ease.

Anne, who had been watching the little scene, drew a relieved breath. She saw that Miss Lavendar and Paul had 'taken' to each other, and that there would be no constraint or stiffness. Miss Lavendar was a very sensible person, in spite of her dreams and romance, and after that first little betrayal she tucked her feelings out of sight and entertained Paul as brightly and naturally as if he were anybody's son who had come to see her. They all had a jolly afternoon together and such a feast of fat things by way of supper as would have made old Mrs Irving hold up her hands in horror, believing that Paul's digestion would be ruined for ever.

'Come again, laddie,' said Miss Lavendar, shaking hands with him at parting.

'You may kiss me if you like,' said Paul gravely.

Miss Lavendar stooped and kissed him.

'How did you know I wanted to?' she whispered.

'Because you looked at me just as my little mother used to do when she wanted to kiss me. As a rule, I don't like to be kissed. Boys don't. *You* know, Miss Lewis. But I think I rather like to have you kiss me. And of course I'll come to see you again. I think I'd like to have you for a particular friend of mine, if you don't object.'

'I ... I don't think I shall object,' said Miss Lavendar. She turned and went in very quickly; but a moment later she was waving a gay and smiling good-bye to them from the window.

'I like Miss Lavendar,' announced Paul, as they walked through the beech woods. 'I like the way she looked at me, and I like her stone house, and I like Charlotta the Fourth. I wish Grandma Irving had a Charlotta the Fourth instead of Mary

Joe. I feel sure Charlotta the Fourth wouldn't think I was wrong in my upper storey when I told her what I think about things. Wasn't that a splendid tea we had, teacher? Grandma says a boy shouldn't be thinking about what he gets to eat, but he can't help it sometimes when he is real hungry. *You* know, teacher. I don't think Miss Lavendar would make a boy eat porridge for breakfast if he didn't like it. She'd get things for him he did like. But of course' . . . Paul was nothing if not fairminded . . . 'that mightn't be very good for him. It's very nice for a change though, teacher. *You* know.'

CHAPTER 24

A Prophet in His Own Country

ONE May day Avonlea folks were mildly excited over some 'Avonlea Notes', signed 'Observer', which appeared in the Charlottetown *Daily Enterprise*. Gossip ascribed the authorship thereof to Charlie Sloane, partly because the said Charlie had indulged in similar literary flights in times past, and partly because one of the notes seemed to embody a sneer at Gilbert Blythe. Avonlea juvenile society persisted in regarding Gilbert Blythe and Charlie Sloane as rivals in the good graces of a certain damsel with grey eyes and an imagination.

Gossip, as usual, was wrong. Gilbert Blythe, aided and abetted by Anne, had written the notes, putting in the one about himself as a blind. Only two of the notes have any bearing on this history.

Rumour has it that there will be a wedding in our village ere the daisies are in bloom. A new and highly respected citizen will lead to the hymeneal altar one of our most popular ladies.

Uncle Abe, our well-known weather prophet, predicts a violent storm of thunder and lightning for the evening of the twenty-third of May, beginning at seven o'clock sharp. The area of the storm will extend over the greater part of the Province. People travelling that evening will do well to take umbrellas and machintoshes with them.

'Uncle Abe really has predicted a storm for some time this spring,' said Gilbert, 'but do you suppose Mr Harrison really does go to see Isabella Andrews?'

'No,' said Anne, laughing, 'I'm sure he only goes to play checkers with Mr Harmon Andrews, but Mrs Lynde says she knows Isabella Andrews must be going to get married, she's in such good spirits this spring.'

Poor old Uncle Abe felt rather indignant over the notes. He suspected that 'Observer' was making fun of him. He angrily denied having assigned any particular date for his storm, but nobody believed him.

Life in Avonlea continued on the smooth and even tenor of its way. The 'planting' was put in; the Improvers celebrated an Arbour Day. Each Improver set out, or caused to be set out, five ornamental trees. As the society now numbered forty members, this meant a total of two hundred young trees. Early oats greened over the red fields; apple orchards flung great blossoming arms about the farmhouses and the Snow Queen adorned itself as a bride for her husband. Anne liked to sleep with her window open and let the cherry fragrance blow over her face all night. She thought it very poetical. Marilla thought she was risking her life.

'Thanksgiving should be celebrated in the spring,' said Anne one evening to Marilla, as they sat on the front door steps and listened to the silver-sweet chorus of the frogs. 'I think it would be ever so much better than having it in November when everything is dead or asleep. Then you have to remember to be thankful; but in May one simply can't help being thankful ... that they are alive, if for nothing else. I feel exactly as Eve must have felt in the garden of Eden before the trouble began. *Is* that grass in the hollow green or golden? It seems to me, Marilla, that a pearl of a day like this, when the blossoms are out and the winds don't know where to blow from next for sheer crazy delight, must be pretty near as good as heaven.'

Marilla looked scandalized and glanced apprehensively around to make sure the twins were not within earshot. They came around the corner of the house just then.

'Ain't it an awful nice-smelling evening?' asked Davy, sniffing delightedly as he swung a hoe in his grimy hands. He had been working in his garden. That spring Marilla, by way of turning Davy's passion for revelling in mud and clay into useful channels, had given him and Dora a small plot of ground for a garden. Both had eagerly gone to work in a characteristic fashion. Dora planted, weeded, and watered carefully, systematically, and dispassionately. As a result, her plot was already green with prim, orderly little rows of vegetables and annuals. Davy, however, worked with more zeal than discretion; he dug and hoed and raked and watered and transplanted so energetically that his seeds had no chance for their lives.

'How is your garden coming on, Davy-boy?' asked Anne.

'Kind of slow,' said Davy with a sigh. 'I don't know why the things don't grow better. Milty Boulter says I must have planted them in the dark of the moon and that's the whole trouble. He says you must never sow seeds or kill pork or cut your hair or do any 'portant thing in the wrong time of the moon. Is that true, Anne? I want to know.'

'Maybe if you didn't pull your plants up by the roots every other day to see how they're getting on "at the other end", they'd do better,' said Marilla sarcastically.

'I only pulled six of them up,' protested Davy. 'I wanted to see if there was grubs at the roots. Milty Boulter said if it wasn't the moon's fault it must be grubs. But I only found one grub. He was a great big juicy curly grub. I put him on a stone and got another stone and smashed him flat. He made a jolly squash, I tell you. I was sorry there wasn't more of them. Dora's garden was planted same time's mine and her things are growing all right. It *can't* be the moon,' Davy concluded in a reflective tone.

'Marilla, look at that apple-tree,' said Anne. 'Why, the thing is human. It is reaching out long arms to pick its own pink skirts daintily up and provoke us to admiration.'

'Those Yellow Duchess trees always bear well,' said Marilla complacently. 'That tree'll be loaded this year. I'm real glad . . . they're great for pies.'

But neither Marilla nor Anne nor anybody else was fated to make pies out of Yellow Duchess apples that year.

The twenty-third of May came ... an unseasonably warm day, as none realized more keenly than Anne and her little beehive of pupils, sweltering over fractions and syntax in the Avonlea schoolroom. A hot breeze blew all the forenoon; but after noon hour it died away into a heavy stillness. At half past three Anne heard a low rumble of thunder. She promptly dismissed school at once, so that the children might get home before the storm came.

As they went out to the playground Anne perceived a certain shadow and gloom over the world in spite of the fact that the sun was still shining brightly. Annetta Bell caught her hand nervously.

'Oh, teacher, look at that awful cloud!'

Anne looked and gave an exclamation of dismay. In the north-west a mass of cloud, such as she had never in all her life beheld before, was rapidly rolling up. It was dead black, save where its curled and fringed edges showed a ghastly, livid white. There was something about it indescribably menacing as it gloomed up in the clear blue sky; now and again a bolt of lightning shot across it, followed by a savage growl. It hung so low that it almost seemed to be touching the tops of the wooded hills.

Mr Harmon Andrews came clattering up the hill in his truck wagon, urging his team of greys to their utmost speed. He pulled them to a halt opposite the school.

'Guess Uncle Abe's hit it for once in his life, Anne,' he shouted. 'His storm's coming a leetle ahead of time. Did ye ever see the like of that cloud? Here, all you young ones that are going my way, pile in, and those that ain't scoot for the post office if ye've more'n a quarter of a mile to go, and stay there till the shower's over.'

Anne caught Davy and Dora by the hands and flew down the hill, along the Birch Path, and past Violet Vale and Willowmere, as fast as the twins' fat legs could go. They reached Green Gables not a moment too soon and were joined at the door by Marilla, who had been hustling her ducks and chickens under shelter. As they dashed into the kitchen the light seemed to vanish, as if blown out by some mighty breath; the awful cloud rolled over the sun and a darkness as of late twilight fell across the world. At the same moment, with a crash of thunder and a blinding glare of lightning, the hail swooped down and blotted the landscape out in one white fury.

Through all the clamour of the storm came the thud of torn branches striking the house and the sharp crack of breaking glass. In three minutes every pane in the west and north windows was broken and the hail poured in through the apertures, covering the floor with stones, the smallest of which was as big as a hen's egg. For three-quarters of an hour the storm raged unabated and no one who underwent it ever forgot it. Marilla, for once in her life shaken out of her composure by sheer terror, knelt by her rocking-chair in a corner of the kitchen, gasping and sobbing between the deafening thunder peals. Anne, white as paper, had dragged the sofa away from the window and sat on it with a twin on either side. Davy at the first crash had howled, 'Anne, Anne, is it the Judgement Day? Anne, Anne, I never *meant* to be naughty,' and then had buried his face in Anne's lap and kept it there, his little body quivering. Dora, somewhat pale but quite composed, sat with her hand clasped in Anne's, quiet and motionless. It is doubtful if an earthquake would have disturbed Dora.

Then, almost as suddenly as it began, the storm ceased. The hail stopped, the thunder rolled and muttered away to the eastward, and the sun burst out merry and radiant over a world so changed that it seemed an absurd thing to think that a scant three-quarters of an hour could have effected such a transformation.

Marilla rose from her knees, weak and trembling, and dropped on her rocker. Her face was haggard and she looked ten years older.

'Have we all come out of that alive?' she asked solemnly.

'You bet we have,' piped Davy, cheerfully quite his own man again. 'I wasn't a bit scared either ... only just at the first. It come on a fellow so sudden. I made up my mind quick as a wink that I wouldn't fight Teddy Sloane Monday as I'd promised; but now maybe I will. Say, Dora, was you scared?'

'Yes, I was a little scared,' said Dora primly, 'but I held tight to Anne's hand and said my prayers over and over again.'

'Well, I'd have said my prayers too if I'd have thought of it,' said Davy; 'but,' he added triumphantly, 'you see I came through just as safe as you for all I didn't say them.'

Anne got Marilla a glassful of her potent currant wine ... *how* potent it was Anne, in her earlier days, had had all too good reason to know ... and then they went to the door to look out on the strange scene.

Far and wide was a white carpet, knee deep, of hailstones; drifts of them were heaped up under the eaves and on the steps. When, three or four days later, those hailstones melted, the havoc they had wrought was plainly seen, for every green growing thing in field or garden was cut off. Not only was every blossom stripped from the apple-trees but great boughs and branches were wrenched away. And out of the two hundred trees set out by the Improvers by far the greater number were snapped off or torn to shreds.

'Can it possibly be the same world it was an hour ago?' asked Anne, dazedly. 'It *must* have taken longer than that to play such havoc.'

'The like of this has never been known in Prince Edward Island,' said Marilla, 'never. I remember when I was a girl there was a bad storm, but it was nothing to this. We'll hear of terrible destruction, you may be sure.'

'I do hope none of the children were caught out in it,' murmured Anne anxiously. As it was discovered later, none of the children had been, since all those who had any distance to go had taken Mr Andrews' excellent advice and sought refuge at the post office.

'There comes John Henry Carter,' said Marilla.

John Henry came wading through the hailstones with a rather scared grin.

'Oh, ain't this awful, Miss Cuthbert? Mr Harrison sent me over to see if yous had come out all right.'

'We're none of us killed,' said Marilla grimly, 'and none of the buildings were struck. I hope you got off equally well.'

'Yas'm. Not quite so well, ma'am. We was struck. The lightning knocked over the kitchen chimbly and come down the flue and knocked over Ginger's cage and tore a hole in the floor and went into the sullar. Yas'm.'

'Was Ginger hurt?' queried Anne.

'Yas'm. He was hurt pretty bad. He was killed.'

Later on Anne went over to comfort Mr Harrison. She found him sitting by the table, stroking Ginger's gay dead body with a trembling hand.

'Poor Ginger won't call you any more names, Anne,' he said mournfully.

Anne could never have imagined herself crying on Ginger's account, but the tears came into her eyes.

'He was all the company I had, Anne ... and now he's dead. Well, well, I'm an old fool to care so much. I'll let on I don't care. I know you're going to say something sympathetic as soon as I stop talking ... but don't. If you did I'd cry like a baby. Hasn't this been a terrible storm? I guess folks won't laugh at Uncle Abe's predictions again. Seems as if all the storms that he's been prophesying all his life that never happened came all at once. Beats all how he struck the very day though, don't it? Look at the mess we have here. I must hustle round and get some boards to patch up that hole in the floor.'

Avonlea folks did nothing the next day but visit each other and compare damages. The roads were impassable for wheels by reason of the hailstones, so they walked or rode on horseback. The mail came late with ill tidings from all over the province. Houses had been struck, people killed and injured; the whole telephone and telegraph system had been disorganized, and any number of young stock exposed in the fields had perished.

Uncle Abe waded out to the blacksmith's forge early in the morning and spent the whole day there. It was Uncle Abe's hour of triumph and he enjoyed it to the full. It would be doing Uncle Abe an injustice to say that he was glad the storm had happened; but since it had to be he was very glad he had predicted it ... to the very day, too. Uncle Abe forgot that he had ever denied setting the day. As for the trifling discrepancy in the hour, that was nothing.

Gilbert arrived at Green Gables in the evening and found

Marilla and Anne busily engaged in nailing strips of oilcloth over the broken windows.

'Goodness only knows when we'll get glass for them,' said Marilla. 'Mr Barry went over to Carmody this afternoon but not a pane could he get for love or money. Lawson and Blair were cleaned out by the Carmody people by ten o'clock. Was the storm bad at White Sands, Gilbert?'

'I should say so. I was caught in the school with all the children and I thought some of them would go mad with fright. Three of them fainted, and two girls took hysterics, and Tommy Blewett did nothing but shriek at the top of his voice the whole time.'

'I only squealed once,' said Davy proudly. 'My garden was all smashed flat,' he continued mournfully, 'but so was Dora's,' he added in a tone which indicated that there was yet balm in Gilead.

Anne came running down from the west gable.

'Oh, Gilbert, have you heard the news? Mr Levi Boulter's old house was struck and burned to the ground. It seems to me that I'm dreadfully wicked to feel glad over *that*, when so much damage has been done. Mr Boulter says he believes the A.V.I.S. magicked up that storm on purpose.'

'Well, one thing is certain,' said Gilbert, laughing. ' "Observer" has made Uncle Abe's reputation as a weather prophet. "Uncle Abe's storm" will go down in local history. It is a most extraordinary coincidence that it should have come on the very day we selected. I actually have a half guilty feeling, as if I really had "magicked" it up. We may as well rejoice over the old house being removed, for there's not much to rejoice over where our young trees are concerned. Not ten of them have escaped.'

'Ah, well, we'll just have to plant them over again next spring,' said Anne philosophically. 'That is one good thing about this world ... there are always sure to be more springs.'

CHAPTER 25

An Avonlea Scandal

ONE blithe June morning, a fortnight after Uncle Abe's storm, Anne came slowly through the Green Gables yard from the garden, carrying in her hands two blighted stalks of white narcissus.

'Look, Marilla,' she said sorrowfully, holding up the flowers before the eyes of a grim lady, with her hair coifed in a green gingham apron, who was going into the house with a plucked chicken, 'these are the only buds the storm spared . . . and even they are imperfect. I'm so sorry . . . I wanted some for Matthew's grave. He was always so fond of June lilies.'

'I kind of miss them myself,' admitted Marilla, 'though it doesn't seem right to lament over them when so many worse things have happened . . . all the crops destroyed as well as the fruit.'

'But people have sown their oats over again,' said Anne comfortingly, 'and Mr Harrison says he thinks if we have a good summer they will come out all right though late. And my annuals are all coming up again . . . but oh, nothing can replace the June lilies. Poor little Hester Gray will have none either. I went all the way back to her garden last night but there wasn't one. I'm sure she'll miss them.'

'I don't think it's right for you to say such things, Anne, I really don't,' said Marilla severely. 'Hester Gray has been dead for thirty years and her spirit is in heaven . . . I hope.'

'Yes, but I believe she loves and remembers her garden here still,' said Anne. 'I'm sure no matter how long I'd lived in heaven I'd like to look down and see somebody putting flowers on my grave. If I had had a garden here like Hester Gray's it would take me more than thirty years, even in heaven, to forget being homesick for it by spells.'

'Well, don't let the twins hear you talking like that,' was

Marilla's feeble protest, as she carried her chicken into the house.

Anne pinned her narcissi on her hair and went to the lane gate, where she stood for a while sunning herself in the June brightness before going in to attend to her Saturday morning duties. The world was growing lovely again; old Mother Nature was doing her best to remove the traces of the storm, and, though she was not to succeed fully for many a moon, she was really accomplishing wonders.

'I wish I could just be idle all day today,' Anne told a blue-bird, who was singing and swinging on a willow bough, 'but a schoolma'am, who is also helping to bring up twins, can't indulge in laziness, birdie. How sweet you are singing, little bird. You are just putting the feelings of my heart into song ever so much better than I could myself. Why, who is coming?'

An express wagon was jolting up the lane, with two people on the front seat and a big trunk behind. When it drew near Anne recognized the driver as the son of the station agent at Bright River; but his companion was a stranger ... a scrap of a woman who sprang nimbly down at the gate almost before the horse came to a standstill. She was a very pretty little person, evidently nearer fifty than forty, but with rosy cheeks, sparkling black eyes, and shining black hair, surmounted by a wonderful beflowered and beplumed bonnet. In spite of having driven eight miles over a dusty road she was as neat as if she had just stepped out of the proverbial bandbox.

'Is this where Mr James A. Harrison lives?' she inquired briskly.

'No, Mr Harrison lives over there,' said Anne, quite lost in astonishment.

'Well, I *did* think this place seemed too tidy ... *much* too tidy for James A. to be living here, unless he has greatly changed since I knew him,' chirped the little lady. 'Is it true that James A. is going to be married to some woman living in this settlement?'

'No, oh no,' cried Anne, flushing so guiltily that the stranger looked curiously at her, as if she half suspected her of matrimonial designs on Mr Harrison.

'But I saw it in an Island paper,' persisted the Fair Unknown.

'A friend sent a marked copy to me ... friends are always so ready to do such things. James A.'s name was written in over "new citizen".'

'Oh, that note was only meant as a joke,' gasped Anne. 'Mr Harrison has no intention of marrying *anybody*. I assure you he hasn't.'

'I'm very glad to hear it,' said the rosy lady, climbing nimbly back to her seat in the wagon, 'because he happens to be married already. *I* am his wife. Oh, you may well look surprised. I suppose he has been masquerading as a bachelor and breaking hearts right and left. Well, well, James A.,' nodding vigorously over the fields at the long white house, 'your fun is over. I am here ... though I wouldn't have bothered coming if I hadn't thought you were up to some mischief. I suppose,' turning to Anne, 'that parrot of his is as profane as ever?'

'His parrot ... is dead ... I *think*,' gasped poor Anne, who couldn't have felt sure of her own name at that precise moment.

'Dead! Everything will be all right then,' cried the rosy lady jubilantly. 'I can manage James A. if that bird is out of the way.'

With which cryptic utterance she went joyfully on her way and Anne flew to the kitchen door to meet Marilla.

'Anne, who was that woman?'

'Marilla,' said Anne solemnly, but with dancing eyes, 'do I look as if I were crazy?'

'Not more so than usual,' said Marilla, with no thought of being sarcastic.

'Well then, do you think I am awake?'

'Anne, what nonsense has got into you? Who was that woman, I say?'

'Marilla, if I'm not crazy and not asleep she can't be such stuff as dreams are made of ... she must be real. Anyway, I'm sure I couldn't have imagined such a bonnet. She says she is Mr Harrison's wife, Marilla.'

Marilla stared in her turn.

'His wife! Anne Shirley! Then what has he been passing himself off as an unmarried man for?'

'I don't suppose he did, really,' said Anne, trying to be just. 'He never said he wasn't married. People simply took it for granted. Oh, Marilla, what will Mrs Lynde say to this?'

They found out what Mrs Lynde had to say when she came up that evening. Mrs Lynde wasn't surprised! Mrs Lynde had always expected something of the sort! Mrs Lynde had always known there was *something* about Mr Harrison!

'To think of his deserting his wife!' she said indignantly. 'It's like something you'd read of in the States, but who would expect such a thing to happen right here in Avonlea?'

'But we don't know that he deserted her,' protested Anne, determined to believe her friend innocent till he was proved guilty. 'We don't know the rights of it at all.'

'Well, we soon will. I'm going straight over there,' said Mrs Lynde, who had never learned that there was such a word as delicacy in the dictionary. 'I'm not supposed to know anything about her arrival, and Mr Harrison was to bring some medicine for Thomas from Carmody today, so that will be a good excuse. I'll find out the whole story and come in and tell you on my way back.'

Mrs Lynde rushed in where Anne had feared to tread. Nothing would have induced the latter to go over to the Harrison place; but she had her natural and proper share of curiosity and she felt secretly glad that Mrs Lynde was going to solve the mystery. She and Marilla waited expectantly for that good lady's return, but waited in vain. Mrs Lynde did not revisit Green Gables that night. Davy, arriving home at nine o'clock from the Boulter place, explained why.

'I met Mrs Lynde and some strange woman in the Hollow,' he said, 'and gracious, how they were talking both at once! Mrs Lynde said to tell you she was sorry it was too late to call tonight. Anne, I'm awfully hungry. We had tea at Milty's at four and I think Mrs Boulter is real mean. She didn't give us any preserves or cake . . . and even the bread was skursce.'

'Davy, when you go visiting you must never criticize anything you are given to eat,' said Anne solemnly. 'It's very bad manners.'

'All right . . . I'll only think it,' said Davy cheerfully. 'Do give a fellow some supper, Anne.'

Anne looked at Marilla, who followed her into the pantry and shut the door cautiously.

'You can give him some jam on his bread, Anne. I know what tea at Levi Boulter's is apt to be.'

Davy took his slice of bread and jam with a sigh.

'It's a kind of disappointing world after all,' he remarked. 'Milty has a cat that takes fits . . . she's took a fit regular every day for three weeks. Milty says it's awful fun to watch her. I went down today on purpose to see her have one but the mean old thing wouldn't take a fit and just kept healthy as healthy, though Milty and me hung round all the afternoon and waited. But never mind' . . . Davy brightened up as the insidious comfort of the plum jam stole into his soul . . . 'maybe I'll see her in one some time yet. It doesn't seem likely she'd stop having them all at once when she's been so in the habit of it, does it? This jam is awful nice.'

Davy had no sorrows that plum jam could not cure.

Sunday proved so rainy that there was no stirring abroad; but by Monday everybody had heard some version of the Harrison story. The school buzzed with it and Davy came home full of information.

'Marilla, Mr Harrison has a new wife . . . well, not ezackly new, but they've stopped being married for quite a spell, Milty says. I always s'posed people had to keep on being married once they'd begun, but Milty says no, there's ways of stopping if you can't agree. Milty says one way is just to start off and leave your wife, and that's what Mr Harrison did. Milty says Mr Harrison left his wife because she throwed things at him . . . *hard* things . . . and Arty Sloane says it was because she wouldn't let him smoke, and Ned Clay says it was 'cause she never let up scolding him. I wouldn't leave *my* wife for anything like that. I'd just put my foot down and say, "Mrs Davy, you've just got to do what'll please *me* 'cause I'm a *man*." *That'd* settle her pretty quick I guess. But Annetta Clay says *she* left *him* because he wouldn't scrape his boots at the door and she doesn't blame her.

I'm going right over to Mr Harrison's this minute to see what she's like.'

Davy soon returned, somewhat cast down.

'Mrs Harrison was away . . . she'd gone to Carmody with Mrs Rachel Lynde to get new paper for the parlour. And Mr Harrison said to tell Anne to go over and see him 'cause he wants to have a talk with her. And, say, the floor is scrubbed, and Mr Harrison is shaved, though there wasn't any preaching yesterday.'

The Harrison kitchen wore a very unfamiliar look to Anne. The floor was indeed scrubbed to a wonderful pitch of purity and so was every article of furniture in the room; the stove was polished until she could see her face in it; the walls were white-washed and the window-panes sparkled in the sunlight. By the table sat Mr Harrison in his working clothes, which on Friday had been noted for sundry rents and tatters but which were now neatly patched and brushed. He was sprucely shaved and what little hair he had was carefully trimmed.

'Sit down, Anne, sit down,' said Mr Harrison, in a tone but two degrees removed from that which Avonlea people used at funerals. 'Emily's gone over to Carmody with Rachel Lynde . . . she's struck up a lifelong friendship already with Rachel Lynde. Beats all how contrary women are. Well, Anne, my easy times are over . . . all over. It's neatness and tidiness for me for the rest of my natural life, I suppose.'

Mr Harrison did his best to speak dolefully, but an irrepressible twinkle in his eye betrayed him.

'Mr Harrison, you are glad your wife is come back,' cried Anne, shaking her finger at him. 'You needn't pretend you're not, because I can see it plainly.'

Mr Harrison relaxed into a sheepish smile.

'Well . . . well . . . I'm getting used to it,' he conceded. 'I can't say I was sorry to see Emily. A man really needs some protection in a community like this, where he can't play a game of checkers with a neighbour without being accused of wanting to marry that neighbour's sister and having it put in the paper.'

'Nobody would have supposed you went to see Isabella Andrews if you hadn't pretended to be unmarried,' said Anne severely.

'I didn't pretend I was. If anybody'd have asked me if I was married I'd have said I was. But they just took it for granted. I wasn't anxious to talk about the matter ... I was feeling too sore over it. It would have been nuts for Mrs Rachel Lynde if she had known my wife had left me, wouldn't it now?'

'But some people say that you left her.'

'She started it, Anne, she started it. I'm going to tell you the whole story, for I don't want you to think worse of me than I deserve ... nor of Emily neither. But let's go out on the veranda. Everything is so fearful neat in here that it kind of makes me homesick. I suppose I'll get used to it after a while, but it eases me up to look at the yard. Emily hasn't had time to tidy *it* up yet.'

As soon as they were comfortably seated on the veranda, Mr Harrison began his tale of woe.

'I lived in Scottsford, New Brunswick, before I came here, Anne. My sister kept house for me and she suited me fine; she was just reasonably tidy and she let me alone and spoiled me ... so Emily says. But three years ago she died. Before she died she worried a lot about what was to become of me and finally she got me to promise I'd get married. She advised me to take Emily Scott because Emily had money of her own and was a pattern housekeeper. I said, says I, "Emily Scott wouldn't look at me." "You ask her and see," says my sister; and just to ease her mind I promised her I would ... and I did. And Emily said she'd have me. Never was so surprised in my life, Anne ... a smart pretty little woman like her and an old fellow like me. I tell you I thought at first I was in luck. Well, we were married and took a little wedding trip up to St John for a fortnight and then we went home. We got home at ten o'clock at night, and I give you my word, Anne, that in half an hour that woman was at work house-cleaning. Oh, I know you're thinking my house needed it ... you've got a very expressive face, Anne; your thoughts just come out like print ... but it didn't, not that bad. It had got pretty mixed up while I was keeping bachelor's hall, I admit, but I'd got a woman to come in and clean it up before I was married and there'd been considerable painting and fixing done. I tell you if you took Emily into a brand-new white marble palace she'd be into the scrubbing as soon as she could get an old dress on. Well, she cleaned house till one o'clock that night and at four she was up and at it again. And she kept on that way ... far's I could see she never stopped. It was scour and sweep and dust everlasting, except on Sundays, and then she was just longing for Monday to begin again. But it was her way of amusing herself and I could have reconciled myself to it if she'd left me alone. But that she wouldn't do. She'd set out to make me over but she hadn't caught me young enough. I wasn't allowed to come into the house unless I changed my boots for slippers at the door. I darsn't smoke a pipe for my life unless I went to the barn. And I didn't use good enough grammar. Emily'd been a school teacher in her early life and she'd never got over it. Then she hated to see me eating with my knife. Well, there it was, pick and nag everlasting. But I s'pose, Anne, to be fair, *I* was cantankerous, too. I didn't try to improve as I might have done ... I just got cranky and disagreeable when she found fault. I told her one day she hadn't complained of my grammar when I proposed to her. It wasn't an overly tactful thing to say. A woman would forgive a man for beating her sooner than for hinting she was too much pleased to get him. Well, we bickered along like that and it wasn't exactly pleasant, but we might have got used to each other after a spell if it hadn't been for Ginger. Ginger was the rock we split on at last. Emily didn't like parrots and she couldn't stand Ginger's profane habits of speech. I was attached to the bird for my brother the sailor's sake. My brother the sailor was a pet of mine when we were little lads and he'd sent Ginger to me when he was dying. I didn't see any sense in getting worked up over his swearing. There's nothing I hate worse'n profanity in a human being, but in a parrot, that's just repeating what it's heard with no more understanding of it than I'd have of Chinese, allowances might be made. But Emily couldn't see it that way. Women ain't logical. She tried to break Ginger of swearing but she hadn't any better success than she had in trying to make me stop saying, "I seen" and "them things". Seemed as if the more she tried the worse Ginger got, same as me.

'Well, things went on like this, both of us getting raspier till the cl*imax* came. Emily invited our minister and his wife to tea, and another minister and *his* wife that was visiting them. I'd promised to put Ginger away in some safe place where nobody would hear him ... Emily wouldn't touch his cage with a ten-foot pole ... and I meant to do it, for I didn't want the ministers to hear anything unpleasant in my house. But it slipped my mind ... Emily was worrying me so much about clean collars and grammar that it wasn't any wonder ... and I never thought of that poor parrot till we sat down to tea. Just as minister number one was in the very middle of saying grace, Ginger, who was on the veranda outside the dining-room window, lifted up *his* voice. The gobbler had come into view in the yard and the sight of a gobbler always had an unwholesome effect on Ginger. He surpassed himself that time. You can smile, Anne, and I don't deny I've chuckled some over it since, myself, but at the time I felt almost as much mortified as Emily. I went out and carried Ginger to the barn. I can't say I enjoyed that meal. I knew by the look of Emily that there was trouble brewing for Ginger and James A. When the folks went away I started for the cow pasture and on the way I did some thinking. I felt sorry for Emily and kind of fancied I hadn't been so thoughtful of her as I might; and besides, I wondered if the ministers would think that Ginger had learned his vocabulary from *me*. The long and short of it was, I decided that Ginger would have to be mercifully disposed of and when I'd druv the cows home I went in to tell Emily so. But there was no Emily and there *was* a letter on the table ... just according to the rule in storybooks. Emily writ that I'd have to choose between her and Ginger; she'd gone back to her own house and there she would stay till I went and told her I'd got rid of that parrot.

'I was all riled up, Anne, and I said she might stay till dooms-day if she waited for that; and I stuck to it. I packed up her belongings and sent them after her. It made an awful lot of talk ... Scottsford was pretty near as bad as Avonlea for gossip ... and everybody sympathized with Emily. It kept me all cross and cantankerous and I saw I'd have to get out or I'd never have any peace. I concluded I'd come to the Island. I'd been here when I was a boy and I liked it; but Emily had always said she wouldn't live in a place where folks were scared to walk out after dark for fear they'd fall off the edge. So, just to be contrary, I moved over here. And that's all there is to it. I hadn't ever heard a word from or about Emily till I come home from the back field Saturday and found her scrubbing the floor, but with the first decent dinner I'd had since she left me all ready on the table. She told me eat first and then we'd talk ... by which I concluded that Emily had learned some lessons about getting along with a man. So she's here and she's going to stay ... seeing that Ginger's dead and the Island's some bigger than she thought. There's Mrs Lynde and her now. No, don't go, Anne. Stay and get acquainted with Emily. She took quite a notion to you Saturday ... wanted to know who that handsome red-haired girl was at the next house.'

Mrs Harrison welcomed Anne radiantly and insisted on her staying to tea.

'James A. has been telling me all about you and how kind you've been, making cakes and things for him,' she said. 'I want to get acquainted with all my new neighbours just as soon as possible. Mrs Lynde is a lovely woman, isn't she? So friendly.'

When Anne went home in the sweet June dusk, Mrs Harrison went with her across the fields where the fireflies were lighting their starry lamps.

'I suppose,' said Mrs Harrison confidentially, 'that James A. has told you our story?'

'Yes.'

'Then I needn't tell it, for James A. is a just man and he would tell the truth. The blame was far from being all on his side. I can see that now. I wasn't back in my own house an hour before I wished I hadn't been so hasty, but I wouldn't give in. I see now that I expected too much of a man. And I was real foolish to mind his bad grammar. It doesn't matter if a man does use bad grammar so long as he is a good provider and doesn't go poking round the pantry to see how much sugar you've used in a week. I feel that James A. and I are going to be real happy now. I wish I knew who "Observer" is, so that I could thank him. I owe him a real debt of gratitude.'

Anne kept her own counsel and Mrs Harrison never knew that her gratitude found its way to its object. Anne felt rather bewildered over the far-reaching consequences of those foolish 'notes'. They had reconciled a man to his wife and made the reputation of a prophet.

Mrs Lynde was in the Green Gables kitchen. She had been telling the whole story to Marilla.

'Well, and how do you like Mrs Harrison?' she asked Anne.

'Very much. I think she's a real nice little woman.'

'That's exactly what she is,' said Mrs Rachel with emphasis, 'and as I've just been sayin' to Marilla, I think we ought to all overlook Mr Harrison's peculiarities for her sake and try to make her feel at home here, that's what. Well, I must get back. Thomas'll be wearying for me. I get out a little since Eliza came and he's seemed a lot better these past few days, but I never like to be long away from him. I hear Gilbert Blythe has resigned from White Sands. He'll be off to college in the fall, I suppose.'

Mrs Rachel looked sharply at Anne, but Anne was bending over a sleepy Davy nodding on the sofa and nothing was to be read in her face. She carried Davy away, her oval girlish cheek pressed against his curly yellow head. As they went up the stairs Davy flung a tired arm about Anne's neck and gave her a warm hug and a sticky kiss.

'You're awful nice, Anne. Milty Boulter wrote on his slate today and showed it to Jennie Sloane,

> Roses red and vi'lets blue,
> Sugar's sweet, and so are you,

and that 'spresses my feelings for you ezackly, Anne.'

CHAPTER 26

Round the Bend

THOMAS LYNDE faded out of life as quietly and unob-trusively as he had lived it. His wife was a tender, patient, unwearied nurse. Sometimes Rachel had been a little hard on her Thomas in health, when his slowness or meekness had provoked her; but when he became ill no voice could be lower, no hand more gently skilful, no vigil more uncomplaining.

'You've been a good wife to me, Rachel,' he once said simply, when she was sitting by him in the dusk, holding his thin, blanched old hand in her work-hardened one. 'A good wife. I'm sorry I ain't leaving you better off; but the children will look after you. They're all smart, capable children, just like their mother. A good mother . . . a good woman . . .'

He had fallen asleep then; and the next morning, just as the white dawn was creeping up over the pointed firs in the hollow, Marilla went softly into the east gable and wakened Anne.

'Anne, Thomas Lynde is gone . . . their hired boy just brought the word. I'm going right down to Rachel.'

On the day after Thomas Lynde's funeral Marilla went about Green Gables with a strangely preoccupied air. Occasionally she looked at Anne, seemed on the point of saying something, then shook her head and buttoned up her mouth. After tea she went down to see Mrs Rachel; and when she returned she went to the east gable, where Anne was correcting school exercises.

'How is Mrs Lynde tonight?' asked the latter.

'She's feeling calmer and more composed,' answered Marilla, sitting down on Anne's bed . . . a proceeding which betokened some unusual mental excitement, for in Marilla's code of household ethics to sit on a bed after it was made up was an unpardonable offence. 'But she's very lonely. Eliza had to go home today . . . her son isn't well and she felt she couldn't stay any longer.'

'When I've finished these exercises I'll run down and chat awhile with Mrs Lynde,' said Anne. 'I had intended to study some Latin composition tonight but it can wait.'

'I suppose Gilbert Blythe is going to college in the fall,' said Marilla jerkily. 'How would you like to go too, Anne?'

Anne looked up in astonishment.

'I would like it, of course, Marilla. But it isn't possible.'

'I guess it can be made possible. I've always felt that you should go. I've never felt easy to think you were giving it all up on my account.'

'But, Marilla, I've never been sorry for a moment that I stayed home. I've been so happy ... Oh, these past two years have just been delightful.'

'Oh yes, I know you've been contented enough. But that isn't the question exactly. You ought to go on with your education. You've saved enough to put you through one year at Redmond and the money the stock brought in will do for another year ... and there's scholarships and things you might win.'

'Yes, but I can't go, Marilla. Your eyes are better, of course; but I can't leave you alone with the twins. They need so much looking after.'

'I won't be alone with them. That's what I want to discuss with you. I had a long talk with Rachel tonight. Anne, she's feeling dreadful bad over a good many things. She's not left very well off. It seems they mortgaged the farm eight years ago to give the youngest boy a start when he went west; and they've never been able to pay much more than the interest since. And then of course Thomas' illness has cost a good deal, one way and another. The farm will have to be sold and Rachel thinks there'll be hardly anything left after the bills are settled. She says she'll have to go and live with Eliza and it's breaking her heart to think of leaving Avonlea. A woman of her age doesn't make new friends and interests easy. And, Anne, as she talked about it the thought came to me that I would ask her to come and live with me, but I thought I ought to talk it over with you first before I said anything to her. If I had Rachel living with me you could go to college. How do you feel about it?'

'I feel ... as if ... somebody ... had handed me ... the moon ... and I didn't know ... exactly ... what to do ... with it,' said Anne dazedly. 'But as for asking Mrs Lynde to come here, that is for you to decide, Marilla. Do you think ... are you sure ... you would like it? Mrs Lynde is a good woman and a kind neighbour, but ... but ...'

'But she's got her faults, you mean to say? Well, she has of course; but I think I'd rather put up with far worse faults than see Rachel go away from Avonlea. I'd miss her terrible. She's the only close friend I've got here and I'd be lost without her. We've been neighbours for forty-five years and we've never had a quarrel ... though we came rather near it that time you flew at Mrs Rachel for calling you homely and red-haired. Do you remember, Anne?'

'I should think I do,' said Anne ruefully. 'People don't forget things like that. How I hated poor Mrs Rachel at that moment!'

'And then that "apology" you made her. Well, you were a handful, in all conscience, Anne. I did feel so puzzled and bewildered how to manage you. Matthew understood you better.'

'Matthew understood everything,' said Anne softly, as she always spoke of him.

'Well, I think it could be managed so that Rachel and I wouldn't clash at all. It's always seemed to me that the reason two women can't get along in one house is that they try to share the same kitchen and get in each other's way. Now, if Rachel came here, she could have the north gable for her bedroom, and the spare room for a kitchen as well as not for we don't really need a spare room at all. She could put her stove there and what furniture she wanted to keep, and be real comfortable and independent. She'll have enough to live on of course ... her children'll see to that ... so all I'd be giving her would be houseroom. Yes, Anne, far as I'm concerned I'd like it.'

'Then ask her,' said Anne promptly. 'I'd be very sorry myself to see Mrs Rachel go away.'

'And if she comes,' continued Marilla, 'you can go to college as well as not. She'll be company for me and she'll do for the twins what I can't do, so there's no reason in the world why you shouldn't go.'

Anne had a long meditation at her window that night. Joy and regret struggled together in her heart. She had come at last ... suddenly and unexpectedly ... to the bend of the road; and college *was* round it, with a hundred rainbow hopes and visions; but Anne realized as well that when she rounded that curve she must leave many sweet things behind ... all the little simple duties and interests which had grown so dear to her in the last two years and which she had glorified into beauty and delight by the enthusiasm she had put into them. She must give up her school . . . and she loved every one of her pupils, even the stupid and naughty ones. The mere thought of Paul Irving made her wonder if Redmond were such a name to conjure with after all.

'I've put out a lot of little roots these two years,' Anne told the moon, 'and when I'm pulled up they're going to hurt a great deal. But it's best to go, I think, and, as Marilla says, there's no good reason why I shouldn't. I must get out all my ambitions and dust them.'

Anne sent in her resignation the next day; and Mrs Rachel, after a heart-to-heart talk with Marilla, gratefully accepted the offer of a home at Green Gables. She elected to remain in her own house for the summer, however; the farm was not to be sold until the fall and there were many arrangements to be made.

'I certainly never thought of living as far off the road as Green Gables,' sighed Mrs Rachel to herself. 'But really, Green Gables doesn't seem as out of the world as it used to do . . . Anne has lots of company and the twins make it real lively. And anyhow, I'd rather live at the bottom of a well than leave Avonlea.'

These two decisions being noised abroad speedily ousted the arrival of Mrs Harrison in popular gossip. Sage heads were shaken over Marilla Cuthbert's rash step in asking Mrs Rachel to live with her. People opined that they wouldn't get on together. They were both 'too fond of their own way', and many doleful predictions were made, none of which disturbed the parties in question at all. They had come to a clear and distinct understanding of the respective duties and rights of their new arrangements and meant to abide by them.

'I won't meddle with you nor you with me,' Mrs Rachel had said decidedly, 'and as for the twins, I'll be glad to do all I can for them; but I won't undertake to answer Davy's questions, that's what. I'm not an encyclopedia, neither am I a Philadelphia lawyer. You'll miss Anne for that.'

'Sometimes Anne's answers were about as queer as Davy's questions,' said Marilla dryly. 'The twins will miss her and no mistake; but her future can't be sacrificed to Davy's thirst for information. When he asks questions I can't answer I'll just tell him children should be seen and not heard. That was how *I* was brought up, and I don't know but what it was just as good a way as all these new-fangled notions for training children.'

'Well, Anne's methods seem to have worked fairly well with Davy,' said Mrs Lynde smilingly. 'He is a reformed character, that's what.'

'He isn't a bad little soul,' conceded Marilla. 'I never expected to get as fond of those children as I have. Davy gets round you somehow ... and Dora is a lovely child, although she is ... kind ... of ... well, kind of ...'

'Monotonous? Exactly,' supplied Mrs Rachel. 'Like a book where every page is the same, that's what. Dora will make a good, reliable woman, but she'll never set the pond on fire. Well, that sort of folk are comfortable to have round, even if they're not as interesting as the other kind.'

Gilbert Blythe was probably the only person to whom the news of Anne's resignation brought unmixed pleasure. Her pupils looked upon it as a sheer catastrophe. Annetta Bell had hysterics when she went home. Anthony Pye fought two pitched and unprovoked battles with other boys by way of relieving his feelings. Barbara Shaw cried all night. Paul Irving defiantly told his grandmother that she needn't expect him to eat any porridge for a week.

'I can't do it, Grandma,' he said. 'I don't really know if I can eat *anything*. I feel as if there was a dreadful lump in my throat. I'd have cried coming home from school if Jake Donnell hadn't been watching me. I believe I will cry after I go to bed. It wouldn't show on my eyes tomorrow, would it? And it would be such a relief. But anyway, I can't eat porridge. I'm going to need all my strength of mind to bear up against this, Grandma, and I won't have any left to grapple with porridge. Oh, Grandma, I don't know what I'll do when my beautiful teacher goes away. Milty Boulter says he bets Jane Andrews will get the school. I suppose Miss Andrews is very nice. But I know she won't understand things like Miss Shirley.'

Diana also took a very pessimistic view of affairs.

'It will be horribly lonesome here next winter,' she mourned one twilight when the moonlight was raining 'airy silver' through the cherry boughs and filling the east gable with a soft, dream-like radiance in which the two girls sat and talked, Anne on her low rocker by the window, Diana sitting Turk-fashion on the bed. 'You and Gilbert will be gone . . . and the Allans too. They are going to call Mr Allan to Charlottetown and of course he'll accept. It's too mean. We'll be vacant all winter, I suppose, and have to listen to a long string of candidates . . . and half of them won't be any good.'

'I hope they won't call Mr Baxter from East Grafton here, anyhow,' said Anne decidedly. 'He wants the call, but he does preach such gloomy sermons. Mr Bell says he's a minister of the old school, but Mrs Lynde says there's nothing whatever the matter with him but indigestion. His wife isn't a very good cook, it seems, and Mrs Lynde says that when a man has to eat sour bread two weeks out of three his theology is bound to get a kink in it somewhere. Mrs Allan feels very badly about going away. She says everybody has been so kind to her since she came here as a bride that she feels as if she were leaving lifelong friends. And then, there's the baby's grave, you know. She says she doesn't see how she can go away and leave that . . . it was such a little mite of a thing and only three months old, and she says she is afraid it will miss its mother, although she knows better and wouldn't say so to Mr Allan for anything. She says she has slipped through the birch grove back of the manse nearly every night to the graveyard and sung a little lullaby to it. She told me all about it last evening when I was up putting some of those early wild roses on Matthew's grave. I promised her that as long as I was in Avonlea I would put flowers on the baby's grave and when I was away I felt sure that . . .'

'That I would do it,' supplied Diana heartily. 'Of course I will. And I'll put them on Matthew's grave too, for your sake, Anne.'

'Oh, thank you. I meant to ask you to if you would. And on little Hester Gray's too? Please don't forget hers. Do you know, I've thought and dreamed so much about little Hester Gray that she has become strangely real to me. I think of her back there in her little garden in that cool, still, green corner; and I have a fancy that if I could steal back there some spring evening, just at the magic time 'twixt light and dark and tiptoe so softly up the beech hill that my footsteps could not frighten her, I would find the garden just as it used to be, all sweet with June lilies and early roses, with the tiny house beyond it all hung with vines; and little Hester Gray would be there, with her soft eyes, and the wind ruffling her dark hair, wandering about, putting her finger-tips under the chins of the lilies and whispering secrets with the roses; and I would go forward oh, so softly, and hold out my hands and say to her, "Little Hester Gray, won't you let me be your playmate, for I love the roses too?" And we would sit down on the old bench and talk a little and dream a little, or just be beautifully silent together. And then the moon would rise and I would look around me ... and there would be no Hester Gray and no little vine-hung house, and no roses ... only an old waste garden starred with June lilies amid the grasses, and the wind sighing, oh, so sorrowfully in the cherry-trees. And I would not know whether it had been real or if I had just imagined it all.'

Diana crawled up and got her back against the headboard of the bed. When your companion of the twilight hour said such spooky things it was just as well not to be able to fancy there was anything behind you.

'I'm afraid the Improvement Society will go down when you and Gilbert are both gone,' she remarked dolefully.

'Not a bit of fear of it,' said Anne briskly, coming back from dreamland to the affairs of practical life. 'It is too firmly established for that, especially since the older people are becoming so enthusiastic about it. Look what they are doing this summer for their lawns and lanes. Besides, I'll be watching for hints at Redmond and I'll write a paper for it next winter and send it over. Don't take such a gloomy view of things, Diana. And don't grudge me my little hour of gladness and jubilation now. Later on, when I have to go away, I'll feel anything but glad.'

'It's all right for you to be glad ... you're going to college and you'll have a jolly time and make heaps of lovely new friends.'

'I hope I shall make new friends,' said Anne thoughtfully.

'The possibilities of making new friends help to make life very fascinating. But no matter how many new friends I make they'll never be as dear to me as the old ones ... especially a certain girl with black eyes and dimples. Can you guess who she is, Diana?'

'But there'll be so many clever girls at Redmond,' sighed Diana, 'and I'm only a stupid little country girl who says "I seen" sometimes ... though I really know better when I stop to think. Well, of course these past two years have really been too pleasant to last. I know *somebody* who is glad you are going to Redmond, anyhow. Anne, I'm going to ask you a question ... a serious question. Don't be vexed and do answer seriously. Do you care anything for Gilbert?'

'Ever so much as a friend and not a bit in the way you mean,' said Anne calmly and decidedly; she also thought she was speaking sincerely.

Diana sighed. She wished, somehow, that Anne had answered differently.

'Don't you mean *ever* to be married, Anne?'

'Perhaps ... some day ... when I meet the right one,' said Anne, smiling dreamily up at the moonlight.

'But how can you be sure when you do meet the right one?' persisted Diana.

'Oh, I should know him ... *something* would tell me. You know what my ideal is, Diana.'

'But people's ideals change sometimes.'

'Mine won't. And I *couldn't* care for any man who didn't fulfil it.'

'What if you never meet him?'

'Then I shall die an old maid,' was the cheerful response. 'I dare say it isn't the hardest death by any means.'

'Oh, I suppose the dying would be easy enough; it's the living an old maid I shouldn't like,' said Diana, with no intention of being humorous. 'Although I wouldn't mind being an old maid *very* much if I could be one like Miss Lavendar. But I never could be. When I'm forty-five I'll be horribly fat. And while there might be some romance about a thin old maid there couldn't possibly be any about a fat one. Oh, mind you, Nelson

Atkins proposed to Ruby Gillis three weeks ago. Ruby told me all about it. She says she never had any intention of taking him, because anyone who married him will have to go in with the old folks; but Ruby says that he made such a perfectly beautiful and romantic proposal that it simply swept her off her feet. But she didn't want to do anything rash so she asked for a week to consider; and two days later she was at a meeting of the Sewing Circle at his mother's and there was a book called *The Complete Guide to Etiquette* lying on the parlour table. Ruby said she simply couldn't describe her feelings when in a section of it headed, "The Deportment of Courtship and Marriage", she found the very proposal Nelson had made, word for word. She went home and wrote him a perfectly scathing refusal; and she says his father and mother have taken turns watching him ever since for fear he'll drown himself in the river; but Ruby says they needn't be afraid; for in "The Deportment of Courtship and Marriage" it told how a rejected lover should behave and there's nothing about drowning in *that*. And she says Wilbur Blair is literally pining away for her, but she's perfectly helpless in the matter.'

Anne made an impatient movement.

'I hate to say it ... it seems so disloyal ... but, well, I don't like Ruby Gillis now. I liked her when we went to school and Queen's together ... though not so well as you and Jane of course. But this last year at Carmody she seems so different ... so ... so ...'

'I know,' nodded Diana. 'It's the Gillis coming out in her ... she can't help it. Mrs Lynde says that if ever a Gillis girl thought about anything but the boys she never showed it in her walk and conversation. She talks about nothing but boys and what compliments they pay her, and how crazy they all are about her at Carmody. And the strange thing is, they *are*, too ...' Diana admitted this somewhat resentfully. 'Last night when I saw her in Mr Blair's store she whispered to me that she'd just made a new "mash". I wouldn't ask her who it was, because I knew she was dying to *be* asked. Well, it's what Ruby always wanted, I suppose. You remember even when she was little she always said she meant to have dozens of beaus when she grew up and have the very gayest time she could before she settled down. She's so different from Jane, isn't she? Jane is such a nice, sensible, lady-like girl.'

'Dear old Jane is a jewel,' agreed Anne, 'but,' she added, leaning forward to bestow a tender pat on the plump, dimpled little hand hanging over her pillow, 'there's nobody like my own Diana after all. Do you remember that evening we first met, Diana, and "swore" eternal friendship in your garden? We've kept that "oath", I think ... we've never had a quarrel nor even a coolness. I shall never forget the thrill that went over me the day you told me you loved me. I had had such a lonely, starved heart all through my childhood. I'm just beginning to realize how starved and lonely it really was. Nobody cared anything for me or wanted to be bothered with me. I should have been miserable if it hadn't been for that strange little dream-life of mine, wherein I imagined all the friends and love I craved. But when I came to Green Gables everything was changed. And then I met you. You don't know what your friendship meant to me. I want to thank you here and now, dear, for the warm and true affection you've always given me.'

'And always, always will,' sobbed Diana. 'I shall *never* love anybody ... any *girl* ... half as well as I love you. And if I ever do marry and have a little girl of my own I'm going to name her *Anne*.'

CHAPTER 27

An Afternoon at the Stone House

'WHERE are you going, all dressed up, Anne?' Davy wanted to know. 'You look bully in that dress.'

Anne had come down to dinner in a new dress of pale green muslin ... the first colour she had worn since Matthew's death. It became her perfectly, bringing out all the delicate, flower-like tints of her face and the gloss and burnish of her hair.

'Davy, how many times have I told you that you mustn't use that word?' she rebuked. 'I'm going to Echo Lodge.'

'Take me with you,' entreated Davy.

'I would if I were driving. But I'm going to walk and it's too far for your eight-year-old legs. Besides, Paul is going with me and I fear you don't enjoy yourself in his company.'

'Oh, I like Paul lots better'n I did,' said Davy, beginning to make fearful inroads into his pudding. 'Since I've got pretty good myself I don't mind his being gooder so much. If I can keep on I'll catch up with him some day, both in legs and goodness. 'Sides, Paul's real nice to us second primer boys in school. He won't let the other big boys meddle with us and he shows us lots of games.'

'How came Paul to fall into the brook at noon hour yesterday?' asked Anne. 'I met him on the playground, such a dripping figure that I sent him promptly home for dry clothes without waiting to find out what had happened.'

'Well, it was partly a zacksident,' explained Davy. 'He stuck his head in on purpose but the rest of him fell in zacksidentally. We was all down at the brook and Prillie Rogerson got mad at Paul about something . . . she's awful mean and horrid anyway, if she *is* pretty . . . and said that his grandmother put his hair up in curl rags every night. Paul wouldn't have minded what she said, I guess, but Gracie Andrews laughed, and Paul got awful red, 'cause Gracie's his girl, you know. He's *clean gone* on her . . . brings her flowers and carries her books as far as the shore road. He got as red as a beet and said his grandmother didn't do any such thing and his hair was born curly. And then he laid down on the bank and stuck his head right into the spring to show them. Oh, it wasn't the spring we drink out of . . .' seeing a horrified look on Marilla's face . . . 'it was the little one lower down. But the bank's awful slippy and Paul went right in. I tell you he made a bully splash. Oh, Anne, Anne, I didn't mean to say that . . . it just slipped out before I thought. He made a *splendid* splash. But he looked so funny when he crawled out, all wet and muddy. The girls laughed more'n ever, but Gracie didn't laugh. She looked sorry. Gracie's a nice girl, but she's got a snub nose. When I get big enough to have a girl I won't have one with a snub nose . . . I'll pick one with a pretty nose like yours, Anne.'

'A boy who makes such a mess of syrup all over his face when he is eating his pudding will never get a girl to look at him,' said Marilla severely.

'But I'll wash my face before I go courting,' protested Davy, trying to improve matters by rubbing the back of his hand over the smears. 'And I'll wash behind my ears too, without being told. I remembered to this morning, Marilla. I don't forget half as often as I did. But' . . . and Davy sighed . . . 'there's so many corners about a fellow that it's awful hard to remember them all. Well, if I can't go to Miss Lavendar's I'll go over and see Mrs Harrison. Mrs Harrison's an awful nice woman, I tell you. She keeps a jar of cookies in her pantry a-purpose for little boys, and she always gives me the scrapings out of a pan she's mixed up a plum cake in. A good many plums stick to the sides, you see. Mr Harrison was always a nice man, but he's twice as nice since he got married over again. I guess getting married makes folks nicer. Why don't *you* get married, Marilla? I want to know.'

Marilla's state of single blessedness had never been a sore point with her, so she answered amiably, with an exchange of significant looks with Anne, that she supposed it was because nobody would have her.

'But maybe you never asked anybody to have you,' protested Davy.

'Oh, Davy,' said Dora primly, shocked into speaking without being spoken to, 'it's the *men* that have to do the asking.'

'I don't know why they have to do it *always*,' grumbled Davy. 'Seems to me everything's put on the men in this world. Can I have some more pudding, Marilla?'

'You've had as much as is good for you,' said Marilla; but she gave him a moderate second helping.

'I wish people could live on pudding. Why can't they, Marilla? I want to know.'

'Because they'd soon get tired of it.'

'I'd like to try that for myself,' said sceptical Davy. 'But I guess it's better to have pudding only on fish and company days than none at all. They never have any at Milty Boulter's. Milty says when company comes his mother gives them cheese and cuts it herself ... one little bit apiece and one over for manners.'

'If Milty Boulter talks like that about his mother at least you needn't repeat it,' said Marilla severely.

'Bless my soul' ... Davy had picked this expression up from Mr Harrison and used it with great gusto ... 'Milty meant it as a compelment. He's awful proud of his mother 'cause folks say she could scratch a living on a rock.'

'I ... I suppose them pesky hens are in my pansy bed again,' said Marilla, rising and going out hurriedly.

The slandered hens were nowhere near the pansy bed and Marilla did not even glance at it. Instead, she sat down on the cellar hatch and laughed until she was ashamed of herself.

When Anne and Paul reached the stone house that afternoon they found Miss Lavendar and Charlotta the Fourth in the garden, weeding, raking, clipping, and trimming as if for dear life. Miss Lavendar herself, all gay and sweet in the frills and laces she loved, dropped her shears and ran joyously to meet her guests, while Charlotta the Fourth grinned cheerfully.

'Welcome, Anne. I thought you'd come today. You belong to the afternoon, so it brought you. Things that belong together are sure to come together. What a lot of trouble that would save some people if they only knew it. But they don't ... and so they waste beautiful energy moving heaven and earth to bring things together that *don't* belong. And you, Paul ... why, you've grown! You're half a head taller than when you were here before.'

'Yes, I've begun to grow like pigweed in the night, as Mrs Lynde says,' said Paul, in frank delight over the fact. 'Grandma says it's the porridge taking effect at last. Perhaps it is. Goodness knows ...' Paul sighed deeply ... 'I've eaten enough to make anyone grow. I do hope, now that I've begun, I'll keep on till I'm as tall as Father. He is six feet, you know, Miss Lavendar.'

Yes, Miss Lavendar did know; the flush on her pretty cheeks deepened a little; she took Paul's hand on one side and Anne's on the other and walked to the house in silence.

'Is it a good day for the echoes, Miss Lavendar?' queried Paul anxiously. The day of his first visit had been too windy for echoes and Paul had been much disappointed.

'Yes, just the best kind of a day,' answered Miss Lavendar, rousing herself from her reverie. 'But first we are all going in to have something to eat. I know you two folks didn't walk all the way back here through those beech woods without getting hungry, and Charlotta the Fourth and I can eat any hour of the day ... we have such obliging appetites. So we'll just make a raid on the pantry. Fortunately it's lovely and full. I had a presentiment that I was going to have company today and Charlotta the Fourth and I prepared.'

'I think you are one of the people who always have nice things in their pantry,' declared Paul. 'Grandma's like that too. But she doesn't approve of snacks between meals. I wonder,' he added meditatively, 'if I *ought* to eat them away from home when I know she doesn't approve.'

'Oh, I don't think she would disapprove after you have had a long walk. That makes a difference,' said Miss Lavendar, exchanging amused glances with Anne over Paul's brown curls. 'I suppose that snacks *are* extremely unwholesome. That is why we have them so often at Echo Lodge. We ... Charlotta the Fourth and I ... live in defiance of every known law of diet. We eat all sorts of indigestible things whenever we happen to think of it, by day or night; and we flourish like green bay-trees. We are always intending to reform. When we read any article in a paper warning us against something we like we cut it out and pin it up on the kitchen wall so that we'll remember it. But we never can somehow ... until after we've gone and eaten that very thing. Nothing has ever killed us yet; but Charlotta the Fourth has been known to have bad dreams after we had eaten doughnuts and mince pie and fruit cake before we went to bed.'

'Grandma lets me have a glass of milk and a slice of bread and butter before I go to bed; and on Sunday nights she puts jam on the bread,' said Paul. 'So I'm always glad when it's Sunday night ... for more reasons than one. Sunday is a very long day on the shore road. Grandma says it's all too short for her and that Father never found Sundays tiresome when he was a little boy. It wouldn't seem so long if I could talk to my rock-people, but I never do that because Grandma doesn't approve of it on Sundays. I think a good deal; but I'm afraid my thoughts are worldly. Grandma says we should never think anything but religious thoughts on Sundays. But teacher here said once that every really beautiful thought was religious, no matter what it was about, or what day we thought it on. But I feel sure Grandma thinks that sermons and Sunday School lessons are the only things you can think truly religious thoughts about. And when it comes to a difference of opinion between Grandma and teacher I don't know what to do. In my heart' . . . Paul laid his hand on his breast and raised very serious blue eyes to Miss Lavendar's immediately sympathetic face . . . 'I agree with teacher. But then, you see, Grandma has brought Father up *her* way and made a brilliant success of him; and teacher has never brought anybody up yet, though she's helping with Davy and Dora. But you can't tell how they'll turn out till they *are* grown up. So sometimes I feel as if it might be safer to go by Grandma's opinions.'

'I think it would,' agreed Anne solemnly. 'Anyway, I dare say that if your grandma and I both got down to what we really do mean, under our different ways of expressing it, we'd find out we both meant the same thing. You'd better go by her way of expressing it, since it's been the result of experience. We'll have to wait until we see how the twins do turn out before we can be sure that my way is equally good.'

After lunch they went back to the garden, where Paul made the acquaintance of the echoes, to his wonder and delight, while Anne and Miss Lavendar sat on the stone bench under the poplar and talked.

'So you are going away in the fall?' said Miss Lavendar wistfully. 'I ought to be glad for your sake, Anne . . . but, I'm horribly, selfishly sorry. I shall miss you so much. Oh, sometimes I think it is of no use to make friends. They only go out of your life after a while and leave a hurt that is worse than the emptiness before they came.'

'That sounds like something Miss Eliza Andrews might say, but never Miss Lavendar,' said Anne. '*Nothing* is worse than emptiness . . . and I'm not going out of your life. There are such things as letters and vacations. Dearest, I'm afraid you're looking a little pale and tired.'

'Oh . . . hoo . . . hoo . . . hoo,' went Paul on the dyke, where he had been making noises diligently . . . not all of them melodious in the making, but all coming back transmuted into the very gold and silver of sound by the fairy alchemists over the river. Miss Lavendar made an impatient movement with her pretty hands.

'I'm just tired of everything . . . even of the echoes. There is nothing in my life but echoes . . . echoes of lost hopes and dreams and joys. They're beautiful and mocking. Oh, Anne, it's horrid of me to talk like this when I have company. It's just that I'm getting old and it doesn't agree with me. I know I'll be fearfully cranky by the time I'm sixty. But perhaps all I need is a course of blue pills.'

At this moment Charlotta the Fourth, who had disappeared after lunch, returned, and announced that the north-east corner of Mr John Kimball's pasture was red with early strawberries and wouldn't Miss Shirley like to go and pick some.

'Early strawberries for tea!' exclaimed Miss Lavender. 'Oh, I'm not so old as I thought . . . and I don't need a single blue pill! Girls, when you come back with your strawberries we'll have tea out here under the silver poplar. I'll have it all ready for you with home-grown cream.'

Anne and Charlotta the Fourth accordingly betook themselves back to Mr Kimball's pasture, a green remote place where the air was as soft as velvet, and fragrant as a bed of violets and golden as amber.

'Oh, isn't it sweet and fresh back here?' breathed Anne. 'I just feel as if I were drinking in the sunshine.'

'Yes, ma'am, so do I. That's just exactly how I feel, too, ma'am,' agreed Charlotta the Fourth, who would have said precisely the same thing if Anne had remarked that she felt like a pelican of the wilderness. Always after Anne had visited Echo Lodge, Charlotta the Fourth mounted to her little room over the kitchen and tried before her looking-glass to speak and look and move like Anne. Charlotta could never flatter herself that she quite succeeded; but practice makes perfect, as Charlotta had learned at school, and she fondly hoped that in time she might catch the trick of that dainty uplift of chin, that quick, starry outflashing of eyes, that fashion of walking as if you were a bough swaying in the wind. It seemed so easy when you watched Anne. Charlotta the Fourth admired Anne whole-heartedly. It was not that she thought her so very handsome. Diana Barry's beauty of crimson cheek and black curls was much more to Charlotta the Fourth's taste than Anne's moonshine charm of luminous grey eyes and the pale, ever-changing roses of her cheeks.

'But I'd rather look like you than be pretty,' she told Anne sincerely.

Anne laughed, sipped the honey from the tribute, and cast away the sting. She was used to taking her compliments mixed. Public opinion never agreed on Anne's looks. People who had heard her called handsome met her and were disappointed. People who had heard her called plain saw her and wondered where other people's eyes were. Anne herself would never believe that she had any claim to beauty. When she looked in the glass all she saw was a little pale face with seven freckles on the nose thereof. Her mirror never revealed to her the elusive, ever-varying play of feeling that came and went over her features like a rosy illuminating flame, or the charm of dream and laughter alternating in her big eyes.

While Anne was not beautiful in any strictly defined sense of the word she possessed a certain evasive charm and distinction of appearance that left beholders with a pleasurable sense of satisfaction in that softly rounded girlhood of hers, with all its strongly felt potentialities. Those who knew Anne best, felt, without realizing that they felt it, that her greatest attraction was the aura of possibility surrounding her ... the power of future development that was in her. She seemed to walk in an atmosphere of things about to happen.

As they picked, Charlotta the Fourth confided to Anne her fears regarding Miss Lavendar. The warm-hearted little handmaiden was honestly worried over her adored mistress's condition.

'Miss Lavendar isn't well, Miss Shirley, ma'am. I'm sure she isn't, though she never complains. She hasn't seemed like herself this long while, ma'am ... not since that day you and Paul were here together before. I feel sure she caught cold that night, ma'am. After you and him had gone she went out and walked in the garden for long after dark with nothing but a little shawl on her. There was a lot of snow on the walks and I feel sure she got a chill, ma'am. Ever since then I've noticed her acting tired and lonesome like. She don't seem to take an interest in anything, ma'am. She never pretends company's coming, nor fixes up for it, nor nothing, ma'am. It's only when you come she seems to chirk up a bit. And the worst sign of all, Miss Shirley, ma'am ...' Charlotta the Fourth lowered her voice as if she were about to tell some exceedingly weird and awful symptom indeed ... 'is that she never gets cross now when I break things. Why, Miss Shirley, ma'am, yesterday I bruk her green and yaller bowl that's always stood on the bookcase. Her grandmother brought it out from England and Miss Lavendar was awful choice of it. I was dusting it just as careful, Miss Shirley, ma'am, and it slipped out, so fashion, afore I could grab holt of it, and bruk into about forty millyun pieces. I tell you I was sorry and scared. I thought Miss Lavendar would scold me awful, ma'am; and I'd ruther she had than take it the way she did. She just come in and hardly looked at it and said, "It's no matter, Charlotta. Take up the pieces and throw them away." Just like that, Miss Shirley, ma'am ... "take up the pieces and throw them away", as if it wasn't her grandmother's bowl from England. Oh, she isn't well and I feel awful bad about it. She's got nobody to look after her but me.'

Charlotta the Fourth's eyes brimmed up with tears. Anne patted the little brown paw holding the cracked pink cup sympathetically.

'I think Miss Lavendar needs a change, Charlotta. She stays here alone too much. Can't we induce her to go away for a little trip?'

Charlotta shook her head, with its rampant bows, disconsolately.

'I don't think so, Miss Shirley, ma'am. Miss Lavendar hates visiting. She's only got three relations she ever visits and she says she just goes to see them as a family duty. Last time when she come home she said she wasn't going to visit for family duty

no more. "I've come home in love with loneliness, Charlotta,"
she says to me, "and I never want to stray from my own vine
and fig-tree again. My relations try so hard to make an old lady
of me and it has a bad effect on me." Just like that, Miss Shirley,
ma'am. "It has a very bad effect on me." So I don't think it
would do any good to coax her to go visiting.'

'We must see what can be done,' said Anne decidedly, as she
put the last possible berry in her pink cup. 'Just as soon as I
have my vacation I'll come through and spend a whole week
with you. We'll have a picnic every day and pretend all sorts of
interesting things, and see if we can't cheer Miss Lavendar up.'

'That will be the very thing, Miss Shirley, ma'am,' exclaimed
Charlotta the Fourth in rapture. She was glad for Miss Lavendar's sake and for her own too. With a whole week in which to
study Anne constantly she would surely be able to learn how to
move and behave like her.

When the girls got back to Echo Lodge they found that Miss
Lavendar and Paul had carried the little square table out of the
kitchen to the garden and had everything ready for tea. Nothing
ever tasted so delicious as those strawberries and cream, eaten
under a great blue sky all curdled over with fluffy little white
clouds, and in the long shadows of the wood with its lispings
and its murmurings. After tea Anne helped Charlotta wash the
dishes in the kitchen, while Miss Lavendar sat on the stone
bench with Paul and heard all about his rock-people. She was a
good listener, this sweet Miss Lavendar, but just at the last it
struck Paul that she had suddenly lost interest in the Twin
Sailors.

'Miss Lavendar, why do you look at me like that?' he asked
gravely.

'How do I look, Paul?'

'Just as if you were looking through me at somebody I put
you in mind of,' said Paul, who had such occasional flashes of
uncanny insight that it wasn't quite safe to have secrets when he
was about.

'You do put me in mind of somebody I knew long ago,' said
Miss Lavendar dreamily.

'When you were young?'

'Yes, when I was young. Do I seem very old to you, Paul?'

'Do you know, I can't make up my mind about that,' said Paul confidentially. 'Your hair looks old ... I never knew a young person with white hair. But your eyes are as young as my beautiful teacher's when you laugh. I tell you what, Miss Lavendar' ... Paul's voice and face were as solemn as a judge's ... 'I think you would make a splendid mother. You have just the right look in your eyes ... the look my little mother always had. I think it's a pity you haven't any boys of your own.'

'I have a little dream-boy, Paul.'

'Oh, have you really? How old is he?'

'About your age I think. He ought to be older because I dreamed him long before you were born. But I'll never let him get any older than eleven or twelve; because if I did some day he might grow up altogether and then I'd lose him.'

'I know,' nodded Paul. 'That's the beauty of dream-people ... they stay any age you want them. You and my beautiful teacher and me myself are the only folks in the world that I know of that have dream-people. Isn't it funny and nice we should all know each other? But I guess that kind of people always find each other out. Grandma never has dream-people and Mary Joe thinks I'm wrong in the upper storey because I have them. But I think it's splendid to have them. *You* know, Miss Lavendar. Tell me all about your little dream-boy.'

'He has blue eyes and curly hair. He steals in and wakens me with a kiss every morning. Then all day he plays here in the garden ... and I play with him. Such games as we have. We run races and talk with the echoes; and I tell him stories. And when twilight comes ...'

'*I* know,' interrupted Paul eagerly. 'He comes and sits beside you ... *so* ... because of course at twelve he'd be too big to climb into your lap ... and lays his head on your shoulder ... *so* ... and you put your arms about him and hold him tight, tight, and rest your cheek on his head ... yes, that's the very way. Oh, you do know, Miss Lavendar.'

Anne found the two of them there when she came out of the stone house, and something in Miss Lavendar's face made her hate to disturb them.

'I'm afraid we must go, Paul, if we want to get home before dark. Miss Lavendar, I'm going to invite myself to Echo Lodge for a whole week pretty soon.'

'If you come for a week I'll keep you for two,' threatened Miss Lavendar.

CHAPTER 28

The Prince Comes Back to the Enchanted Palace

THE last day of school came and went. A triumphant 'semi-annual examination' was held and Anne's pupils acquitted themselves splendidly. At the close they gave her an address and a writing-desk. All the girls and ladies present cried, and some of the boys had it cast up to them later on that they cried too, although they always denied it.

Mrs Harmon Andrews, Mrs Peter Sloane, and Mrs William Bell walked home together and talked things over.

'I do think it is such a pity Anne is leaving when the children seem so much attached to her,' sighed Mrs Peter Sloane, who had a habit of sighing over everything and even finished off her jokes that way. 'To be sure,' she added hastily, 'we all know we'll have a good teacher next year too.'

'Jane will do her duty, I've no doubt,' said Mrs Andrews rather stiffly. 'I don't suppose she'll tell the children quite so many fairy tales or spend so much time roaming about the woods with them. But she has her name on the Inspector's Roll of Honour and the Newbridge people are in a terrible state over her leaving.'

'I'm real glad Anne is going to college,' said Mrs Bell. 'She has always wanted it and it will be a splendid thing for her.'

'Well, I don't know.' Mrs Andrews was determined not to agree fully with anybody that day. 'I don't see that Anne needs any more education. She'll probably be marrying Gilbert Blythe, if his infatuation for her lasts till he gets through college, and what good will Latin and Greek do her then? If they taught you at college how to manage a man there might be some sense in her going.'

Mrs Harmon Andrews, so Avonlea gossip whispered, had never learned how to manage her 'man', and as a result the Andrews household was not exactly a model of domestic happiness.

'I see that the Charlottetown call to Mr Allan is up before the Presbytery,' said Mrs Bell. 'That means we'll be losing him soon, I suppose.'

'They're not going before September,' said Mrs Sloane. 'It will be a great loss to the community ... though I always did think that Mrs Allan dressed rather too gay for a minister's wife. But we are none of us perfect. Did you notice how neat and snug Mr Harrison looked today? I never saw such a changed man. He goes to church every Sunday and has subscribed to the salary.'

'Hasn't that Paul Irving grown to be a big boy?' said Mrs Andrews. 'He was such a mite for his age when he came here. I declare I hardly knew him today. He's getting to look a lot like his father.'

'He's a very smart boy,' said Mrs Bell.

'He's smart enough, but' ... Mrs Andrews lowered her voice ... 'I believe he tells queer stories. Gracie came home from school one day last week with the greatest rigmarole he had told her about people who lived down at the shore ... stories there couldn't be a word of truth in, you know. I told Gracie not to believe them, and she said Paul didn't intend her to. But if he didn't, what did he tell them to her for?'

'Anne says Paul is a genius,' said Mrs Sloane.

'He may be. You never know what to expect of them Americans,' said Mrs Andrews. Mrs Andrews' only acquaintance with the word 'genius' was derived from the colloquial fashion of calling any eccentric individual 'a queer genius'. She probably thought, with Mary Joe, that it meant a person with something wrong in his upper storey.

Back in the schoolroom Anne was sitting alone at her desk, as she had sat on the first day of school two years before, her face leaning on her hand, her dewy eyes looking wistfully out of the window to the Lake of Shining Waters. Her heart was so wrung over the parting with her pupils that for the moment college had lost all its charm. She still felt the clasp of Annetta Bell's arms about her neck and heard the childish wail, 'I'll *never* love any teacher as much as you, Miss Shirley, never, never.'

For two years she had worked earnestly and faithfully, making many mistakes and learning from them. She had had her reward. She had taught her scholars something, but she felt that they had taught her much more ... lessons of tenderness, self-control, innocent wisdom, lore of childish hearts. Perhaps she had not succeeded in 'inspiring' any wonderful ambitions in her pupils, but she had taught them, more by her own sweet personality than by all her careful precepts, that it was good and necessary in the years that were before them to live their lives finely and graciously, holding fast to truth and courtesy and kindness, keeping aloof from all that savoured of falsehood and meanness and vulgarity. They were, perhaps, all unconscious of having learned such lessons; but they would remember and practise them long after they had forgotten the capital of Afghanistan and the dates of the Wars of the Roses.

'Another chapter in my life is closed,' said Anne aloud, as she locked her desk. She really felt very sad over it; but the romance in the idea of that 'closed chapter' did comfort her a little.

Anne spent a fortnight at Echo Lodge early in her vacation and everybody concerned had a good time.

She took Miss Lavendar on a shopping expedition to town and persuaded her to buy a new organdie dress; then came the excitement of cutting and making it together, while the happy Charlotta the Fourth basted and swept up clippings. Miss Lavendar had complained that she could not feel much interest in anything; but the sparkle came back to her eyes over her pretty dress.

'What a foolish, frivolous person I must be,' she sighed. 'I'm wholesomely ashamed to think that a new dress ... even if it is a forget-me-not organdie ... should exhilarate me so, when a good conscience and an extra contribution to Foreign Missions couldn't do it.'

Midway in her visit Anne went home to Green Gables for a day to mend the twins' stockings and settle up Davy's accumulated store of questions. In the evening she went down to the shore road to see Paul Irving. As she passed by the low, square window of the Irving sitting-room she caught a glimpse of Paul on somebody's lap; but the next moment he came flying through the hall.

'Oh, Miss Shirley,' he cried excitedly, 'you can't think what has happened! Something so splendid. Father is here ... just think of that! Father is here! Come right in. Father, this is my beautiful teacher. *You* know, Father.'

Stephen Irving came forward to meet Anne with a smile. He was a tall, handsome man of middle age, with iron-grey hair, deep-set, dark blue eyes, and a strong, sad face, splendidly modelled about chin and brow. Just the face for a hero of romance, Anne thought with a thrill of intense satisfaction. It was so disappointing to meet someone who ought to be a hero and find him bald or stooped, or otherwise lacking in manly beauty. Anne would have thought it dreadful if the object of Miss Lavendar's romance had not looked the part.

'So this is my little son's "beautiful teacher" of whom I have heard so much,' said Mr Irving with a hearty handshake. 'Paul's letters have been so full of you, Miss Shirley, that I feel as if I were pretty well acquainted with you already. I want to thank you for what you have done for Paul. I think that your influence has been just what he needed. Mother is one of the best and dearest of women; but her robust, matter-of-fact Scotch common sense could not always understand a temperament like my laddie's. What was lacking in her you have supplied. Between you, I think Paul's training in these two past years has been as nearly ideal as a motherless boy's could be.'

Everybody likes to be appreciated. Under Mr Irving's praise Anne's face "burst flower-like into rosy bloom", and the busy weary man of the world, looking at her, thought he had never seen a fairer, sweeter slip of girlhood than this little 'down East' school teacher with her red hair and wonderful eyes.

Paul sat between them blissfully happy.

'I never dreamed Father was coming,' he said radiantly. 'Even Grandma didn't know it. It was a great surprise. As a general thing' ... Paul shook his brown curls gravely ... 'I don't like to be surprised. You lose all the fun of expecting things when you're surprised. But in a case like this it is all right. Father came last night after I had gone to bed. And after Grandma and Mary Joe had stopped being surprised he and Grandma came upstairs to look at me, not meaning to wake me up till morning. But I woke right up and saw Father. I tell you I just sprang at him.'

'With a hug like a bear's,' said Mr Irving, putting his arm around Paul's shoulder smilingly. 'I hardly knew my boy, he had grown so big and brown and sturdy.'

'I don't know which was the most pleased to see Father, Grandma or I,' continued Paul. 'Grandma's been in kitchen all day making the things Father likes to eat. She wouldn't trust them to Mary Joe, she says. That's *her* way of showing gladness. *I* like best just to sit and talk to Father. But I'm going to leave you for a little while now if you'll excuse me. I must get the cows for Mary Joe. That is one of my daily duties.'

When Paul had scampered away to do his 'daily duty', Mr Irving talked to Anne of various matters. But Anne felt that he was thinking of something else underneath all the time. Presently it came to the surface.

'In Paul's last letter he spoke of going with you to visit an old ... friend of mine ... Miss Lewis, at the stone house in Grafton. Do you know her well?'

'Yes, indeed, she is a *very* dear friend of mine,' was Anne's demure reply, which gave no hint of the sudden thrill that tingled over her from head to foot at Mr Irving's question. Anne 'felt instinctively' that romance was peeping at her round a corner.

Mr Irving rose and went to the window, looking out on a great, golden, billowing sea where a wild wind was harping. For a few moments there was silence in the little, dark-walled room. Then he turned and looked down into Anne's sympathetic face with a smile, half whimsical, half tender.

'I wonder how much you know,' he said.

'I know all about it,' replied Anne promptly. 'You see,' she explained hastily, 'Miss Lavendar and I are very intimate. She

222

wouldn't tell things of such a sacred nature to everybody. We are kindred spirits.'

'Yes, I believe you are. Well, I am going to ask a favour of you. I would like to go and see Miss Lavendar if she will let me. Will you ask her if I may come?'

Would she not? Oh, indeed she would! Yes, this was romance, the very, the real thing, with all the charm of rhyme and story and dream. It was a little belated, perhaps, like a rose blooming in October which should have bloomed in June; but none the less a rose, all sweetness and fragrance, with the gleam of gold in its heart. Never did Anne's feet bear her on a more willing errand than on that walk through the beech woods to Grafton the next morning. She found Miss Lavendar in the garden. Anne was fearfully excited. Her hands grew cold and her voice trembled.

'Miss Lavendar, I have something to tell you . . . something very important. Can you guess what it is?'

Anne never supposed that Miss Lavendar *could* guess; but Miss Lavendar's face grew very pale and Miss Lavendar said in a quiet, still voice, from which all the colour and sparkle that Miss Lavendar's voice usually suggested had faded.

'Stephen Irving is home?'

'How did you know? Who told you?' cried Anne disappointedly, vexed that her great revelation had been anticipated.

'Nobody. I knew that must be it, just from the way you spoke.'

'He wants to come and see you,' said Anne. 'May I send him word that he may?'

'Yes, of course,' fluttered Miss Lavendar. 'There is no reason why he shouldn't. He is only coming as any old friend might.'

Anne had her own opinion about that as she hastened into the house to write a note at Miss Lavendar's desk.

'Oh, it's delightful to be living in a story-book,' she thought gaily. 'It will come out all right of course . . . it must . . . and Paul will have a mother after his own heart and everybody will be happy. But Mr Irving will take Miss Lavendar away . . . and dear knows what will happen to the little stone house ... and so there are two sides to it, as there seems to be to everything in this world.'

The important note was written and Anne herself carried it to the Grafton post office, where she waylaid the mail-carrier and asked him to leave it at the Avonlea office.

'It's so very important,' Anne assured him anxiously. The mail-carrier was a rather grumpy old personage who did not at all look the part of a messenger of Cupid; and Anne was none too certain that his memory was to be trusted. But he said he would do his best to remember and she had to be contented with that.

Charlotta the Fourth felt that some mystery pervaded the stone house that afternoon ... a mystery from which she was excluded. Miss Lavendar roamed about the garden in a distracted fashion. Anne, too, seemed possessed by a demon of unrest, and walked to and fro and went up and down. Charlotta the Fourth endured it till patience ceased to be a virtue; then she confronted Anne on the occasion of that romantic young person's third aimless peregrination through the kitchen.

'Please, Miss Shirley, ma'am,' said Charlotta the Fourth, with an indignant toss of her very blue bows, 'it's plain to be seen you and Miss Lavendar have got a secret and I think, begging your pardon if I'm too forward, Miss Shirley, ma'am, that it's real mean not to tell me when we've all been such chums.'

'Oh, Charlotta, dear, I'd have told you all about it if it were my secret ... but it's Miss Lavendar's, you see. However, I'll tell you this much ... and if nothing comes of it you must never breathe a word about it to a living soul. You see, Prince Charming is coming tonight. He came long ago, but in a foolish moment went away and wandered afar and forgot the secret of the magic pathway to the enchanted castle, where the princess was weeping her faithful heart out for him. But at last he remembered it again and the princess is waiting still ... because nobody but her own dear prince could carry her off.'

'Oh, Miss Shirley, ma'am, what is that in prose?' gasped the mystified Charlotta.

Anne laughed.

'In prose, an old friend of Miss Lavendar's is coming to see her tonight.'

'Do you mean an old beau of hers?' demanded the literal Charlotta.

'That is probably what I do mean ... in prose,' answered Anne gravely. 'It is Paul's father ... Stephen Irving. And goodness knows what will come of it, but let us hope for the best, Charlotta.'

'I hope that he'll marry Miss Lavendar,' was Charlotta's unequivocal response. 'Some women's intended from the start to be old maids, and I'm afraid I'm one of them, Miss Shirley, ma'am, because I've awful little patience with the men. But Miss Lavendar never was. And I've been awful worried, thinking what on earth she'd do when I got so big I'd *have* to go to Boston. There ain't any more girls in our family and dear knows what she'd do if she got some stranger that might laugh at her pretendings and leave things lying round out of their place and not be willing to be called Charlotta the Fifth. She might get someone who wouldn't be as unlucky as me in breaking dishes, but she'd never get anyone who'd love her better.'

And the faithful little handmaiden dashed to the oven door with a sniff.

They went through the form of having tea as usual that night at Echo Lodge; but nobody really ate anything. After tea Miss Lavendar went to her room and put on her new forget-me-not organdie, while Anne did her hair for her. Both were dreadfully excited; but Miss Lavendar pretended to be very calm and indifferent.

'I must really mend that rent in the curtain tomorrow,' she said anxiously, inspecting it as if it were the only thing of any importance just then. 'Those curtains have not worn as well as they should, considering the price I paid. Dear me, Charlotta has forgotten to dust the stair railing *again*. I really *must* speak to her about it.'

Anne was sitting on the porch steps when Stephen Irving came down the lane and across the garden.

'This is the one place where time stands still,' he said, looking around him with delighted eyes. 'There is nothing changed about this house or garden since I was here twenty-five years ago. It makes me feel young again.'

'You know time always does stand still in an enchanted palace,' said Anne seriously. 'It is only when the prince comes that things begin to happen.'

Mr Irving smiled a little sadly into her uplifted face, all astar with its youth and promise.

'Sometimes the prince comes too late,' he said. He did not ask Anne to translate her remark into prose. Like all kindred spirits he 'understood'.

'Oh, no, not if he is the real prince coming to the true princess,' said Anne, shaking her red head decidedly, as she opened the parlour door. When he had gone in she shut it tightly behind him and turned to confront Charlotta the Fourth, who was in the hall, all 'nods and becks and wreathed smiles'.

'Oh, Miss Shirley, ma'am,' she breathed, 'I peeked from the kitchen window ... and he's awful handsome ... and just the right age for Miss Lavendar. And oh, Miss Shirley, ma'am, do you think it would be much harm to listen at the door?'

'It would be dreadful, Charlotta,' said Anne firmly, 'so just you come away with me out of the reach of temptation.'

'I can't do anything, and it's awful to hang round just waiting,' sighed Charlotta. 'What if he don't propose after all, Miss Shirley, ma'am? You can never be sure of them men. My oldest sister, Charlotta the First, thought she was engaged to one once. But it turned out *he* had a different opinion and she says she'll never trust one of them again. And I heard of another case where a man thought he wanted one girl awful bad when it was really her sister he wanted all the time. When a man don't know his own mind, Miss Shirley, ma'am, how's a poor woman going to be sure of it?'

'We'll go to the kitchen and clean the silver spoons,' said Anne. 'That's a task which won't require much thinking, fortunately ... for I *couldn't* think tonight. And it will pass the time.'

It passed an hour. Then, just as Anne laid down the last shining spoon, they heard the front door shut. Both sought comfort fearfully in each other's eyes.

'Oh, Miss Shirley, ma'am,' gasped Charlotta, 'if he's going away this early there's nothing into it and never will be.'

They flew to the window. Mr Irving had no intention of going away. He and Miss Lavendar were strolling slowly down the middle path to the stone bench.

'Oh, Miss Shirley, ma'am, he's got his arm around her waist,' whispered Charlotta the Fourth, delightedly. 'He *must* have proposed to her or she'd never allow it.'

Anne caught Charlotta the Fourth by her own plump waist and danced her around the kitchen until they were both out of breath.

'Oh, Charlotta,' she cried gaily, 'I'm neither a prophetess nor the daughter of a prophetess, but I'm going to make a prediction. There'll be a wedding in this old stone house before the maple leaves are red. Do you want that translated into prose, Charlotta?'

'No, I can understand that,' said Charlotta. 'A wedding ain't poetry. Why, Miss Shirley, ma'am, you're crying! What for?'

'Oh, because it's all so beautiful ... and story-bookish ... and romantic ... and sad,' said Anne, winking the tears out of her eyes. 'It's all perfectly lovely ... but there's a little sadness mixed up in it too, somehow.'

'Oh, of course there's a resk in marrying anybody,' conceded Charlotta the Fourth, 'but, when all's said and done, Miss Shirley, ma'am, there's many a worse thing than a husband.'

CHAPTER 29

Poetry and Prose

FOR the next month Anne lived in what, for Avonlea, might be called a whirl of excitement. The preparation of her own modest outfit for Redmond was of secondary importance. Miss Lavendar was getting ready to be married and the stone house was the scene of endless consultations and plannings and discussions, with Charlotta the Fourth hovering on the outskirts of things in agitated delight and wonder. Then the dressmaker came, and there was the rapture and wretchedness of choosing fashions and being fitted. Anne and Diana spent half their time at Echo Lodge and there were nights when Anne could not sleep for wondering whether she had done right in advising Miss Lavendar to select brown rather than navy blue for her travelling dress, and to have her grey silk made princess.

Everybody concerned in Miss Lavendar's story was very happy. Paul Irving rushed to Green Gables to talk the news over with Anne as soon as his father had told him.

'I knew I could trust Father to pick me out a nice little second mother,' he said proudly. 'It's a fine thing to have a father you can depend on, teacher. I just love Miss Lavendar. Grandma is pleased, too. She says she's real glad Father didn't pick out an American for his second wife, because, although it turned out all right the first time, such a thing wouldn't be likely to happen twice. Mrs Lynde says she thoroughly approves of the match and thinks it's likely Miss Lavendar will give up her queer notions and be like other people now that she's going to be married. But I hope she won't give her queer notions up, teacher, because I like them. And I don't want her to be like other people. There are too many other people around as it is. *You* know, teacher.'

Charlotta the Fourth was another radiant person.

'Oh, Miss Shirley, ma'am, it has all turned out so beautiful. When Mr Irving and Miss Lavendar come back from their tower I'm to go up to Boston and live with them . . . and me only fifteen, and the other girls never went till they were sixteen. Ain't Mr Irving splendid? He just worships the ground she treads on and it makes me feel so queer sometimes to see the look in his eyes when he's watching her. It beggars description, Miss Shirley, ma'am. I'm awful thankful they're so fond of each other. It's the best way, when all's said and done, though some folks can get along without it. I've got an aunt who has been married three times and she says she married the first time for love and the last two times for strictly business, and was happy with all three except at the times of the funerals. But I think she took a resk, Miss Shirley, ma'am.'

'Oh, it's all so romantic,' breathed Anne to Marilla that night.

'If I hadn't taken the wrong path that day we went to Mr Kimball's I'd never have known Miss Lavendar; and if I hadn't met her I'd never have taken Paul there ... and he'd never have written to his father about visiting Miss Lavendar just as Mr Irving was starting for San Francisco. Mr Irving says whenever he got that letter he made up his mind to send his partner to San Francisco and come here instead. He hadn't heard anything of Miss Lavendar for fifteen years. Somebody had told him then that she was to be married and he thought she was and never asked anybody anything about her. And now everything has come right. And I had a hand in bringing it about. Perhaps, as Mrs Lynde says, everything is foreordained and it was bound to happen anyway. But even so, it's nice to think one was an instrument used by predestination. Yes, indeed, it's very romantic.'

'I can't see that it's so terribly romantic at all,' said Marilla rather crisply. Marilla thought Anne was too worked up about it and had plenty to do with getting ready for college without 'traipsing' to Echo Lodge two days out of three helping Miss Lavendar. 'In the first place two young fools quarrel and turn sulky; then Steve Irving goes to the States and after a spell gets married up there and is perfectly happy from all accounts. Then his wife dies and after a decent interval he thinks he'll come home and see if his first fancy'll have him. Meanwhile, she's been living single, probably because nobody nice enough came along to want her, and they meet and agree to be married after all. Now, where is the romance in all that?'

'Oh, there isn't any, when you put it that way,' gasped Anne, rather as if somebody had thrown cold water over her. 'I suppose that's how it looks in prose. But it's very different if you look at it through poetry ... and *I* think it's nicer ...' Anne recovered herself and her eyes shone and her cheeks flushed ... 'to look at it through poetry'.

Marilla glanced at the radiant young face and refrained from further sarcastic comments. Perhaps some realization came to her that after all it was better to have, like Anne, 'the vision and the faculty divine' ... that gift which the world cannot bestow or take away, of looking at life through some transfiguring ...

or revealing? . . . medium, whereby everything seemed apparelled in celestial light, wearing a glory and a freshness not visible to those who, like herself and Charlotta the Fourth, looked at things only through prose.

'When's the wedding to be?' she asked after a pause.

'The last Wednesday in August. They are to be married in the garden under the honeysuckle trellis . . . the very spot where Mr Irving proposed to her twenty-five years ago. Marilla, that *is* romantic, even in prose. There's to be nobody there except Mrs Irving and Paul and Gilbert and Diana and I, and Miss Lavendar's cousins. And they will leave on the six o'clock train for a trip to the Pacific coast. When they come back in the fall Paul and Charlotta the Fourth are to go up to Boston to live with them. But Echo Lodge is to be left just as it is . . . only of course they'll sell the hens and cow, and board up the windows . . . and every summer they're coming down to live in it. I'm so glad. It would have hurt me dreadfully next winter at Redmond to think of that dear stone house all stripped and deserted, with empty rooms . . . or far worse, with other people living in it. But I can think of it now, just as I've always seen it, waiting happily for the summer to bring life and laughter back to it again.'

There was more romance in the world than that which had fallen to the share of the middle-aged lovers of the stone house. Anne stumbled suddenly on it one evening when she went over to Orchard Slope by the wood cut and came out into the Barry garden. Diana Barry and Fred Wright were standing together under the big willow. Diana was leaning against the grey trunk, her lashes cast down on very crimson cheeks. One hand was held by Fred, who stood with his face bent towards her, stammering something in low, earnest tones. There were no other people in the world except their two selves at that magic moment; so neither of them saw Anne, who, after one dazed glance of comprehension, turned and sped noiselessly back through the spruce wood, never stopping till she gained her own gable room, where she sat breathlessly down by her window and tried to collect her scattered wits.

'Diana and Fred are in love with each other,' she gasped. 'Oh, it does seem so . . . so . . . so *hopelessly* grown up.'

Anne, of late, had not been without her suspicions that Diana was proving false to the melancholy Byronic hero of her early dreams. But as 'things seen are mightier than things heard', or suspected, the realization that it was actually so came to her with almost the shock of perfect surprise. This was succeeded by a queer, little lonely feeling ... as if, somehow, Diana had gone forward into a new world, shutting a gate behind her, leaving Anne on the outside.

'Things are changing so fast it almost frightens me,' Anne thought, a little sadly. 'And I'm afraid that this can't help making some difference between Diana and me. I'm sure I can't tell her all my secrets after this ... she might tell Fred. And what *can* she see in Fred? He's very nice and jolly ... but he's just Fred Wright.'

It is always a very puzzling question ... what can somebody see in somebody else? But how fortunate after all that it is so, for if everybody saw alike ... well, in that case, as the old Indian said, 'Everybody would want my squaw.' It was plain that Diana *did* see something in Fred Wright, however Anne's eyes might be holden. Diana came to Green Gables the next evening, a pensive, shy young lady, and told Anne the whole story in the dusky seclusion of the east gable. Both girls cried and kissed and laughed.

'I'm so happy,' said Diana, 'but it does seem ridiculous to think of me being engaged.'

'What is it really like to be engaged?' asked Anne curiously.

'Well, that all depends on who you're engaged to,' answered Diana, with that maddening air of superior wisdom always assumed by those who are engaged over those who are not. 'It's perfectly lovely to be engaged to Fred ... but I think it would be simply horrid to be engaged to anyone else.'

'There's not much comfort for the rest of us in that, seeing that there is only one Fred,' laughed Anne.

'Oh, Anne, you don't understand,' said Diana in vexation. 'I didn't mean *that* ... it's so hard to explain. Never mind, you'll understand some time, when your own turn comes.'

'Bless you, dearest of Dianas, I understand now. What is an

imagination for if not to enable you to peep at life through other people's eyes?'

'You must be my bridesmaid, you know, Anne. Promise me that . . . wherever you may be when I'm married.'

'I'll come from the ends of the earth if necessary,' promised Anne solemnly.

'Of course, it won't be for ever so long yet,' said Diana, blushing. 'Three years at the very least . . . for I'm only eighteen and Mother says no daughter of hers shall be married before she's twenty-one. Besides, Fred's father is going to buy the Abraham Fletcher farm for him and he says he's got to have it two-thirds paid for before he'll give it to him in his own name. But three years isn't any too much time to get ready for housekeeping, for I haven't a speck of fancy work made yet. But I'm going to begin crocheting doilies tomorrow. Myra Gillis had thirty-seven doilies when she was married and I'm determined I shall have as many as she had.'

'I suppose it would be perfectly impossible to keep house with only thirty-six doilies,' conceded Anne, with a solemn face but dancing eyes.

Diana looked hurt.

'I didn't think you'd make fun of me, Anne,' she said reproachfully.

'Dearest, I wasn't making fun of you,' cried Anne repentantly. 'I was only teasing you a bit. I think you'll make the sweetest little housekeeper in the world. And I think it's perfectly lovely of you to be planning already for your home o' dreams.'

Anne had no sooner uttered the phrase, 'home o' dreams', than it captivated her fancy and she immediately began the erection of one of her own. It was, of course, tenanted by an ideal master, dark, proud, and melancholy; but oddly enough, Gilbert Blythe persisted in hanging about too, helping her arrange pictures, lay out gardens, and accomplish sundry other tasks which a proud and melancholy hero evidently considered beneath his dignity. Anne tried to banish Gilbert's image from her castle in Spain, but, somehow, he went on being there, so Anne, being in a hurry, gave up the attempt and pursued her aerial architecture with such success that her 'home o' dreams' was built and furnished before Diana spoke again.

'I suppose, Anne, you must think it's funny I should like Fred so well when he's so different from the kind of man I've always said I would marry . . . the tall, slender kind? But somehow I wouldn't want Fred to be tall and slender . . . because, don't you see, he wouldn't be Fred then. Of course,' added Diana rather dolefully, 'we will be a dreadfully pudgy couple. But after all that's better than one of us being short and fat and the other tall and lean, like Morgan Sloane and his wife. Mrs Lynde says it always makes her think of the long and short of it when she sees them together.'

'Well,' said Anne to herself that night, as she brushed her hair before her gilt-framed mirror, 'I am glad Diana is so happy and satisfied. But when my turn comes . . . if it ever does . . . I do hope there'll be something a little more thrilling about it. But then Diana thought so too, once. I've heard her say time and again she'd never get engaged any poky commonplace way . . . he'd *have* to do something splendid to win her. But she has changed. Perhaps I'll change too. But I won't . . . I'm determined I won't. Oh, I think these engagements are dreadfully upsetting things when they happen to your intimate friends.'

CHAPTER 30

A Wedding at the Stone House

THE last week in August came. Miss Lavendar was to be married in it. Two weeks later Anne and Gilbert would leave for Redmond College. In a week's time Mrs Rachel Lynde would move to Green Gables and set up her lares and penates in the erstwhile spare room, which was already prepared for her coming. She had sold all her superfluous household plenishings by auction and was at present revelling in the congenial occupation of helping the Allans pack up. Mr Allan was to preach his farewell sermon the next Sunday. The old order was changing rapidly to give place to the new, as Anne felt with a little sadness threading all her excitement and happiness.

'Changes ain't totally pleasant but they're excellent things,' said Mr Harrison philosophically. 'Two years is about long enough for things to stay exactly the same. If they stayed put any longer they might grow mossy.'

Mr Harrison was smoking on his veranda. His wife had self-sacrificingly told him that he might smoke in the house if he took care to sit by an open window. Mr Harrison rewarded this concession by going outdoors altogether to smoke in fine weather, and so mutual good-will reigned.

Anne had come over to ask Mrs Harrison for some of her yellow dahlias. She and Diana were going through to Echo Lodge that evening to help Miss Lavendar and Charlotta the Fourth with their final preparations for the morrow's bridal. Miss Lavendar herself never had dahlias; she did not like them and they would not have suited the fine retirement of her old-fashioned garden. But flowers of any kind were rather scarce in Avonlea and the neighbouring districts that summer, thanks to Uncle Abe's storm; and Anne and Diana thought that a certain old cream-coloured stone jug, usually kept sacred to doughnuts, brimmed over with yellow dahlias, would be just the thing to set in a dim angle of the stone house stairs, against the dark background of red hall paper.

'I s'pose you'll be starting off for college in a fortnight's time?' continued Mr Harrison. 'Well, we're going to miss you an awful lot, Emily and me. To be sure, Mrs Lynde'll be over there in your place. There ain't nobody but a substitute can be found for them.'

The irony of Mr Harrison's tone is quite untransferable to paper. In spite of his wife's intimacy with Mrs Lynde, the best that could be said of the relationship between her and Mr Harrison, even under the new *régime*, was that they preserved an armed neutrality.

'Yes, I'm going,' said Anne. 'I'm very glad with my head . . . and very sorry with my heart.'

'I s'pose you'll be scooping up all the honours that are lying round loose at Redmond.'

'I may try for one or two of them,' confessed Anne, 'but I

don't care so much for things like that as I did two years ago. What I want to get out of my college course is some knowledge of the best way of living life and doing the most and best with it. I want to learn to understand and help other people and myself.'

Mr Harrison nodded.

'That's the idea exactly. That's what college ought to be for, instead of turning out a lot of B.A.s, so chock full of book-learning and vanity that there ain't room for anything else. You're all right. College won't be able to do you much harm, I reckon.'

Diana and Anne drove over to Echo Lodge after tea, taking with them all the flowery spoil that several predatory expeditions in their own and their neighbours' gardens and yielded. They found the stone house agog with excitement. Charlotta the Fourth was flying around with such vim and briskness that her blue bows seemed really to possess the power of being everywhere at once. Like the helmet of Navarre, Charlotta's blue bows waved ever in the thickest of the fray.

'Praise be to goodness you've come,' she said devoutly, 'for there's heaps of things to do ... and the frosting on that cake *won't* harden ... and there's all the silver to be rubbed up yet ... and the horsehair trunk to be packed ... and the roosters for the chicken salad are running out there beyant the henhouse yet, *crowing*, Miss Shirley, ma'am. And Miss Lavendar ain't to be trusted to do a thing. I was thankful when Mr Irving came a few minutes ago and took her off for a walk in the woods. Courting's all right in its place, Miss Shirley, ma'am, but if you try to mix it up with cooking and scouring everything's spoiled. That's *my* opinion, Miss Shirley, ma'am.'

Anne and Diana worked so heartily that by ten o'clock even Charlotta the Fourth was satisfied. She braided her hair in innumerable plaits and took her weary little bones off to bed.

'But I'm sure I shan't sleep a blessed wink, Miss Shirley, ma'am, for fear that something'll go wrong at the last minute ... the cream won't whip ... or Mr Irving'll have a stroke and not be able to come.'

'He isn't in the habit of having strokes, is he?' asked Diana, the dimpled corners of her mouth twitching. To Diana, Charlotta the Fourth was, if not exactly a thing of beauty, certainly a joy for ever.

'They're not things that go by habit,' said Charlotta the Fourth with dignity. 'They just *happen* ... and there you are. *Anybody* can have a stroke. You don't have to learn how. Mr Irving looks a lot like an uncle of mine that had one once just as he was sitting down to dinner one day. But maybe everything'll go all right. In this world you've just got to hope for the best and prepare for the worst and take whatever God sends.'

'The only thing I'm worried about is that it won't be fine tomorrow,' said Diana. 'Uncle Abe predicted rain for the middle of the week, and ever since the big storm I can't help believing there's a good deal in what Uncle Abe says.'

Anne, who knew better than Diana just how much Uncle Abe had to do with the storm, was not much disturbed by this. She slept the sleep of the just and weary, and was roused at an unearthly hour by Charlotta the Fourth.

'Oh, Miss Shirley, ma'am, it's awful to call you so early,' came wailing through the keyhole, 'but there's so much to do yet ... and oh, Miss Shirley, ma'am, I'm skeered it's going to rain and I wish you'd get up and tell me you think it ain't.'

Anne flew to the window, hoping against hope that Charlotta the Fourth was saying this merely by way of rousing her effectually. But alas, the morning did look unpropitious. Below the window Miss Lavendar's garden, which should have been a glory of pale virgin sunshine, lay dim and windless; and the sky over the firs was dark with moody clouds.

'Isn't it too mean!' said Diana.

'We must hope for the best,' said Anne determinedly. 'If it only doesn't actually rain, a cool, pearly grey day like this would really be nicer than hot sunshine.'

'But it will rain,' mourned Charlotta, creeping into the room, a figure of fun, with her many braids wound about her head, the ends, tied up with white thread, sticking out in all directions. 'It'll hold off till the last minute and then pour cats and dogs. And all the folks will get sopping ... and track mud all over the house . . . and they won't be able to be married under the honeysuckle . . . and it's awful unlucky for no sun to shine on a bride, say what you will, Miss Shirley, ma'am. I *knew* things were going too well to last.'

Charlotta the Fourth seemed certainly to have borrowed a leaf out of Miss Eliza Andrews' book.

It did not rain, though it kept on looking as if it meant to. By noon the rooms were decorated, the table beautifully laid; and upstairs was waiting a bride, 'adorned for her husband'.

'You do look sweet,' said Anne rapturously.

'Lovely,' echoed Diana.

'Everything's ready, Miss Shirley, ma'am, and nothing dreadful has happened *yet*,' was Charlotta's cheerful statement as she betook herself to her little back room to dress. Out came the braids; the resultant rampant crinkliness was all plaited into two tails and tied, not with two bows alone, but with four, of brand-new ribbon, brightly blue. The two upper bows rather gave the impression of overgrown wings sprouting from Charlotta's neck, somewhat after the fashion of Raphael's cherubs. But Charlotta the Fourth thought them very beautiful, and after she had rustled into a white dress, so stiffly starched that it could stand alone, she surveyed herself in her glass with great satisfaction . . . a satisfaction which lasted until she went out in the hall and caught a glimpse through the spare-room door of a tall girl in some softly clinging gown, pinning white, star-like flowers on the smooth ripples of her ruddy hair.

'Oh, I'll *never* be able to look like Miss Shirley,' thought poor Charlotta despairingly. 'You just have to be born so, I guess . . . don't seem's if any amount of practice could give you that *air*.'

By one o'clock the guests had come, including Mr and Mrs Allan, for Mr Allan was to perform the ceremony in the absence of the Grafton minister on his vacation. There was no formality about the marriage. Miss Lavendar came down the stairs to meet her bridegroom at the foot, and as he took her hand she lifted her big brown eyes to his with a look that made Charlotta the Fourth, who intercepted it, feel queerer than ever. They went out to the honeysuckle arbour, where Mr Allan was awaiting them. The guests grouped themselves as they pleased.

Anne and Diana stood by the old stone bench, with Charlotta the Fourth between them, desperately clutching their hands in her cold, tremulous little paws.

Mr Allan opened his blue book and the ceremony proceeded. Just as Miss Lavendar and Stephen Irving were pronounced man and wife a very beautiful and symbolic thing happened. The sun suddenly burst through the grey and poured a flood of radiance on the happy bride. Instantly the garden was alive with dancing shadows and flickering lights.

'What a lovely omen,' thought Anne, as she ran to kiss the bride. Then the three girls left the rest of the guests laughing around the bridal pair while they flew into the house to see that all was in readiness for the feast.

'Thanks be to goodness, it's over, Miss Shirley, ma'am,' breathed Charlotta the Fourth, 'and they're married safe and sound, no matter what happens now. The bags of rice are in the pantry, ma'am, and the old shoes are behind the door, and the cream for whipping is on the sullar steps.'

At half past two Mr and Mrs Irving left, and everybody went to Bright River to see them off on the afternoon train. As Miss Lavendar . . . I beg her pardon, Mrs Irving . . . stepped from the door of her old home, Gilbert and the girls threw the rice and Charlotta the Fourth hurled an old shoe with such excellent aim that she struck Mr Allan squarely on the head. But it was re-served for Paul to give the prettiest send-off. He popped out of the porch ringing furiously a huge old brass dinner bell which had adorned the dining-room mantel. Paul's only motive was to make a joyful noise; but as the clangour died away, from point and curve and hill across the river came the chime of 'fairy wedding bells', ringing clearly, sweetly, faintly and more faint, as if Miss Lavendar's beloved echoes were bidding her greeting and farewell. And so, amid this benediction of sweet sounds, Miss Lavendar drove away from the old life of dreams and make-believes to a fuller life of realities in the busy world beyond.

Two hours later Anne and Charlotta the Fourth came down the lane again. Gilbert had gone to West Grafton on an errand and Diana had to keep an engagement at home. Anne and

Charlotta had come back to put things in order and lock up the little stone house. The garden was a pool of late golden sunshine, with butterflies hovering and bees booming; but the little house had already that indefinable air of desolation which always follows a festivity.

'Oh dear me, don't it look lonesome?' sniffed Charlotta the Fourth, who had been crying all the way home from the station. 'A wedding ain't much cheerfuller than a funeral after all, when it's all over, Miss Shirley, ma'am.'

A busy evening followed. The decorations had to be removed, the dishes washed, the uneaten delicacies packed into a basket for the delectation of Charlotta the Fourth's young brothers at home. Anne would not rest until everything was in apple-pie order; after Charlotta had gone home with her plunder Anne went over the still rooms, feeling like one who trod alone some banquet hall deserted, and closed the blinds. Then she locked the door and sat down under the silver poplar to wait for Gilbert, feeling very tired but still unweariedly thinking 'long, long thoughts'.

'What are you thinking of, Anne?' asked Gilbert, coming down the walk. He had left his horse and buggy out at the road.

'Of Miss Lavendar and Mr Irving,' answered Anne dreamily. 'Isn't it beautiful to think how everything has turned out . . . how they have come together again after all the years of separation and misunderstanding?'

'Yes, it's beautiful,' said Gilbert, looking steadily down into Anne's uplifted face, 'but wouldn't it have been more beautiful still, Anne, if there had been *no* separation or misunderstanding . . . if they had come hand in hand all the way through life, with no memories behind them but those which belonged to each other?'

For a moment Anne's heart fluttered queerly and for the first time her eyes faltered under Gilbert's gaze and a rosy flush stained the paleness of her face. It was as if a veil that had hung before her inner consciousness had been lifted, giving to her view a revelation of unsuspected feelings and realities. Perhaps, after all, romance did not come into one's life with pomp and

239

blare, like a gay knight riding down; perhaps it crept to one's side like an old friend through quiet ways; perhaps it revealed itself in seeming prose, until some sudden shaft of illumination flung athwart its pages betrayed the rhythm and the music; perhaps ... perhaps ... love unfolded naturally out of a beautiful friendship, as a golden-hearted rose slipping from its green sheath.

Then the veil dropped again; but the Anne who walked up the dark lane was not quite the same Anne who had driven gaily down it the evening before. The page of girlhood had been turned, as by an unseen finger, and the page of womanhood was before her with all its charm and mystery, its pain and gladness.

Gilbert wisely said nothing more; but in his silence he read the history of the next four years in the light of Anne's remembered blush. Four years of earnest, happy work ... and then the guerdon of a useful knowledge gained and a sweetheart won.

Behind them in the garden the little stone house brooded among the shadows. It was lonely but not forsaken. It had not yet done with dreams and laughter and the joy of life; there were to be future summers for the little stone house; meanwhile, it could wait. And over the river in purple durance the echoes bided their time.